GEEKERELLA

GEEKERELLA

A Novel

By Ashley Poston

QUIRK BOOKS
PHILADELPHIA

First published in the United States of
America in 2017 by QUIRK BOOKS

ISBN: 978-1-59474-993-3

Printed in China
Typeset in Arkhip, Avenir, and Sabon LT Std

Designed by Timothy O'Donnell
Cover illustration by Dan Sipple
Production management by John J. McGurk

Quirk Books
215 Church Street
Philadelphia, PA 19106
quirkbooks.com

10 9 8 7 6 5 4 3 2

To the Fellowship:
Here's to many more
great adventures

PART ONE

LOOK TO THE STARS

"As the Black Nebula swallowed each world in darkness, stories are told of a single spark of light blazing brighter than a star that gave people hope when all hope was lost. This is the story of the starship Prospero, and this its final flight.

Look to the stars. Aim. Ignite."

—Ending monologue, Starfield, Episode 54

ELLE

The stepmonster is at it again.

Raffles, discount coupons, and magazine sweepstakes lay strewn across the kitchen table. My stepmom sits straight-backed in one of the creaky wooden chairs, delicately cutting out another coupon, dyed blonde hair piled on top of her head in perfect ringlets, lipstick the color of men's heartblood. Her white blouse is spotless, her dark pencil skirt neatly ironed. She must have a meeting with a potential client today.

"Sweetie, a little faster this morning." She snaps her fingers for me to hurry up.

I shuffle over to the counter and pry open the coffee tin. The smell is strong and cheap—the only kind I was raised on. Which is all the better, seeing as we can't afford expensive coffee, although I know that never stops the stepmonster from ordering her double-shot dirty chai soy latte no whip every morning and charging it to one of her dozens of credit cards.

Catherine—my stepmom—picks up another magazine to cut. "No carbs this morning. I'm feeling bloated and I have a meeting with a couple this afternoon. Big wedding plans. She's a debutante, if you could believe that!"

In Charleston? I can believe it. Everyone's either a debutante, a Daughter of the Confederacy, or a politician's kid—Thornhill or

Fishburne or Van Noy or Pickney or a handful of old Charlestonian names. And I couldn't care less.

I dump two scoops of coffee into the machine—plus an extra one for good measure. It feels like a three-scoop kind of day. Maybe adding more caffeine to their morning will get my stepmother and the twins out before nine. That's not too much to wish for, is it?

I glance up at the clock on the microwave. 8:24 a.m. Unless the twins start moving at warp speed, I'll be cutting it real close. I say a silent prayer to the Lord of Light or Q or whoever is listening: *Please, for* once, *let the stepmonster and the twins leave the house on time. Starfield* history will be made today at 9 a.m. sharp on *Hello, America*, and I won't miss it. I *refuse*. Finally, after years of delays and director changes and distribution snafus, the movie is happening—a reboot, but beggars can't be choosers—and today they're making the long-awaited announcement of the official film platform. The lead actors, the plot, everything. I've missed *Starfield* marathons and midnight rereleases of the final episode in theaters and convention appearances because of Catherine and the twins, but I'm not missing *this*.

"They want to say their vows under the magnolia trees at Boone Hall Plantation," Catherine goes on. "You know, ever since Ryan Reynolds and his wife got married there, that place is always booked."

Catherine is a wedding planner. I've watched her spend entire weekends hand-sewing sequins onto table toppers and hand-pressing invitations at the print shop downtown. The way she plans a venue, down to the type of cloth on the tables and the color of flowers in the vases, making every wedding look like a magical land of unicorns. You'd think she does it because of her own happily-ever-after cut short, but that's a lie. She wants her weddings in *Vogue* and *InStyle*, the kind you Instagram and Pinterest a hundred times over. She wants the renown of it, and she's sunk all of Dad's life insurance payout into her business. Well, her business and everything she claims is "essential" to her "image."

"I want to at least *look* like I shop at Tiffany's," she says, talking more to herself than to me.

It's the same spiel again and again. How she used to shop at Tiffany's. How she used to attend galas at Boone Hall Plantation. How she used to be happily married with two wonderful daughters. She never mentions me, her stepdaughter.

Catherine finishes cutting her coupon with a sigh. "But that was all *before*. Before your father left me and the twins here in this dreadful little house."

And there it is. Like it's my fault that she's blown all her savings. Like it's *Dad's* fault. I take out Dad's *Starfield* mug—the only thing left of his in our house—and pour myself a cup of coffee.

Outside, the neighbor's dog begins to bark at a passing track-suited jogger. We live on the outskirts of the famous historical district, the house not quite old enough to be a tourist attraction but not new enough to be renovated—not that we could afford it anyway. Two streets over and you run into the College of Charleston. Our house was one of the last ones left after Hurricane Hugo decimated the coast of South Carolina before I was born. The house has its leaks, but all good and old things do. I've lived here my whole life. I don't know anything else.

Catherine absolutely hates it.

The coffee smell is rich and nutty. I take a sip, and I almost melt. It's heaven. Catherine clears her throat, and I pour coffee into her favorite mug: white with pink flowers. Two sugars (the only sweetness she splurges on each day), lightly stirred, with three ice cubes.

She takes it without even looking up from her magazine. And then, when the neighbor dog lets out a sharp howl, she sets down her cup. "You would *think* dogs would learn when to shut up. Giorgio has enough on his plate without that dog barking."

Catherine likes to pretend she's on a first-name basis with everyone, but especially people she deems important. Mr. Ramirez—Giorgio—is a banker, which means he has a lot of money, which means he's an influential part of the country club, which means he's important.

"If it doesn't shut up soon," she goes on in that cool, detached voice of hers, "I'll muzzle it myself."

"His name's Franco," I remind her. "And he doesn't like being tied up."

"Well, we all must get used to disappointment," she replies, and takes another sip of coffee. Her blood-colored lips turn into a scowl and she shoves the mug back at me. "Too bitter. Try again."

Begrudgingly, I put in another cube of ice to water it down. She takes the coffee and tries another sip. It must be sufficiently soulless, because she sets it down beside her stack of coupons and goes back to scanning the gossip column in her magazine.

"*Well?*" She prods.

I hesitate, looking from her coffee to her, wondering if I've forgotten something. I've been doing this for seven years—I don't think I'm missing anything.

Outside, the dog gives a pitiful howl. *Oh.*

She raises a pencil-thin eyebrow. "How am I supposed to have a calm morning with *that* racket?" she goes on in that overworked, all-knowing voice of hers. "If Robin was still here . . ."

I glance back at her. Open my mouth. Begin to say that I miss Dad too. I want him here too—but something stops me. Or I stop myself. I blame it on the lack of coffee. One sip doesn't give you the insta-courage a cup does. Besides, I'm not trying to make Catherine mad. I'm trying to get her caffeinated, placated, and *out the door.*

She flips the page in her magazine and picks up the scissors again to cut out a coupon for a winter coat. It's June. In South Carolina.

But then Catherine clears her throat. "Danielle, *do something* to get that mutt to quiet down."

"But—"

"*Now,*" Catherine says, flicking her hand for me to hurry up.

"Sure, *my queen,*" I mutter under my breath. While Catherine puts down her coupons and picks up an article about Jessica Stone's latest red carpet look, I slip last night's steak tips out of the fridge and hurry through the back door.

Poor Franco sits in the mud outside of his doghouse, thumping his tail in a puddle. He looks at me through the broken slat in the fence, a muddy brown Dachshund in a dirty red collar. It rained last night and his doghouse flooded, just like I told Mr. Ramirez—sorry, *Giorgio*—it would.

Mr. Ramirez brought Franco home a few weeks after he married his second ex-wife, I guess as a dry run for having a kid. But since his divorce a few years ago, he pretty much lives at work, so Franco is this forgotten idea that never panned out, with the flooded doghouse to prove it. At least the poor Frank can float.

I slide the container through the slat and rub the dog behind the ears, slathering my fingertips in mud. "You're a good boy, yes you are! Once I save up enough, I'll spring the both of us out of here. Whatcha think of that, copilot?" His tail pat-pats excitedly in the mud. "I'll even get us matching sunglasses. The whole nine yards."

Franco's tongue lolls out of the side of his mouth in agreement. Maybe they don't even make doggy sunglasses, but for a while I've had this picture in my head: me and Franco crammed into a beat-up car, heading out on the only highway out of town—wearing sunglasses, of course—and headed straight for L.A.

Ever since I can remember, my fingers have itched to make things. To write. I have filled journals, finished fanfics, escaped again and again into the pages of someone else's life. If Dad was right—if I could do anything, be *anyone*—I would make a show like *Starfield* and tell other weird kids that they aren't alone. And after next year—my senior year—I'm going to do it. Or start to. Study screenwriting. Write scripts. I've already got a portfolio, kind of. Right now I satisfy my need to write by blogging on my site *Rebelgunner,* where I cover the one thing I know for certain: *Starfield*. That and the money I'm scraping together from my job at the food truck are gonna be my ticket out of here. One day.

"Danielle!" my stepmom screeches from the kitchen window.

I push the steak tips under the fence and Franco dives headfirst into the bowl.

"Maybe in another universe, boy," I whisper. "Because for now, my home is here."

This place is too full of memories to leave, even if I wanted to. Dad technically left the house to me, but Catherine's in charge of it while I'm still a minor. So until then—

"*Danielle!*"

Until then I'm here with my stepmother and her daughters.

"All right! Coming!" With one last scratch behind Frank's ear, I say goodbye, make a mental note to return later for the dish, and dart back to the kitchen.

"Girls!" Catherine calls again, slinging a Gucci purse over her shoulder. "Hurry up or you'll be late for Mr. Craig's lesson! Girls? *Girls!* You better be awake or so help me I'll . . ." Her footsteps thud up to their room and I glance at the clock. 8:36. There's no *way* they'll be out of here in time. Not unless I speed things along.

Begrudgingly, I assemble kale and strawberries and almond milk to fix the twins' morning smoothies. Catherine has, of course, left her magazine splayed on the counter, so Darien Freeman's face is grinning up at me. My lips curl into a sneer. There were rumors that he had signed on to the new *Starfield* remake, but that's about as big of a joke as saying Carmindor will be played by a pug riding a skateboard. You don't put a soap opera star in charge of an entire galaxy.

Ugh. I press BLEND and try not to think about it.

Upstairs, there are muffled thumps as Catherine drags the twins out of bed. This happens every morning, like clockwork.

My summertime morning routine goes like this: Wake up—coffee, extra scoop for Mondays. Catherine stoops over the morning papers, cutting out coupons. Lingers too long on purses and pretty dresses. Says something passive-aggressive about her old life. Orders me to fix breakfast. Instead, I feed the Frank. Catherine goes upstairs to yell at the twins for "forgetting" to set their alarms. I still don't fix breakfast. Ten minutes later, the twins are fighting over the shower, and Catherine reminds me that she is the one with the deed to the house, *Danielle,* and unless I want her to cash in this place for a *luxury condo*—as if this house would ever get that much—I had better fix breakfast. So I blend up their Grinch vomit, the twins grab their matching tumblers, and Catherine shoves them out the door for tennis lessons.

The rest of my day is never much better. I'll be five minutes late to work, but my coworker Sage—the food-truck owner's daughter—is too engrossed in her Harajuku fashion magazines to even notice. Then it's eight hours in the Magic Pumpkin, doling out healthy food-truck fritters to bankers in tight business suits and soccer moms with babies bouncing on their hips. Then I'm elbowing my way through the supermarket armed with coupons that make the cashier roll her eyes when I get in line (everyone hates coupons). Then home again for "family dinner," made by me. Cue the twins' mean comments on my cooking, then their disappearance upstairs to film a beauty vlog about the perfect cat eye or best eyeshadow pairing with ruby lips or whatever. Then dishes, leftovers, one last check on Franco, and bed.

Well, sorta. Then late-night reruns of *Starfield* on my Dad's boxy TV in the corner of my room. Maybe I write a blog post about the episode, if I'm feeling inspired. Check all my Stargunner fansites for news. I fall asleep to the Federation Prince's voice. *"Look to the stars. Aim. Ignite."*

The next morning I wake up, and we do everything all over again. But this time—plot twist!—I get to work on time. Maybe Sage actually talks to me for once. Maybe the twins are nice. Maybe someone stuffs two airplane tickets to L.A. into the tip jar. Maybe I write a love-letter to episode 43 instead of criticizing the integrity of the characters as the colony blows up. Maybe I dream about Dad.

The blender growls as though it's in pain. I let it rest and shake the kale smoothie into two separate tumblers, nervously glancing at the microwave clock. 8:41 a.m.

After sliding the twins' breakfasts across the counter like the seasoned food service employee I am, I root around in the cabinet for the jar of peanut butter I tucked away last night. I protect my peanut butter like Smeagol protects the One Ring—*mine, precious*—no matter what diet "we" are on as a household. Right now, Catherine's on a paleo kick, but last month it was raw foods. Before that South Beach—or was it

Atkins? Something with bacon. Next week will be low-fat or low-salt or . . . whatever she's craving. Whatever food she can make *me* make by threatening to sell this house—Dad's house.

I scrape out the last bit of peanut butter from the bottom of the jar, savoring its taste on my tongue. I take my victories wherever I can get them.

Upstairs, the shower turns off with a groaning of pipes. *Finally.* The twins are taking their sweet time this morning. Usually they enjoy tennis practice at the country club because their friends are always there. It's the hangout spot if you're popular and rich. As for me? Catherine's always not-so-subtly insisting that the only thing I'm fit for at the club is toting someone's golf clubs.

I dispose of the peanut butter jar in the garbage and check my indestructible brick phone, which I "inherited" after Dad died. Another grand idea from the stepmonster, another way to save the money we barely have: the twins were allowed to buy new ones, but if I wanted a phone, I had to take what I could find in the house. It's huge—you can practically fend off a ship full of Reavers with it—but at least it tells the time.

8:43 a.m. Can't they leave any sooner? Just once. Just once be out of the house by 9 a.m.

They're upstairs, but Chloe's nasally voice can be heard clear as a bell. "But, *Mom*, Darien Freeman's going to be on TV this morning! I will *not* miss that."

My heart sinks. If Chloe commandeers the TV, there's no way I'll get to watch *Hello, America.*

"We can be a few minutes late," echoes Calliope. Cal sides with Chloe on everything. They're the same age as I am—rising seniors—but we might as well be on different planets. Chloe and Calliope are starters on the varsity tennis team. Organizers of the homecoming committee. Prom leaders. And they don't mind using their popularity to remind everyone at school that I'm practically dirt. That without their family, I'd be an orphan.

Thanks. Like I could forget that.

"We *can't* miss this," Chloe says. "We have to watch it and vlog about it or *everyone* else will get their reactions up before us. And that would kill us, Mom. It would *kill us*."

"Sweeties, I'm paying Mr. Craig a *handsome* tuition to teach you girls tennis. I am *not* wasting your varsity positions next year for a television program!" Catherine descends the stairs and reenters the kitchen, rustling through her purse. "Danielle, have you seen my cell phone?"

I reach over the counter to unhook it from the wall charger. "Here it is."

"Now why did you put it there?" She takes the phone from me without a second glance and begins scrolling through her Facebook feed. "Oh," she adds, "and remember, tomorrow is—"

"Yeah," I say. "I know." Like I'd forget the day my own father died. "Should I get orchids this year or—"

"*Girls!*" Catherine yells, checking her watch. "Get down here *now!*"

"*Fine!*" They trample down the stairs in their tennis whites and grab their smoothies from the counter. The twins are the spitting image of Catherine. Light hair, hazel eyes, pouty heartbreaker lips. Chloe and my stepmom are cut from the same cloth, but Cal's cut a little different, a little quieter. I think that's because she takes after her own dad, who ran off when the girls were young and married the daughter of some Atlantic City casino owner.

Right now, they both have their blonde hair pulled back into tight ponytails, and they'd be impossible to tell apart if you didn't know Calliope always matches her earrings to her purple glasses, and Chloe has a new nail color every day—today, a sweet summer blue. Sometimes evil comes in disguise.

"This isn't fair! Why doesn't Elle have to go to these stupid lessons?" Chloe whines.

"Girls." My stepmother *tsk*s, putting on a patient smile. "Elle has to make do with the talents she does have."

I try to ignore her as I grab my house keys from the bowl in the foyer and put them in my satchel, pretending like I'm getting ready for work. Sometimes I think Catherine just forgets I'm in the room.

"You're going to ruin our career," Chloe accuses, sucking on her green smoothie. "We *need* to be on top of this."

"Everyone else will be tweeting about it," Calliope adds.

"Ever since we got a hundred thousand views because of our *Seaside Cove* makeup tutorial, people expect us to be on our game!"

"GIRLS!" Catherine jabs a pink nail toward the door. "Four hundred dollar lessons. NOW!"

Calliope rolls her eyes, grabs her purse from the rack in the foyer, and storms out the door to the red Miata (another "necessity" for Catherine's "image"). Catherine glares at the remaining twin. If there is one thing Chloe can't stand up to, it's her mother's disapproval. She grabs her purse too—the exact same as Cal has, except pink—and stomps out after her sister. I don't envy *that* ride to practice.

My stepmom gives one last victory fluff to her hair in the foyer mirror. "Are you sure you don't want me to put in a good word for you at the club, Danielle? I'm sure they'd take you back even after your . . . incident . . . last year. You've learned, haven't you?"

To never trust a guy again? Sure. I pull on a polite smile. "No, thanks."

"It's the best place for someone like you, you know." She shakes her head. "You'll see I'm right in the end."

With that, she closes the door.

I wait until the Miata pulls out of the driveway before I dart into the living room and turn on the TV. 8:57. Perfect. The food truck's supposed to pick me up at ten to head to the RiverDogs baseball game across town, so I have plenty of time. For the next hour, I will be basking in perhaps the biggest news in *Starfield* history.

This moment to end all moments—or maybe begin them. A new *Starfield* for a new generation. I like the possibility in that.

Grabbing the remote from the coffee table, I sit down cross-legged in front of the 54-inch TV. The black screen flickers, and anticipation blooms in my chest. I wish Dad could be here to see this. I wish he could be sitting beside me. He'd be just as excited—no, he'd be *more* excited. But the reality is, I don't really have anyone to fangirl about this with. About who will finally don the Federation starwings and follow in the legendary footsteps of David Singh, the original Prince Carmindor. I've been blogging about it for months in my little corner of the world, but no one really reads it. *Rebelgunner* is therapeutic, more like a journal. The closest I have to friends is the online Stargunner community, where everyone's been speculating about the casting: maybe the guy from the latest *Spider-Man* movie? Or maybe that cute Bollywood star who's in all the Tumblr GIFsets? Whoever it is, they'd better not whitewash my prince.

On the TV, *Hello, America* is wrapping up a segment about pets doing goofy things on the internet. The host beams, and then the camera cuts to the audience. It's full of girls—lots of girls—and all of them are cheering. Holding signs. Wearing T-shirts with the same name scribbled across them. A name that makes the anticipation in my chest grow cold and drop like an atomic bomb into my stomach.

Darien Freeman.

The girls throw up their hands for the camera, screaming his name. One person's name. Some look like they're literally going to swoon.

I don't swoon.

My excitement makes a U-turn into dread.

No—no, this can't be right. I must have the wrong channel.

I jab the remote INFO button. *Hello, America*, the caption states, and I want nothing more than for the Black Nebula to swallow me whole.

What are the odds? What are the odds of him being on the same morning talk show? What are the odds of *him* being the guest appearance on the show that will announce the *Starfield* cast?

But the host is smiling, and says a few choice words, and suddenly all my fears come to light.

The *Starfield* logo blazes across the screen behind her. This moment has become a train wreck I can't look away from. It's my entire fandom crashing into a burning, bubbling pit of despair.

No. No, it's not him. It can't be *him*.

Darien Freeman is *not* my Federation Prince Carmindor.

DARIEN

THE CROWD IS FULL OF MONSTERS.

Okay, not actual monsters. But *you* try flying to New York City on a red-eye, subsisting on nothing but burnt coffee and half a grapefruit, sitting for thirty minutes in a makeup chair just so your stylist can get your curly hair *just right* (for God's sake, man, it's *hair*), in designer jeans that are pinching you in places that aren't even awake this early while you're trying to remember the answers to all the questions the cohosts are going to ask you—all on three hours of sleep, *three*—and then being excited to see a crowd of fans.

Breathe, I tell myself. It's fine.

I pace back and forth behind the outside stage. No one has spotted me yet, but my skin's crawling as if I'm being watched. It comes with the territory.

Now I know why Gail, my handler, told me to pop two Advil before the show. I've been to rock concerts (and, back in the day, convention panels), but this audience is *ridiculous*. Gail said they've been standing out here since four this morning. What person in their right mind would stand in line that early for *me*?

Beside me, Gail bounces on her well-worn sneakers. I don't think she's had the chance to unlace them since the second episode of *Seaside Cove*. She's scrolling through her emails, nodding. "Everything's set. We've got your flight booked for tonight, your ride to and from the airport, two assistants running interference for paparazzi . . ." Then she looks up at me and smiles. "We're golden."

She hands me a water bottle, and I put it against my neck. Her strawberry-blonde hair is pulled back into a too-tight frizzy bun, a sure sign she's just as stressed as I am. "Just breathe. You'll be fine. This is just the starter course for the media blitz. You can do it."

"You could say I'm *leveling up*," I joke.

She gives me a blank look.

"Like in video games? When you get enough experience points you—shutting up now." I unscrew the bottle and take a swig. Through the gap in the backstage curtains, I watch my fans shift impatiently. I squint. "Is that girl wearing my face on her shirt?"

"Don't pay too much attention," she replies. Her phone beeps and she pulls it out again. She frowns.

I give her a side-eye. "Everything all right?"

She scrolls through her email.

"Earth to Gail?"

Nothing.

"*Gail Morgan O'Sullivan.*"

"What? Oh!" She shoves her phone into her back pocket. "Sorry, sorry. Do you ever feel like you're forgetting something?"

"My underwear. All the time," I say with dead seriousness. "Sometimes I give myself a wedgie just to make sure I have them on."

Her worry cracks open into a small smile. "You do *not*."

Gail is older—twenty-five or so—with a brushing of freckles on her cheeks that darken in the summer, and almost glow when she blushes. Aside from my signed copy of *Batman: Year One*, she's the best friend I've got. When you're me, real friends don't come all that easy. Or at all. They used to, but I learned the hard way that things change. Especially when you're famous.

A stagehand comes over to mic me. I thread it under my blazer and clip the receiver to the back of my jeans. "Two minutes," he says, and rushes away.

"*Oh*-kay!" Gail says. "Remember to smile and just be the best you you can be." She looks me over with an eagle eye, putting a lock of hair back in place and straightening the blazer over my T-shirt. It's the most expensive thing I own—the blazer, not the T-shirt—as per my agent's request. He wants me to look *approachably geeky* but still Burberry-wearing *Seaside Cove* material. Which, as far as I'm concerned, are two streams that you shouldn't ever cross.

"Look to the stars. Aim. Ignite." Gail chants. She hugs me tightly. "I'm so proud of you, Darien. Your dad is too."

"Proud of the money," I mumble.

Her mouth twitches. "I don't think it's just—"

The audience's shrill cheer cuts through her words. Just shrill, all-hell-loose screams. I'm pretty sure my costar Jessica Stone—sweet, popular, with an indie-film track record that's way more impressive than my *Seaside Cove* stint—gets a crowd that's a lot . . . *calmer*. Her dude followers don't draw I HEART JESS on T-shirts, they just . . . well, never mind. I don't really want to think about the creepy Google searches of Jess Stone fans. Our crowds are different, end of story. The *Starfield* director, Amon Wilkins, of giant robot movie fame, probably figured she would bring in the coveted awards attention and accolades. But I guess I'll find out soon enough, since we start filming tomorrow.

As for me? I apparently bring an army of monsters to a beloved cult fandom. My fans call themselves SeaCos—or maybe it's Darienites. And today? This is a publicity stunt. This is my manager and PR team at their finest.

Scotty can beam me up anytime now.

That's the thing too. I know I'm not the first young guy to take over a character that people already love. I'm sure Chris Pine had people who didn't like him because he was Kirk 2.0. But I'm different. I'm eighteen. He was twenty-something. He had time to refine his *No Fraks Given*. I still worry about matching my socks and making sure no one uncovers my *Star Wars* boxers. Plus, right now, my hands are clammy and I think I'm starting to sweat, and sweating during a televised interview is the *worst* possible thing you can do.

Breathe in, breathe out. You can do this, Darien.

The stagehand rounds back and corrals me up the steps to the stage. He starts counting down with his fingers.

Five . . . four . . .

I smooth my blazer. Swallow my anxiety.

"And now let's welcome our next guest to the stage," one of the cohosts says, quieting the crowd, "the young actor better known as the king of *Seaside Cove*"—Holy Ego-Crusher, Batman, *that* knocks off all my street-cred—"and now picking up the mantle as our favorite *royal* from the stars, Federation Prince Carmindor . . . *Darien Freeman!*"

Breathe in. Breathe out. Put on a smile.

Like a superhero donning a mask, I step out of me and into Darien Freeman, swallowed up by the ravaging screams of five hundred teenage girls.

ELLE

THE BEAUTIFUL FACE—ANNOYINGLY BEAUTIFUL, the kind you'll remember because it'll be plastered on every fragrance ad and billboard for the next ten years—of Darien Freeman stretches across the entirety of my stepmother's 54-inch plasma TV, grinning in an easygoing sort of way. Brown skin, long eyelashes, curly hair. He might look the part, but his smile's so bright it's almost blinding. Not dour, brooding Federation Prince material. Not even cut from the same cloth.

Carmindor smiled only once in all fifty-four episodes. At Princess Amara in episode 53. The episode before—

No, *no*. No one *thinks* about that last episode, let alone talks about it. It never happened. I even blacklisted any mention of it from my blog.

Rockefeller Center is crowded with *Starfield* blue and silver. A gaggle of fangirls in the front row wave around STARCRUSH ME! and I WANT TO WABBA-WABBA WITH YOU signs like they've all watched the interstellar missions against the Nox firsthand. Which they haven't.

Even *I* haven't.

Dad, though . . . *he* was there from the beginning. The original fanboy. He even started a convention for it. ExcelsiCon. We went every year. I remember meeting the aging cast, getting my stargun signed. Hiding it in my book bag during school. Waking up every morning to Dad's alarm clock playing the theme song. Eating Wabba-Wabba Flakes for breakfast (which were really Frosted Flakes, but six-year-old me didn't know the difference). Stargazing in the summers and pretending to defeat the Nox in our backyard. Saving the galaxy from being sucked into the Black Nebula . . . Living with Dad was like living in a universe where the Federation Prince Carmindor existed.

And then—in the blink of an eye—that universe vanished.

My finger hovers over the POWER button on the remote, but I can't seem to look away. How will *Seaside Cove* fans clash with us Stargunners? It's like seeing two souped-up racecars headed for a collision at full speed—I have to watch.

Leaning back in the comfy-looking chair, Darien Freeman waves—a little shy, a little taken aback—to his sea of fans as the cohosts welcome him to the show. I'm sure he thinks it's cute.

"It's great to be here," Darien Freeman begins. His fans screech like ambulance sirens: "I love you, Darien!" and "Marry me!"

Ugh, gag me.

One of the cohosts, a guy with a massive chin, says, "We're so excited to have you! I remember—and this might date me—but I remember staying up late just to watch the show. It's a classic! How do you feel stepping into a role as big as Carmindor?"

The actor smiles. His teeth are too white, his lips too balanced—I bet he practices it in the mirror. "It's an honor, for sure," he says, even though he wouldn't know a classic if it shot phaser cannons at him. "And I'm looking forward to stepping into Carmindor. Big shoes to fill."

"Big boots, you mean," I say to no one. David Singh was phenomenal. A barrier breaker in the days when almost no other sci-fi shows had a lead actor of color. An advocate for human rights, onscreen and off. A man who tell truly believed in the philosophy of *Starfield*.

"Well, unlike Rick here, I never watched *Starfield*," says the second cohost, a petite woman in a white pantsuit who probably doesn't mean to look like a Stormtrooper but totally does. "But it seems like everyone knows about it these days! That motto—how does it go?"

"Look to the stars. Aim. Ignite," Darien says. "And I hope you become a fan. *Starfield* has a little something for everyone. It's a story about the good ship *Prospero* and its crew as they fight to protect the galaxy and uphold the standards of peace and equality. Oh"—he grins—"*and* fight aliens."

"That sounds downright terrifying!" The cohost gasps. I roll my eyes. "Fight aliens" is not how I'd describe facing down the Nox King—technically the humans are the aliens in the series. But then again, I'm an *actual* Stargunner.

"Now, don't hate us for this," the cohost goes on, "but we like to play little games on our show, and since you seem to know so much about *Starfield*, I thought I could challenge you to Dunk Tank!"

The camera pans wide to a water-filled booth with a bull's-eye on the side. The camera cuts back to Darien, looking—well, faking—a shocked expression. "Oh man! Really?"

"Of course!" Then the cohost reaches behind her chair and pulls out a water gun. "Let's see how well you can school us in *Starfield*! Every time you get an answer wrong, I get to take a shot at you."

Oh, I think. *This'll be* good. There's no way he knows anything about the series beyond its name.

The crowd begins to chant in a loud, raucous voice. "Dunk tank! Dunk tank! Dunk tank!"

Darien throws his arms out to the crowd dramatically. "Really? Really? You want to see me get dunked?"

"Dunk tank! Dunk tank!" the crowd chants, and I have to agree.

"What do you say, Darien?" the woman host asks, grinning.

He sighs, hanging his head—acting all *oh, fine, let's get this over with*. Then he slaps his hands on the side of the armchair and stands, shrugging out of his expensive-looking blazer. "All right! You're on."

Oh yeah? Let's see what you'll get wrong, Darien Freeman. I fold my arms and settle back in my chair. Onscreen, Darien climbs up onto the dunk tank, securing goggles around his eyes, and gives the thumbs-up.

The woman cocks her water gun and looks at a card in her hand.

"Question one! What is the name of the government that Carmindor is a part of?"

"Seriously? Too easy!" Darien shouts back at her. "The Federation!"

A buzzer dings, signaling the right answer, and the audience boos, shouting to dunk him already. Something goes flying past Darien's head—I think it's underwear. He doesn't look fazed in the least, grinning from ear to ear, swinging his feet underneath the plank he's sitting on.

"Fine, we'll get a little tougher!" the big-chin cohost shouts. He reads the next question. "Who is Carmindor's best friend?"

"Euci! A little harder than that!" Darien eggs them on.

"How about what Euci *does* on the ship? Or in which episode does he betray Carmindor to the Nox to save his colony? Or which episode does that colony blow up anyway?" I mutter. "How about *that* question, pretty boy?"

The crowd chants louder. "Dunk tank, dunk tank, dunk tank!"

"What's the name of the ship?"

"*Prospero!*"

"What is the Federation salute called?"

"The promise-sworn!"

The female cohost grins and whips out the final card, clearly about to go in for the kill. I edge to the front of my seat.

"What does Carmindor call his love interest in the final episode of the series?" she asks.

Darien hesitates on that one. He looks around, out at the crowd.

"No cheating!" the cohost cries. "Are you stumped? Ten, nine . . ."

Up on the plank, Darien chews on his cheek, rocking back and forth. I snort. Of course he doesn't know this one. He's never watched an episode of *Starfield* in his life.

"Five! Four! Three!" The crowd begins to count along. The cohost spreads her feet apart and aims with one hand—very dramatically, which is not at all a good way to aim a water gun—as Darien scrubs the back of his neck, looking puzzled.

"Two . . . ONE!" The crowd cheers.

The female cohost fires her shot and it hits the bull's-eye directly. A siren wails and a flashing light spins above Darien Freeman's perfectly groomed head, and the plank slips out from beneath him. He goes tumbling into the water, and the crowd goes wild. They're loving it.

Strangely, though, I'm not.

"It's *ah'blena*," I mutter, even though he's underwater. Even though I'm seeing him through a TV. Even though he definitely can't hear me and I'm just talking to a plasma flat screen. Still. If he's going to be Carmindor, it's something he should know. Dunk tank or no dunk tank. "*Ah'blena* is what he calls her."

Onscreen, Darien emerges from the tank soaking wet and flips his wet hair out to the crowd, and they scream, reaching up their hands. He grins at them.

I scowl. At this point, the only way the movie can salvage itself is by announcing the perfect villain. Obviously, it should be the Nox King, because how cool would that be? The Nox are the natural enemies of the Federation, but unfortunately the early-'90s SFX in the original series didn't do so hot with their giant ears. A reboot could make them look way better. Plus—let's be honest—think of the *slash fiction* potential. I glance at my phone, just to check the time, but I've still got a good twenty minutes before I'm on Pumpkin duty.

Onscreen, Darien takes a towel handed to him by a PA and begins to dry off. But then someone yells at him to take his shirt off. He pauses, turning back to the crowd.

"Really?" he asks them.

They scream in reply.

The screams get louder as he reaches for the bottom of his soaked shirt. I can already see the definition of his chest through the fabric. Everyone can. I groan. Why can't life have a fast-forward button?

Unlike the twins, I'm not a Darien Freeman fangirl. And I'm *definitely* not a fan of that teenage wet dream of a show *Seaside Cove*.

But then Darien Freeman peels off his shirt, and my mouth falls open. His abs and chest beam across Catherine's plasma TV, piercing through my sleepy brain like a ray of hope in this godless universe.

"He . . . he's certainly buffed up for the Federation Prince," I mutter. "I'll give him that."

I stare longer than I want to. Longer that I'll ever—*ever*—admit. Darien, clearly loving every minute, spreads his arms and then, after a moment, flourishes a bow toward the audience.

The woman cohost begins fanning herself with her water gun. "*Well.* That makes up for you losing! Can I touch them?"

Outside, a rumble rips through the air so loud that it quakes the pictures on the mantel and I jump. *Crap.* I'd know that sound anywhere.

The Magic Pumpkin is coming.

Quickly, I turn back to the TV, clasping the remote like a prayer. "C'mon, just announce who the villain is!" I beg. "Please let it be the Nox King! Please! *Please!*"

"So, as the hero of the galactic Federation"—big-chin guy gives his cohost a pitying *little lady* look as Darien pulls his T-shirt back on—"you need a nemesis . . ."

"Think of the monologues! Think of the OT3s!" I cry out to no one. "Just give me *something*, universe!"

Big Chin goes on as though I'm not making a very compelling case. "Now I hear the villain has been very hush-hush and there have been some . . . *rumors* . . . going around. About a certain . . . *lady.*"

My mouth falls open wordlessly. If it's a lady, it's not the Nox King. But then it'll have to be . . .

I lean in closer to hear over the rumble of the Pumpkin, holding the candle on the coffee table to keep it from rattling in its jar. Darien Freeman says something snarky, fiddles with his blazer cuffs, and wait for it . . . *wait for it* . . .

I squint to read his lips. They're nice lips, at least. And I recognize the syllables that push around them. The way his mouth forms the villain's name, the way his tongue curves around the sound.

The Pumpkin honks from the driveway, and next door, Franco begins yapping. The horn blares again, but Sage is going to have to wait—

she's way early, anyway. I just sit back, stunned. I can't believe it. They picked the one villain—the one character—I never want to think about again. In the original *Starfield*, Prince Carmindor shouts her name to the skies with fist-shaking agony, in an image you may recognize from the internet meme "Angry Shouting Soul-Crushing Angst."

Then again, she's the only villain who makes sense for a movie reboot. The only one who *could* rip your weak human heart out of your chest and use your spine like floss against the teeth of agony and bitterness. Prince Carmindor's one and only love interest.

Princess Amara.

Big Chin looks at the screen. "And if you want to be one of the lucky few to meet the Federation Prince himself, Midlight Entertainment is teaming up with ExcelsiCon this year to host a fan competition! Dress up as your favorite *Starfield* character and you could win once-in-a-lifetime tickets to ExcelsiCon's masquerade ball, where the winners will be treated to an exclusive meet-and-greet with our man Darien Freeman, plus tickets to the premiere of *Starfield* in L.A.!"

I shake my head. The only part of that prize I'd want are the tickets to L.A. And maybe the chance to tell Darien Freeman what I think of his stupid, vapid Carmindor to his stupid, vapid face.

Darien Freeman gives the host a weird look. "I . . . what?"

The host just stares at him, open mouthed. There's an awkward pause. Then Darien Freeman looks at the TV again. At me. An emotion crosses his face I can't quite recognize—something he's trying to hide—and millions of Americans are watching.

"You know, Darien. ExcelsiCon!"

Darien nods distractedly. "Right, right. Sorry. Of course."

The female cohost puts a hand on his knee. "Darien, it was so nice to have you on the show and we can't wait for *Starfield,* coming to theaters next spring!"

Suddenly, there's a noise off-camera. Shouting. Someone climbs onto the stage and takes a running start for the actor. A girl in a homemade I'LL SEA YOU AT THE COVE T-shirt and bikini bottoms.

Her mouth connects to his with such force that it sends them both tumbling over the sofa. Security swoops in. The camera cuts to a Huggies commercial.

I sink even deeper into Catherine's squishy chair. This is *Starfield* now? All of these SeaCos and Darienites flocking to my *Starfield*? Where they treasure abs and golden sunsets more than lifelong promise-sworns and celebrating your own weirdness?

Fine. If the universe thinks they can dish it, then I can dish it right back. I shove myself to my feet and thunder up the stairs, hurtling into my room. I wrench open my laptop just as Sage lays on the Magic Pumpkin's horn in my driveway.

I ignore it and pull up my blog. Honestly, Chloe and Cal weren't wrong—when it comes to the internet, you *do* need to get your reaction up as soon as possible. And if I do anything in this life, it's this: writing about the catastrophe that will become *Starfield*. Documenting it. After forty years *this* is how Hollywood repays us Stargunners? By giving us Darien Freeman?

FAN-TASTIC OR FAN-SERVICE? I bang out into the "title" field. Perfect.

My fingers shake as they fly across the keyboard. Words just pour out of me. I don't know where they're coming from. Maybe years of pent-up rage of not being appreciated. Of having to watch reruns on a secondhand TV for *years* just to see the HD face of some idiot heartthrob wreck my father's favorite character.

My favorite character.

The horn blares again, and I know the neighbors are wondering what a food truck is doing in the driveway.

"I'm coming!" I shout. With a click, I post the article, sending it out into the netherverse.

Thirty seconds later, I've pulled my work shirt over my head, slung my satchel over my shoulder, and hopped in shotgun to the ostentatiously orange monstrosity that is my place of employment.

"You're late," she says in a voice that matches her chlorine-green hair. Dull. Pretty weird. Not interested in talking to me. It was probably once a deep green, because she's the type of person who would dye her hair the color of her name—Sage. "I've been waiting here for *ever*."

"Sorry," I say quickly. A creepy laughing pumpkin hangs from the rearview mirror that my coworker adjusts as she backs out. "I had to . . . do something." In a million years, or a million universes, I would never admit to Sage that I'm a Stargunner. I'm sure she'd just laugh. "Wait, isn't the RiverDogs stadium the other way?" I add as she turns down one of Charleston's notorious one-way streets.

"Change of plans."

"I . . ." My voice trails off as I glance at a passing street sign. "I think this is one way the *other* way."

Sage says nothing, just grips the wheel tighter, a grin curving her hot-pink lips. On her otherwise expressionless face, it looks . . . out of place. Like a stuffed animal in the middle of a blood puddle. Demonic almost.

"Tally-ho!" Sage shouts—so loud that I jump—and yanks around on the gearshift.

I scramble for my seatbelt. I have my license, but since her mom is the owner—and thus our boss—Sage is the one who gets the driver's seat. The downside is that she's also a lunatic behind the wheel. And everywhere else, too. Honestly, if I *could* work anywhere else, I *would*. But since the only thing on my resume is my ill-fated stint at the country club—which I am *not* going to return to, no matter what Catherine says—I'm probably lucky the Pumpkin even wanted me at all.

There are worse jobs, I guess. I could be getting attacked by fangirls like poor, pretty Darien Freeman.

DARIEN

"I'm so, so, so sorry." Gail hands me an ice pack as soon as I make it to the green room.

"What just happened?" I take it and wince as I press the pack against the back of my neck.

Gail shakes her head. "I thought security had her . . ."

"I mean, they did," I say. "Right after she had me. On the floor. I thought I'd choke on her tongue." My damp hair—no longer perfectly curled—sticks to my neck like seaweed.

The fangirl had come at me so fast, I barely knew what—or *who*—hit me until I was already flipping over the rock-hard sofa and onto my already bad back. Which is ridiculous, I know: I'm eighteen, I shouldn't *have* a bad back. But after two years of carrying my costar around on *Seaside Cove*—it was supposed to be romantic, the fans loved it—my chiropractor told me to lay off the stunts for a while. I'm pretty sure that includes random girls lip-locking me in the middle of *Hello, America*.

Gail rubs her hands together nervously. "I'll make sure it doesn't happen again. I'm sorry. Was my fault *completely*. I should've had more security. I should've said something."

"Hey," I interrupt, gently touching her elbow. "I'm sure it's not your fault, you know that. We both knew these abs were killer."

She gives me a pained look, but smiles. "Don't make me laugh! I'm your handler; I should've handled this before they surprised you on live TV. Mark's gonna shank me right up the middle this time."

I sink onto the green room couch. Mark. My manager, my number one cheerleader, my bailer-out-of-jail, and—somewhere far, far *down* that list in a galaxy far, far away—my father. Gail's been on his bad side for quite a while now. To him, she's a fumbling idiot and sometimes she does fray at the edges, but everyone does. And if he thinks *she* is a fumbling idiot, I don't even want to know what he thinks of me.

Besides, Gail's the only person left from B.S.C.—Before *Seaside Cove*. Everyone else, my assistants and their assistants and Gail's assistants, have all gone through Mark's wringer, but Gail stayed. She's a monument to where I came from. A piece of history from a time when I never thought a fan would tackle me on the stage of *Hello, America*.

I also never thought I'd purposefully miss a *Starfield* question. I knew the answer too—it was *so* easy. But that was the script. I'd miss *ah'blena*, get dunked, and show my abs. All in a day's work.

Gail motions to my neck. "Hurt bad?"

"I can feel it, so I think that's a good sign."

Nodding, she sits down beside me. Once security pried off the fan, the producers ushered me into my dressing room to get checked out and go over the legal jargon I signed to go on the show. Mainly so I won't sue them for injuries. Of course *I* wouldn't sue, but the second Mark found out what happened, he ordered us to stay in the studio until he arrived. *He'd* sue *Hello, America* in a heartbeat.

But that's not even what I'm most worried about.

"So . . . ," I say, turning to Gail, "who was supposed to tell me about that ExcelsiCon contest?"

"I'm sorry. I just . . ." Gail usually meets my eyes when she talks, but now she takes out her phone. "There's a lot going on and it slipped my mind."

"Gail?"

She begins to check her email. Another good thing about working with her for so long—I can tell when she's lying.

"Is it hot in here?" She starts fanning herself. "It's hot in here. I'll go ask someone to turn on the air—"

I put a hand on her shoulder to keep her from getting up, then offer her my ice pack. She takes it and presses it against her flushed cheeks.

"I'm not cut out for this," she says.

"You kidding? I'd be lost without you, Gee. You know that."

"This is my fault." She shakes her head, burying her face in the ice pack. "I mess everything up."

"You do not," I reply. "No one could've predicted Fishmouth."

"Fishmouth? That's a horrible nickname, Darien."

I shrug. "I mean, it's not like she took the time to introduce herself. Usually when someone lands one on me I at least get her name first. . . . Did you see the look on the one guy?"

"Rick Daley?"

"He covered his face so fast, you'd think he had his chin insured for half a mil."

That was, apparently, the wrong thing to say. Panicked, Gail drops the ice pack and begins to inspect me again, lifting up my now-floppy hair, checking my arms. "Crap, crap, crap! Your face! Is your face okay? Bruised? You're filming tomorrow! I told Mark to not let you strip on the show. I told him it was a bad idea! Mark's gonna murder me if—"

I grab her hands and clasp them together. "Gee, it's fine," I say, lying.

"B-b-b-but—"

"I'm *fine*," I repeat, gently easing her down into the couch, and return the ice pack to her hand. Gail is the closest thing I have to a friend, after my actual friends turned into, well, assholes. I know Gail. I *trust* her. She's that little voice in the back of my head telling me when something isn't a good idea. Like taking flying lessons from Harrison Ford, or buying a house on the same street as Justin Bieber. And she always seems to Houdini me out of pits of fan hell or stalker paparazzi just in the nick of time.

"But I forgot to tell you about that convention!" she cries. "Excelsi-Con. I completely forgot."

The name punches a shard of ice through my stomach. She must see my face twist because she begins to fret again.

"Oh crap—oh no, that's the one you used to go to. With—"

"It's fine," I lie again. "Actually, you sit tight. I'll be right back."

Slowly, I back out of the green room and close the door quietly behind me. I touch my mouth, feeling the wound from where Fishmouth's teeth collided with the inside of my lip. Maybe Mark's right. Maybe I do need someone who can keep the fans at arm's length, provide a little muscle just in case—

"No," I tell myself. "Stop it. You are trusting. You love your fans. You're cool and funny and chill. You are Jennifer Lawrence."

But even as I say it, my heart begins to sink into my gut. Because ExcelsiCon may be a con—but it isn't *just* a con. It's ExcelsiCon. The con I used to fly across the country for with my best friend, Brian. Back before I had to start covering my face to meet a date at a restaurant. Back when I *could* date. Back when it wasn't a publicity stunt. Back before my abs had more screen time than the rest of me.

I scratch my stomach at the thought of it. The airbrushed makeup—I mean, "contouring"—makes my skin itch like hell. Even thinking about going back to a con hurts. If I go back, it means I'm really not that Darien anymore. The normal—well, geeky and obscure—guy with normal friends who didn't betray him.

So I've just always said I don't do cons. Everyone knows this little factoid—Gail, my publicist Stacey, Mark, the countless assistants he's fired over the course of my career. This isn't a secret. It's probably even in my personal file at the agency, highlighted and underlined with scented marker. So, yeah, this is kind of ticking me off.

I've barely leaned back against the green room door when a thunderous voice makes me jump.

"DARIEN!"

It's my father. My throat tightens.

"Old man!" I try for a joke because he hasn't let me call him "Dad" in three years. To protect my image, he said. I also try to sound like I'm happy to see him, which is the even bigger joke. "Finally managed to hobble out of L.A.?"

His face falls, looking tense and unfriendly under the low-watt institutional-like lighting, and he drops his outstretched arms. At this point I'm sure he's more plastic than person, but most people who hate wrinkles become Daleks over time, anyway. "What're you doing without Gail? I knew I should've gotten you a bodyguard."

"She's in there," I say, jabbing my thumb toward the door, "and I don't need a bodyguard. My fans are . . . well, passionate, but—"

"What if someone was coming down the hallway that wasn't me? You can't just go anywhere anymore. It's too risky. You *know* this," he stresses, "especially now that you'll be Prince, uh . . ." He waves a hand around.

"Carmindor."

"Exactly!" Mark smirks. "The lead guy. Everybody wants a piece. You're valuable now. You're a million-dollar man."

"I'd have taken the part for free," I mutter.

Mark snaps his fingers in my face. "Don't say that. Don't you *ever* say that." He looks left and right down the hall, as if he's worried someone might have overheard me daring to express enthusiasm for my part. "What're you doing out here, anyway?"

I hesitate. I have to just lay it out for him—no ExcelsiCon. No way. Because instead of wandering the aisles and waiting for autographs, it'll be photos. Aching, smiling muscles. Flash blindness. Carpal Tunnel. Fake friends pretending they know me. And dredging up bad memories. That's not what I want from a con.

"Well . . . ," I begin. "I kinda want to talk to you about the—"

"Where's Gail?"

Once again I thumb toward the door.

He mutters something under his breath and adjusts his cufflinks. "I'm not paying her for panic attacks."

"She's had a long day."

"*I've* had a long day. *You've* had a long day. And it isn't even Monday."

"Actually it is—"

"The press junkets after filming are supposed to be the tough-as-balls part, not this," he goes on. "*This* was supposed to be easy."

"It was pretty easy for Fishmouth to get onstage," I point out.

"Actually, I want to talk to you about—"

"Can it wait?" he interrupts, pulling out his phone. It dings again. Either an email or a text, I don't know. "I'm gonna handle this. Why don't you go get some lunch, yeah? We can talk about it later, promise."

My shoulders slump. Whatever the opposite of promise-sworn is, that's Mark. *Later* is never going to come. "Yeah."

"Good. Oh—and Darien?"

"Yeah?"

"Diet. Don't forget. I think the third floor has a cafeteria."

I make a face. "Cafeteria food? That's cardboard, bro."

"*Bro*, get a salad."

I purse my lips. With my new workout regimen and my personal trainer (who reminds me of Wolverine with the personality of a wet cat . . . so basically just Wolverine), I've existed on protein shakes and rabbit food. And chicken. So much chicken I could sprout feathers. And it's not even seasoned. All to keep me looking like the however many million dollars my body's apparently worth.

David Singh—the original Federation Prince—never had to worry about crunches, or cardio, or airbrushing, or fangirl ambushes on live TV. The original *Starfield* show barely made the ratings, and yet it somehow inspired a cult following. He got fans for his work, for inspiring people to think bigger than the Earth and ignite the stars.

I get fans for my abs.

If I were David Singh, if I were *really* Carmindor, I'd tell Mark to shove off. Diplomatically, of course. And he'd listen, and I'd go get a burger down at Shake Shack.

But I'm not Carmindor. Not in this universe, anyway.

———

THE CAFETERIA ON THE THIRD FLOOR is *worse* than cardboard. It's an entire table of absolute gluttony and sin. Because doughnuts. Nothing but doughnuts. Doughnuts as far as the eye can see. And sitting to the side, like an emo kid in a high school cafeteria, is one sad and lonely fruit cup.

"It's you and me, buddy." I take the fruit cup and find a table.

There's a few other people eating breakfast—doughnuts, to be exact—but I bypass them all to the far corner of the cafeteria. It overlooks Rockefeller Center. The blue and silver *Starfield* crowd has almost dissipated. It's hard to think they all came for me. *Me.* My stomach twists, and it has nothing to do with the fruit cup.

I give a pineapple chunk a poke. Out of the corner of my eye, I notice a guy walking toward me. The one who until a moment ago was eating a heavenly looking chocolate-sprinkled doughnut. He's older than I am, with thick-rimmed glasses and a sweat mustache.

"Hey," he says. "You're Darien Freeman."

People say this to you all the time when you're famous. What do they expect me to say back—*Yeah, you caught me.* Instead, I just stick out a hand to shake. "Hi there. Nice to meet you."

He doesn't take my hand. "*Great* show today."

I know sarcasm when I hear it. "Thanks, man," I reply, giving him a tight-lipped smile.

"Me and some of my PA buddies were just talking about it." He leans in a little closer. "Can I ask you a question? Just between us."

I don't like where this is going, but there's no way for me to say no, is there? And Gail isn't here to distract him while I make a break for the door. I shift uncomfortably. "Uh, sure."

"Do you actually know *anything* about *Starfield?*"

My eyebrows shoot up.

"Because you might have all those *Seaside* fans fooled, but they wouldn't know a decent TV show if it hit them upside the head. I bet you couldn't even tell Carmindor from Captain Kirk."

It's not a question. He just assumes.

"You know, there's a lot of us who actually love *Starfield*. It's not a fad. Or a cash cow. It's not just a chance for you to get your face on a billboard. It *matters* to people. So don't ruin it, dude." He starts to walk away, then stops and half-turns back to me. "Oh, and just so you know, I'm not the only one who thinks it. You're a joke."

"I've never been good at jokes." I try to crack a smile. "I'm not that funny."

He doesn't smile back. "*Starfield* isn't a game to us. We're a family, not a franchise. Just look online."

Then he stalks away before I can even formulate a polite, movie-star-worthy reply.

I clench my fork. I want to grab him by his starched shirt collar, turn him around, and shove the promise-sworn salute—pointer and pinky fingers out, middle two together, thumb down—into his eye sockets. And while I have his attention I want to lay down in excruciating detail the synopsis of all fifty-four episodes I watched *religiously* as a nobody teenager in the suburbs of L.A. From the Nox King to Princess Amara to every moon orbiting Galactic Six and every dwarf planet from the Helix Nebula to Andromeda. I want to tell him what that ending monologue meant to me. What it meant to see someone who looked like me in command of the *Prospero*. I want to cut out my fanboy heart and show him that it bleeds like every other Stargunner's. I want to tell him that the Federation Prince Carmindor saved my life.

But I don't. Because Mark is in the back of my head saying, *Don't lose your cool. Follow the director. Cash the check. Be a star.* And more than anything: *Don't become a headline.*

"Just look online," the so-called "true fan" had said. I push aside my depressing fruit cup and pull out my phone so I can search for whatever he was talking about. Did some A-lister tweet about me? Or did one of the gossip websites put something out already?

It doesn't take long. A few searches through *Starfield*-related hashtags and I've found it. A blog post, linked to by one of the bigger social media outlets, entitled "FAN-TASTIC OR FAN-SERVICE?"

Against my better judgment, I open the link.

The choice of teen heartthrob Darien Freeman as the noble Carmindor can only be seen as a slight against the true Starfield *fans.*

It has over a thousand retweets. Hundreds of comments. Great.

I copy the link to the post and begin to text it to Gail, ready to point out that *this* is why I shouldn't go to a con. The fans will eat me alive. But then I pause. Mark's with Gail, and if he hears that there's bad press—even if it's just a blogger—he'll probably put me under 24-7 surveillance. And force me to go to the con. And if that con is full of people like Mr. True Fan here and whoever writes this *Rebelgunner* blog, well, then, I'm screwed. It'll be humiliating. Worse than any dunk tank. But if Gail can't get me out of it, and Mark *won't* . . .

What would Carmindor do?

I thump my phone against the table, annoyed. He wouldn't blame others for his problems, that's for sure. He'd take things into his own hands. Maybe *I* can call ExcelsiCon instead. Pose as my own assistant. I'm an actor, aren't I? I can speak with the con director and get this whole ordeal sorted out. Googling ExcelsiCon, I start scrolling through their website again. I try the number for the corporate event management company, but I get lost in a phone tree. I need a *human being.* After even more scrolling, I find the con's About Us page, which doesn't have phone numbers but does have the name of the guy who founded it. One quick white pages search later and I've got his info.

Score.

I clear my throat, punch in the number, and listen to it ring. Maybe the fans don't think I'm anything more than "a brainless soap actor with more hair gel than talent," as that blog post so eloquently put it, but I *am* an actor—so I'd better get to acting.

ELLE

SAGE PARKED US IN THE VERY CORNER of the public parking lot, the one surefire way around Isle of Palm's "no food truck" ordinance. Despite the crowd at the beach, it's a pretty slow day. June in Charleston is sticky and heavy, like the syrup at Waffle House. Not even the beach breeze dents the humidity, so no one wants to move. Tourists just lie on the sand like slabs of meat, grilling in the sun.

I chew on the end of my pen, staring down at my journal. Beside me, Sage is doodling something in her notebook, her pencil making soft *tch-tch-tch*es across the page.

I peek over. It's an illustration of a girl—no, she's faceless; it's an illustration of a *dress*.

"Wow, that's a nice drawing," I say. Sage looks up, her dark-stenciled eyebrows drawn tight. "Not that I'm surprised," I quickly add, feeling my ears burn red. "What I mean is that I didn't know you could draw that *well*—no, I mean, just, I can't draw, so . . ."

Another brilliant conversation between coworkers. I swear, I try to be friendly to everyone—except the twins and their country club friends—but I suck at being social. I think one thing and my mouth says something completely different, like I'm possessed. By a whole lot of stupid.

After a long moment, Sage goes back to her sketchbook, etching a long line down the curve of the dress.

"Who do you think did the pumpkin on the side of the truck?" she asks without looking up. I begin to answer when she cuts me off. "Spoiler: it was me." Then she nudges her head toward a customer coming up to the truck. "Your turn."

I sigh, closing my journal, and turn to the order window. The guy's young and tall, his shaggy hair in such bad need of a trim that it's begun to curl around his ears.

He recognizes me at the same time. "Oh. Hey. Elle."

I purse my lips. "James."

The back of my neck prickles with sweat, and a little panic. James Collins is one of the twins' country club cronies. Relatedly, he's the reason I'm sworn off trusting boys—ever. Maybe it was my fault for assuming that someone like James would ever be interested in me, but I'm not the one who *filmed* our ill-fated country club rendezvous and sent the YouTube link to the entire school. No, that would be my charming twin step-vloggers. You know, because they weren't already making my life miserable enough. And James was all just part of their plan.

He's in dark blue swim trunks and a T-shirt that reads I'D RATHER BE ON PROSPERO with the silhouette of the starship *Prospero* whirling around the last word, warping into light speed.

I clear my throat, pointing to his shirt. "I hear the observation deck is nice this time of year."

"Huh?" He glances from me to Sage, but she isn't even paying attention. Then he looks down to his shirt. "Oh, this? It's my brother's old shirt. He's into that dumb nerd stuff."

"Dumb," I echo, and for a moment I want to shove a cold and soulless vegan fritter down his throat. Dumb. He's totally lying. He didn't call it dumb last summer. "What's so dumb about—"

Sage kicks me beneath the counter.

I shoot her a glare. She returns it under glittery fake eyelashes. I turn back to him.

"What would you like?" I say between a tight-lipped smile.

"He wants the chimichangas," Sage says, putting down her sketchbook. "Don't you?"

"Uh . . ." James looks like what he wants, even more than vegan food, is just to get away from the crazy *Starfield* girl and her colorful, piercing-covered companion. "Sure."

He pays—with his own credit card, of course—takes some chimichangas from Sage, and leaves at warp speed. I sit down on a cooler and open my notebook again, still angry at James, and use that vehemence to draft another scalding blog post about other uses for Darien Freeman's deceptively perfect body.

Number one: A washboard.

Number two: A skin suit for criminals.

Number three: The mold for real-life Ken dolls.

Number four: *Not* being Carmindor.

Across the truck, Sage's pencil makes quick *tic-tic-tic*s across the paper. A leaf of green hair falls into her face and she scoops it back absently.

"That guy seemed like a douche-bro."

It's one of the longest sentences she's ever said to me. I don't even know how to answer.

"You two have some history?"

When I don't answer, she shrugs and juts her chin in the direction James left.

"Don't you go to high school with me? I'm sure you saw the video."

She just frowns, and from the way she scrunches her pink mouth against the orange ring pierced into her lower lip, I can't tell if she *did* see it or not. But if she wants to press the issue, she doesn't—and I'm glad. Last summer's better left tossed into the Black Nebula. It's better off gone.

Thankfully, my phone chooses that exact moment to vibrate on the counter. But when I pick it up, I don't recognize the number—which doesn't surprise me. Since I inherited Dad's phone number, I've gotten calls and texts from random people, usually about ExcelsiCon. And usually—actually, *every time*—I ignore them. They'll get through to the right person eventually, and it's best to ignore things you don't want to remember. It's not because I don't want to be reminded of Dad, but because every time I think of ExcelsiCon—of not going—it feels like I'm letting him down.

But as soon as I let it go to voicemail, I feel bad. It's not this person's fault ExcelsiCon left Dad's bio up on the site for so long. They miss him as much as I do. And a part of me, so small I can normally squash it out, thinks that it could be Dad, phoning in from another universe.

So when my phone buzzes again—a text, this time—I pick it up.

Unknown 11:36 AM

—*Hi there. Could you take the Federation Prince off your schedule?*

—*He sincerely apologizes, but something came up.*

My annoyance quickly turns to curiosity. It must be one of the dudes on the cosplay panels. After the announcement today, everybody and their mothers will probably be playing Carmindor, so professional cosplays will probably want to cosplay as someone *else*.

Before I can even answer, the phone buzzes again.

Unknown 11:39 AM

—*Please? He will be very tired. He has a lot of work to do.*

Today just wants to give me a face full of *Starfield*, doesn't it. I type back a reply before even really thinking about it.

11:40 AM

—*Work? Like what? Last I heard, Carmindor doesn't give excuses.*

The number pings me back almost immediately.

Unknown 11:41 AM

—*Oh I beg to differ.*

—*Do I have the right number? For ExcelsiCon?*

11:42 AM

—*Nope.*

—*But hey, I can offer you an out-of-this-world deal on vegan chimichangas.*

Unknown 11:42 AM

—*Sounds galactic. Maybe some other time.*

—*Do you know who I should contact?*

Yes. Maybe.

I could point him in the right direction. I haven't been in touch with Dad's colleagues at ExcelsiCon since . . . well, not in a really long time. But I could probably get in touch with someone. I've never offered to before. I never wanted to.

11:43 AM

—*Afraid not.*

—*Maybe it won't be so bad.*

—*You know, boldly go.*

Unknown 11:43 AM

—*Wrong show, but thanks.*

—*And may the force be with those chimichangas.*

"Look, *look!*" Sage crows. I jerk my head up from my phone. Out in front of us, James rounds out of one of the beachwear shops, pushes a hairy guy in trunks out of the way, and sprints toward the public bathrooms.

Wide-eyed, I stare at Sage. "Did you . . ."

Sage smiles her demon grin. "Were those the new batch of chimichangas? Or were they chimichangas from last week?" She heaves a big shrug. "Who's to say? Wibbly wobbly timey space stuff." She wiggles her fingers, making her many bracelets jangle.

Did my coworker just exact vegan food-poisoning revenge on my behalf? I don't know whether to be grateful or terrified. My phone vibrates again.

"Sorry, I . . ." I hold up my phone. "This wrong number keeps texting me—"

But then I look at my texts again and my stomach plummets.

> *StepMOMster 11:44 AM*
>
> —*The neighborhood watch called me about a food truck in our driveway.*
> —*We'll speak about this tonight.*
> —*After you pick up this grocery list.*
> —*[1 attachment]*

When I look up again, Sage is back at her sketchbook, totally silent. And for the next four hours, the mystery number doesn't text back either.

Once again, I'm completely alone.

———————

APPARENTLY MR. RAMIREZ COMPLAINED ABOUT A noise violation on his peaceful day off, aka basically tattled on me to Catherine. So when Sage drops me off at the end of the street—so Catherine doesn't hear the truck—my punishment is cleaning out the attic. And coupon duty for the next month. And dish duty. And grocery duty. Basically every chore I do already, but now considered "punishment."

Catherine hands me rubber gloves and a dust mask.

"You're lucky I don't ground you for the rest of summer vacation," she says. "The *humiliation* of having to apologize to Giorgio! I'm barely going to be able to look him in the eye at Pilates. This is a *respectable* community, Danielle. You can't just go around parking nasty trucks in the driveway. Honestly, sweetie, what would your father think?"

Dad would think she was a monster for siding with someone who leaves their poor wiener dog out in the weather. Dad would adopt the Frankenwiener in an instant, probably. But most of all, Dad would chastise her for throwing his things away, for wasting our money, for pretending like things were still perfect.

I still don't understand how or why he fell in love with her.

"And working with someone with so many piercings! I'm sure that green-haired girl is rubbing off on you."

I finally glance up, afraid for a moment that she would make me quit. "I like my job."

But she goes on like I haven't said anything at all. "I told Robin you would grow up to be a troublemaker. I guess it can't be helped."

My hands begin to shake. "I was going to work! To my job! I was being responsible!"

"Don't argue with me."

"You're acting like I committed a crime!"

She gives me a surprised look. "Go," she says calmly, pointing up the stairs. "Clean out *your* attic. Before it gets too late."

Fine.

I march out of the kitchen and up the stairs, snapping the dust mask over my mouth as I pass the twins' bedroom, when a ridiculously upbeat song blasts from their stereo. It makes me pause, and I backtrack. Through the crack in the door, Chloe and Cal stand in the middle of their room, facing their Mac, waiting for the song to start again. I stare, slack-jawed, as Chloe starts lip-syncing into a comb, wearing a ridiculous pink . . . *thing* . . . clamped around her chin. Whatever the contraption is—the twins are obsessed with Korean beauty products— she can barely move her mouth but still bops her hip and rolls her head.

And Cal mimics her, wearing a purple facemask that makes her look more like a *luchador* than a beauty vlogger.

They get halfway through the song before Cal notices me out of the corner of her eye. She freezes midslide. Chloe slams into her. They stumble.

"Oh my god! What the hell?" Chloe snaps at her. Well, she kinda snaps. It all sounds like a jumble of words since she can't move her jaw. "Klutz!"

Cal quickly looks away from the door, but it's too late. *Uh-oh.*

Chloe glances over to see what distracted her and, upon seeing me, pales. She lunges for the computer and puts the video on pause. "Freak! Don't you understand *privacy?*" She shouts, storming toward me.

"The door was open," I argue, "and I heard the Spice Girls. Have you been practicing?"

She scowls. "Ugh. When we get our new house, I'm going to ask Mom to put you under the stairs."

I roll my eyes. "Whatever." I begin toward my room when I pause, finally hearing what she said, and backtrack. "What did you say?"

Crossing her arms smugly, she leans against the doorway. "I guess Mom hasn't told you."

Behind her, Cal begins to pull off her mask and winces. "Chloe, leave her alone."

"No, I think *someone* should tell her."

"Tell me what?"

She leans toward me out of the room. The twins are tall and long-legged, so when Chloe wants to tower, she's like the Eye of Sauron. "Why do you think Mom wants you to clean the attic, huh?"

"It's dirty," I fill in, perplexed. "It probably hasn't been touched in seven years—"

"She's selling the house, genius," she says.

My eyes widen. I glance from her to Cal, who never lies. Cal, who's cut from a slightly different cloth. Cal, who's ripping all the hair off her face as she peels off the mask. Cal, who can't meet my gaze.

Chloe smirks. "Now you know."

My parents' house? This house? I take a step back. Chloe's lying. She has to be.

I whirl on my heels and rush back downstairs and into the kitchen. The walls are a blur. Catherine glances up from her coupons.

"You're selling it?" I tug the dust mask off my mouth, trying to gulp down enough air, but I can't seem to. "You—you're selling the house?"

My stepmother tilts her head like she has positively no idea what I'm talking about. For a moment I take that as a good sign. Like she couldn't have done something so awful. But then she says, "Oh, Danielle, it's for the best. You understand."

My throat begins to constrict, too tight for words.

She goes on. "It's so big and drafty. When the twins go off to college what will we do with the place? I think it's best to sell it."

"When are you selling it?"

She gives me a patient, pitying look. "Sweetie, that's why I asked you to clean the attic. It's already on the market."

I lean against the doorframe to steady myself. The room begins to close in around me, warping, melting, like the universe is changing again. Like it did when Dad died. Doorways slamming closed. Bolting. Roads disappearing. What-ifs blowing away like dust in the wind.

I take a step back. Then another.

Catherine gives me a patient look. "Danielle, we all have to make sacrifices. Struggle builds character, after all."

Blinking back tears, I turn back toward the stairs and climb them again. I don't bother with the attic tonight. The attic can wait. It has for seven years. It can wait until we're gone.

I pass Chloe on the way to my room. "Told ya," she says.

I spin around and squint at her. She's taken the ridiculous chin-thinner off, but I can see the impression on her face. "You know, I think your chin's thinner."

Her eyes lighten. "Really?"

"*No.*" Then I close the door to my room. Lock it.

What am I going to do now? Where am I going to go? This is my home. This house, these walls. I wipe my nose, determined not to cry, and sit down at my old desktop computer. My room is small—just big enough to fit a twin bed and a desk. The twins don't come in, and Catherine can't stand tiny spaces. It's the only place in the universe that is strictly *mine*.

And even this won't be mine for much longer.

I wiggle my mouse until the computer comes to life, then take a Hershey's Kiss from my secret stash at the bottom of my drawer—above the $721 I've saved up between last summer working at the country club and this summer. It's the only safe place I could think of, where neither the twins nor Catherine'll look.

For a brief moment, I imagine catching the first Greyhound out of here, with Franco in tow. Do Greyhounds take dogs? They're named after a dog, so I don't see why not. I begin to Google it when I notice my email has a lot of notifications. From my blog.

Great. More spammers. And here I thought my day couldn't get any worse. I log on, getting ready to hit mass-delete. It takes me a moment to realize something's different. That the comments on my latest post aren't spam. The post about Darien Freeman as Carmindor.

But no one ever comments on my blog. No one knows it even exists.

And there are over *two hundred* comments.

I take out another Hershey's Kiss and click on my post, fearfully scrolling down to the comments.

At least he wasn't whitewashed

But he SUX at acting

I click over to my page view and almost choke on my chocolate. Over *a hundred thousand*. And it's hot-linked back to news sites. Actual news sites.

"FAN'S ELOQUENT REACTION TO STARFIELD CASTING REVEAL," one headline reads.

"FAN-TASTIC OR FAN-TROUBLE?" another asks.

And they have excerpts to *my* blog post. What . . . what in the world?

"You're dreaming, Elle," I tell myself, checking my subscribers—then *ten thousand*—and my other posts? Twenty-seven thousand. Thirteen thousand. And so many comments.

Seaside is the worst!!!!

cant BELEIVE they are letting him into ECon lolol

yeah srsly gunners are NOT gunna be happy that d-free is at their con

i wouldn't let him autograph ANY of my SF stuff!!!! NO WAY

My heart gives a funny lurch in my chest. My parents met in an autographing line, twenty-some years ago. As Dad told it, Mom came up to him as they waited in line for the cast—David Singh, plus Ellen North, Carl Thompson, and Kiki Sanchez, the original Carmindor, Amara, Euci, and CLE-o. As the story went, Mom smiled at Dad and said, "I hear the observation deck is nice this time of year," and that was that.

Together, they were unstoppable. The way Dad told it, he barely knew how to darn pants, never mind sew cosplay, but Mom was a pro. She was known through the circuits as one of the queens of cosplay. She made Dad's Federation Prince uniform as an anniversary present, and he looked great in it (that was also back when he had hair). He always said he was the studdiest muffin. I laughed, but in all the pictures Catherine threw away he really was handsome. In a 1980s, Marty McFly sort of way.

In the *Starfield* world, Mom and Dad became celebrities in their own right—Big Name Fans before the internet was even a thing—and then Dad went on to found ExcelsiCon.

I keep scrolling. There are more comments, but it's just too overwhelming to read. I ease away from my computer, change into my pajamas, and face-plant on my bed. There's no way that I have that many page views. It's a trick. Someone's playing games. But Chloe's friends aren't that smart, and I don't know of anyone else who *would*.

Out the attic window, heat lightning streaks across the ocean. Through the damp wood of the attic, I can smell the rain in the air. Dad loved thunderstorms. He would sit with me out on the porch and we would watch them together.

"They're starfights, starlight," he would tell me. *Starlight*—his nickname for me. Like in the rhyme.

Star light, star bright, first star I see tonight . . .

How many times did we used to look out these windows together? I turn my face into my pillow so I can't see the sky anymore. Without this house, I have no reason to stay. Catherine doesn't want me, and the twins certainly don't either. But I don't have anywhere to *go*. What I need is for the *Prospero* to come sweep me up. What I need is a ticket to another universe.

Outside, the thunderhead slowly crosses the ocean, eating up all the stars in the sky.

DARIEN

THE HOTEL MATTRESS IS TOO SOFT. They're always too soft. I sometimes dream I'm drowning in them. Those are the worst nightmares, but not as bad as the ones where I'm falling. I didn't have falling nightmares until a stunt went wrong during filming of the climax of *Seaside Cove*'s first season. My harness broke and I fell twenty feet—onto foam, but still. For two seconds I forgot the camouflaged foam wasn't cement.

How am I going to film *Starfield*, whirling around in harnesses in "deep space," if I can't even get over a twenty-foot fall? Worse, what if that dude in the cafeteria was right?

I fluff up my pillow again and roll over onto my back, trying to forget about him. The ceiling's absolutely spotless. That's how you can really tell how expensive a place is. I remember when Mark didn't put me up in five-star hotels, back when I first auditioned for *Seaside Cove*. He drove me to the casting call in Santa Barbara and booked me into a shoddy Motel 6 that had roaches crawling across the ceiling.

It's no use. I can't sleep. I sit up, scratching my stomach from where the airbrush makeup irritated my skin, and wander over to the mini-fridge. Low-calorie beer, bottles of water. I actually don't want beer, though I'm pretty sure the entire population of eighteen-year-old guys would disown me for that, and the water's the weird kind with added electrolytes.

What I *want* is an Orange Crush. It's my one and only kryptonite, diet or no diet. One of these floors has to have a soda machine, and even a walk down the hall beats being holed up in a hotel room.

I'm pulling a hoodie over my head when the door lock clicks green and Mark strides in, coming off a call from some other agent or producer or whoever.

"Hey! Yo, ever heard of knocking?" I grumble, tugging my hoodie down in aggravation.

"Heard of it." He takes a no-taste beer out of the mini-fridge and pops it open on the half-kitchen counter. "Enjoying the hotel room?"

"I was just about to go get a soda."

"Call room service," he replies, taking out the menu from behind the phone on the desk in the sitting area. Yeah, my hotel room has a *sitting area.* "What do you want? I'll do it—"

"Never mind. I'll just have a bottle of water." I sulk over to grab one from the fridge. Electrolyte water tastes as bland as my soul feels. "What'd *you* want?"

"What, a father can't spend some quality time with his son?"

I give him a look.

"Fine." He takes another swig before setting his beer on the coffee table. He sits down in one of the plush velvet chairs. I take the one opposite of him.

We look alike, from our brown skin to our black hair. But I got my nose from my mom, and apparently my temperament from her father. At least that's what Mark said. They split up a long time ago, in the B.S.C. (Before *Seaside Cove*) days. Mom went back to her socialite family in London, and I can't say I blame her—if being Mark's son is this bad, I can't imagine what being married to him was like. These days she's always doing charity work with her new husband in India or modeling for Italian magazines or something. She used to invite me to family reunions to meet the Dayal side of the family. I went once, but because I grew up with my dad, I didn't know how to address my grandparents, I didn't know table etiquette (you use your right hand, never pour your own drink, eat only after the eldest at the table has eaten). The Dayals were open and welcoming, but I felt like an idiot, like a jigsaw piece that didn't fit into their big picture.

After that disastrous reunion I stopped going, and after a while Mom stopped inviting me, the son of a Hollywood social climber—I'm sorry, *manager*. Now it's just me and Mark, united under the Freeman brand.

"So, here's the deal," he says. "We're moving your vacation to the weekend *after* you wrap filming."

"Surprise," I deadpan, waiting for the rest. I want him to bring it up—ExcelsiCon. Because he sure as hell hasn't yet. I failed miserably this morning when I called—well, texted—that stranger. I didn't get the person at the con, and I practically blew my cover besides. It was, certifiably, one of the worst ideas I've ever had.

"We had some last-minute gig come up. A photo shoot for *Entertainment Today,* a car commercial—assuming those clowns at BMW USA sharpen their pencils a little—and that appearance at the . . . you know. The thing." He waves his hand in a spiral.

"The con," I say shortly.

He snaps. "That's it. Look, I know *Hello, America* spoiled the surprise, but—"

"Spoiled the surprise? I'm not an idiot, Mark. I know you didn't tell me so that they'd corner me and I'd basically have no choice but to agree on camera!"

He sighs. "Come on, kid. You love cons, don't you? You always went with that buddy of yours. Billy or Bucky—"

"Brian."

"Yeah, him. And you haven't been to one in a while. I thought, hey! Let's give him something he'll actually like doing!"

I massage the bridge of my nose. "Mark, you know I don't—"

"Yes yes, you 'don't do cons.' I get it—"

"Did you just air-quote me?"

"—but hey, you know what? It'll perfect timing at the end of summer to remind everyone that you're in *Starfield*. You're coming right off filming! You'll be in great shape! And it's great press to get out there and meet the fans."

"The fans," I repeat. Like the *Rebelgunner* blogger, ready to slug me in the face for besmirching Carmindor's good name.

"C'mon. It'll be good for you to get out and do something normal." He's trying to reason with me—which, props for that, at least. "All you gotta do is show up—"

"No."

"And do a meet-and-greet—"

"No."

"—with one lucky contest winner, and make an appearance at their weird dance party afterward—"

I jerk to my feet. "How many times do I have to tell you? *No.*"

"Well, hate to break it to you, buddy, but you agreed to do it on live television. If you cut out now, it'll look bad. Like you're temperamental. A diva." He lowers his voice. "Hard to work with."

"Whatever."

He gives me an appalled look. "What's gotten into you, kiddo? You know how important these things are for your image." He softens. "And you love conventions."

"*Loved*. Past tense. I also loved *making my own decisions,* but I guess that doesn't get me enough good press, huh?" Turning on my heels, I snatch the room's keycard from the counter and shove it into my back pocket.

"Where the hell are you going?"

"To get a soda," I grind out, yanking open the door.

"Remember your diet—"

I slam the door.

The hallway's quiet, white and immaculate like a lot of these new-age hotels. The hallway actually reminds me of the *Seaside* set, stark white walls with halogen lighting. Empty. Except the set was fake and I could pull back the plywood that made up most of our "houses" and peek at the tech guys behind them. Here, I can't get away from it.

There isn't a vending machine on my floor, so I take the stairwell down to the tenth, and then the ninth. By the eighth floor, still no vending machine, but no people, either. At this point, the less people in my life, the better.

On the seventh-floor landing, though, I hear voices. I quickly press myself against the side of the wall as they get louder, drawing near the stairwell. I sink down on the bottom step of the landing, and there I sit, waiting for them to leave.

Maybe they're just regular people. Maybe they won't recognize me. Or maybe I'm crazily paranoid. Long story short, there are people like my dad who want to channel your fame and help you rise to the top. Then there are people like Brian, who take damning pictures of you when you invite them to visit the set and sell them to TMZ. That's what hurt, more than the yacht fall. And no, despite what the "IS *SEASIDE COVE'S* DARIEN FREEMAN IN A FREEFALL?" article said, I wasn't drunk, or high, or tripping on anything besides my own feet. It wasn't some publicity stunt.

And *yes*, I have a scar to prove it.

I put my face in my hands, getting impatient. All I wanted was an Orange Crush. Just one. It's been a *day*. I deserve one.

I do.

Getting to my feet, I pull my hoodie over my head and wrench open the stairwell door and—slam into one of the guys loitering in the hallway. There's three of them, one girl. My age, maybe a year or two younger. Tourists, by their sandals and backpacks.

"Sorry," I mutter, and duck my head as I pass.

Don't recognize me, don't recognize me, I pray. These days, when everyone's got a jillion-megapixel camera in their pocket, you don't even have to worry about official paparazzi. Why couldn't I live during the days of flip phones?

Phones. My hand goes to my pocket—empty. I turn around. The tourists are still there.

"Hey, dude," one of them calls.

I turn back around, go in the other direction, speed up.

"Wait a sec!" the girl adds, a slight tilt to her words. French, or Canadian. Of course the girl would be the one to recognize me. I hear her start running down the hallway toward me. "Hey—hey, dude, you dropped your phone."

She holds it out and I take it, trying not to look her in the eye without seeming rude.

"Thanks," I mutter.

She frowns. "You look really familiar—"

"I get that a lot," I reply, and quickly spin on my heels again, making my exit down the hallway.

"Weird guy," one of her friends murmurs.

"Whatever, it's New York. Everyone's weird."

Yeah, *understatement*. They keep talking and I force myself not to listen as I follow the signs toward the snack machines. I push open the door and the iridescent lights of the soda machine shine eerily in the dark room. *Bingo*. I don't bother to turn on the lights as I dig into my pockets for spare change and pop the coins into the machine.

"Take *that*, luck," I mutter, pressing the button for orange soda.

OUT reads the machine display.

I jab it again.

OUT.

OUT.

OUT.

"*Nox's crack*, come on," I plead, jabbing the button with the fervor of a man on death row.

Sighing, I opt for water instead, and the vending machine groans as it operates, rolling out a sparkling bottle of nothingness. Have you ever noticed how vending machines are never out of water?

I lean against the wall, taking a swig. I don't want to go back to the room yet, but I also don't want to pass that group of friends again, and they're between me and both the stairwell and the elevator.

If I had friends, or a girlfriend—there's a hilarious idea—now's when

I'd fire off a text message to catch up, say hey, complain about my day. I settle on the vending-machine-room floor and idly thumb through my messages from the bottom up, contact after contact after contact. A few odd texts with the *Seaside* cast from last March, but I was never close with them—they're all, like, twenty-five and on the opposite coast. Then some with the *Seaside* publicist, my publicist Stacey, Gail, Mark . . . all people I work for, or people who work for me.

I'm not lonely. I'm not, I swear.

Then, at the top, there's that wrong number. The chimichanga girl— or guy, I guess, but for some reason I assumed it was a girl.

I sip my soulless water. There's no reason to text the number again. Absolutely none. But I'm bored, and I'm stuck, and my fingers type up a quick message and hit SEND before my head can catch up.

ELLE

I ROLL OVER ON THE BED, taking my phone out of my back pocket, and slide my thumb across the cracked screen to the message.

It's the stranger. Well, the cosplayer. Carmindor.

Unknown 9:42 PM

—*How were those chimichangas?*

I chew on my lip. This guy could be a stalker. Or some weird old geezer with a Carmindor fetish. Or just someone who wants to know about Mexican food on my spaceship *el pumpkin*.

9:47 PM

—*Very vegan.*

—*Did you get in contact with who you were looking for?*

Unknown 9:48 PM

—*Sadly not.*

—*Haven't had time to track them down.*

I sit up. The convention was a part of me I walled off after Dad died. I didn't want to be a part of it, didn't want to walk in through those glass doors and almost see Dad standing in the lobby, Carmindor coat starched, starwings gleaming. Besides, the people at ExcelsiCon haven't been much in contact with me either. Pretty much dropped me cold turkey after Dad died. Some community *that* was.

But Dad always believed in helping everyone no matter what. In being kind and going the distance. I wish I was half the person he was, but he always said he learned it from Mom. So if Mom was kindness and Dad was half of her, what did that leave me? A quarter?

Chewing on the inside of my cheek, I reply, wondering why I'm making an exception.

> *9:48 PM*
>
> —*Maybe I can help?*
> —*Although the REAL Carmindor doesn't give excuses, you know.*

> *Unknown 9:48 PM*
> —*What do you call episode 26?*

> *9:48 PM*
> —*Uh, he was mind-warped by a Nox?? Please.*
> —*Unless I'm wrong and you'd like to set me straight, your Federation highness.*

> *Unknown 9:48 PM*
> —*Somehow correcting you about Starfield feels like a bad idea.*
> —*As I tend to have.*

9:50 PM

—*You wouldn't be Carmindor without your bad ideas.*

—*. . . No offense.*

Unknown 9:51 PM

—*None taken. I pity the poor galaxy that falls under my rule.*

—*Muha. Ha.*

—*So . . . you're a Stargunner?*

9:51 PM

—*I bleed Federation blood.*

—*You?*

Unknown 9:52 PM

—*Born from the Brinx Devastation itself.*
  I promise-swear.

—*\m/*

Like I believe his promise-sworn . . . whoever he is. Lightning cracks across the sky again, closer this time. I wait to hear thunder. One-one thousand. Two-two thousand. Three-three thousand . . . Then it comes, slow and soft like a song.

Dad always liked thunderstorms. The way it rattled the house, like a heart rattling in a ribcage.

Unknown 9:59 PM

—*Can I ask you a weird question?*

10:00 PM

—*Uh . . . I guess??*

Unknown 10:00 PM

— *What do you think of the new Carmindor?*

Uh-oh. I think back to my blog post. My viral blog post. I'd lie to him if I said anything other than what was absolutely true.

10:00 PM

— *You mean Darien Freeman?*

Unknown 10:00 PM

— *Yeah.*

I tilt my head back to watch the storm roll in out the window. I could link him to my blog post, but chances are if he's a Stargunner he already knows my feelings. Or the author's feelings. That no matter the universe, Darien Freeman will *never* be Carmindor. Instead, I decide to stall.

10:01 PM

— *Why, are you a Seaside Cove fan?*

Unknown 10:01 PM

— *Please, give me Gilmore Girls. Coffee. Quick wit.*
— *So you don't think he can pull it off?*
— *Darien, I mean.*

I don't know why I say what I do next. I guess because if he's asking, he genuinely likes the casting.

10:01 PM

— *I . . . think if he tries, maybe he could do it.*

—*I mean, that's what Carmindor would do. Try. Even when the odds seem hopeless.*

—*But who knows if Darien Freeman cares enough to try.*

Unknown 10:01 PM

—*So you DO think he'll be good? As a fan?*

10:01 PM

—*Can I take a rain check on that answer?*

Unknown 10:01 PM

—*Depends. How long's the rainstorm?*

I look out the window, at the water whipping through the night sky. *Never ending,* I want to say. But instead I reply:

10:02 PM

—*Until he does something to change my mind, I guess.*

—*Show he's going to try.*

DARIEN

Mark's still sitting where I left him, sipping on his beer. He lifts an eyebrow as soon as I slip back through the door.

"So the prodigal son returns," he says in greeting. "Cooled your jets?"

"Yeah, they're cool." I sit down opposite him in the room's sitting area. His thumbs fly across his antique Blackberry, the clicks on the keyboard eating up the silence between us. I tap my half-empty water bottle against my thigh, thumping out the *Starfield* theme.

If Stargunners want me to prove that I'm their Carmindor, that I'm one of them—even after missing the *ah'blena* question on *Hello, America*, which I'm sure will come back to haunt me—then I have to be a fan. And there's only one way I know how to be a fan.

There will be people like Fishmouth and that guy from the cafeteria and whoever blogs at *Rebelgunner* who scream so loud it's hard to hear anything else. But then there'll be people like the person on the other end of those texts, whispering in a steady cadence. *Those* are the people I signed the contract for. Because I know what that's like. *Starfield* was there for me when my shitty parents and my shitty friends weren't. That's why I took this job. Because I'm a fan.

"I'll do the con," I say.

He glances up from his Blackberry. "You will?"

"I just said so."

He begins to stand up. "Great! I'm glad to hear it—"

I put up a hand. "On one condition."

He sits back. "Of course. Are you sure it's not two? Three?" He flicks his eyes to the ceiling—almost rolling them, but not quite. "Well, what is it?"

Here goes. *Aim. Ignite.* "I want to help judge the cosplay contest. I don't just want to be some aloof movie star posing for photos. I want to be part of this fandom."

"Part of the . . . what? Fandom?" Dad's too-smooth forehead gets the tiniest crease—his expression at its most emotional. "It's not on brand, Darien."

"Please, just this once. To show I'm one of them."

"But you're not."

I purse my lips. "I'll be there already. We could make it on brand."

Mark shifts in his chair and I can tell he's doing some mental calculus. Would Chris Pine condescend to judge a costume contest? Would Chris Evans? Chris Hemsworth?

"It would be hard," he says at last.

"But if you'll just let me—"

"*But.*" He holds up a finger to stop me. "I think we can make it work. And ExcelsiCon will be more than happy to agree to that." He takes another sip of beer. "Yeah . . . yeah I think we can make it on brand. Keep you front and center. You're a genius."

I don't like the look that slowly slides across his face, half smug, half scheming. What is he thinking up? I'm not sure I want to know. Still— he didn't say no. For once I got through.

"Thanks," I say.

And for a moment, I almost add *Dad.*

ELLE

I DON'T KNOW WHEN I FINALLY FALL ASLEEP after the last text message, but I know exactly when I wake up.

"Danielle!" my stepmother snaps as she yanks the covers off me. "Danielle, get up!"

"Whaaa . . . ," I murmur, and wince when she shines a flashlight into my face.

Hard rain pounds against the window as zigzags of lightning flash across the sky. I squint at the clock, but it's completely dark. The storm must've knocked out power. The howl of the wind almost drowns out her words—almost—but Catherine would never allow something to be louder than she is.

"Get *up!*" she roars, barely giving me a chance to take in her hair in fat foam rollers and her ridiculous silk bathrobe before she yanks me out of bed by the arm. I rub the sleep from my eyes and stumble after her, her nails digging into my forearm until she lets me go at the end of the hallway.

"What's wrong?"

She jabs her pink-polished claw upward. I blink sleepily. A dark stain is spreading across the ceiling. My heart sinks. A leak. In the attic. "I thought I told you to fix it last time!"

Down the hall, the twins peek out of their bedroom. Great. Now we have an audience.

"Can't you do anything right?" she fumes, folding her arms over her chest, where her bathrobe has a few wet splotches. It must be leaking into her room or else she wouldn't have bothered waking me up.

"I did," I mutter. It's not like it matters. Isn't she selling the house anyway? "The wind must've knocked the shingles loose again—"

"*Apparently* you didn't." She glares at me as I shift from one foot to the other. "Well?"

I glance over at her, confused.

She jabs her finger toward the ceiling again. "Get up there and fix it!"

I blanch. "*Now?*"

"Before it gets worse!" she cries, and hands me a flashlight. "First your attitude this evening and now *this*. Honestly, Danielle, you're lucky I am being this forgiving."

Half of me wants to tell her it's absolutely *bonkers* for me to go searching for a leak in the middle of the night during a storm. And I have work early tomorrow morning—they don't.

"Now, you are going to crawl up there and stop the leak. And I think you should pay for the damages, don't you? I can't very well sell a house like this."

My mouth falls open. "That makes no sense! This could have happened to any house—it's a freaking thunderstorm!"

"Oh? And did the thunderstorm forget to repair the leak the first time?"

I clamp my mouth shut. How the hell do you argue with crazy?

"That's what I thought," Catherine replies, and then turns on her heels swiftly and stalks back to her room. "Go back to bed, girls. Danielle is taking care of it."

The twins look at each other and close the door. Sighing, I reach for the string and pull down the stairs until the dark mouth of the attic yawns open above me. I shine the flashlight into the darkness to banish the ghosts and climb up.

Even though I've lived in this house my whole life, the attic feels for-
bidden. My entire childhood home feels like a stranger now, just like the
Federation Prince felt after being rescued from the Nox. Familiar, but
foreign. No longer how I remembered. No more tabletop games in the
living room. No more swords and shields above the mantel. When Dad
married Catherine he boxed it all away, and when Dad died she donated
everything. Erased the last bit of history that belonged to me. Or tried
to. You can't erase a house, or the stories in the walls.

But Catherine found a way around that, I guess. You can sell it instead.

The attic is hot, dark, and damp. There's definitely a leak somewhere. But there's also a surprising amount of clutter, which, on second
thought, makes total sense. It's just like Catherine to be a secret pack
rat—"perfect" house below, all her broken-down junk stuffed up here
out of sight.

I shine the light across the plastic bins that are stacked to the gabled
ceiling as a clap of thunder rattles the house. I jump, my heart balloon-
ing in my throat. The rain is pounding so hard, it sounds as if water is
seeping in everywhere. How in the world am I supposed to find a leak
in a downpour?

I crawl across the plywood floorboards, quietly scooting aside cardboard boxes labeled WINTER CLOTHES and BABY TOYS, searching for wet
areas. The wood gets damper the farther I crawl.

This is ridiculous. Look at me—creeping through an attic in the middle of the night searching for a leak. I'm not sure how I'm going to stop
it if I do find one. Maybe just shout at it until it does something. Works
for Catherine.

A shadowy box pushed into the corner catches my eye. The glint of
an iron hinge. I shine my flashlight on it. A trunk. No—no, not just any
trunk. I *remember* this trunk. From a long time ago. A faded memory,
old.

I crawl up and put the end of the flashlight in my mouth and dig my
fingernails under the lock. My hands are shaking. The lock pops open,

unnaturally loud against the rain pelting the roof. Another roll of thunder vibrates the rafters as I push up the lid, the flashlight illuminating a beautiful blue jacket.

I remember the fabric before I even touch it. I remember how it feels, and how it rustled when Dad walked, trailing like a cape. Dad's Federation Prince cosplay. I pull on the jacket, unveiling it inch by inch as though I'm easing it back into existence.

Slowly, half afraid it'll turn to dust, I slip it on.

The coat's too big, of course. The buttons need to be resewn, the tassels rethreaded. I turn my nose into the collar, inhale. It still smells like him too, mixed with the starch he used on the coattails.

But then the flashlight beam catches glitter and dark-purple cloth. Can't be—Catherine threw all this stuff out. She said she did. Donated it with the twins' clothes and her clutter.

I sink my hands into the trunk and take hold of a dress that could have been made from a midnight sky, the fabric a rich plum, soft and silky. I lift it up, wisps of gauzy silk slipping between my fingers. In the shadows, it sparkles like a galaxy caught in the threads.

Tears brim in my eyes. It's Mom's dress. Princess Amara's dress. I never really knew her, not like I knew Dad. But I wish with all my heart that I did.

I hug it tightly, squeezing my eyes closed. For a moment, it feels like I'm not alone in the attic. It feels like they're here.

An idea begins to dawn on me. Catherine can sell the house. She can take away my parents and put them in boxes. She can make me do the chores. She can berate me for working at a food truck . . . But besides what's here, in this trunk, I'm the last bit of my dad the world has left. I might be no one, but my father was extraordinary. And he loved me more than anything.

What kind of daughter would let that fade?

Then again, what can I do when the only thing I really own in the world are my parents' old costumes?

The answer hits me like a lightning strike.

I'll go to ExcelsiCon and enter that contest. I'll *win* that contest. And I'll get my tickets out of here, away from Catherine and the twins, and create a new universe where I can be whoever I want to be and not what everyone thinks I am.

I'll be my father's daughter.

It'll be work. I'll have to clean these things up, alter them so they fit, somehow find a way to get to Atlanta for the convention. But Dad taught me a long time ago that it takes much more than a few good pieces of costume to be worthy of the Federation insignia. It takes courage and perseverance. It takes all the good things I still feel in Dad's old cosplay uniform. All the kind things in Mom's galaxy dress.

And with their help, I'll make them proud.

I'll ignite the stars.

PART TWO

AIM

_____

"When you can't win the fight, you get bigger guns."

—*Episode 14, "Better Space Than Never"*

DARIEN

I'VE MET MY DOOM, AND IT isn't even breakfast yet.

Six foot eight, as broad as a New York Jets linebacker with sausage fingers that could snap me—even buff, gained-twenty-pounds-of-muscle-for-a-movie Darien 2.0 me—in half. A tribal tattoo winds across the side of his mostly shaved head.

Holy looming nose hairs, Batman.

Mark looks between me and my doom with this proud grin on his face. Like he's won the county fair with a stolen prized pig.

"So?" he says, egging on a compliment that I will not give him. He can call me petulant. He can tell me I'm showing my age. I don't care. "What do you think, Darien?"

"I don't need a bodyguard," I reply, crossing my arms over my chest. I try to stand as tall as I can, but even then Mr. Doom towers over me by a good six inches. Think half the Rock, half Terry Crews. All three hundred pounds of muscle. And when I stand up straighter, so does he. *Showoff.*

"He's not here for your benefit," Mark replies through a smile. His teeth are clenched. "He's here because our insurance company insisted on it."

"It's not my fault you insured my abs. They never asked for that. If you hadn't made me do that stupid stunt on *Hello, America—*"

"I'm thinking of your future, Darien. You don't want to mess it up more, do you?" He taps my chin—the same spot where I have a "career-ending" scar. After my unfortunate boat fail, Mark tossed around names of plastic surgeons like NFL quarterbacks throw Hail Mary passes. I didn't think the stitches were that bad, but the showrunner had to go back and reshoot almost every scene in the finale to incorporate them. Needless to say, the resulting scar did *not* end my career. The only thing that ended was my last and only friendship.

I tear my eyes away from Terry Crews Jr. to glare at my dad.

"Don't give me that look, Darien," he says with a sigh. "I just want to do best by you. I just want you to get jobs in this town. You understand that, right?"

"Fine. *Fine.*" There's no point arguing. "For how long?"

"Now see, that's the thing—"

"How long? And what does Gail say about it?"

"Gail agrees it's a good idea. And indefinitely." He takes out his vibrating phone and glances at the number. "I need to take this. You two get to know each other. This'll be an adventure, right?"

I don't even answer before Mark spins off, phone nestled against his shoulder. "Hello, yes, this is Mark. Harrison! How are you? How's the ankle?"

The door can't slam behind him quick enough.

My bodyguard and I exchange the same expectant look. I size up his crisp black suit and his neat tie and his silver Rolex—which makes you wonder how well bodyguards get paid—and I scowl. When he doesn't flinch I give up, pull off my day-old T-shirt, and stomp over to the corner where I stashed my suitcase.

We rolled into Atlanta late last night. I couldn't sleep a wink because the plane powered through a monstrous thunderstorm. The moment I got to the hotel I fell asleep in my clothes, and I'm still tired. The glaring red clock on the bedside table reads 8:31 a.m., which means I only slept four hours.

"You're probably good at taking lip, aren't you?" I mutter more to myself than to my bodyguard, clawing through the suitcase for a T-shirt that isn't tight on me. "Like a CIA operative, right? Do bodyguards go to bodyguard school? Are you like the hitman in *Hitman*?"

He adjusts his cuffs. "You know the rule about fight club?"

I give him a surprised look. "So you *can* talk!"

He raises a single eyebrow. "I will be right outside your door if you need me. You have to be down at the lot in twenty minutes. I suggest you hurry." Then he takes his burly frame and saunters out of the room.

I shove my head into a clean shirt and pull my arms through just as my phone blips.

There's a message. Well, two messages.

> *Gail 8:36 AM*
>
> —*HIS NAME IS LONNY. BE NICE.*

"Lonny?" That name definitely is not fit for a three-hundred-pound machine of total annihilation, but okay. I find a clean pair of gym shorts and socks. My phone dings again, and that's when I remember the other message.

> *Unknown 8:44 AM*
>
> —*Okay, sorry to bother you but I thought you might know this. What do you call it when Eucinedes does that thing to the ship's guns? Correcting? Fixing?*
>
> —*Bah.*

Right. The stranger. My lips twist into a half grin as I respond.

> *8:44 AM*
>
> —*Writing fanfic this early in the morning?*

Unknown 8:44 AM

—*NO.*

—*That sounded too strong, didn't it?*

8:44 AM

—*Slightly. I'll give you a hint.*

—*It starts with a C.*

Unknown 8:44 AM

—*Crap, I knew it was a C! Let me think.....*

I pull on my gym shorts and socks, stick the phone in my pocket, and run my hands through my hair while looking in the bathroom mirror. The scar on my chin is more prominent in harsh lights, a razor-white line against my brown skin.

Mark's right. Carmindor doesn't have a scar. Just another reason on my list of why the casting director was crazy to pick me. Crazier to think I could pick up where David Singh left off.

Another message flashes and I sort of dread it. I hate text messaging. Especially with strangers. But somehow . . . I don't know . . . there's something comforting about texting this person. Being completely anonymous. I don't have to be anyone. They haven't even asked for my name—I haven't asked for theirs. I don't need to make excuses for why I have a bodyguard or my weird diet or why I insist on wearing my favorite T-shirts even though they have holes in the armpits.

We're just . . . we're just *talking.*

Unknown 8:45 AM

—*Correcting? Calculating?*

—*Come on, Carmindor!*

—*Collecting? Catering? I have NO idea*

—wait

—OH MY GOD IT'S CALIBRATING.

—I am terrible.

8:46 AM

—And you call yourself a fan...

Unknown 8:46 AM

—A TERRIBLE one!

—I'll never forgive myself for this.

—Thank you, Your Highness.

"Ten minutes, boss." Lonny-aka-My-Doom has poked his head in from the hallway.

"What are you, a timer too?"

"I'm whatever I'm paid to be."

"Can I pay you to disappear?"

He gives me a deadpan look.

"It was a joke," I say, shoving the phone in my pocket and grabbing my keys. I wouldn't say that I make my way out of my room *fast*, but I don't take my time putting on my shoes, if you're wondering. And just before I leave, I send one final message.

8:56 AM

—Just Car is fine. :)

ELLE

Calibrating.

I'm going to kick myself for eons.

"Euci *calibrates* his guns, Elle," I grouse to myself, scribbling it in my notebook. "Why the hell was I thinking with *calculating*?"

The high Tuesday sun bakes over our heads as I watch tourists wander down the Battery. My brick of a phone rests in the shade, struggling to play a YouTube video about how to measure and sew darts on its ancient screen. I must've watched this one about forty times. There's a lot of weird sewing vocabulary I don't understand, and the tutorial lady is using a sewing machine, which I don't have and have no way to buy. All my savings is already going toward materials and, eventually, a bus ticket and convention pass. I'll be lucky if I can afford a needle and thread, let alone figure out how to use it.

"Why couldn't it be a fanfiction contest," I grumble. Writing is easier. When I'm a screenwriter, I'll get to draft dialogue and describe characters all I want, and someone *else* can handle the costumes.

But for now, I'm a one-woman shop.

I've decided to enter as Carmindor, stupid as that may be. Mom's Amara dress probably fits better, but there's something about it that keeps me at arm's length. I always needed permission to wear that dress. Dad would pull it down from the top of the closet and make me promise to tread lightly or else the galaxy sewn into the seams would swallow me up. But really he was asking me not to ruin the costume that held the memory of Mom. To treat it cautiously. To pretend it was spun gold. Besides, you cosplay who you *want* to be, and I've wanted to be Carmindor for as long as I can remember.

The problem, of course, is that Dad's jacket swamps me. He was a big guy, but I must've forgotten just how big. Memory becomes funny after a while. In my head, he's this broad-shouldered hero, with a soft smile that tugs up one side of his mouth more than the other and eyes as deep and dark as the Atlantic Ocean. I got Mom's brown eyes. He used to hum "Brown-Eyed Girl" as he danced her around the living room. Her head fit against his shoulder like a lock and key.

I wonder if he ever waltzed Catherine around the living room. My stepmother has blue eyes, and I can't think of any happy songs about blue-eyed women. Were Dad and Catherine ever happy? They must have been at some point. After the first night I met her—when she showed up on our doorstep in a tiny white dress, holding a bottle of wine in a fancy little bag—Dad asked me what I thought of her. I was eight. Mom had been gone four years. I wanted to shake him and remind him that Princess Amara dies at the end—that Mom *died* at the end. That stories shouldn't get sequels. That sequels are always bad. A rotten on the Rotten Tomatoes critic scale.

But I didn't.

"I like her," I said.

Seven months later they were married. Then the impossible happened and Catherine and I were stuck with each other. Stuck together in a world where he no longer exists. Or at least I thought he didn't. In the jacket, I feel him. In the seams and buttons and epaulets I can hear him humming "Brown-Eyed Girl."

Maybe everything does die—but maybe, somehow, everything that dies someday comes back.

The door to the Pumpkin swings open and I hide my phone under the notebook. Sage climbs in, two cups of ice cream in hand.

"Oof, remind me *never* to take a lunch to run across town to the ice cream store," she says, breathless, and offers me a melting cup. The spoon wedged inside has already begun to tilt to the side. "Butterscotch? Or praline?"

I look at her, confused. "For . . . me?"

She rolls her eyes and puts both cups on the counter. "No, for the *other* coworker we have around here. Jeez. I'm eating the butterscotch." She sits down on the water bucket and begins to eat. "The line was *ridiculous*. Anyone come while I was gone?"

I shake my head, claiming the praline. I actually really like praline. But something about this feels . . . weird. And not just the part where Sage is talking to me.

"You bought ice cream," I say stupidly.

"Uh, yeah. It's hot outside." Sage stirs her ice cream soup.

"But ice cream has . . . cream."

She blinks her purple-shaded eyelids. "And? Oh"—she grins big— "you thought *I* was a vegan? No way. That's just boss lady. I don't get it at all."

"Same," I agree. "I'm too much of a bacon fan."

"Mmh, bacon-flavored ice cream. Now *that* would be a sin in a vegan truck." Sage laughs. "We'd go straight to vegan hell. Though I don't know how much of a hell that'd be if we're already in it."

"You don't like working here?"

She looks away guiltily. "I mean, if I say no it makes me a bad kid, right? That I don't want to inherit boss lady's pride and joy." She pats the counter like she would a dog, like *good boy, it's nothing against you.*

"So . . . what would you do instead?"

She shrugs. "I try not to think about it."

"You draw, right? And make your own clothes?"

She glances down at her skirt, which is seven different colors sewn together in vertical panels with tulle underneath. It reminds me of those Japanese fashion magazines she reads, as if she jumped out of the pages. "You can tell?"

"Not in a bad way!" I amend quickly. "You just always look so cool."

She snorts. I try again. "Do you want to be a fashion designer?"

She eats another spoonful of ice cream and hums. "I want to marry this ice cream is what I want. We'll abscond to Tahiti."

For a split second, I think about asking her to explain the sewing video, but before I can even articulate the thought, a voice interrupts me.

"Oh look, it's our gross sister in her natural habitat."

Chloe and Cal are sneering into the order window. In the three weeks I've worked at the Pumpkin, the twins had yet to find me. Of course that had to end today. Naturally, they're flanked by the whole Country Club Crew: their mutual best friend Erin, her boyfriend, and a few guys from the football team whose parents own yachts down at the harbor. And, standing a little farther behind, James. Great.

Sage sets down her cup of ice cream and stands. "Can we help you?" she asks, spoon tucked into the corner of her mouth.

Chloe ignores her. Her blonde hair is pulled up into a loose ponytail; she's wearing short pink shorts and a College of Charleston T-shirt—the college she wants to go to next year. Beside her, a tall and broad guy—linebacker on the football team, buzz cut, stinks like his father's got money—nods at Sage. "You the only one working with her?"

Sage leans against the counter toward them. "What's it to you?"

"Might want to be careful around her. She's crazy," he says, turning his gaze to me. At the back of the crowd, James shrugs and looks away. The tips of my ears burn with embarrassment.

Sage either ignores them or doesn't hear. "We have pumpkin fritters, tofu pumpkin spread sandwiches, pumpkin tacos, and pumpkin fries," she intones dryly. "We're all out of chimichangas. Although I'm sure we could make an exception if you'd like to be on the menu too."

The linebacker really looks at Sage this time, from her green hair down to the ring in her lip. "Hey, you're the chick in my homeroom, yeah?"

"And *you* are holding up the line," she replies.

He looks behind him. "There's no one here."

She smiles a tight-lipped smile. "Which means you're scaring the customers away. Now run along. Go chase tail somewhere else."

Chloe squints at her. "Excuse you, who do you think you are?"

My coworker feigns shock. "I'm sorry, I didn't introduce myself, did I?" Then she pauses for a long, long moment as they wait for her to introduce herself. Finally, Sage goes, "Oh, I'm not going to."

Behind Chloe, Cal chews on her bottom lip, trying to hide a smile.

"*Freak*," Chloe sneers, grabs James by the arm, who is also kind of smiling because *no one* makes Chloe look like an idiot the way Sage just did, and drags him away. The rest of the posse follows like a herd of cattle. Cal lingers for a moment, her gaze fixated on Sage as if she's trying to puzzle out what she's made of, until her sister calls her name and she hurries away too.

Sage rolls her eyes and turns to me. "Your sisters are the bane of all existence. Bet you can't wait to graduate."

"I guess," I reply, but the words put a sour taste in my mouth because I don't know what'll happen after senior year. No—I *do* know. I'm going to win this contest and fly out of here, straight to L.A. And never come back.

She picks up her ice cream again and turns to me. "Anyway. What were you saying?"

"Oh . . . nothing."

I can't bring myself to ask her about the sewing video. I know Sage isn't like the others—I just saw as much—but she'll want to know why I'm asking and there's no way someone like Sage is going to care about *Starfield*. If I'm going to fail, I don't want to drag someone as cool as Sage down with me.

She shrugs. "Suit yourself."

Besides, I can do it myself. I've always done everything myself.

DARIEN

I SQUINT IN THE DRESSING ROOM mirror, messing with the golden star-wings on my lapel.

"Gail, this costume's all wrong."

Gail is sitting in a hard red chair, scrolling through emails and itineraries and fan mail—everything that I don't want to do—while chewing on the string of her IGNITE THE STARS hoodie. She looks about as tired as I feel.

The film's shooting in a studio lot outside of Atlanta, Georgia, under the codename *Kingship*. It'll be my home for the next twenty-three days of principal photography. The director insists on using practical effects whenever we can, which means shooting on an actual bridge made in a sound studio and doing actual stunts and . . . and kissing Jessica Stone on said bridge in that soundstage while doing my own stunts.

I'm most nervous about that. The kissing, not the stunts. Well, okay, maybe the stunts too.

"Huh?" Gail looks up from her smartphone and squints at my Federation Prince uniform. "What's wrong with it?"

"It's the wrong color. The blue's not—it's not blue enough."

"It's the same color it was when wardrobe fitted you."

"No, it's bluer, Gee. It's definitely bluer."

"It is *not*." She sends off an email and sets down her phone, finally turning her full attention to me. "It's just the lighting in here. Trust me."

"But you lied about Lonny. He's great company, by the way. Loquacious even."

The tips of her ears go red and she squirms in her chair. "Mark gave me strict instructions to keep him a . . . surprise."

"Because I'd say no."

"Surprise?" she offers weakly. I give her a knowing look and she quickly averts her gaze to her phone. "Let's argue about it later, okay? You've got makeup in ten minutes. Do you need anything? Water? Or we could go over today's script while we wait, help calm your nerves—"

The dressing room door flies open.

Sunlight streaks in, making me wince. At first I think it's Donna, the makeup artist, come to yell at me for being late. But last time I checked, Donna the Makeup Artist doesn't have long dark hair braided into a perfect royal Anorian braid. Or legs that go on for days. Or a female Federation uniform.

Gail jumps to her feet, looking flustered as ever. "Oh! Oh hello!"

"Mind if I hide in here for a while?" The amazingly beautiful girl plops down in Gail's empty seat and pulls one golden leg over the other. Me, I'm trying not to stare. Because holy even tan lines, Batman.

"It's troll o'clock and the paparazzi are out in *droves*," she continues, leaning toward the mirror to fix her lipstick. "I'm already up to *here* with all the heckling. I had to get away. You don't mind?"

Gail looks at me hesitantly. "Well, actually we were—"

"No," I croak, giving Gail a meaningful look. Doesn't she even know who this girl is?

Jessica Stone. *The* Jessica Stone. My costar. As in, indie film poster child, beloved by the internet for being sexy and cute and funny, sure to snag an Oscar one day *Jessica Stone*. I think I saw her last movie in theaters fifteen times, and not just because it was based on a graphic novel.

Don't fanboy, I order myself. *Don't fanboy*.

Gail looks at me, surprised. "But Dare, we were—"

I cough. Twice. Gail looks between Jessica Stone and me, widens her eyes, and finally gets it. Her ears go even redder.

"Oh. *Oh*." She grabs her backpack and makes a hasty retreat. "I . . . um. I'll be around if you need me, Dare."

After the door closes, Jessica Stone turns her eyes—which are super, freakishly, ice-water blue—to me. "I didn't mean to intrude."

My tongue ties into ten hundred knots. She can intrude as much as she wants. I mean, not intrude—like, let me politely be in her presence for the rest of my life—but intruding works too. Into my life. As much as she wants.

Is that weird? It's probably weird. But it's *Jessica Stone*.

Damn it, man, don't fanboy.

"I have a bad habit of doing that," she goes on. "Just barging in places. My therapist says I have no sense of personal space. Really, you can tell me to leave if you want. I'm Jess, by the way."

"N-n-n—" I stammer, then bite the inside of my cheek. *Stay. Cool.* I try again, channeling Sebastian, my character on *Seaside Cove*. "No, Gail really was just legging—*leaving*."

Her eyes widen, and for a moment I worry she's about to take one of her heels and shove it through my eye socket like she did in *Huntress Rising*, but then she throws her head back and laughs. It's a no-holds-barred laugh, the kind where if I get her laughing too much I guarantee she'll snort. The edges of her eyes crinkle when she smiles. She's beautiful in all the traditional ways—obviously the legs—but her personality helps, and her acting chops. She could quote Shakespeare in circles around me and I'd be none the wiser. It's a respect thing, I decide, not a fanboy thing.

Her laughter dies down and she shakes her head. "You're cute. No wonder they chose you for the lead. Equal parts dorky and sexy. A winning combo. If I were a guy, I'd be nervous. You'll start taking all the good roles."

I look back at the mirror, still fiddling with the lapel of my uniform. "Nervous? I'm the one who should be nervous. You'll make me look like a sham. You were amazing in *Huntress*. You *were* Sylvia. You channeled her perfectly from the comic books."

She shrugs. "Thank you. But I never actually read them."

"You didn't?"

"No time," she says simply. She cocks her head and surveys my uniform. "How come the men get to wear pants while I have to wear these stupid things?" She motions to her mile-high heels.

"Sexism?" I offer. Jess smiles. *With* me, not at me, this time.

"Sadly," she says. "It's just ludicrous."

"Yeah," I say in agreement. "Because, I mean, the Federation never puts its female officers in heels, so it's not even canon, right?"

Jess gives me a blank look. "No," she says, not unkindly. "Because they expect me to run in them."

"Oh," I say. "Right. Of course."

"In heels! With all those physical stunts! Seriously, I was telling Nicky"—our costume director—"didn't you see the Golden Globes? Heels and I don't have a great track record. But he told me to put them on anyway." She looks down at her manicured nails and shrugs. "It'll be hell. But it's not like I didn't know that when I signed up. Just a means to an end, you know?"

"To . . . what end?" I ask.

Jess looks up. "To something better."

"Better than *Starfield*?" I say before I can stop myself. Jess opens her mouth, then shuts it.

"So you're a fan, huh?" she says.

I shrug, even though it's pretty obvious now that I am. "And you're not?"

She snorts. "I'm a fan of paychecks." I must look disappointed because she rushes to add, "Not that I don't respect the *Starfield* fans! They're the ones who're going to propel this thing, after all." She indulges me with another gloriously perfect smile. "And this kind of big-budget stuff—well, it's not art but it's fun, you know? At least at first. It's new, it's shiny, it's colorful. Before you get bored. And move on to the next one." She fixes me with an intense look, and suddenly I'm not sure if we're talking about the same thing anymore. "You know what I'm saying, Darien?"

Oh. Right. *That.* I shift uncomfortably. Another brilliant idea to drum up publicity—keep it in the air that Jess and I are, well, a thing. Which might explain why I'm so freaking nervous to meet her.

"Gail—my handler—she mentioned that we're dating, yeah," I say.

"For the twenty-three days we're filming," Jess corrects. "And that's it. I don't want anything after, okay? Unless we become good friends and then I *might* kiss you at the premiere."

"I'm not sure I can kiss someone who isn't a Stargunner," I joke.

One side of her mauve lips twists up. "Maybe you can convert me."

"On the Federation's starwings, I'll try." I give her the promise-sworn salute.

"Dork." She laughs. "No wonder you got cast for this role. You're born for it."

Born for it. The phrase makes my stomach curl—as if there isn't enough already riding on this. I quickly look away. "Ha, right."

Jessica squints at me for a moment before she pulls her legs off the side of the chair and sits properly. She looks me dead in the eye. "Darien, can I be real for a second?"

I can't look away—her gaze is too intense. They're going to need to give her contacts. Princess Amara has green eyes, green like the radiation from superheated quasars in space. "Um, yeah."

She breathes in. "So, you've never done a big role before—"

What does she think *Seaside Cove* is? An after-school special?

"—but I have, and I know fans are the worst sometimes. The best, but also the worst. And you *are* a fan. So you're going to be the worst to yourself. You're going to judge yourself the harshest. My advice to you is—don't. This is just one role. It doesn't have to define you. Trust your instincts, trust your director, and it'll be a cakewalk. And then you can go on to bigger, better things. This is a springboard, not a glue trap. Make sense?"

"Uh," I say. But she's already standing, and when she bends to kiss me on the cheek I feel the tackiness of her lipstick come off on my skin.

"I'll see you on set, okay?"

"Sure thing, Princess," I mumble.

She grins. "You're not one of those method actors, are you?"

I mimic her grin, even though I don't feel it. "Nah. If I really wanted to get into character, I'd call you *ah'blena*."

"Isn't that the *Starfield* question you missed?"

I give her a wounded look. "Did *everyone* watch that?"

"YouTube is forever, trust me. You're looking at the most GIF'd red carpet moment in Golden Globes history." She grimaces at her heels. "See you, Darien."

And with that, Jessica Stone—my costar, my Amara, my fake girl-friend for the next twenty-some days—waves goodbye, one finger at a time, and leaves my trailer. But even after she's gone, her words stick like tar on the walls.

Bigger, better things. This is just a springboard.

I turn back to the mirror and stare at the wannabe Carmindor in a uniform that is definitely the wrong color blue. And I have to wonder if I'm any different from her—or if I should be. Am I doing this just for a paycheck too?

That's why Mark wants me to do it. He wouldn't have booked me for the audition if he hadn't seen dollar signs. Wouldn't have hired a bodyguard if he didn't picture my face on a billboard.

On the counter my phone buzzes, and I grab for it blindly, praying that it isn't Mark wanting me to do another convention.

But it isn't Mark.

> *Unknown 8:32 AM*
>
> —*How do you get a one-armed Nox out of a tree?*
> —*You wave at it!!!*

I chew on my bottom lip to keep from smiling. At least I know one person who believes in *Starfield* as more than just a cash cow. I square my shoulders in the mirror and tuck my phone into Carmindor's pocket.

Maybe it is a springboard. Maybe as a fan I'm the worst person for this role. Maybe I'll screw it up more than someone who doesn't care that way. Jessica wants artistic cred, serious roles, golden statues lined up on her mantel—and she'll make a fine Amara. Serviceable, and certainly beautiful. The fans will accept her. Me, I've had posters of *Starfield* in my room since I was seven. I know every galaxy and every world in Federation space. I know the prince's tics inside and out. I know his ending monologue. I know what he orders from the bartender at Belowgaze.

I don't want Oscar nods or award speeches—well, not yet. I just want to be good. I just want to do the fandom justice. I could keep my head down and waltz through this shoot like the Darien Freeman the world thinks I am, but that's not how my fanboy heart beats.

Because, most of all, I want to be good enough for a sequel.

ELLE

After work, I take Frank to Our Blessed Days cemetery, a bouquet of daffodils cradled in my arm. Because it's that day—The Day—and because . . . well, because I feel like I need permission. Or their blessing. Or something.

The graveyard is deserted and quiet. It's one of the smaller ones in Charleston, not touristy because it isn't as old as the haunted ones, but just as beautiful, with lazy weeping willows and oaks with large, gnarled roots. Franco and I are the only ones in the entire place, besides the night watchman. I pull out the droopy flowers from the Wittimer vase and replace them with the vibrant yellow daffodils.

I sit back on the damp grass. Franco pants beside me, rubbing his head against my arm.

The tombstones are quaint and gray. Lily Wittimer and Robin Wittimer in crisp letters, newer than a lot of the other plots around them. Dad's funeral is brighter in my head, Mom's is a shadowy blur, but I remember the preacher's words like an echo coming back from a dark, steep cliff.

Too young. Too soon. Too, too, *too.*

Too everything. Too little time. Too few memories. Too few "I love you"s exchanged from me to Mom to Dad. Mostly Dad. I miss Mom too, but I miss her like you miss a distant, beautiful place you've heard about but never actually visited. Her face is blurry, her smile a blank. I can't even remember what she sounded like.

But in my head, Dad's voice is still there. I hold on to it like a buoy, afraid I'll lose it in the storm of time.

"I found your costumes," I tell the tombstone. "I wondered for a minute if you caused the leak because it kind of felt like you were there, you know? Like you're still . . ."

I wipe my eyes with the back of my hand. Franco puts his head on my knee, his tail swishing against the ground, begging me to rub him behind the ears. I begin to but then my phone dings in my hoodie pocket. I pull it out as Franco whines, so I switch the phone to the opposite hand and adhere to the beast's commands.

> *Unknown 8:36 PM*
>
> —*Do you think the people on Prospero ever get homesick?*

I slide my thumb across the unlock screen. This is the first time they've texted me first, aside from the first time.

> *8:36 PM*
>
> —*Missing home, Carmindor?*

> *Unknown 8:36 PM*
>
> —*It was blown up, remember? Episode 43. The Last Turn of Time.*

> *8:37 PM*
>
> —*Doesn't mean you can't miss it.*

> *Unknown 8:37 PM*
>
> —*I miss parts of it. I don't miss the actual place. That's never as good as you remember it.*
>
> —*Sorry, I don't know what I'm saying. It's stupid.*

Not as stupid as he thinks.

8:37 PM

—*Would it be weird to say I know how you feel?*

Unknown 8:38 PM

—*We can be weird together then.*

—*What place would you go back to?*

What a question. Because the place wouldn't be as good as I remember it. And now, knowing what I know, there's only one place I'd go back to.

I want to text back that I don't know—that it's a hard question.

But that's a lie. I know exactly where I'd go back to—to the exact moment, seven years ago, when I sat on the steps of the veranda, the story I'd written that day in hand, waiting for Dad to come home. I would tell that little girl to go inside. To lock the door. To keep the bad news out.

My phone buzzes again.

Unknown 8:43 PM

—*Let me guess. You'd go back to when Starfield was still on TV, right?*

I smile.

8:44 PM

—*Never saw it live. Too young.*

I realize too late that I've just revealed to a total stranger that I'm a teenager, which I know you should never, ever do. But then they ping back.

Unknown 8:44 PM

—*Same. Syfy reruns? 11 to midnight? Falling asleep in homeroom the next morning?*

8:45 PM

—*Every. Day.*

Whoever this unknown number is, they don't feel like a stranger. Or even unknown. Clumsily, on the stupid number pad, I hit SAVE CONTACT and type in the name, one letter at a time.

CARMINDOR.

Franco sits with me as the sun sets behind the tree line. In the dusky darkness, the night watchman begins his rounds.

When he gets to me, he tips his hat. "Closing time, Miss Danielle."

"Just a few more minutes?"

His rigid gray eyebrows soften. "Just don't let that fat rat pee on any tombstones."

"You wouldn't pee on a tombstone, would you?" I ask Franco once the night watchman is gone. In reply, the dog slurps at my cheek, tail whipping through the air. "Not unless its Catherine's gravestone, no you wouldn't, no you wouldn't!"

Frank woofs and jumps onto my lap, and we settle in for a moment longer. To be honest, the night watchman will let me stay as long as I want—and if I could, I would stay for hours. I would curl up by the gravestone and just talk with the dirt.

But tonight, I won't. Tonight, for once, I actually have someone else who knows how I feel.

DARIEN

FIRST I FIND OUT THAT I have a bodyguard named Lonny, then the hottest girl in Hollywood tells me we're dating for the next twenty-three days, and now I'm about to die. Probably.

Is it too late to cash in my insured abs?

"I think I need a moment," I tell the stunt coordinator—who is, I'm pretty sure, *insane*, a thirty-something woman with dark hair and a dead-eyed stare. I adjust the strap that's digging into my left little guy. As stunts go, this is the one I have been looking forward to the least.

"What, getting scared, hero?" She claps me on the shoulder. *Hero* is her nickname for me, which, given how scared I am, is probably ironic. Like calling Lonny "Shrimp." Really flattering, in other words.

"I just want to, uh, write my will first," I reply. Or at least I think I do. My pulse thrums so loud in my ears that I can't hear anything else. I stare down, down, down the fifty-foot drop onto the green-screen landing.

If I fall now, I'll land flatter than a pancake. At least my only consolation is that the camera guy filming me is coming along.

"You know, maybe we should take a break. Who's hungry? You hungry?" I ask the camera guy.

He pops on his chewing gum, giving me a bored no-bullshit gaze. Am I the only one who thinks this is nuts?

"Can it, hero." My stunt coordinator tugs on the wires of my harness, triple-checking that I won't in fact hit the ground flatter than a pancake.

"We—we haven't established a safe word yet," I say. *Stall for time,* my mind chants. *Stall for life.* "I mean, you've got me into his compromising position, and I barely know you!"

She rolls her eyes and radios to the assistant director. "I told you we should've let Luis do the stunt."

"Luis?"

"Your double."

"Wait, he wanted to?"

"Want me to get him, *hero?*" She drawls out the last word.

Yes. "Nope," I squeak.

"Good." The stunt coordinator turns back to the cameraman and begins checking his harness too. He keeps messing with the settings on his camera as they talk about the scene.

I tug on my collar, staring down, down, down at all the people below me. I'm beginning to regret my decision to do most of my own stunts.

The scene *sounds* simple enough. Carmindor's running for safety. In this part of the movie, the Nox lay siege to a council hearing, and the entire building on Andromeda Earth—the homeworld of the Federation—goes up in flames. Carmindor (me) rushes down a hallway, pursued by seven Nox knights. He's heading toward a dead end, but because Carmindor is genetically enhanced, he can bust through the window at the end of the hall, hurtling himself to the next building's rooftop to escape.

That's where I find myself now. Running away from the Nox, busting through the glass window, and letting the cables take me fifty feet down onto a landing pad. Fifty feet doesn't sound that high until you're looking down at where you're supposed to land. But I must've failed to realize that I'm not the Federation Prince, and my bones are not made of titanium, and I *will* break just as easily as the next guy.

I swallow the bile rising in my throat.

Run, spin, knee, wall, I keep reminding myself, remembering the rehearsal for this shot. *Run, elbow, back-step, jump. Run, kiss ass good-bye, jump*—

Suddenly, I feel something buzz in my tattered uniform. It's been made to look singed at the edges and caked in soot, like I've just—you now—been through a siege.

I reach into my jacket.

Unknown 3:47 PM

—*So, about your question yesterday…*

—*Where would YOU go?*

—*Anywhere, any time, in the history of you?*

"Hey, hero, you ready to rock and roll?" Ms. Scary Eyes calls to me.

God bless my poor unfortunate soul. "Do I have a choice?"

Down below, Amon, the director, barks a laugh. "We got the paramedics standing by. You've got brass balls, Darien! I respect you!"

I follow the stunt coordinator back down the hallway specially built for this fight scene. It's one continuous camera shot, so no mistakes.

Run, spin, knee, wall. Run, elbow, back-step, jump. Run, kiss ass goodbye, jump.

I've practiced this. I can *do* this.

3:48 PM

—*I honestly don't know.*

—*I wouldn't go anywhere alone—it's a big universe out there.*

—*I'd need a buddy system.*

Unknown 3:48 PM

—*LOL scaredy-cat. Then where would WE go?*

"Quit texting your girlfriend, hero! Get ready."

3:49 PM

—*The frozen tundra of the Arteysa Galaxy is supposed to be nice.*

Unknown 3:49 PM

—*Brisk! I like it.*

"*Loverboy*!" the stunt coordinator snaps. "Can someone take the kid's phone away?"

Kid. I try not to let the word sting as Gail rushes up and snatches the phone out of my hand. "I was just making sure my will was in place. And my insurance," I add under my breath.

The cameraman moves his hundred-thousand-dollar equipment closer, bracing to follow me down the hallway. Is it too late to opt out? I'm not good at this. I should probably just—

"Get ready," Ms. Scary Eyes says, and radios down to Amon. "We're set!"

"Three, two . . . ," the AD says. I turn around, rocking back and forth on my feet.

Get into the moment. Slip on Carmindor like a Halloween mask that still smells like rubber. Breathe in. Breathe out.

"Start running. Go!" the AD directs, and then shouts "Action!" A horn blares.

I take off down the hall. A Nox comes out of the first doorway. I spin on my heels, ducking his punch. A piece of stucco wall pops over my head—fake gunshot—and three more go off down the hallway. I grab the Nox by the collar and send his face into the fake wall.

"And BOOM!" the AD shouts.

I stumble on command, feet slipping out from under me. Another Nox emerges from the next doorway and slams the tip of his rifle against my forehead. Fires.

I dodge, grabbing the gun, and elbow him in the side. I back-step, aim, *fire*. The Nox is blown backward on ripcords.

"FINAL CUE!" roars the AD.

Tossing the gun to the side I hurtle the downed Nox, dodging another knight trying to grapple onto me. I can feel the harness digging into me. My heart's in my throat.

I can almost see the fire, the taste of fake blood in my mouth, the stucco falling from the ceiling, the screams of people trapped in the Federation building as it goes up in flames, the titanium in my bones hurting—because for Carmindor they never stop hurting, never will, his humanity rebelling against the unnatural inside of him—and for a moment, I look at the window and I'm not afraid.

Run, kiss ass goodbye, and—

I launch myself out the window, arms pin-wheeling, air rushing around me faster and faster. The green-screen floor comes so close so fast, between one heartbeat and the next, my life flashes before my eyes. I don't regret most of it—except one minor, inconsequential thing.

I never asked my mystery friend's name.

The harness tightens, pressing against my chest, squeezing the breath out of me. I land, feet spread like I've been practicing on the green-screen ground. Right where they want me.

Nailed it.

I hold the landing for one second—two—

"And CUT!" Amon yells from the ground. He runs up to me and slaps me on the back. "Amazing! Great job. That was *sick*."

"Thanks," I wheeze, tugging at the harness. I relish my feet planted on sweet, sweet ground. My hands are shaking; I push my thumbs into the harness so the director doesn't notice.

From the window the stunt coordinator applauds. "*Perfect*! You could be a stunt man," she adds. I feel the ropes on my harness begin to tighten again. As if they're about to hoist me up. "Except next time, try not to scream like a girl."

"That's not very PC," I yell up, my voice shaking, before I realize what she's said. "Wait—*next* time?"

Amon claps me on the shoulder. "Word of advice? Don't grimace like the harness is pinching those pretty brass balls. You don't wanna have to record sound for this scene in post, right? That'd be embarrassing." He motions for my stunt coordinator to set me down again, and one of the assistants comes to unharness me. "Okay, five-minute recess!"

Thank the gods of special effects. The moment the assistant unstraps me, I make a break for the restroom in the corner of the building, because all the jostling has *not* been kind to my bladder. But as I sidle through the crowd of PAs loitering around the snack bar, I get this weird déjà vu, like I've passed someone familiar. When I look again there's no one I recognize—no one besides all the lucky PAs cramming doughnuts in their faces.

I duck into the bathroom and do my business, but my hands are still shaking from the stunt. It's the adrenaline messing with my eyes, my brain, making me hallucinate that I'm seeing people.

"Shake it off, Darien," I tell myself. I would splash water on my face but it'll ruin the special-effects makeup on my forehead: a shard of glass embedded into my hairline, a line of blood curving down my temple. I'm just being paranoid. No one's here trying to snap pictures of me. I mean, I don't even *have* any friends left to sell me out.

The longer I spend in this oasis of conflicting aromas—one of the PAs stationed bowls of mango potpourri everywhere—the longer I prolong going back out there and doing it again. Mark told me that doing my own stunts would be good press—and I did most of my own stunts on *Seaside Cove*—but this is different.

Just another way I'm not the Federation Prince. He isn't scared of heights, or firefights, or flying through space with a 0.1 percent possibility of landing his target.

Darien Freeman? He's scared of it all.

ELLE

WHEN MY PHONE PULSES WITH THE wake-up alarm at its usual ungodly hour, I reach for it, swiping clumsily for the UNLOCK button to shut the alarm up. But it's not just the alarm. I have a message.

From Carmindor.

I roll over in my bed with my cell phone. The morning light peeks in through star-patterned blackout curtains, creating yellow ribbons across the carpet. In the distance someone is mowing the lawn at six-thirty a.m. Ah, summer.

I tap the message icon and the text pulls up with a soft *whoosh*.

Carmindor 11:23 PM

—*Hey, sorry I didn't text back earlier. I had to save myself from an assassination attempt.*

—*Twenty-three times.*

—*Anyway, this might seem a bit late in the game but…*

—*what's your name?*

I bite the inside of my lip, trying not to smile.

6:34 AM

—*You were busy saving the galaxy! No need to be sorry.*

—*And I thought Carmindor knew everything?*
—*ps - good morning*

Across the hallway, the twins' alarm goes off, a screeching sound that Chloe will snooze off at least three times before they finally get up.

I roll off the bed, sneaking a look underneath at the costume folded in a cardboard box. I still have to pinch myself. Dad's costume. His actual costume. *Here.* I left Mom's safely in the attic, where no one—not Chloe or Cal or the Nox King himself—will find it.

I grab yesterday's work clothes and a towel from the main closet and pause. I move slowly toward my computer and tap the space bar to wake it up. *Rebelgunner* has thirty thousand followers and climbing. Still not a dream.

I should be wary because this universe never lets me be lucky, but I shove that thought to the back of my mind. I take a quick shower before Chloe or Cal can bully their way into the bathroom, and then wiggle into my day-old uniform. I'll never get the smell of vegan fritters off me.

Carmindor 6:41 AM

—*Ugh, there's nothing good about this morning.*
—*And we both know that I don't know anything.*

6:41 AM

—*So I'm not in CLE-0's files?*
—*Man I feel left out, Carmindor...*

Carmindor 6:42 AM

—*OR you're too important to be in her systems.*
—*You might be classified.*

"Classified as a raging idiot," I mutter, pulling my wet hair into a ponytail. I glance at the reflection in the mirror on the far wall—a girl with red hair from a box, her mom's brown eyes, and a birthmark shaped like a starfish on her neck, wearing a frumpy TREAT YO PUMPKIN T-shirt and holey, greasy thrift-store jeans.

I wonder what Carmindor thinks I look like. Probably better than I do.

6:43 AM

—*Alas! You found my secret.*

—*I am much too important for your trivialness!*

—*You shall address me as Your Supreme Intergalactic Empress.*

Carmindor 6:44 AM

—*So you're a girl.*

—*Sorry—that came out weird.*

—*It's an observation. Casual-like.*

—*You're a girl.*

—*Argh. I'm digging myself a hole, aren't I?*

6:45 AM

—*Yes, yes you are.*

"Danielle!" Catherine's voice calls up from the kitchen. I curse, stuffing the costume into a duffel bag and slinging it over my shoulder. It's missing a few pieces. The starwings, for one, and the crown. I looked everywhere in that trunk, but they weren't there. Catherine probably threw them away when she chucked everything up in the attic.

I start down the stairs as Carmindor sends another text.

Carmindor 6:48 AM

—*I'm really good at that. Digging myself into holes.*

—*Making impossible promises. Groveling. Endangering my*

own mental sanity. More groveling. It's part of the job.
—*So: I am worms, Your Supreme Intergalactic Empress*

I bite the inside of my cheek, trying not to laugh, then hear Chloe in the kitchen.

"God, I know, okay?" she snaps. "I didn't think it'd be so hard to find a stupid costume."

"I don't think they're just costumes," Calliope replies hesitantly as I enter the kitchen. "Like, there's a whole community of people who dress up for conventions."

"It's called cosplay," I say before I can stop myself.

Chloe turns her dark-eyed glare at me. "We get it, Elle. You're a huge nerd. But guess what? *Everyone* likes that star show now. It's, like, retro chic or something." She screws up her mouth. "You probably know where to get a costume, right?"

Fear twists in my stomach. I clutch the strap of my duffel bag.

"No," I say.

"Darlings," Catherine says. "You don't have to click your heels just because everyone else does. You girls like what you like. Don't be like Danielle."

Don't be like Danielle.

If ever I had a cue to leave, that was it. Ducking my head, I pull my duffel bag higher and quickly escape through the front door. I hurry toward the end of the street when, with a roar, the Pumpkin skids onto the pavement and comes to an exhausted stop. Sage leans over. "Get in, loser. We're getting the good spot today!"

I jump in and glance back at the house one last time with unease, remembering the twins' conversation. I grip my bag tightly. It'll be fine.

Starfield is just a phase for them. Soon it'll disappear like Princess Amara through the Black Nebula and never be spoken of again.

DARIEN

"LOOK AT ME."

I glide Jessica to a stop. We've been waltzing through this ballroom for two hours, a herd of PAs following to sprinkle fresh ash and dirt over the map of my failed footprints.

Focus. I cup Jessica's cheeks and whisper, "You ignite me."

She presses her dark-red lips against mine and the world spins.

It spins and spins and spins. I can hear the swell of music in my head, that moment in the TV show, the sweep of the wobbly camera around half-baked costumes with cardboard props. And for a moment I am Carmindor. I am—

"And done!" Amon shouts.

Reality drops on me like the *Prospero* out of the Mars Two skyline, straight and fast. Carmindor is ripped out of me so quickly I'm left breathless and hollow. Or as I like to call it: Darien Freeman everyday.

Jessica steps away and rubs her lipstick off my lips with a thumb. She smiles. "And where did *you* learn how to kiss?"

"Well, I've had about two hours of practice by now," I reply—cheekily, I hope.

"With the best kisser in Hollywood." Her mouth twitches in amusement. Dark lipstick, the same on my mouth. Cherry and whatever was left of her lunch. She taps my chin—the scar—and floats past me off the set. I follow her out to the lot, unbuttoning my sweaty jacket. I need to tell the costume person to steam clean this thing before tomorrow. It's going to start growing trees.

"Thank god *that's* over." She unsnaps her curly hair extensions, tossing them at her assistant. "I thought my lips would—"

"*DARIEN*!"

Our heads turn toward the main gate. The security guard isn't at his post, but then again it's dinnertime and there's a security camera. We see a whole gaggle of girls—not like I think a group of teenagers is a flock or anything, but there's a whole . . . a *group* of them, and they're all staring at me like they're the ducks and I've got a piece of sorta moldy bread to feed them. Or *I* am the piece of moldy bread.

"IT'S HIM! IT'S *DARIEN*!" another girl screams.

They have their phones out, flashes sparking in the dusk as if they want to catch the whole moment on fire. And everyone—from the PAs to the cameramen to frakking Jessica Stone—is staring at them.

"Your adoring fans?" Jess asks.

"I . . . um. Yeah." I rake a hand through my hair. "I should get Gail on it, or my, uh, my Lonny." I cringe again. "I mean, bodyguard."

A couple of the PAs are pointing at the crowd and snickering.

"Wow." Jessica shakes her head. "Makes me glad I didn't take that *Vampire Diaries* part."

Right. Because she's a real actor and I'm just the dude from the soap opera.

"They're just fans," I say. "Don't you ever fangirl?"

"Of course," she replies, folding her arms over her chest. She juts her chin toward the fans. "But I've never stalked anyone."

"It's part of fan culture," I say, trying not to remember the other side of fan culture that is Fishmouth. Fans like that are one in a million. But the memory of that girl charging me creates a sick, sinking feeling in my gut. "They're monsters, but they're *my* monsters."

Jess lifts an eyebrow. "Monsters?"

I spread my arms. "Come to rejoice at the great church of Darien

Freeman."

Her perplexed look slowly devolves into a deviously white smile. She gives me a bracing pat on the shoulder. "Then we should go see your congregation."

"What? Oh, no, I don't think Mark would . . ."

"Who's Mark?"

"My—" I stop. There's no way I'm going to say *dad*, and *manager* isn't much better. He would not approve of me doing this without Lonny. Which makes it enticing. "No one. Never mind. C'mon, let's do it."

We barely make it to the barrier. I give the crowd Sebastian's (my character's) bro nod. The girls go nuts. One shoves a picture into my hands—it's of me shirtless, pulled from the *Teen Vogue* photo shoot last year.

"Hi!" I say, faking enthusiasm as I take her Sharpie and sign it. "How did you guys find me so fast?" I try to make it a joke, which is the best way to frame a serious question.

"The footage," the guy beside her says. Tall, gelled hair. "It was awesome!"

"I can't believe they put it on Twitter," squeals another.

"Oh my god that scene today was *amazing*. I *loved* the kiss!"

I pause mid-autograph (I've already signed three photos and an arm). The kiss today? Footage?

I glance over at Jess, whose big white smile has faltered. She's thinking the same thing as I am: we have a snake in the water. A leak. Even an actor from a dumb teenage soap opera knows that's *not* good.

"Jess, what's it like kissing Darien? Isn't he amazing?" interrupts a girl in pigtails. I hand back her notebook.

Jess laughs. "He's a terrible kisser!"

"Hey," I say. "I am not."

"Oh, did I hurt your feelings?"

"Positively shattered."

"They're so cute together!" someone cries. Cameras flash.

Jess wraps her arm around mine and tugs me toward the costume trailer. I give a guy back his Sharpie, having half-signed his T-shirt. "Well, you guys are awesome, but we should really get going. Dare?"

"Yeah. Hey, it was nice meeting you all!" I say to the group, waving and smiling like we're both in a beauty pageant. I don't think I exhale until we get to the trailer. My jacket sticks to my shoulders when I shrug it off.

"You're way too nice, you know." Jess comes out from behind one of the racks, now wearing into street clothes and pulling her hair into a high ponytail. "You can't waste more than two minutes on stuff like that. Tops."

"Nah," I say with a shrug. "They're nice people." Sometimes, anyway. I step out of my pants, hop into my gym shorts, and pull a hoodie over my head. "Hey, do you think it's someone working for the movie? Who ratted the footage, I mean."

Jess shrugs. "It could be a PA—and if it is, they're going to get a piece of my mind. Trust nobody around here, Dare. Now if you'll excuse me, I have a date."

"A date?" I say. "With . . . ?"

She blinks, twice. "Like I said. Trust *nobody*."

Then she leaves in a twirl of dark hair and cherry blossom perfume.

"She's a firecracker, that one," says Nicky the wardrobe manager, clicking his tongue to the roof of his mouth.

"Tell me about it," I reply, unable to wash her cherry kiss from my lips. I fish into my gym shorts pocket for my phone.

A glowing blue message is waiting for me.

Unknown 6:06 PM

—*It's Elle.*

—*Just Elle.*

—*Elle.*

A name—her name. Elle. A nickname? Short for a horrendously

long name? Eleanor? Janelle? Elle . . . izabeth? There's a whole universe of possibility in it.

Elle.

I add her name to my contacts, able to put a pin into the idea of her and keep it steady because now I know her name. I didn't think a name could do that: turn a wispy idea of a person into, well, a person.

Suddenly I'm wondering what someone named Elle looks like. Blonde hair, brown? Pale skin or dark? Large eyes, but what color? Are her teeth straight or does she have a cute overbite? When she smiles, is it crooked? Is she tall? Short? Curvy or skinny?

Elle.

"What're you smiling at?" Nicky asks loudly.

"Oh—nothing. I'll see you tomorrow," I reply, swiping off the lock screen and exiting the trailer.

The girls begin screaming my name, but it's not my name that I'm thinking about anymore.

ELLE

REBELGUNNER'S AT FORTY-THREE THOUSAND FOLLOWERS and counting.

I'm working on a post instead of working on my cosplay because no matter how many YouTube tutorials I watch, I'm still terrified of slicing through Dad's costume. But I have nineteen days. In the meantime, there's *Starfield* news—movie news—and all forty-three thousand of my followers are waiting for me to pass judgment.

I add a link to a video of the now notorious leaked kissing scene from the reboot next to what I think is its TV show parallel. Episode 33, "A Nox to Remember." It looked like the ballroom scene. The one before Princess Amara's coronation, when the Nox attacked. But I can't be sure.

I rewind the video and replay it. Darien Freeman holding Jessica Stone's face, his mouth moving in words I can't make out and then drawing, slowly, into a kiss—before the camera shakes and cuts away.

Yeah, definitely episode 33. You can tell by the balustrades in the background. The ash on the ballroom floor.

"One thing's for sure," I write in closing, "Darien Freeman's Carmindor uniform is the wrong color blue."

Then I hit POST. 11:34 p.m.

Everyone is gone to bed by now, so I quietly slide out of my chair and pad down the stairs.

The house is so dark I can barely see, but I know it blindfolded, having snuck around in the dark for years. In the kitchen, I open one of the cabinets, reaching in the back for the new jar of peanut butter, and then grab a spoon from the clean dishwasher. I'll have to put away the dishes in the morning, and Catherine will probably scold me for letting them sit all night, but I'm too tired and hungry to care.

As I scrape another spoonful from the bottom of the jar, I hear something shift at the table.

"I wondered where you stashed that," says the cool, soft voice of my stepmother.

I freeze, the spoon stuck in my mouth. I turn slowly toward the darkened figure.

"Turn the light on, sweetie. We aren't Neanderthals."

I reach over to the switch and begrudgingly flip it on. I already know the scene I'll find on that table. The brightness of the light makes my eyes water. Catherine is still in her "work" clothes—a five-hundred-dollar wrap dress she can't afford, with hair curled up on top of her head. She looks tired.

"Sorry, I . . . ," I say, trying to come up with an excuse to explain why I've been caught red-handed with super-creamy Peter Pan peanut butter, but my mind fails me.

"We all have our guilty pleasures," she says, tapping manicured nails on the rim of her empty wineglass. Her cheeks are warmed and her eyeliner faded, flakes of mascara scattered around her eyes. The last time I saw her look this, well, *human* was the day Dad died.

I pull the spoon out of my mouth and quickly screw the top onto the jar, "Yeah, sorry, I just—"

"Don't apologize. I have Rocky Road hidden in the back of the freezer," she replies.

I blink at her. The stepmonster eats Rocky Road? I make a mental note to check the freezer when she's not around.

She tilts her head as if she didn't just admit to having ice cream—which I'm pretty sure is *not* Paleo—in the freezer.

"No matter what I do, I can't get rid of him, you know," she says in a voice so soft I almost don't hear. "First you—but oh, I knew you'd be just like him—and now the twins."

"The twins?"

She waves a hand. "They're obsessed with that thing—*Star Trek?*"

"*Starfield.*"

"The show Robin liked." Her eyelids flutter shut. "He's everywhere."

I fold my arms over my chest. "The twins only like it because of Darien Freeman—"

"What's so special about it?" Catherine snaps, her eyes wide open. "Every time I see the logo for that *stupid* show, I think of Robin. There's no point to it. It's for children."

"Why does it have to be stupid or childish?" I ask, my voice trembling a little. "It taught me a lot of things. Like about friendship and loyalty, and how to think critically and look for all sides of a narrative. It helped me—"

"*Helped* you? *Taught* you?" Catherine shakes her head. "How can a show teach you anything? How can you learn about the world if you're buried in a fantasy?"

"How can you think something's stupid if Dad liked it so much?" I say. "He loved that show."

"Well he should've loved *other* things more!"

The room is deadly silent. Catherine clears her throat, as if she remembers that it's not ladylike to yell and is afraid the neighbors might hear.

"If he cared half as much about his family, we might not be in this mess," she says in her usual sticky-sweet tone. "Scraping by. Cutting coupons. *Alone.*"

"Is that why you're selling the house?" I ask. "Because my dad had the audacity to die in a car accident without buying enough life insurance to pay for all your *stuff*?"

Catherine's eyes turn hard and sharp. "You know nothing about the world."

"I know that you don't have to sell the house!" I say. "I know that you could get a real job!"

"My job *is* real, Danielle."

I ball up my hands. It might not be my decision, but it isn't her house, either.

"You talk a lot about how stupid it is to like a TV show, but *you're* the one living in a fantasy world," I say. "You're the one being childish."

With a *crack*, Catherine's manicured hand strikes the side of my face.

"Go to bed, Danielle," she says ever so softly. "You have work in the morning."

I don't have to be told twice. I throw the spoon on the table, run for my room, and dive into bed. Holding a hand to my stinging cheek, I pull the covers over my head and untuck my phone from my pocket.

> *11:52 PM*
>
> —*Car?*

> *Carmindor 11:52 PM*
>
> —*What are you still doing up?*

> *11:52 PM*
>
> —*I can't sleep.*
>
> —*Why are YOU still up?*

> *Carmindor 11:53 PM*
>
> —*Same.*

I press my phone against my mouth, still angry with Catherine. Angry that she thinks she has to do things alone.

She's not alone. She has the twins and their real dad—wherever he is—and she has Franco's terrible owner Giorgio. She has the country club and her friends at the salon and her clients and her parents (although they live in Savannah and apparently it's such a *chore* to drive to see us). She doesn't understand what being truly alone means.

Her life is crowded compared to mine. And I'm angry that I thought, even for a second, that she had room for me.

Carmindor 11:54 PM

—Do you want to talk about it?

—Not wanting to brag, but I'm the MASTER at listening.

11:55 PM

—Got an award in kindergarten for it, did you.

Carmindor 11:55 PM

—My crowning achievement.

—And I don't tell secrets, either.

—I'm a steel trap.

I lay the phone on my chest. For some reason, all I can think about is that leaked video being replayed again and again. To the people who haven't watched the show, they don't know what he says. His mouth is too blurry to read.

But I know that scene. I know those words by heart.

"*You are not alone*, ah'blena."

And then she kisses him.

In the right universe, the possible one, I don't want to win a contest to see the premiere, to watch that famous scene on the big screen. I wouldn't have to. In a perfect world I'd be buying two tickets to the midnight release at the local theater. I'd wait for Dad to get off work and we'd go together. And maybe at that midnight release I'd see a guy across the theater dressed in a Federation uniform and we'd lock eyes and know that this was the good universe. Maybe a guy with dark hair and chocolate eyes and—

For a moment, Darien Freeman flashes across my mind. Startled, I quickly shake away the image. No. Abort.

Not Darien Freeman. Not that it matters. I pick up my phone and answer Carmindor.

> *11:57 PM*
> — *Thanks, but I'm good.*
> — *Goodnight, Car*

His reply lights up my phone almost instantly.

> *Carmindor 11:57 PM*
> — *Goodnight, Your Supreme Intergalactic Highness.*

I hide the phone under my pillow. Because I'm not a princess. And this is the impossible universe, where nothing good ever happens.

DARIEN

I'VE BEEN CHECKING MY PHONE ALL day. That is, when I'm allowed to have my phone on me. And yet here I am, checking my phone again. Nothing. Not since last night.

Did I say something wrong?

Underneath a parking light on the lot I rub my eyes in exhaustion, waving to Jess and her entourage of equally gorgeous girlfriends. I don't even know their names, and I think she met two of them today on set. Everyone's leaving, filtering out of the looming black gates like a river of bobbing, tired heads. My stunt coordinator claps me on the arm as she passes.

"Good work today," she says with a smile. "A few more takes and your footwork would've been almost as good as Cary Elwes."

"I almost stabbed Calvin in the face with my sword," I remind her. Calvin Rolfe is our reboot Euci, and from what I can tell he's less than thrilled about playing second fiddle to a kid almost ten years his junior.

"He had it coming, hero. Get some shut-eye, you look terrible."

"Night shoots aren't my favorite."

"Aw, poor wittle hero," she teases, and gives my head a scrubbing before strolling off toward the parking lot.

Lonny pulls up to the gates in a black SUV. At three-thirty in the morning, my fans are nowhere to be seen, but he still assists me into the vehicle like I'm about to get assassinated.

My phone beeps.

Elle?

I glance at the clock on the dash. 3:32 a.m. She shouldn't be awake at this hour.

I pull out my phone anyway and frown. Not Elle, but another unknown number.

Unknown 3:32 AM

—*Killer skills, bro.*

—*[link]*

Against my better judgment, I tap the link. It goes straight to a video of today's shoot—basically me almost stabbing Calvin in the eye. I wince. But even worse than my poor swordsmanship are the comments. I close out of the link and delete the text for good measure.

"Something wrong?" Lonny asks.

"Long day," I reply.

He drives me back to the hotel and parks in the back. We enter through the emergency exit and he follows me all the way to my room, where he tells me he'll pick me up at seven-thirty sharp. Then he hands me a protein bar.

"You look weak," he says.

I take it, kind of touched by his thoughtfulness. "Thanks."

Even after I shower off the eight hours of failed footwork—after a night of being blown out of a spaceship hatch—and put on clean clothes, I'm not tired enough to go to bed. I should be; it's been an exhausting day, and usually whenever we're shooting *Seaside* I crash harder than a cow shot with an elephant tranquilizer.

But I lie awake and keep thinking about that video. Who could have filmed it? Jess already asked the PA manager to rake everyone through the gutters. I heard him screaming at the PAs from the soundstage. Half of them are probably too traumatized to take another job in production ever again.

I flop onto my back and waste I don't know how long trying to count the popcorn kernels in the stucco ceiling. Eventually my mind wanders. *What's Elle doing?* I wonder if she stares at the ceiling too, counting sheep or doing what I do when I can't sleep, namely, wondering what would've happened if Barbara Gordon never answered the door in *The Killing Joke*.

As the red-lettered clock on my nightstand blinks to 5:58, I roll out of bed.

5:58 AM

—Hey. Are you awake?

She's probably still asleep. I'd be asleep right now but I can't, and this room is suffocating. I grab a hoodie from the floor around my exploded suitcase and pull it on, taking the keycard from the TV stand and slipping out the door.

The hallway is eerily lit, like in those horror movies where an ax murderer is just around the corner. I pull up my hood—by habit, not because I'm emo or anything—and set off toward the stairwell. As in most hotels, the door to the roof is rigged with an alarm. But also as in most hotels, the alarm doesn't work. Probably.

I push the lever timidly to make sure. The door squeaks open, but no alarm, so I shoulder it open the rest of the way and escape onto the rooftop. There's not much up here—air-conditioners, a water tower, a storage hut of sorts. I slide off one of my shoes and wedge it in the doorway so I don't get locked out and sit at the edge of the building.

Mark would flip. "You're too close!" he'd rage. "What if you fell off?"

I look down, and down, and down, along the side of the building. My heart thrums in my throat. I hate heights, but there's something quiet about rooftops. Peaceful. The way the city sounds like a distant, muted ambience.

It might sound stupid, but up here I feel most myself, and these days I don't feel that way often. Between having to put on a face for the cameras or for other industry people or for the paparazzi—Darien Freeman seems to always be "on."

The only other time I feel myself is when . . . well, when I talk to Elle, and that's stupid because she's the only person who doesn't know I'm me. How could I be most myself when I'm lying?

My phone buzzes.

Elle 6:04 AM

—*Sadly, I am.*

—*Why're you up?*

6:04 AM

—*I haven't gone to sleep yet.*

Elle 6:04 AM

—*OMG GO TO SLEEP*

—*Weirdo*

6:05 AM

—*Haha*

—*It's busy work saving the galaxy.*

The moment I send the message, I wish I hadn't. I've been trying to fill Carmindor's shadow for eight hours today. For a moment, I just want to be me.

6:05 AM

—*No, not saving the galaxy. That was stupid. I don't really do that.*

Elle 6:06 AM

—*So you're a REAL person behind your strapping exterior?*

—*Color me shocked, really.*

6:06 AM

—*I'm sensing some sarcasm here.*

Elle 6:07 AM

—*It's okay, I can forgive you.*

—*As long as you're not really, like, bald.*

I sigh, knowing exactly where this conversation is heading. To what I look like, who I am. It's best to just stick to Carmindor. I *do* look like him more often than usual these days, thanks to my makeup artist.

Elle 6:09 AM

—*You ARE bald, aren't you? That's your big secret.*

—*You're really bald.*

6:10 PM

—*I am ashamed you think that. I promise you I have hair.*

—*It's darkish. Curly.*

Elle 6:11 AM

—*Like Carmindor's?*

6:11 AM

—*Surprisingly, yes.*

Elle 6:12 AM

—*Are you as tall as him, too?*

— *Like, if I was standing beside you, would I be looking up your nose hairs?*

6:14 AM

— *That's an awkward question.*

Elle 6:15 AM

— *It's also awkward to be so short you can see all the way up into someone's cerebral cortex, but welcome to my life.*

I laugh quietly, even though there's no one else up here. I feel like this is a secret, so I have to be quiet, ensuring that the universe won't find this little bubble and burst it into nothing.

6:15 AM

— *I guess it depends on how short you are.*

Elle 6:16 AM

— *I'm like super short. 5'3"*

— *The worst height. Always get lost in crowds.*

— *Great height for proms though. No one sees you're alone.*

Dawn's just beginning to break across the cityscape. Orange light spreads across the night sky like an inferno, stretching pink and yellow fingers across the stars. The sun's so bright I have to squint, but it's rising all the same. I wonder what the sunrise looks like from Elle's side of the world.

6:16 AM

— *I'm 6'1" but I'd be able to see you.*

— *Even in a crowd, I'd know.*

Elle 6:17 AM

—*Know what?*

6:18 AM

—*That I'd want to dance with you.*

It's the delirium from a lack of sleep. I don't really say that, do I? Do I really think that? I remember the moment when I was kissing Jess, and her secretive smile, and asking me who I had thought about.

The truth is, it wasn't just when we kissed that I'd thought about Elle. I'd thought about her during every step of that dance.

I'd meant those words. Every one of them.

I turn around and take a photo of myself against the sunrise. You can't see my face—the sunrise is so bright I'm just a silhouette. Protecting my image, like Mark has taught me to do for years. But you can see my hair.

6:18 AM

—*To prove I'm not bald.*

—*[1 attachment]*

—*Good morning.*

Then I notice him—the guy standing in the doorway, holding up a camera and obscuring his face. I almost drop my phone.

"Hey—hey *you!*" I shout, lurching forward.

The stranger whirls around, kicks out my shoe, and slams the door before I get halfway across the roof. I bang my fist into the door, cursing. There's no handle. I'm locked out, on a rooftop, basically about to reenact *The Hangover*.

And what's worse, I'm not hallucinating. There really is a rat on the set of *Starfield*.

ELLE

THE JUNE SUN BURNS AGAINST my neck like an iron brand as I sit outside and slowly, painfully, make stitches in the blue material. It's miserable, but after the fight with Catherine, there's no way I'm working on the costume at home, and I am *not* bringing my dad's coat into the grease-bomb Pumpkin. Besides, I'm way too embarrassed to sew in front of Sage.

My phone hums, startling me. The needle slides into the thick shoulder—and also my finger. "Ow!" I yank out my hand and shove my bleeding finger into my mouth. It stings. And tastes like copper and the Magic Pumpkin's special for the day, a spicy Asian pumpkin fritter.

Sage pops her head around the back of the truck. "Yo. Everything okay?"

My heart leaps into my throat. I shove the coat beside the crate I'm sitting on. "Fine! I'm fine! Just, uh, dropped my phone—"

She comes around, wiping her hands on her WHAT'S EATING YOU, PUMPKIN? apron. Someone's supposed to handle the grill at all times, but Sage doesn't care about protocol. And since there's a fried grits balls vendor across the street, no one's even blinking at us.

I try and scoot the jacket as far behind me as I can, but her eyes fall on a sleeve snaking out beside my foot.

"You're going to get it dirty."

Ashamed, I take the jacket up in my arms, remembering that the Magic Pumpkin bleeds oil like it's in a food-truck version of a Tarantino movie.

"It's nothing. Just . . . just something I'm working on. Is my lunch break over yet? I should probably—" I try to dodge around Sage, but she steps in front of me. I try the other way, but she blocks me there, too. I frown. "What're you doing?"

"I know what you're up to, you know." Her glittery eyes dart to the wimpy sewing kit I bought at the drugstore. I gather the needles and thread into the plastic case, clamp it closed, and stick it under my arm, but Sage won't let me off that easily. "That's really nice material," she says. "You can't just tack up the hem. You'll ruin the trim."

"I won't," I reply defensively, clutching the jacket tighter. "I know what I'm doing."

She blinks.

My shoulders sag. "Well . . . sorta."

"Mm-*hmmm*." She reaches out to take the jacket. I hesitate for a moment, like Frodo with his Ring, but then I remember how much crap Frodo walked into and I'd rather not end up like Frodo. So I give it to Sage.

She takes it by the collar and flips it around, studying the hems inside the back and sleeves. Her magenta lips fold downward, slowly but surely, into a serious frown.

"And how exactly are you planning to take this in? Yourself?"

I pull out my cell phone with the YouTube video still on the screen.

"Oh no! My eyes! It burns!" Sage cries. "*No.* Put that away."

I pocket my phone as a blush rushes into my cheeks. She turns the jacket inside out, showing me the seams.

"See, you need to take the shoulders apart, cut it, and then sew it back together if you want to resize it properly. The shoulder pads will be a beast because this is hella fine work." Is that *awe* in her voice? And not even bored awe. This is a first. "Is this handmade? Who drafted the pattern?"

"No one—I mean, *someone* made it. But it's not really important."
I squirm, training my eyes on the grease-stain splotch on my Doc Martens. "It's just a . . . it's just dumb."

"I thought you said that if someone likes something, then it's not dumb."

She has me there. Defeated, I try to grab the jacket out of her hands, but she steps back, turns it right side out again with an expert flip of the wrist, and fits the coat over her shoulders like a cape.

The blue accentuates the green of her hair, making her look strange and ethereal and awesome all at the same time. I hate how it looks good on her, oversized and all. Anything would. She wears life like Elvis wore sequins, with no apology laced into the seams. I don't even want to think how it looks on me. Clownish. Frumpy. I'm sure I would be the laughing stock of the cosplay competition.

"It's *really* well made," she goes on. "Is this a costume for something?"

I sigh. "Yeah. *Starfield*? The Federation Prince?"

Sage bunches her lips together. "I didn't know you dressed up."

"It's called cosplaying, and I don't—I mean, I haven't. But I want to." I lower my eyes again to my shoes, and the words come out in a torrent. "There's this cosplay competition in like two weeks at ExcelsiCon in Atlanta, and the prize is two tickets to the premiere of *Starfield* and some cash and . . . and it's a long story but I really want to win. I *need* to win. I mean, I probably won't but—but my dad said that the impossible is only impossible if you don't even try. So I want to try." I swallow the lump rising in my throat. "But yeah. I can't sew."

She cocks her head and doesn't say anything for a long moment.

My cheeks begin to burn red. I spin around toward the Pumpkin. "Never mind. It was stupid—forget I said anything—"

"Sounds like fun."

I stop. Turn around.

Sage, the girl who barely even looks at me while we're working, wants to help me? Right, *that'll* happen when Princess Amara comes out of the Black Nebula (i.e., never).

She takes off the coat gingerly. "You're in luck because I need more pieces for my portfolio."

"Really?"

The service bell chirps. A customer at the truck window. Neither of us moves to leave.

She hands the jacket back to me. The starch is almost gone, the coattails droopy. It doesn't smell like Dad much anymore, more like me and vegan burgers and that particular musty old-coat smell. When I first got this hare-brained idea, I didn't think about *how* I would wear the costume. I just thought that I could find a little of Dad in me again. Maybe whenever I pushed my arms through the sleeves, or buttoned it up, or looked myself in the mirror . . . but I'm built of different lengths than my dad. Different curves and edges.

"Really really," she replies after a moment. "You don't have to always do everything alone, you know."

I smile, hugging the coat—as blue as the ocean, the perfect shade, the perfect color—tighter to my chest. "Thanks."

The customer at the service window dings again.

I half-expect Sage to rescind her offer, tell me to go back to staring at people through the order window and scrolling through the forums on my phone because I'm asking the impossible. Get a costume together in a week? Compete in a *professional-level* competition? It's crazy. There isn't enough time in the world to disassemble this jacket and put it back together.

Sage juts out her hand for me to shake. "My house. This evening."

I unravel one arm from the coat and take her hand, shaking it. "Deal."

She squeezes it tightly, and for the first time since I met her she smiles—not a demonic grin, but a real human-person smile. "Now that wasn't so hard, was it?"

It was. It was and it wasn't. But I'm glad I said yes. "You made an offer I couldn't refuse," I say truthfully.

The customer at the front window impatiently dings the customer bell again, like she's trying to send us a message in Morse code. "*Hell-oh*!" she calls.

Sage rolls her eyes, letting go of my hand. "Ugh, *soccer moms*. Your turn."

I gather up my crappy sewing kit, fold up Dad's jacket, and return to the truck where a very aggravated young mother is standing at the window, banging on the service bell.

My phone buzzes again as I hop into the truck and stash the jacket in a safe cubby. It's from Carmindor, from this morning—I must have fallen back asleep. A sun-drenched picture comes up beside the text. I can see bits of him, curly hair, the shadows of a strong jaw, but not really his face. I don't think he took it to show me who he was, actually, but the sunrise behind it.

This morning's sunrise was pretty spectacular.

"*Hello*," the woman calls. She's wearing a white visor and a determined frown. A tourist. "Don't you work here?"

"I do," I reply, putting on my apron. "Would you like to try our pumpkin fritters today? It's our specialty—"

She shoves a five-dollar bill at me. "A bottle of water. *That's all.*"

"All right, all right," I mutter, reaching for her water and change. Someday customers at the Pumpkin will learn to be nice. Or better yet, someday I'll get out of this food truck entirely.

For the first time in a long time, *someday* actually feels possible.

DARIEN

I RUN THROUGH THE FIGHT SCENE in my head while the rest of the crew preps for another take.

Left, right, dodge. Pick up, ram, back-step, back-step, back-step—

My heel slides off the edge of the set piece. I almost lose my balance and fall, but manage to lean forward just in time. Calvin-slash-Euci looks up before tucking his phone into his jacket. No one yells at *him* for having a phone on set.

"Take twenty-three!" Amon yells. "Darien, let's see a little more Carmindor in this one."

"Like I haven't already," I mutter, rolling my shoulders.

We're on the ship's bridge, for one of the major scenes of the film, but right now it just looks like a bunch of plywood with fancy running lights and one huge green screen behind me. Everything will be added in post.

We take our places on the far side of the set. I can do this footwork in my sleep. Calvin hops back and forth, the camera lights shining against his waxed Euci forehead.

"You cool?" he asks.

"I'm cool," I say. We haven't exchanged more than a few words since arriving on set, but I don't think we'd be friends in real life, anyway. He's the sports-playing type. Got his start on some family show, then migrated to Hollywood. Plus he's, like, almost thirty. "Why?"

He shrugs nonchalantly. "Just wanna make sure this isn't too hard for you."

I look at him strangely.

"Since everything's come so easy to you," he adds, adjusting his fingerless gloves. "Rich mama, good connections through your daddy. It's not exactly a secret."

"I—" I almost stammer. "Hey, I'm not my parents."

"Just their biggest investment, right?" He shrugs. "Hey, don't worry. After this thing bombs you'll be back to gigs more in your league."

I open my mouth to object, but nothing comes out. I don't know what should come out. Is he right? That this is out of my league?

"Okay, let's start." Amon gives a signal with his hand to start rolling.

Don't think about it. Just act. I try to shake off his words, but he's got this smirk on his face that is more menacing than friendly, and it throws me off.

Does everyone think that? That I didn't bust my chops to get here like the rest of them? That because my mom is a zillionaire socialite and my dad an agent I've had it easy? Or is Calvin just salty because—

—because I'm Carmindor, I realize. I'm Carmindor, and he's not. No matter that I *auditioned*, that the casting director *picked* me, or that Calvin's white and Carmindor definitely *isn't*. Maybe none of that matters. Maybe Calvin Rolfe is the kind of person the fans would accept as their Federation Prince.

I start back-stepping, sliding my feet across the plywood. Calvin advances, gaining momentum, tensing.

"And . . . GO!" Amon shouts.

There's an explosion behind us—bright lights, the actual effects to be added later—as half the ship blows. Calvin lunges at me. I dodge left, grab his right hook, but he powers through it and sends me careening backward. I slam against the floor, pulling my weight back, scrambling to get my feet under me. He picks me up by the collar; I grab his hand and wrench it away.

Quickly, I reach for my gun. Too slow. He rams his shoulder into my chest and I stumble into the console. The entire structure shakes. He grabs hold of my neck and pretends to squeeze—one second, two . . . okay it's getting a little tight now, actually.

Holy throttle, Batman, any moment now—

"And CUT!" Amon says.

Calvin lets go and bumps my shoulder. "Good footwork."

I rub my neck. "You think you could've been a little gentler?"

"Then it wouldn't've looked real, eh? You can take it."

Amon motions for everyone to reset the scene as he looks at the take in a small monitor. "Okay, we're doing good. Euci—I mean Calvin—could you look less menacing? You're brain-dead. You don't know what you're doing. The Nox has control of your mind."

"Sure thing, boss."

"And Darien"—he doesn't even confuse me with the Federation Prince, that can't be a good sign—"can you be more . . ." He motions to the air with his hands. A PA jumps onto the set to fix the fake blood on my forehead. "More *Carmindor*?"

Yep. Not a good sign. I put my hands on my hips, nodding. "Yeah, sure thing."

"Okay, good. Everyone, let's try that again—"

Suddenly, Gail's phone begins to ring. Amon shoots an annoyed look at her as she flounders to silence it—why doesn't she just turn it off?—and answers the call quietly. Her face goes pale.

This is going from bad to worse.

She hops off the chair and shuffles up to me, her hand over the receiver. "It's Mark," she whispers. Her eyes are wide and she's shaking her head. "You're in the news."

I blink at her once. Twice. Before it sinks in. "Oh, *shit*."

"Hey, what's this?" Amon asks.

"I—uh—it's an emergency, sorry," I say.

The director throws his hands in the air. "Fine!" he cries, suddenly sounding exhausted. "Take ten, everyone."

The set breaks, PAs and gaffers relaxing as a bell shrills overhead. Calvin jostles his shoulder against mine as he passes to the refreshments. "Real professional, *Carmindor*."

When he's gone, Gail mouths, *Your dad,* and hands me the phone. Of course it is. I take a deep breath, unmute it, and answer. "Mark?"

"How old are you, Darien?" he asks in a voice so cold and clipped, I get a wind chill.

"Um, well. Eighteen, but—"

"Eighteen. So you can read?"

"I mean, yeah—"

"So when you went up to that roof, did the door say *no exit?*"

The muscles in my shoulder tense. I move away from Gail so she can't hear him screaming through the phone. "Yes, sir."

"Good," Mark says. "I just wanted to make sure before we have this conversation, because now I know exactly how stupid you're being."

"What's happening?" I ask. "What's everyone saying?"

"Does it matter? You have an image to uphold, Darien. You have a career. You can't be a stupid kid anymore." He says the last part slower. "Do you understand?"

I can hear the undercurrent of his voice, the words squeezed between the ones he said. I have a part to play, I have a career, but it's not mine to steer. I'm strapped to the pilot chair of my life, and my hands are tied. I swallow, fisting and unfisting my hands. The other actors laugh at the water cooler at something Jess said. I bet they don't get scolded by their managers. "Yes, sir. I understand."

"Good. Because I'm two seconds away from firing that idiot handler of yours and getting someone who actually knows what they're doing."

I shoot a look at Gail, who's sitting in my actor's chair, screwing and unscrewing a water bottle cap. "She's not the problem. It's me."

"Then *you* make sure this doesn't happen again, or I'm flying out there to watch you *personally* until the end of the shoot."

"Okay. I'll talk to you lat—" I begin to reply, but he's already hung up. I press END anyway and walk the phone over to Gail.

She looks up from her water bottle and takes her phone back. "I'm sorry, Dare. What did he say?"

"He . . . just told me to be careful," I lie, with a shrug. He'll never fire Gail, not while I'm around. "It's fine. Besides, you manage me better than he ever did."

She goes silent, not sure what to say. She looks like she might cry.

I squeeze her shoulder. "You deserve better than Mark for a boss—"

Amon shouts that our ten minutes are up, and I crack my knuckles and walk onto the set again, for once ready as hell to play the Federation Prince. Because being Carmindor means I don't have to be me.

ELLE

"*And in more startling news, Hollywood's latest heartthrob had a run-in with danger this morning when he was discovered locked on a hotel rooftop . . . ,*" the radio personality's voice blares in her I-Hate-My-Life monotone as Sage pulls the Pumpkin into her driveway.

You wouldn't expect that inside the home on the corner of Cypress and Mulberry there would be a shrine to electrified punk rock in the basement. I must've biked past this house a hundred times on my way to and from work and never once did I suspect that Sage lived here. It looks so . . . *unassuming.*

Sage flicks off the radio and hops out.

"Really, if you don't want to, you don't have to," I say. "You can duck out—"

"Elle." She comes around to my side of the truck and extends a hand inside. "Let us flee to yonder basement room and sew thy starry helm."

When I don't move, she yanks the passenger door open and grabs the duffel bag, pulling me out with it. She pushes me up the steps and swings open the front door, corralling me inside, and then leads me down to the basement, which is finished and strangely cozy, with its beanbag chairs and stack of records and crooked TV stand. Covering the walls are posters of fashiony people in brightly colored clothing, some I recognize from the magazines she reads, but mostly they're of

David Bowie. The Goblin King smolders at me as I sink into a green beanbag. It hisses softly, smelling like old hackeysacks kicked around for too long. A puff of dust rushes up between the cloth.

"Okay, so give me the lowdown," she says. "What do I need to know?"

"Um." I'm not sure what she means. "About sewing?"

"About the show!" Sage replies. "Gimme the deets."

"Really?"

"Really really. If I'm going to sew this costume for you, I want to do it right."

"It's, um, it's fifty-four episodes."

"So start at episode 1?" she asks, cueing up the TV.

"Aren't we going to sew?" There's a little over two weeks until the convention, and as exciting as it is to have help, I'm not super confident about Sage's ability to stay on task.

"Yeah, but you can't sew without the TV on. It's, like, boring." She unrolls the jacket and shakes it out. "You take the helm, Captain, and I'll start working on our masterpiece."

I shift on my feet for a moment, hesitant.

"Elle?" Sage glances back at me.

The thing is, I've never introduced anyone to *Starfield* before. It's only ever been Dad and me, and then the internet people I sort of know from *Rebelgunner,* but never someone in person. A thrill begins to creep up my spine, like the *Prospero* warming up to light speed, heading for destinations unknown. I grab the remote off the floor.

"Actually, we'll do the crash course starting at episode 3. Then we'll jump back to 1, and then go forward to 12 and then hit 22 and—"

"Um, why?"

I slowly blink. Right. I'm not talking to a fan but a soon-to-be fan. I need to lay out the rules of *Starfield.* "The TV series was made for syndication. It didn't follow a linear storyline, so things just happened whenever the writers decided to include them. We're watching them in order of the history of *Starfield.*"

She laughs. "Right! I'll pretend I understand that." She goes to the little workstation in the corner—where, I note with happiness, there is a sewing machine—and gets out a bin of tools. I flick through the various streaming networks until I find one with *Starfield,* select the episode, and then crawl back to sit on my squishy green throne to wait for the opening credits. I can't help but look over at Sage as she handles Dad's jacket.

She touches it so gently, like each thread is made of pure silk, tracing her fingers across the seams as though she knows the coat as well as I do. The starched tails are no longer stiff and the collar's kind of fraying, but she smooths it out anyway to take stock of the cut.

"Okay." She waves me to standing. "Up."

I hit PAUSE and get out of the beanbag. Sage nods and whips around me, lifting one arm and then another, measuring everything from my waist to my neck. When she's done, she turns one of the jacket arms inside out, marking with chalk and pinning things into little tents. When she's done with that, she lays the jacket flat on the ground and fishes into her tool bin for scissors. Then she lines up the scissors with the chalk, her face composed and relaxed—probably how a serial killer looks, devoid of all humanity as they begin to ruin something beautiful—

"Stop!" I yelp. "What are you doing?"

She gives me a side-eye. "Alterations, Elle."

"But you're cutting it!"

"For alterations."

"But . . ."

She sighs. "Look, do you want this to fit or don't you? I told you. You can't just hem it up, you have to get into the seams and stuff. Either stop me and try to win with nostalgia, or let me do this and help you clinch your victory."

I hesitate, glancing between her and the jacket. Maybe she's right. Pursing my lips, I nod and let her cut the fine seams that Mom sewed years ago. I watch as, thread by thread, Sage unravels the history of my parents and the opening credits of *Starfield* begin.

In the middle of the third episode, a raspy voice calls from the top of the basement, "Sage! You down there?"

"Yeah, Mom!" she replies as footsteps come down the stairs. I don't say anything, seeing as I'm trapped inside the coat with a forest of pins preventing my moving even an inch.

A graying-haired woman reaches the bottom step. She looks as surprised as I am to see her, but then her smile turns warm. "Ah—well! Elle, right?"

"Hi, Miss Graven."

"Please, call me Wynona." She extends her hand to shake. "Sage's mom."

"I think she figured that out," Sage states, crossing her arms over her chest. "Seeing as you hired her?"

"She could've thought I was your sister." Sage's mom leans toward me with a mock-whisper. "I still get carded at bars, you know."

Sage rolls her eyes.

"Don't let her give you any mouth," Sage's mom goes on. "She's really a sentimental brat under all that hair and makeup."

"Mom," Sage whines. "*Stop it*. We're kinda busy right now."

"All right, all right. Well, Elle, you staying for dinner?" she says with a lopsided smile. "It's wheat-meat night!"

I glance at the clock—and then curse. How'd it get to be eight-thirty already? Jerking to my feet, I quickly begin to gather up the costume. "I have to get home—I'm sorry. It's almost my curfew."

Sage waves her hand. "Leave the costume here. And be careful, there's still pins in the shoulder!" she adds when I pick up the jacket and yelp. I drop it, sticking my poked finger in my mouth. She looks at me patiently. "Told you."

I hesitate, glancing down at the jacket.

"It'll be fine here, daisy," Sage's mom says with a laugh. "It's in the best hands."

I nod, gathering my empty duffel bag. "All right."

We climb the stairs out of the basement. A sweet aroma wafts from the kitchen, making my stomach grumble. Nothing at the Wittimer household ever smells half as good as wheat-meat night does. Probably because I season our dinners with tears for the carbs we'll never eat.

Sage sees me to the door as her mom calls out from the kitchen, "Was a pleasure, Elle! Come back anytime!"

"You'll see her tomorrow!" Sage yells back. She sees me out the door. "Sorry. My mom can get up in everyone's business sometimes."

"I like her," I reply. "She's cool."

"Yeah, try living with her. You sure you don't want me to drive you home?"

I shake my head, thinking of Catherine and Giorgio and their hatred of the Pumpkin's faulty muffler. "Nah, it's nice out tonight. I'd like to walk. But, um, thank you."

"Suit yourself." She gives me a salute, and I head down the porch stairs and toward the end of the block. After a few steps, I realize I'm grinning. For the first time, I'm looking forward to tomorrow—and I can't remember looking forward to anything since the twenty-fifth anniversary of *Starfield* two years ago. And even then I looked forward to watching the recording while Catherine and the twins were on a ski retreat two weeks after it aired.

This feels different. Like something I can control. *Happiness* I can control. Happiness that is solely mine. I didn't realize there was such a thing anymore. I didn't think it existed in this universe. I thought that when Dad died, it moved to the other universe, the one where he's still alive.

"Hey!" It's Sage, yelling all the way from her porch. "Elle! When's your contest again?"

"Two weeks from Friday. Is that . . ." I clear my throat. "Enough time?"

"Fifteen days?"

There's a long pause. But then she gives me a thumbs-up.

"Are you kidding? Nothing's impossible with me."

DARIEN

WE FILM FOR TEN HOURS STRAIGHT, not to mention the two hours in the makeup chair and the time spent waiting on Calvin to get his freaking lines right (maybe they're a little harder between Euci's shark teeth, but no one forced him to sign on as Euci, so I don't feel the least bit bad).

When the director finally calls it a wrap for the day, Calvin shrugs out of his coat so fast that his assistant doesn't have time to catch it before it hits the dusty ground. He jumps off the soundstage, pulling his pointy teeth out of his mouth. He couldn't at least wait to disrobe before reaching the costume trailer? Jeez.

Gail rushes up instantly, digging into her jacket pocket. "It's been going off like crazy," she says. "Who's wanting to contact you so badly?"

"Dunno." I take the phone and slide open the lock screen, a cascade of blue messages filling the screen.

Elle 6:42 PM

—*Introducing a friend to Starfield*

—*this is going to be tres interesting*

—*I'll keep you updated*

Elle 7:02 PM

—*Yesterday's thoughts: she is not impressed*

— kept asking questions like "What's a solar flux capacitor and why is it broken?"

— Pssssh, Earthenders.

My lips turn up without my consent. *Earthenders* is what anyone from the stars calls people who prefer a planet. The people who stay in one place forever, stuck in their narrow ways. It's like calling a person a *Muggle* in the Harry Potter world.

I scroll down. There are so many texts; she wrote an entire novel. Entirely to me.

Elle 7:32 PM

— TODAY: Fifth episode, not as many questions.

— Thought the general's sawed-off horns looked like boobs on his head.

— oh, oh Carmindor

— they actually kinda do.

— huh.

— (also I know you're probably busy but I have to tell someone or I'll bust.)

Elle 7:35 PM

— pee break. Also, sixth episode or skip to ten?

— skipping to ten, executive decision.

Elle 8:10 PM

— BEST IDEA EVER.

— also it's the episode with Carmindor in the shower

— I mean, not you in the shower—i'm sure you take showers

— and not that I'm repulsed by you being in a shower

— I was just saying it's the one with the other Carmindor being sexy in the shower.

—Not that YOU couldn't be sexy either...

—oh, gosh

—I'll shut up now.

That's the end of the texts, but my lips are straining so far over my teeth they're beginning to hurt. Suddenly, getting my ass kicked by Calvin I'm-Better-Than-You Rolfe doesn't seem too terrible.

"You're smiling. What is it?" Gail stands on her tiptoes to sneak a peek at the messages, but I click off the phone and stash it in my pocket before she can read about me in a shower. "Is it that girl from *Seaside?*"

"No," I say. "Just someone I met."

"Randomly?" Gail's eyebrows shoot up. "Like, a stranger? You don't think she could be the one who—"

"She's *not* the snitch. I'm going to get changed." I exit the soundstage, with Gail following to ask more questions. The night air is humid and sticky as I cross the lot to the costume trailer. On the other side of the chain fence surrounding the compound, a girl cries out my name. "I love you, Darien! Look over here! Darien!"

I look over, pulling on my Darien Freeman mask, and wave to them. They squeal.

"Don't antagonize them," Gail scolds.

"I'm just saying hello. Can't I do that?"

She fakes a smile to the fans, teeth clenched together. "Not without your bodyguard."

"Spoilsport."

In the costume trailer, Nicky, the costumes manager, is beating the dirt off Calvin's costume, muttering darkly. Of course Calvin had to go and put him in a bad mood, so he'll be in an even worse mood when I tell him that a button's fraying on my coat. The same button. Again.

"Is this girl anyone I have to worry about?" Gail asks, following me into the costume racks. I decide to wait and tell Nicky about the button tomorrow. I'll pretend I didn't notice until then—I'm an actor, right?

"I don't think so." I shrug out of the coat and grab a hanger.

Gail's face scrunches in suspicion. "How'd you meet her?"

I shrug. "The internet?" Sort of true.

"Darien!" she gasps.

"What? It's cool."

"It is *not* cool," she stresses as I hang up my costume under the nametag FREEMAN, D. "You don't know who she could be."

"She's funny, and nice, and caring." I unclasp the mandarin collar of my shirt and begin to unbutton it, tugging the tails out of my pants as I think about the girl on the other end of the messages. "And she's honest. Actually, I think I know her pretty well."

"Do you two talk about . . . ?" Gail waves a hand around us.

"The costume trailer?" When she gives me a stony look, I grin. "I'm joking. I know what you mean, and no, not really. I mean, she doesn't know I'm *me*, if that's what you're asking."

"So you're lying to her?"

"I'm not *lying*," I say quickly. Except now I wonder if that's true. "She just . . . she just assumed I was, I don't know, *normal*, and I didn't want to correct her. Don't give me that look."

But she's giving me the eye of disapproval anyway—like she's my mom or something. Not that I've seen my actual mom act like that. I just assume. I shrug out of my shirt, my arm muscles aching from the day's swordplay. "I will tell her. I mean, someday. I just sort of wanted someone to treat me like a normal person for a while."

"Oh woe is you being the famous abs-insured actor who wants to be *normal*." Gail rolls her eyes. "You're really in deep, Dare."

"I'll tell her," I assure her. "When it comes up, you know . . . in natural conversation."

"No," Gail says. "You have to end it."

"End it?" Alarmed, I almost drop my shirt. "Why? That's not fair!"

"I don't care if it's fair. It's for your own good and you know it." She looks back at me, her gaze almost entirely steady.

"What are you, my mom? You can't just tell me who my friends are."

Gail's mouth quivers. "If I don't, Mark will. Dare"—her voice cracks—"I just don't want any more trouble, you know? No more photos. No more—"

"I *know*," I say. "I know, I know."

I feel horrible, making Gail play the authoritarian. She doesn't like it and can barely pull it off. On the one hand, I know she's right, that what I'm doing is stupid and dangerous and can't last anyway.

But on the other hand . . . there's Elle.

"Good," she murmurs, more to herself than to me, and checks her phone again. "So Lonny'll be here to pick you up at the front gate. Don't stand him up."

"Yeah yeah, roger that—wait, pick *me* up? What about you?"

Gail squirms, blushing. "Well, I . . . I'm going, ah, out, and—"

"You've got a date!" I accuse. "You've got a date and you're ditching me!"

"Shhhhh!" She slaps a hand over my mouth to muffle the rest of my words. If Mark found out that she was dating while I was on a job, he would flip. Not to say that she can't, but she shouldn't during principal photography. "Don't say it so loud!"

I pull her hand away, grinning. "It's that gaffer, isn't it?" When she turns beet red, I laugh. "It's the gaffer! You traitor!"

"Shush you! Not a word or I'll—"

"How about this," I fish my phone out of my jacket pocket and hold it up. "I won't tell Mark if you won't?"

I wiggle my eyebrows encouragingly and Gail chews her lip, clearly caught between her loyalties. But apparently whoever this gaffer guy is must be worth it, because eventually she wilts. "This is a bad idea." She sighs. "But okay."

After making sure that I've got my marching orders for the night, Gail takes off, informing Nicky that I'm in the trailer. Gail, you *traitor*.

Before I know it, Nicky has zipped over to grab the shirt out of my hands. "You don't just *hang* these up!" he screeches—guy's got a really high voice considering how burly he is. "And where's your coat? You didn't get it dirty, did you?"

He snatches the coat out of my hands and holds it at arm's length. The loose button catches his eye and his mustache twitches. "Putting on weight, are you?"

"No," I say, stepping out of my pants as defensively as I can. "I mean, if I was, could you blame me? All that protein's adding up."

"Hmph." He sniffs, eyeing me one more time—the muscular slab of meat that I am—and turns promptly on his heels, presumably back to his sewing desk where he'll fix my busted coat. I pull on my civilian uniform—gym shorts, a LOOK. AIM. IGNITE. T-shirt, hoodie—and leave before he notices the muddied hem at the bottom of my pants leg.

Outside, the girls call my name again, but I flip up my hoodie and head toward the front gate, where a small gathering of fans still loiters with posters and T-shirts with I HEART DARIEN on their boobs.

As I wait for Lonny to pick me up, I take my phone out of my gym shorts pocket. Elle's messages illuminate the night around me. Her last message was sent three hours ago. She must be absolutely mortified. I pull up the keyboard and try to come up with something witty to say.

Think of me in the shower a lot, do you?

No, can't say that. I hit backspace.

I assure you, Carmindor would be jealous of ME in the shower.

Ugh, definitely not. My thumb jabs on the backspace button as I head to the edge of the lot. A few other responses flit through my head—some of them involving her in the shower. Which is silly because I don't have the slightest clue what she looks like, or how old she is, or where she's from. I don't even know how to picture her. I guess I've always just thought of Princess Amara.

Finally, by the time I reach the gate, my brain throws together some words and I manage to type something that I won't regret in the morning.

11:13 PM

—I'm flattered that you think of me.

It's lame and boring, but it's something. And perfect timing too, because as soon as I look up, Lonny's tank-sized SUV is looming outside the gates.

"Boss," he says with a nod as I slide in.

"Hey," I reply. It's quiet except for the soft murmuring of an NPR show. No sooner have I shoved my phone into my gym shorts than the soft sound of Elle's reply dings above the murmur of the radio. She's still awake?

"Girlfriend?"

I look up, surprised. Lonny's face is unreadable as always, like he's been specifically trained to avoid emoting. I don't really know what to say, so I pull my phone out, its screen illuminating my face.

Elle 11:13 PM
—I think of you a lot, actually

I click the phone locked again. I must look embarrassed or flustered or something, because in the rearview mirror Lonny's eyebrow raises.

"Thought so." He straightens in the driver's seat. "She the real deal?"

For some reason I can't lie to him. "Yeah. She is."

He nods. "Don't worry, boss. Secret's safe."

We lumber off into the night and I read Elle's text a second time. A cold shower might not be such a bad idea.

ELLE

OVER THE PAST SEVEN DAYS, I'VE gotten extremely good at sneaking back into the house. Tonight, it's close to nine—cutting it close to curfew, but sewing the shoulder seams is tricky, and Sage kept making me try on the jacket so she could pin and repin and get the curves to lie right. Plus, okay, we might have gotten a little distracted watching *Starfield*. But we still have a week—if I don't get in any more trouble, anyway.

Catherine shoots me a look from the couch as soon as I slip in the door, and her dark eyes follow me the length of the hallway as I head for the stairs. *Vogue Weddings* is splayed out on her lap, a glass of wine in her hand.

"Where have you been?" comes her cool voice, just as I'm almost across the hall. "I had the girls clean the attic because you were gone."

"I was washing out the truck, like yesterday." I glance up the stairs. Just get to my room. That's all I have to do.

"Still?"

"Yes, ma'am. We're going to need to do more tomorrow." I pile on lies like a buffet. "You know, to keep everything sanitary."

She sips her wine. "I told you the truck was a horrible place to work. At the country club, you wouldn't have to do those nasty things."

I pull a fake smile across my lips. "I don't mind." I hurry up the stairs.

As I pass the twins' closed door, it opens.

"Hey, weirdo, can we use your help for a minute?"

It's Chloe, smiling ever so pleasantly. Like how a cat would smile at a canary.

"No, we're fine!" Cal shouts from somewhere in their room. She sounds strange. "We don't need help!"

"Shut it," Chloe snaps at her sister, then turns back to me. "Because *you* didn't do it, I thought we'd never get done cleaning the attic, but it turned out to be *so* worth it. And now we *finally* have something for that stupid contest."

My eyebrows crinkle. "You're going to enter?" I try not to laugh, I really do. "Come on, Chloe. You don't even watch *Starfield*!"

She smirks. "Which is why we want your opinion on our costume."

Oh this should be good. Catherine couldn't have given them the money for a well-made costume from Etsy—she hates *Starfield*, there's no way she would. So I *have* to see what nylon-spandex hybrid monstrosity they bought. The sooner I do this, the sooner I can write about that idiot Darien Freeman getting himself trapped on a roof.

"All right," I say. "What are you cosplaying—"

But the moment I step into their room, the words die in my throat.

Cal can't even turn to me as she frantically braids her hair down her shoulder, standing in front of their full-length mirror in a beautiful silk dress.

My mother's cosplay costume.

"What do you think?" Chloe asks, smirking.

What do I think? I think my heart is breaking. I remember the way the dress looked when Mom twirled, like the galaxy was spinning, stars sparkling across the living room. Now a ghost, twirling, twirling, dancing around the living room, the heels of her starshine shoes clipping across the hardwood like a heartbeat.

Chloe waves her hand dismissively toward Cal's feet. "*I* couldn't fit into the stupid shoes—who makes *glass* shoes?—but Cal looks nice in them, doesn't she?"

"Where did you . . ." My heart thumps in my throat, swelling, making it harder to breathe. "Where did you find this?"

"In a trunk full of a lot of trash," Chloe replies.

Her words cut a searing pain through me, snapping me to my senses. "That's my mom's cosplay!" I cry. "It's not *trash*!"

That must've been what she was looking for me to say, because her face brightens and she smiles. "So it *is* one of those stupid costumes from the show! I told you, Cal."

"We just need it for a week," Cal adds, as if that makes things better. "Then we'll give it back."

"But it's not yours!" I protest.

Cal winces, but Chloe scoffs. "Like it's *yours* either. I don't see your name on it."

"It was my mom's!"

"Yeah, well." Chloe shrugs. "So was the house."

My mouth falls open as though she physically slapped me. "But . . . but Catherine'll never let you go to the con."

Chloe clicks her tongue to the roof of her mouth. "See, we might've lied and said we had a tennis tournament that weekend. Cal here will enter the contest and we'll win and record ourselves meeting Darien Freeman, which'll skyrocket our vlog to fame. We'll be famous. And you never know," she adds, her grin growing, "Darien might fall in love with me."

My hands clench into fists. "I won't let you go. I'll tell Catherine—"

"And we'll tell her why you've been coming home so late. You've been smoking weed or doing whatever nasty things that girl—what's her name?—*Sage* does."

"How do you—"

"James saw you going into her house today. So, what, did you just give up on men entirely?" She smirks, knowing the words dig under my skin. They do, like briars. "Because it's pathetic that you went with *her*."

"Chloe, stop it," Cal says, looking down at the floor.

"No," Chloe says simply. "She threatened to snitch on us, so if she snitches—*we* snitch. We're going to that contest, and we're going to win and meet Darien, even if we have to play along with this ridiculous *Star Wars* thing—"

"*Starfield*," Cal corrects.

"Whatever. We'll win and meet Darien and it'll be perfect—and I won't let a nobody like *you* ruin it for us."

Then she slams the door, trapping my mom's dress in a room of nightmares.

"Danielle!" Catherine calls from downstairs. "Dishes!"

If I tell Catherine, then I don't know what they'll do to Mom's cosplay, but if I don't . . . then what? Then they win. Maybe not the competition—because cosplay is more than putting on a costume—but they'll enter. With my mom's cosplay.

Clenching my fists, I hurry downstairs to do the dishes and put away the food, my hands shaking. If I don't finish fixing Dad's costume, if I don't prove that there's more to cosplaying than just putting on the right clothes, then they'll win. Maybe not the competition, but they'll win against me. And I can't let that happen—not with Mom's cosplay.

Not at Dad's convention.

Not in this universe.

DARIEN

"Darien, Mark's on the line," Gail says, extending her phone to me. "He says he's been trying to call for the last few days."

I turn the page in *Batman: Year One*. "Oh, is *that* who's been calling me? I thought it was a telemarketer or—"

"Darien," she says my name flatly, with the no-bull-right-now kind of inflection.

I close my book with a sigh and take the phone. "Hi there, M—"

"Who are you dating, again?" Mark interrupts.

My mouth falls open. "Um, I . . ." Is this a trick question? "Jess?"

"Oh good, so you remember."

"Of course I remem—"

"Then *why* is TMZ reporting that you're cheating on her?" he asks tersely.

I shoot a look at Gail, who's sitting on the side of my bed, nibbling on her thumbnail, knees bopping up and down from nerves. She couldn't have told. She wouldn't have. I pull myself up in my chair.

What is it? she mouths.

We're in my hotel room, spacious and beautiful thing that it is. But the walls are paper thin and Jess is in the room next door. We have a shoot in an hour with a star-chase scene, and I don't want it to be awkward.

I mouth, *Mark knows about the texts.*

Paling, Gail shakes her head. *Wasn't me,* she says. I know it wasn't. I have dirt on her now too, thanks Gaffer Dude. Lonny, then? No, he strikes me as a man of his word.

"There's no one," I say. "It's just rumors, you know?"

"Rumors," Mark echoes. "Then why are multiple sources saying you can't get your nose out of your phone?"

I brace for impact, like he's going to order Gail to take away my phone; the thought of not texting Elle leaves me with a panicky hollowness.

But then he laughs, as if trying to diffuse the situation. "You have to be careful, kiddo. You're the face of *Starfield.* It'll look bad if you're dating your costar and getting a little something on the side. You know what you should do?" He's going to tell me anyway, even though I don't want to know. "You should put whoever's on the other end of that phone on hold. Have some good times with Jess. I just talked with her manager and we're setting up a nice date for you two, okay? Tonight after the shoot. You can do that, yeah?"

I'm quiet for a moment, looking down at my phone in my lap. Not talk to Elle? For, what, the week left until we wrap up? Until Excelsi-Con? A week doesn't seem that long, and the moment after wrap-up Jess and I will end our "relationship" and go our separate ways but . . .

As if Elle knows we're talking about her, my phone blips with a message. Her name.

8:47 AM

—*Oh no, Car.*

—*Oh no.*

—*There's a dog next door and I went out to feed him because he barks and*

—*Car, it's so bad. I hate my stepmom.*

—*I hate her so much.*

—The neighbor's taking him to the pound.
—THE POUND.

I tap out of my call with Mark to answer her.

8:49 AM

—O, shit. I'm so sorry.

Elle 8:49 AM

—I just don't know what to do Car
—This isn't Frank the Tank's fault
—She always wins. She ALWAYS does.
—I'm powerless. I'm always so powerless.

Powerless. I know a thing or two about that. I feel useless, half-thinking that I'm actually going to sit here and let Mark tell me whom I can and can't talk to. But he's my dad, and shouldn't dads know best? Don't they know best?

"Darien? Are you still there?" My phone speaker crackles with Mark's voice. "Did I drop you? Did you hear me? Stupid phone . . ."

"I get it, Mark," I reply, picking up my phone again.

"I knew you'd come around!" He cheers as though this is some breakthrough in our relationship. "Now don't forget that date tonight. Be on your best. Shine like you always do, yeah?"

"Yeah," I grind out, and hang up with a look at Gail. "Next time he calls, I'm busy."

Gail frowns. "Darien, maybe he's right. It's just a week . . ." She looks down at her phone hesitantly. "I mean, just listen to him for a week—"

My phone vibrates again.

Elle 8:52 AM

—I don't know what to do.

I glance back to Gail, who simply puts up her hands and returns to the couch to watch the morning news. "I don't see anything."

8:52 AM

—*It's okay. Let's think.*

—*Do you have anywhere to put him? Take care of him for a while?*

Elle 8:52 AM

—*Nowhere.*

—*I can't do anything.*

8:52 AM

—*How about your friend? The one you're showing Starfield to?*

Elle 8:53 AM

—*Are you saying that I STEAL Frank??*

8:53 AM

—*I'm saying let's stop being powerless.*

—*Sometimes we shouldn't be Carmindor.*

—*Sometimes we should be Amara.*

ELLE

At least Frank likes the food truck. He's tucked in the one cool place by the refrigerator, which we lovingly (okay, well lovingly on my part; Sage was very begrudging) gave up for him. On hot summer days, Charleston is a cesspool of sweat and gnats, and being locked in a tin can is downright stifling. Not only stifling—it's *hot as balls.*

I fan myself with a spatula, pressing a cheek against the cool countertop, and I'm literally about to pass out from the heat when I remember something. I snap to attention and check my phone for the date, but I have it right. With expedited shipping, today's the day.

"Frank the Tank is getting more attention than our food," Sage mutters, glaring at the dog as another heart-eyed tourist walks away, cooing about Frank's pudginess.

He looks at her with big brown eyes, tongue lolling out of his mouth. She scowls.

I pet Franco on the head. "Sorry boy, but your charms won't work on her."

"I can't believe you stole him right out of his yard. We're probably violating a billion health codes right now."

"A billion and one," I add, snagging a hot sweet-potato fry from the fryer. I pop it into my mouth and quickly realize my mistake, fanning my tongue. "Hot, hot, hot!"

"Serves you right," Sage crows. Her bright hair is pulled back into a bandana, her mouth working a Dubble Bubble she's been chewing on for the better part of the afternoon.

"So he convinced you to steal it, that mystery boy of yours?" she asks, turning the page in her latest issue of *Vogue*.

"He didn't *convince* me. I was already thinking about it. But he said something weird—that we should stop being so powerless. I wonder what that means? Does he have an evil stepmonster too? Or something else?"

She shrugs. "Why don't you ask him?"

I scoff. "I wish."

"Why?"

"Because he barely talks about himself. I should be lucky to have gotten even *that* from him. I mean, if we're not talking about *Starfield* or the integrity of the solar flux capacitor, then we just . . . I don't know. We talk about me. Not really him. I think he's just very private."

"You think . . . ?"

I look at her hard from my spot beside the fryer and she holds her hands up in surrender. Frank woofs, wagging his tail.

"See? Frank agrees." I give him a scratch behind the ears and look back at my phone. "Hey, um, can I ask you a favor?"

"I'm already babysitting your dog until you can find it a permanent home," Sage intones dryly. "What more could you want from me, oh Queen?"

I grin innocently. "My lovely servant, may we perchance swing by my abode before our drudgery in your basement tonight? The twins won't be home but I'm expecting something in the mail . . ."

Sage heaves a harder-than-needed sigh, fanning through her magazine. "I *guess* we could . . ." Then she looks up and asks, eyebrow quirked, "What's coming?"

"Tickets," I say. "To ExcelsiCon."

"Tickets? Plural?"

A blush creeps across my cheeks. "I mean, yeah. I thought you'd want to come—and it'd be my treat. Because, you know, you're working on the cosplay and . . ."

"But it's for my portfolio. I'm already getting something out of it."

"I know. I just—if you don't want to come, that's okay too." I fumble with my words, wringing my plastic-gloved hands together. "It was silly not to ask you first—"

"Are you kidding?" When I look up, Sage is beaming. "I would *love* to."

Surprised, I meet her gaze. "Really?"

"Yeah! It sounds ballin'!"

Franco barks again.

She thumbs back to him. "See, Frank thinks so too! Thanks. It'll be awesome. I mean, we're going to have to figure out how to get there 'cuz Mom won't let me take the Pumpkin outta city limits—"

"Bus. 6:30 a.m. Then there's one that comes home at 8." I'd biked down to the Greyhound station early that morning and bought the tickets—nonrefundable. Between that and the con passes, my stash of cash was nearly wiped out.

Sage laughs. "You got this all planned out, don't you?"

"I have to. This is like *The Italian Job*. Except we're smuggling me."

"Sounds more like Sam and Frodo sneaking into Mordor to me," she replies. I give her a blank look. She shrugs. "What? So I bleed Hobbit."

"Aragorn or Boromir?"

"I'm more of an Arwen fan, if you know what I mean." Sage winks.

I smile, but then I remember what the twins said—about me and Sage. And then I remember the awful, indelible sight of Cal in my mom's cosplay. I look down to the frying fritters.

"Something wrong?" Sage says. "Oh god, please don't tell me you can't be friends with a lesbian."

"What? *No!*" I say quickly. "It's just . . . they're entering too. The twins."

Her eyebrows jerk up. "I didn't know the hell-twins were *Starfield* fans."

"They aren't."

"Then how are they entering?"

"They, um, found a costume. A dress." I want to be as vague as possible. I don't want her to know it's Mom's cosplay. I don't want to admit that yet. Like a bad haircut you keep trapped under a beanie: if you don't think about it, then it never happened. "And if we don't get this cosplay done they might actually win, and I can't let that happen. But I can't let the twins know I'm entering the contest either. They'll tell my stepmom and it'll be over."

But Sage isn't letting it go. "How did they just *find* a costume? Do you have them lying around the house or something?"

"No," I reply quietly. "It . . . was in the attic. With my parents' stuff."

Slowly, as the words sink in, her eyes widen. She sets down her magazine, shaking her head. "Oh my god. It's your mom's, isn't it?"

"I mean, I . . ." My throat begins to close. I don't want to talk about Mom's dress, the yards of night sky sewn into the hems. It hurts in a place I haven't felt in eight years, like a sore muscle I'd forgotten existed.

"Seriously?" she says when I don't debunk her question. "They're using your mom's cosplay? That's messed up. Why don't you do anything?"

"What *can* I do, Sage?" I argue. "If I go to Catherine then they'll destroy it. And they can't know that I'm entering the contest too, or they'll tell Catherine and I won't be able to go. I can't win with them. I can *never* win."

"But you can't just let them—"

"I'm not. We're entering. *That's* how I'll stop them."

She purses her lips. "All right, fine. We'll swing by and then head over to my house—*Dog*! Stop panting so loudly! Ugh. It's slobbering *everywhere*."

The edges of my lips quirk up at the scowl on her face. "It just means he loves you."

"Mm-hm." She gives Frank the evil eye and goes back to her magazine.

To anyone who's never been in my house, it can be a little . . . jarring. Most houses in historic Charleston are beautiful, elegant. They think of the ones on Rainbow Row that are painted in the pastels of the season, lining the Battery like marching petit-fours. But my house is on the edge of the historical district, and though it's old, it's too young to qualify as "historical" and too old to be torn down. So it sort of exists in this limbo, with a leaky roof and a creaky front door.

I push open the door and hurry up the stairs. Sage marvels at the foyer, the immaculate wood finish, the chandelier, and the spotless living room. At least that's what the twins' friends look at when they first invite them over. They're all astonished that everything is so tidy, so white, so . . .

"It's all so *soulless*," comes Sage's voice as she follows me up the stairs.

I try to think of the best place to hide the con passes. Underwear drawer? No, I've already stashed the bus tickets and cash in there. "Catherine likes things clean."

She wanders down the hallway, with Frank tucked under her arm like a furry football. If Catherine knew that a dog was in her tidy little home, she'd flip. That gives me a mote of satisfaction—she doesn't know everything. She can't *control* everything.

Sage studies the family portraits of Catherine and the twins, lingering a little longer on the ones showing the twins as kids. She cocks her head. "Where're you?"

"I wasn't in those," I reply, glancing around my room. Under the mattress? No, who knows what's under that.

"Hey, is this the twins' room? With the two beds?"

"Yeah." I twirl around my room, searching, searching—until my eyes settle on the framed blue prints of the *Prospero*. Bingo. I take the frame off the wall and tuck the con passes against the back of it.

"Hey, um, Frank needs to take a leak, so I think I'm heading out."

"I'll be out in a minute!"

"Don't hurry!"

I shake the frame to make sure the passes won't fall out and then hang it back on the wall. There's no way they'll find them there. *I* wouldn't find them there. I close the door to my room and hurry through the hallway and down the stairs. I lock up just as Sage comes out from the back of the truck, wiping her hands on her pants.

"Did Frank do his deed?" I ask, rounding to the passenger side.

"Right on your stepmom's petunias. As I'd hoped." She hops into the driver's seat and cranks it up. The engine rumbles to life. "You know, he's not so bad."

"Told ya he'd grow on you."

She adjusts the rearview mirror. "Hmm? Oh, oh yeah."

I give her a strange look as she pulls out of the driveway and starts off toward her house in North Charleston. "Are you okay?"

"Fine. I'm fine. *But*," she adds after a minute, "I do have a question. Those things on Carmindor's jacket. Those two things." She motions to her sleeve and I know exactly what she's talking about. The Federation badges that say what class and what genetic modification you are. Starwings. "Your jacket doesn't have them. And you don't have the crown either."

"Yeah, those were missing from the trunk."

"Can we get them online?"

"The starwings, maybe. But the crown . . ." I shrug, trying to remember how much one goes for on Etsy. " . . . is the price of a small child."

"Well my firstborn's already taken by the Dark Lord, so how about we just make one instead?"

"Make it?" I think she's joking until I realize that I'm the only one laughing. I clear my throat. "No, no, I don't think so."

She drives around a slow economy car, jostling onto the freeway. "Oh come *on*, I'm sewing your jacket back together. I can work miracles. Can you ask on one of your forums or whatever? Fandoms have forums, right?"

"Yeah we have forums."

She raises a dark pierced eyebrow.

"I . . . can try," I finally cave.

She punches me good-humoredly in the shoulder, making the truck swerve. "I knew you could do it!"

"Hey, eyes on the road!"

Grinning, she turns back to the wheel. I feel for my phone, even though I know Car is working. He'll be at the con too, won't he? He had been trying to cancel something, but maybe he never got through.

Would there be a chance of us meeting? Would he even want to meet me? I chew on my bottom lip, nervous. What if he comes to his senses once he sees me? Takes one look and runs for the closest Amara for support?

What if—if we meet—he doesn't like the real me? It's easier to be who you want to be when aren't trying to be who everyone else thinks you are. But why do I care? I hate that I care. I hate that I think about Car when I should be focused on nothing but winning the contest.

I hate that I'm falling for someone I don't even know.

DARIEN

"With the solar flux capacitor breaching critical mass, I don't—I mean, I do—*shit*." Calvin/Euci shoves away from me, shark teeth glinting. "What's my line again?"

I beat his PA to it and intone, "With the solar flux capacitor breaching critical mass, I don't see any other way, *Your Highness*."

Calvin glares at me. "I didn't ask you. What do you want, extra credit for knowing *my* lines too?"

I shrug and adjust my collar as he composes himself. The ADR shakes her head, muttering something to the director. Amon nods, checking his watch, before he signals to her again.

"All right, we'll take an hour. Dinner break!" the ADR shouts at the crew. "And we got barbecue catering tonight! Cal, can you run your lines while you're at dinner?"

"Yeah, yeah," he mutters and hops off the stage.

It's unreal how fast the techs and assistants drop their work and make a beeline for the exit. I sigh, sinking down to the edge of the fake bridge, unbuttoning my jacket collar. The set empties out faster than bleachers during halftime at a high school football game.

A PA comes to take my jacket, but I tell her I can do it myself. She's older, college age, probably interning for cheap—or no—pay. She thumbs back to the door. "Are you coming to eat at least?"

I give her a thankful smile. "Yeah, I'll be there in a few."

When she's gone, I reach into my jacket and fish out my phone. I'm getting better at hiding it. Not texting as often, doing it on breaks when no one's watching. It sucks, and I feel like a jerk for not answering Elle quickly. But at least I answer eventually.

Elle 3:02 PM

—*Day 2 of Frank the Tank at work is amazing*

—*He's such a ham*

—*[1 attachment]*

Elle 4:21 PM

—*I think tonight I'll introduce my friend to the Amara eps.*

—*Let her cry it out*

—*Although I'm not sure if she cries*

—*I mean, I'm going to cry*

—*Maybe she's the crying-because-other-people-cry type*

Elle 6:32 PM

—*Do you ever wonder what would've happened if she had never saved his ass?*

I smirk, because I know the exact answer to that.

7:43 PM

—*He probably would've died.*

—*Also hi ☺ Sorry for not replying sooner*

—*Got in trouble for texting at work ☹*

"Oh look, it's the Ice King doing what he does best—being anti-social."

The sound of Jess's voice makes me jump. I shove my phone into my jacket and spin around to face her. She's changed out of her costume, back into yoga pants and a tank top, her dark hair pulled into a ponytail. In her hands are two plates of barbecue.

I lift a brow. "One of those for me?"

She chuckles, sitting down beside me. "I only share with *social* people."

"I'm social enough."

"You totally aren't, dude." She hands me a plate anyway. "How're you supposed to *work the crowd* if you're sitting over in a corner texting all day?"

"It's not my job," I argue, taking the plate. It smells delicious. Oh and look—she remembered not to put bread or any sort of carbs on my plate. Only protein and greens. I swear, if I can just have *one piece* of bread, I'll never lie about my texting habits again. "And genius sells itself, anyway."

Jess gives me a look. "Watch out, your ego's showing."

"It ain't easy being me."

"Hm." She swings her legs back and forth, looking out over the soundstage. "My agent's in talks with this indie project," she says after a moment.

"Oh yeah?" I say through a full mouth. "Whassit 'bout?"

"This small-town girl who lives a double life as a deejay. I read the script and it's good. It's *really* good. And I'd be so good *in* it."

"You have the talent." I swallow my food. "I mean, no one can run in heels like you can."

"Want me to stab you with one?" she threatens. I raise my hands in surrender. "It's a good project—small but cool, you know? And I'm a perfect fit for the lead."

But she doesn't sound happy about it. I study her for a moment.

"Then what's wrong?"

"*Starfield*," she says simply.

"I'm . . . not following."

She exhales slowly. "*Starfield*'s the matter. It's got this huge following—fans are coming out of the woodwork. Those Stargunners. If they rally around this movie, pay attention to it, make it a success . . ."

Realization dawns. "If there are *Starfield* sequels, you can't do that role."

"It'd conflict with my contract." She sighs. "I'm already twenty-two, Darien. And a woman. I know *you* love this, but my expiration date's coming a little faster than yours. I can't waste another three years being a space princess. Space princesses don't win Oscars." Morosely, she picks at her food, separating the green beans from the barbecue, her lips curved into a frown. "So much for a springboard. Maybe I should just hope it bombs—oh jeez." She gasps and looks over at me with wide, apologetic eyes. "I'm *so* sorry. I didn't mean that. It was word vomit. I know this is your dream role. I'm so sorry. I suck."

"It's okay." I tilt my head up, staring at the dimming orange lights on the set. "When I was younger, I never fit in anywhere. I always felt like that puzzle piece no one knew where to fit it. And then I found *Starfield* and its fandom"—and Brian—"and I thought for the first time hey, Carmindor's like me. And now I get to *be* Carmindor. But what if I'm not cut out to be him after all? What if it does bomb? What if it bombs because of *me*? You might not have anything to worry about."

"Seriously? If the screaming banshees outside the lot every day don't tell you anything—"

"Not them," I interrupt quickly, frustrated. "The *true* fans. Like you said, they're coming out of the woodwork and I don't think they like me much."

Jess cocks her head. "You like *Batman*, right?"

I shrug. "I'm a fan."

She eats a small bit of barbecue, chewing slowly. That's how she eats, I've realized. She savors little pieces, eating bit by bit, like a bird. "So who do you like better, Val Kilmer or Christian Bale?"

I scoff. "No one in their right *mind* likes Val Kil—"

She makes a buzzer sound with her mouth. "Does that mean you aren't a true fan?"

"What?"

"If you like one Batman over another? Which Batman does a *true* fan like?"

"I—" I realize what she means. "I guess it depends on the fan."

Jess nods. "As actors, all we can do is put ourselves in another person for a while and play them the best we can. We're instruments. We read the notes on the page and interpret them." She fashions a violin out of thin air and begins to play a slow, moving song, her eyes closed so delicately, I wonder if in another life she once played the instrument.

"I thought you didn't care," I tease. "Since it's not an 'Oscar movie.'"

She pauses midnote and drops her invisible violin. "I don't. But like I said, we're an orchestra, and if you're out of tune you'll make me look bad too." But she can't meet my gaze.

"Admit it, you like being Amara."

She mock gasps. "*Never!*"

"Jessica!" An assistant calls from the exit, her voice echoing in the now-empty warehouse. "Phone call!"

Jess hops off the set so quickly; she must've been expecting the call. "For the fans, right?" she says, and hurries out of the lot, grabbing the cell phone from her assistant's hand as she goes.

I flip out my own phone, remembering blog posts on *Rebelgunner*. All the scathing comments online. Jess paints a pretty picture of an orchestra, but if we are one, then I'm the first chair violinist . . . who's been doused in gasoline and handed a match by the fans to watch me play while going up in flames.

I have a bunch of new messages, all from Elle.

> *Elle 7:47 PM*
>
> —Oh no! Did I get you in trouble??
>
> —I'm sorry!
>
> —I won't text you as much anymore, promise-sworn!

But then there are fans like Elle—*people* like Elle. Even if she ends up not liking my version of Carmindor, I'm going to give it my all. Because somehow she makes me want to be better. She makes me want to play my heart out while I'm on fire, play and play until I burn up like a dying red giant.

7:49 PM

—Pshhh, let them riot.

—I'd rather you promise-swear that you'll never stop.

Elle 7:50 PM

—Really?

7:50 PM

—Really. I like talking to you.

Elle 7:51 PM

—Why?

"Ten minutes!" someone calls, and I jump. My hands are actually shaking a little on my phone, dying to type all the things I'm thinking. Before I can stop myself, I start to type.

7:52 PM

—Because I can't stop thinking about you.

—But that's crazy right, because we don't know each other? But I feel like I want to know you.

—...I'm just making a fool out of myself, aren't I?

"Darien?" It's Amon. "Where is that kid?"

"Here!" I jump to my feet. "Coming."

But before I go, I sneak one last look at my phone.

Elle 7:53 PM

—*I want to know you too, Car.*

—*I wish you were here.*

—*For real.*

A knot swells in my throat. Because I wish I was there too, for real, but there are a hundred thousand reasons why it would never work. Why it *could* never work.

"Hey, hero!" my stunt coordinator hollers from the other end of the soundstage, holding up a harness. I put my phone into a pocket inside Carmindor's jacket, trying to figure out how to tell Elle that if she ever met me, she wouldn't like who she saw.

IT'S ANOTHER TWO HOURS BEFORE I'M free. And by free, I mean out in Olympic Park, running laps. Because apparently when you're a movie star, even when you're not working, you're working.

Lonny grunts behind me. "You okay?"

"Yeah, why wouldn't I be?" Besides the fact that my heart won't stop pounding, and it's got nothing to do with exercise.

Even though Olympic Park is in the heart of Atlanta, the world is mute. The park's supposed to be closed at night, but when the night guard recognized me, he let me slip the fence. Perks to having a recognizable face, I suppose. Or having a gigantic bodyguard. Only me, my breath pumping in and out of my lungs, and my feet thumping against the pavement. Enough to make everything feel clear and sharp. Enough to make me want to tell Elle the truth—that I wish I were with her too. But in no universe can that ever happen, can it? All I can do is be there the only way I know how, and it'll never be enough.

It's been over two hours since her last text. She's probably pissed that I haven't texted her back, or she's asleep. Or both.

But still, I have to try.

10:45 PM

—I have an idea.

—Let's play I Spy.

With a whoosh of speed, my bodyguard passes me.

"What the—"

"Too slow!" Lonny throws over his shoulder, pulling ahead of me around the track. The one part of my "fitness regimen" I actually enjoyed doing—running—is the one thing I can't do alone anymore. I'm surprised I can still pee alone, honestly. Soon Lonny'll probably start tailing me to the urinal.

Still no text. I type another message.

10:46 PM

—I'll start.

—I spy something big.

Please answer, I all but beg. After a moment, the typing notification appears beside her name and sends through a message with a soft *ding*.

Elle 10:46 PM

—Inside or outside?

10:46 PM

—Outside.

I don't have to glance up to know it's a clear night. The streetlights don't even need to be on, it's so bright out here. In fact, I can see my bodyguard's shadow rounding up behind me. This feels like the scene from that superhero movie with a certain dude with a shield.

"On your—"

"Left," I deadpan as he passes. "Show-off!"

Elle 10:59 PM

—I don't know—a cloud?

—This is impossible.

—How am I supposed to guess if I'm not there to see, Car?

10:59 PM

—Tsk, tsk, patience!

—You don't always have to be where I am for us to see the same thing, young padawan

"You're smiling," Lonny says as he passes me again.
I wave my hand after him. "Oh go on! Keep lapping me."

Elle 11:01 PM

—I still don't get it.

11:04 PM

—I'll give you a hint.

—Look up.

—When was the last time you did?

I look up, thinking that maybe she is too.

Stars and stars for as far as the eye can see. The inky blackness is so dark it looks purple, bejeweled with abandoned bits of glitter. So many stars, white hot, flaring, burning like candles in the night sky.

I spy . . .

Elle 11:09 PM

—Is it the sky?

11:09 PM

—Not JUST the sky. It's the SAME sky.

—And if we're both looking up at the same sky, how far apart can we REALLY be? What were the odds of us being put on the same slab of rock in this huge universe?

"On your left!" my bodyguard shouts again, skirting around me. "Looks like you only got two speeds—slow and slower!"

I glare after him. "*Excuse* me?"

Lonny spins around and begins jogging backward. "Prove me wrong, pretty boy."

That is *it*.

He has followed me. He has towered over me with that serious, terrifyingly calm face of his. He's been a quiet, stalking Weeping Angel for as long as he's been around. But Hades'll freeze over before I let him throw shade like that.

I shove my phone into my jogging shorts pocket, then take off after him. He begins to pick up speed. We round the first corner, legs pumping. I gain on him, one stride at a time, my heart hammering in my throat.

"On your left!" I shout, sprinting past him to the finish line.

We slow down and double over, putting our hands on our knees. I suck in a painful breath, chest aching. I think I pulled my ego running.

"I win," I wheeze.

Lonny begins to laugh, and once I realize how silly it all is, I begin to laugh too—and then I wince, ribs hurting.

"There you go, boss!" he says after a moment, righting himself. "You're never going to pull ahead unless you really go for it."

He gives his arms a shake, rolling his head to and fro, stretching his massive shoulders. I take the opportunity pull out my phone—still no answer.

Maybe Lonny's right. I need to really go for it.

11:09 PM

—*Elle, we might not know much about each other, and I might not be there, and you might not be here, but I'm glad to share this sky with you.*

—*Maybe we should start looking up together, ah'blena*

ELLE

Ah'blena.

My heart. The words that Carmindor says to Amara in the last episode. The episode when she . . . when the Black Nebula . . .

I hold the phone to my chest and stare out my bedroom window, up and up at the clear and cloudless sky.

"We aren't alone," I say quietly, liking how the words fit around my lips. If this is the impossible universe, then I hope tonight was the good sort of impossible.

I want to believe.

———

Battery Park is already teeming with tourists and horse-drawn carriage tours by the time I race to the truck. Sage doesn't even glance up when I come in, wiping her paring knife on her apron. Today her hair's pulled back with a polka-dotted bandana, her lips a dark, deep purple-black.

"I began to think your stepmom actually cut you up into her salad," she says.

"It's only a matter of time," I reply, dumping my bag in the corner of the truck and grabbing my apron from my peg. I tie it around my waist and pull my hair into a Magic Pumpkin cap. "So my friends online said that you can make the crown and badges with something called Wonderflex."

"Wonderflex."

"Yeah, and we need a heat gun. Or a hair dryer."

"I figured as much." Sage gives a grim nod. Beside her, Frank the Tank sits happily on his little mat on the counter, wagging his tail at all the tourists. A little kid comes up and pets him under the chin, and he gives her a big lick. She runs away screaming.

Sage just keeps chopping. I retie my apron, bunching it into knots. "Or we could skip the crown. I mean, people take cosplay super seriously. They've been doing this for years and we're . . ."

"We're what?" Sage stops chopping and puts her hands on her hips. "Rookies? Because last I heard, Carmindor was a total rookie before he survived the Brinx Devastation."

"You can't compare a cosplay competition to the destruction of an entire colony."

She rolls her eyes, pulling the plastic gloves higher on her hands. "Look, don't you want to win?"

I hesitate, scrubbing Franco behind the ears. "We'll be posers."

"Why, because we're new? So everyone who tries something for the first time's a poser? Come on, Elle, that's crazy."

"But what if . . ." I bite my cheek as I dump a batch of fritters into the fryer beside the sweet potato fries. They hiss and spit like vipers. "What if we *are* posers?"

"Impossible. You're the most *Starfield* person I know," Sage says. "And besides, you're allowed to try new things, Elle. You're allowed to test the waters. Don't you want to try?"

Try. I want to try a lot of things. I want to go to the convention. I want to cosplay. I want to pretend that I have some modicum of courage in me, like Carmindor. What if Car is at the convention? What if he's in the competition too?

And then I realize I'm not thinking about cosplay anymore.

"Well then, what *do* you want?

I half-shrug, half-wince. "I want something . . . I don't think I can have."

"Like what?"

Maybe we should start looking up together, ah'blena.

I don't know how to answer, so I just shrug, shaking the fries to loosen them out of the basket. "I don't want to talk about it."

Sage shrugs and flaps a tired hand at me. "Fine, whatever." Chopping done, she pulls out the costume from underneath the counter, along with a pincushion and thread that matches the deep blue of Carmindor's jacket, and threads the string through the needle. "It's that guy, isn't it? The one you're texting."

"I don't want to talk about it," I repeat.

"You never want to talk about anything!" she says. "Come on, if you can't talk to me, who can you talk to? Why don't can't you just confide in me? Just rant! Tell me things!"

I clench my phone. "I just . . ."

"Am I not a good enough fan or something?" she asks, throwing the jacket onto the counter. "Is that what this is about? Do I not meet your fangirl expectations? Why won't you just let me be your fri—"

"Because it won't change anything!" I say, whirling around to her. "It won't change *anything* if I complain. If I tell you what I want, if I tell you that I hate my family and my life sucks and I'm falling for someone I don't even know and that wish—oh how I *wish*—I was in any other universe, what difference would it make?"

My voice is so loud, the tourists across the street turn to watch. Sage opens her mouth, closes it again, opens—like a fish gobbling for water—before her eyes drift to the counter and the empty pumpkin-orange dog bed. "Where's the fleabag?"

"What?" I blink. Glance over at Franco. Who isn't there. Neither is the jacket.

We lean over the counter just in time to watch a fat brown wiener dog race between a family of tourists' legs, blue fabric fluttering in his wake.

"I'm going to fry him!" Sage cries, ripping off her apron. She dodges past me and swings open the back doors to the truck with a running leap, calling for Franco.

I don't even take off my apron as I dart after her. Franco has my costume—and who knows what he's going to do with it. "*Franco!*"

Tourists line the streets both ways, cars bump by on the cobblestones, horse-drawn carriages stopping frequently to marvel at rainbow-colored houses. So many people—but no Franco. How could I have let him out of my sight?

We shout his name, dodging and weaving through tourists who loiter too long in front of the big houses with steepled roofs and grand verandas. They turn to stare like we're some kind of weird show: two girls—one in an orange EAT ME apron, the other in a tulle tutu and checkered ribbons—tearing down the sidewalk like the Nox are on their heels.

But when we reach Rainbow Row, he's gone. My chest constricts. "Oh no. Oh no oh no oh no."

"Hey mutt! Fleabag!" Sage adds. "Rolly-Polly Olley! Fatso!"

"That's not helping," I hiss.

She shrugs. "He came when I called him Frankzilla last night—oh! There!" She nudges her head toward a side street and what might be Franco's chubbiness rounding the corner. At least we hope it is. How can a fat dog run so fast? She grabs my arm and pulls me into a gallop again, but she trips on a stroller, stumbling. I pull ahead and turn into the cobblestoned alley—and suddenly my worst nightmare is realized.

Franco is sitting, tail wagging happily, as his ears are scratched by none other than Calliope Wittimer. And she has my dad's jacket in her grip.

"Oh!" She glances up through her loosely braided hair and quickly stands. "Elle."

"Cal? What are you . . ." I chance a look at my jacket, which she knows is mine. "Aren't you supposed to be at the country club? For lessons?"

"I skipped today. Sometimes I do that. Chloe doesn't tell as long as I don't tell Mom what she does behind the pool house with that linebacker from school." She pets Franco's little head. "I was wondering where this little guy went, you know, when he disappeared."

"Here." I hurry over and scoop up Franco, hugging him tight, eyeing the jacket, wondering if I should go for it too. Calliope frowns, looking hurt. I shouldn't care. But I can't get the image of her in my mom's dress out of my head, and now she has my dad's jacket?

I shift from one foot to the other. Maybe I can fake her out—toss Franco at her as a distraction. He'll come at her, claws bared, and kung-fu her while I wrestle the jacket out of her grip and then—

Frank whines, wiggling in my grasp as Sage rounds into the side street beside me.

"Case solved, I guess," Calliope says. The buttons on the jacket glint in the sunlight. She glances over at Sage. "Um, hi. I'm—"

"Calliope," Sage replies for her.

"Cal. Elle's stepsister."

Sage glances between us and I can see the thought crossing her face. Cal really doesn't *look* evil or conniving, with her purple glasses and braided hair. But evil rarely looks like evil should.

Hesitantly, Cal holds out the jacket to us. "Is this yours too?"

Sage takes it. "Yeah, mine. The mutt got away with it."

"It's the jacket, isn't it? Carmindor's?"

"Don't say a word," I say stonily. "Don't say a word, Cal."

Her face fractures a little. "Elle, about that dress—"

"It's fine," I force out, my voice tight. "I don't want to talk about it."

"But . . ."

"It's fine. Thanks for catching him," I add, heaving Frankendog higher, and turn to go. "We should get back to work. Sage?" I say when she doesn't follow me out of the alley.

She hesitates for a moment, rubbing the back of her head. "It was nice meeting you," she murmurs to Cal, then turns and follows me out. She doesn't catch up until we're halfway down Rainbow Row. "Hey—

hey wait a second. Do you think maybe you're wrong about her?"

"No. She's going to tell Chloe. I know she will. Usually they're conjoined at the hip."

"Maybe she isn't as bad as you think."

I snort. "Yeah, and Darien Freeman can act. Which reminds me that I have to write a new blog post."

"About Darien's acting skills?"

"His inability to stay out of trouble," I reply. "He and Frank have that in common. You move your fat butt from that cushion ever again and you're going in a fritter, you hear me, Frank? A *fritter*."

"That wouldn't be very vegan," Sage mutters, but then she flashes a grin. "Hey, maybe you should text that guy your blog."

"Dream on!" I've had that blog since practically before I knew how to spell. The very thought of Car reading it is mortifying. "Besides, he works so much, he doesn't have time to read my silly little blog."

"Mm-hmm." Sage sweeps the jacket over her shoulders to wear like a cape. "Whatever you say, Captain."

DARIEN

"You're right. Whoever's writing those blog posts has a serious crush on you." Jess hands me back my phone as we pull into the hotel. Three scheduled "dates"—i.e., us eating food in the same restaurant to the soundtrack of camera flashes—down, one more to go.

I ease us into the carport. "I think you mean has a serious *vendetta* against me."

Jess makes a *tsk*ing sound. "No one is that vicious without some feeling behind it," she says. "And I think she has some fair points. I mean, it's not like she's one of those white dudes saying you just got cast because you're not white."

"One, that's ridiculous. And two, if they even watched the show, they'd know that—wait, how do you know it's a she?"

Jess arches an eyebrow. "Seriously? Read it again. I'm totally right."

I raise my hands in surrender. "Fine, fine. But no one should be that vicious, *period*. She's like a Dalek with a blacklist. Absolutely relentless."

I open the passenger door for her and toss the keys to Lonny, who's squeezing himself into the driver's seat to go park. I wrap my arm around Jess's waist and start for the hotel lobby, paparazzi following like a swarm of bees. Between the constant barrage of flashbulbs and questions, I'd take my fans over this any day.

"Are you two dating?" a paparazzo barks at us.

"What's she like? How about your old costar?"

"Jess! Hey, Jess! What about Carla? Cheating on her now?"

Jess falters a step, but I think only I can tell. *Carla?*

"How do you feel about the other girl he's texting right under your nose?" someone else asks. I whirl around, but Jess yanks me by the arm to the end of the lobby, where they barrage us with questions at the elevator. After an eon, the doors open to reveal a strawberry blonde bouncing on her toes—Gail, because of course she can sniff out trouble like a bloodhound.

I corral Jess into the elevator as Lonny catches up, pushing through the paparazzi like butter.

"Dare!" Gail says, squeezing into the elevator with Lonny. He towers in the corner like a great imposing shadow. "I've been looking everywhere for you. There's messages at the front desk—"

I ignore her and turn to Jess. "Carla?"

Jess jabs the button to her floor, staring straight ahead into the shiny brass doors, her jaw set. "Please don't ask. Please."

"*Darien.*" Gail touches my elbow. She looks agitated. "There's this guy calling you. He keeps leaving messages with the front desk."

"A guy?" Jess asks. "What guy?"

Lonny tenses. "Is he a security threat?"

"An ex-boyfriend?" Jess adds.

"No, no," Gail says. "It's just someone talking about the con—"

The elevator doors *ding* open and I make a break down the hallway before Gail can answer. Jess and Lonny follow, but they don't keep pace. Gail, however, does.

I swipe open my door with the magnetic key and faceplant onto my bed.

"Dare, I know you don't want to handle this right now but—"

"Isn't handling things *your* job?" I say into my pillow.

"You know what I mean."

I roll over, staring at the popcorn ceiling. "Okay. Messages. What did they say?"

"Just that—" Gail falters, sitting down on the edge of the bed. "Just that you should look out for him—whoever this guy is. At ExcelsiCon. And that you should want to talk to him."

"That's it?" I sit up. "Gail, honestly, it's probably just this angry blogger. They've been posting for weeks about how terrible I am as Carmindor."

"But how did he find the hotel?"

"Well . . . dunno," I admit. "I mean, how did the fangirls find the set? These internet people are crazy. They're probably swapping location info on Tumblr right now. Here." I pull up *Rebelgunner* on my phone. "This is what I'm talking about. These people are pretty ruthless—well, Jess thinks this girl has a crush on me but—"

"Girl?" Gail looks up from the blog.

"Or guy," I amend. "I mean, I don't know who writes it. But I bet you they're just some bitter fan with an ax to grind. So he'll come and tell me off. Big deal."

She hands back my phone. "So you don't think it's someone you know?"

I give her a blank look, waiting for her to clarify.

"You don't think it's Brian?"

I blink. I haven't heard that name in months, too busy with training and the shoot and all of the tabloid stuff and . . . Elle. Elle helped me forget. "Nah. He wouldn't dare show his face around here. Besides, what would he be doing in Atlanta?"

"You're right," she agrees quickly, and paces. "Well, maybe it's best if you don't do the contest. You'll be right there with all those fans. Something can easily go wrong.'"

"Wrong?" I echo. "Like *what*?"

"We don't know who left those messages. It could be any crazy person. After what happened on the roof . . . we can beef up security. We can make sure you feel safe and—"

"I'll be fine, Gail," I interrupt. "I don't want to be some aloof star in this fandom."

"But this is your *life*, Darien."

"You really think I'm in danger?"

She throws up her hands, turning on her heels to pace the other way—but then she stops and falls with a *thunk* onto the bed beside me. She heaves out a long sigh. "I don't know. I should tell Mark—"

"No."

Gail goes silent, and I study her. The way she fidgets with her hands, digging the dirt out from under her bitten fingernails. Her plaid shirt is half-untucked from the waistband of her washed-out boyfriend jeans, about as put together as she normally looks but she's missing her earrings. Purple studs. She gets scatterbrained when she's under pressure.

"What if this guy really wants to hurt you, Dare?" she asks softly. "You can't be just a fan anymore."

She's right. I don't know what these people are capable of. Jess's joking about the blogger is all fun and games until one of those fans starts to use more than just words to hurt me. Who knows what the guy on the roof would do if he cornered me again. Take more than just a few bad photos?

I can't take that risk. But I can't avoid the con, either.

"Tell you what, Gee," I say, keeping my voice as steady as I can. "Just double-check that I'm not doing anything one-on-one—no signings or anything. Okay?"

Gail nods. "Okay."

"Perfect. See? Problem solved."

Gail is silent for a moment and puts her head on my shoulder. "And if anyone *does* mess with you, they have to go through Lonny," she says.

"I pity the fool," I reply, trying to pretend like I'm not scared. She laughs and rolls her forehead against my shoulder. Just act like everything is okay. It's my job. I should be brilliant at it.

ELLE

WHEN I GET TO SAGE'S HOUSE the next night—the last night we're working together—I kick off my shoes and dump my bag at the door, just like I would at home. Sage's house is weird like that. It feels like home.

"I want to be back at a reasonable hour tonight," I tell her. "I don't want Catherine to start getting any ideas."

She rolls her eyes. "You're paranoid. We'll get you home at the same time we have every night."

"But what if she begins to suspect something?"

"Then I'll call and say that you were here, dear!" Sage's mom emerges from the living room, all sixties goddess supreme in a tie-dye sarong and bracelets that jingle like new-age maracas. "Don't you worry."

I smile. "Sorry Ms., um, Wynona, but she won't go for that. My stepmom just doesn't . . ."

"Have feelings," Sage finishes for me. "Or, like, know how to mom."

"Oh, Elle." Sage's mom puts a hand to her chest. "You know you can always come here if you need some mothering. Just ask Sage. I'm a natural." She winks.

"Moooooom," Sage groans and grabs me by the elbow. "C'mon, Elle, let's watch that last episode and get you fitted. We don't exactly have time to waste."

She's right. The contest is tomorrow. In less than twelve hours we'll be on a bus bound for Atlanta, costume in tow.

But I still drag my heels. It's because we're about to watch the episode I can't stand. It's because I'm about to relive my nightmare: Princess Amara falling into the Black Nebula again and again, in an endless time paradox. That's why episode 54 doesn't exist to me. Because it's the sticks of bad luck. It's the worst send-off to a character. The worst goodbye. Because Carmindor never gets to say it. And I know better than anyone how that feels.

"You know," I say, as we descend to the basement, "I can just explain it to you. We don't have to actually watch it."

"No, I want to see it! I slogged through all the rest!"

"*Slogged*?"

"Slogged enthusiastically," she corrects.

I hesitate. "But this one's . . ."

"The last one, so yeah *yeah* it's sentimental, blah blah blah." Sage holds out my jacket and trousers. "Whatever. Come stand here. We can watch it while I make the final adjustments."

Hesitantly, I press PLAY. The episode cues up as I wiggle into the trousers, no longer embarrassed for Sage seeing me in my three-year-old underwear with cartoon rabbits on it—we're way past that. Pants on, I climb up onto the step stool as she hands me the jacket, and gingerly, I slip it on.

The opening credits light up the TV—for the last time, the last episode, the last new experience—but it differs from the other intros. Instead of showing random scenes, it shows the best scenes. The climactic ones. Dad said that when it first aired, he knew it would be the last episode because of the opening credits.

"It looked final," he told me. "You could tell—it was a send-off."

Dad's send-off was quieter. Only a handful of people gathered around a small hole in the cemetery. Black umbrellas. Rain. Catherine sobbing into her father's shoulder. The twins crying into each other.

I stood alone. Like an extra in one of those bad nineties punk music videos.

Sage thinks I hate Princess Amara on the principle that she's a lying double-crosser, but I hate her because I can relate to her. I'm the one tossed into the Black Nebula. I'm the one lost, in a life, a world, a universe that is no longer mine.

The phone rings upstairs, and for a terrible moment I think it's Catherine, having sniffed out my lies, ready to ground me for good. But then Sage's mom calls down, "Sagey, it's your father!"

Sage makes a face and goes to the bottom of the stairwell. "Tell him I'll call him later!"

"He'll be working with a client!"

"Tell him I'm busy!"

"Sagey, pleeeease!"

She rolls her eyes and glances back at me. "Sorry, it's my dad-person. He calls, like, once every thirty years and . . . oh Jesus, you can't even talk to your father anymore and here I am complaining—"

I put on a tight-lipped smile. "I'll wait. Not like I'm going anywhere."

"Okay. Don't move!" She climbs the stairs two at a time, her clunky boots thundering against the wooden steps. When she's gone, I step off the podium and pat my clothes for my phone in a back pocket.

7:38 PM

—I have this theory, ah'blen

Ah'blen—the masculine version of "my heart." Car responds as soon as I send it, so quick it surprises me. Like he was waiting, or about to text me, or . . . just on his phone. Probably just on his phone.

Carmindor 7:38 PM

—Theory?

7:39 PM

—Don't laugh. I've had it for a while.

—I have a theory that there's another universe beside ours.

Carmindor 7:39 PM

—Like those fan-theories on where the Black Nebula goes?

Above me, Sage shakes the dust off the rafters as she stomps from one side of the room to the other. It must be the living room. She's arguing with her dad, the kind of argument padded with years and years of well-worn "I love you"s squeezed between the syllables.

Her voice carries down, muffled, through the air vents as I type out a text.

7:40 PM

—Yeah, where everything we thought was impossible happens and then there's a world where everything impossible doesn't.

Carmindor 7:40 PM

—So which universe are we in?

7:40 PM

—The first.

Maybe in that other universe, I'm having those same arguments with Dad. Maybe we're arguing about where I'll go to college or what to eat for dinner or why Darien Freeman is the worst Carmindor known to humankind. But we'll never have those arguments.

We'll never argue again.

Carmindor 7:41 PM

—Oh good, I was scared for a minute there, ah'blena.

—I'm glad we're in the impossible world.

7:42 PM

—*Why?*

Carmindor 7:42 PM

—*Because otherwise I never would've found you.*

I hold the phone close to my chest, closing my eyes.

Oh but isn't that the problem? Which would I choose, if I had to choose between my father and Car? Which universe could I be happy in?

The opening credits fade into the first scene. I know it too well. Amara and Carmindor stand across from each other on the bridge. His face is the picture of heartbreak as he stares at the phaser in his lover's hand.

"You were warned about me, *ah'blen*," Princess Amara will reply to his shocked face, but just as her mouth opens, Sage returns from her phone conversation, grabs the remote, and turns off the TV.

I blink, suddenly thrown out of the moment. "What was that for?"

"Lift your arms," she says, so I do. She pinches and tugs at the fabric, seemingly satisfied. "Good, good. I think we're good."

"Good?" I ask, dumbfounded. I begin to turn toward the mirror. "Why'd you pause it? Are we done?"

"No no! Not yet! No looking!" She darts off to her workbench, which is covered with a white sheet. When she flips it, a gasp escapes my throat.

The crown. She found a crown for me.

Gingerly, like it's made of real gold, she picks it up and brings it over.

"I couldn't help myself," she says. "It's my flaw. I'm a completionist. The outfit wouldn't have looked right without it." When I don't move, her smile begins to falter. "What, did I do something wrong? Is it the wrong crown?"

"No," I whisper, taking the crown. "It's perfect."

She laughs awkwardly. "Seriously, no need to get all mushy. It was nothing."

To her it might be nothing, but to me it means the world—the *universe*. I want to say that, I want to thank her over and over, but my mouth isn't working the way it's supposed to because I'm trying not to cry. And I'm trying not to laugh. And I'm trying to find the right words to describe the light slowly filling me up.

I can never repay her. Never in a hundred thousand light-years.

She squirms. "Okay, okay, now quit hanging on me and put it on! I didn't slave over it just to have you look dopey-eyed at it!"

I pull away, laughing and crying and rubbing my eyes with the back of my hand as she places the crown on my head.

A perfect fit.

She grabs my hand and gently turns me to the mirror. "Your royal Federation Prince Carmindor, esteemed captain of the good ship *Prospero*. It is an honor!"

Then she flourishes a Federation bow, promise-sworn salute and all. Her smile is brighter than any star in the sky. She looks proud, and when I finally shift my gaze to me, someone else stares back. A girl with dyed-red hair, dark roots showing, and thick black glasses, the highest graduate at *Starfield*, the heir to the throne of stars, the general's daughter. Carmindor. I am Carmindor, a crown of stars over my brow.

But something still feels off.

Sage puts her hands on her hips, appraising me in the mirror. "Damn, I'm good."

"Damn," I echo. What's wrong with me? This is beautiful—this is exactly what I wanted. I am Carmindor.

But how come I don't feel like I am? I brush the feeling away. It's just shock, that's all. The shock of seeing myself so different.

Sage walks around me, nodding. "Not bad for a wannabe fashion designer."

"You *are* a fashion designer."

We grin at each other, wide and unabashed, and for a moment I think she's about to say something, but then she averts her gaze. "We even got done early. I think we can get you home by nine?"

My heart sinks. "Oh. Yeah."

"What's wrong? You just went from exuberant to depressed in the time it takes for Boromir to die in the first movie."

"Spoiler!"

"Oh you've seen it. Aren't you excited?"

"I am. It's not that." I take off the crown. So much detail went into it. All of the small ridges, the handmade stars.

"Well? I'm not a mind-reader," Sage adds impatiently.

"It's just . . ." I can't meet her gaze. "I've never really had a friend before. I mean, I have. Online. But not in person. Not in a long time, at least. So . . . we'll be friends after this, right? After the con?"

She puts her hands on her hips and tilts her head. "Now what kind of question is that? Of course we will."

I finally look at her and drink up the only friend I've ever really had. Her chlorine-green hair, her piercings, the way she stands, shoulders back, feet apart, how she can walk into every room and instantly be the coolest person in it. "Thank you."

"The costume was nothing. It was pretty easy, really—"

I stretch out my arms and wrap them around her because she's just too badass to start a hug first. But she returns it. She returns it like the rib-crushing fiend she is.

———————

EVEN THOUGH THE COSTUME'S DONE, we decide to finish *Starfield*. I think that maybe it won't be that bad watching it with someone else. Spoiler: it totally still is. Sage dabs at her eyes as the final credits roll and passes the tissue box to me. I tell her my theory, that the Black Nebula doesn't kill Princess Amara, but sends her away. Like the Time Dragon does to Elphaba in *Wicked*.

"That's a shitty consolation prize," Sage moans.

My cell phone buzzes. I dig it out of my pocket and swipe my thumb over the lock screen instinctively; I was wondering when he'd text me tonight.

"The boy again?" she asks, dabbing at her mascara.

"Yeah, the boy."

She sniffs and shakes off her tears, then turns to me with an eager look. "So what's the deal with him? How did you meet? You just tricked me to the worst snot-fest in the history of me. I demand this as repayment."

She has a point. I fiddle with my phone. "It started out as a wrong number, actually. Like you know those Buzzfeed articles where people text the wrong number while going into labor and then these randos show up with diapers and baby formula and they become besties?"

"No, but I'll take your word that it happened."

"Yeah, so, it's kind of like that. He just texted the wrong number—I think he was looking for my dad because I inherited his phone. But then we just . . . I don't know, we just kept talking and—"

"So you legit don't know him," she interrupts.

"I *do* know him."

"Have you talked, though?"

I hold up my brick phone. "How do you think we're communicating? Smoke signals?"

She waves away my sarcasm. "No, I mean actually *talked*. Like," she holds her hand up like a phone, "*here's my number, call me maybe* talked."

I squirm. "Not exactly."

Sage rolls her eyes. "Elle! He could be a sixty-year-old with a collection of American Girl Dolls in his basement for all you know."

"He isn't!" I cry. "He's our age. And besides, I like *texting* him. It feels more, I don't know, *You've Got Mail*-y."

Sage stares at me quizzically, like I'm a Nox who's just pledged allegiance to the Federation. "But haven't you, like, wondered?"

I can't meet her gaze because the truth is, I *have* wondered. What he sounds like, how he sounds, whether his words are laced with an accent or a lisp, deep or light or reedy or full.

I shrug. "He's never given me any clues that he wants to talk. What if he doesn't feel comfortable talking? Or he's nervous about having a stutter or something?"

"What if he's waiting for you to call first?" she argues.

"Maybe. But I mean . . . I don't even know his real name."

She sits up. Squints. Scrutinizes me. I'm about to add that I at least know he isn't bald when she grabs my phone and in two quick steps reaches the other side of the room.

"Hey, give it back!"

She puts up a finger and lifts the phone to her ear. "Give me a sec."

Panic surges in my chest. "What are you doing?"

"Calling him—"

"STOP!"

I move so fast I don't even realize that I'm yanking the phone out of her hand until I've already done it. We both hear the ringing stop. Carmindor answers the phone.

"Hello?"

It's soft. Deep. Male.

I slam END so fast I think I fracture my thumb. I shove my phone into my pocket so deep she'll *never* be able to get it. I glare at her. "Happy now?"

Sage falls back on her beanbag, laughing. "Oh my god, you were ninja fast!"

"*Not* funny!"

"You *know* I had to." She sits up on her elbows and tilts her head. "He sounds nice, Elle."

I sit down beside her. "Yeah?"

"Yep. Certifiably *not* ax murder-y." She shrugs. "At least I think so."

"Well, thank god." I swallow the lump in my throat. I'm not sure how I'm going to explain this to Carmindor. He did sound nice. Sweet. A voice I could listen to for hours. But would he ever want to listen to me?

I glance down at my phone and suddenly my blood runs cold. "Oh my god," I whisper and jerk up to my feet. "Oh *shit*."

Sage glances over at me. "What?"

"It's ten after nine." My hands start to shake. I stuff the cosplay uniform into my duffel bag and loop it over my shoulder. "I'm so late—*so* late. Can you take me halfway home?"

Sage shambles to her feet and salutes. "I'll get you home faster than Greased Lightning."

With heart pounding, I fly up the stairs after her. We've worked too hard. The con is *tomorrow*. I can't ruin this now.

DARIEN

Last take, I think. Don't ruin it.

"And . . . *action*!" the director yells. The set plunges into deathly silence. The crew looks on. Then we're moving like a machine: graceful, precise, well rehearsed, in the moment. The green screen fades, the boom disappears, the camera becomes a thought in the back of my mind.

I step into Carmindor at the helm of his ship, the good *Prospero*. I'm here, in command of my crew. And shit is about to go down.

"Forty-two clicks to the left," I bark to Euci, "and *ignite*!"

"Aye!" Calvin replies at the head of the bridge, his fingers twitching just enough to ease the ship to the left. And in that moment, he's not the jerk B-lister with a perpetual chip on his shoulder but the Federation's best pilot, my best friend, and navigator of the *Prospero*. Three Nox ships are coming in from our starboard, and we have thirty percent power left. There's no one else I'd trust to get us out of this mess.

The helm of the *Prospero* goes quiet as we wait for the three red dots blinking on the screen to fall off, but they keep pursuing us toward the Black Nebula. It looms against us, the size of three suns, swirling, catching, inhaling everything, growing larger with each atom broken down and absorbed. The galaxy's only hope of stopping it is aboard this ship.

Another torpedo slams into our back hull. Red lights flare across one of the screens. Euci flicks it away.

"Four clicks faster," I order.

"We're already shaking apart as it is," Euci warns. "If we get too close—"

"I said four clicks!" I snap.

He twitches his head slightly—a throwback to the show's Euci, who always tossed his head to the left whenever he knew Carmindor was wrong but did as his captain commanded.

A boom mic hovers above us, the gaping eye of three lenses staring from just off the bridge. One of them, on a pulley, draws closer.

In front of me the navigation panel glows like an oversized keyboard. Beside me, Princess Amara wrings her hands nervously.

"*Ah'blen,*" Jess says, and the word fills me with a strange sort of longing. A reminder of Elle. I push it down.

Not now.

"We can do this," I tell her. "We have to."

"We're going to die—we're all going to die if you get closer."

Another missile slams into the back of the *Prospero*, destroying one of the thrusters. The ship careens out of warp-speed. Everyone is thrown forward with the invisible weight of our descent. The princess stumbles against the controls and catches my hand. She squeezes it tight, and our eyes meet.

One second.

Two.

The set is quiet. We're quiet. The stars, in all their mass and all their time, orbit us. She smiles timidly, and as Carmindor, I know she is the only star in the sky I care about. Red lights flare across all the screens. Warnings boom through the speakers. One more hit and *Prospero* will be space trash.

"You know what I have to do, *ah'blen,*" she whispers.

"No, I won't let you—I can't let you. There has to be another—"

She kisses my forehead. "I hear the Observation Deck is nice this time of year," she tells me, and then she slips her hand out of mine and leaves the bridge.

Watching the show, this is where I scream at the TV. Call Carmindor stupid. Because this is where the princess looks back at him, this is where she waits to see if he'll try to change her mind, waits for him to look back at her. But he doesn't know that he's supposed to look at her. He's trying to decide if his soul could survive killing his entire crew for the sake of the universe. If he'll be damned in the afterlife. If, in the next universe over, he'll get another chance.

He looks back a heartbeat too late, and she's already gone.

I hold on to the scene, looking at the last place I saw her, the last place I'll ever see her, and then—

"Cut!" yells the AD. "And that's a wrap!"

Euci—I mean Calvin—pumps his fist into the air as the crew cheers so loud it rumbles the makeshift set. I lean back against the captain's command module and drop my head back, closing my eyes. I stand amid the triumphant hoots from the crew, the congratulations from the other actors, relishing it all.

You only get one shot, I remind myself, trying to hold on to as much of Carmindor as I can. Just for a little longer.

"You sure had the spirit," comes Jess's sweet honey-and-salt voice. She hops back onto the set and punches me in the shoulder. "You even looked torn when you said *ah'blena*. Tell me, were you thinking about not seeing me every day anymore or the absolute sadness that we didn't make out more?"

I slide on a grin, because she doesn't need to know. "Maybe a little of both."

"My word, are you making jokes, Darien?" She puts her hand on her chest, aghast. "What a pity! Maybe we could've dated for twenty-four days instead of twenty-three."

"You couldn't handle one more day of me," I reply as she leans against the captain's command module with me. We stare out at the set, at the crew beginning to wrap up the wires, at the secondary unit getting notes on what they still need to film. Our parts are done, for the most part. Our parts are done in this building, at least. After tonight, we'll leave this lot and never look back.

She knocks her shoulder against mine. "So how does it feel?"

"How does what feel?"

"To be Darien again?"

I tilt my head. "I'm not sure yet. I'd been waiting to feel like Carmindor for so long—waiting for it all to just sort of click—that I didn't realize I've been him all along."

"Maybe you were Carmindor in another life," she teases.

"Maybe. But right now I'd rather be Darien."

"Yeah?"

I nod. "Because Darien is not on a diet." Then I lean into her and whisper, "*Baaaaccccccccooooooon.*"

She laughs and shoves off the control module, gliding off set. Calvin follows her, giving me a congratulatory slap on the shoulder that almost makes me stumble. Who knows. Maybe now that we're not filming, we're bros.

The PAs are passing out champagne as I walk off set; one of them hands me a glass on her rotation around the room. Amon, grinning ear to ear, shushes the crowd and does his little director speech. I listen half-heartedly to most of it, my attention roaming across everyone, familiar and not, the crew, the actors, the assistants, the interns.

Amon turns to me, his glass raised. "And most importantly, to our Carmindor, the infallible genius boy that he is. Long live the Federation Prince! Here's to the possibility of a sequel!"

At that, I find Jess in the crowd and see that her face is impassive, like stone. But then she raises her cup, slowly, and locks eyes with me. *Told you,* she mouths and winks.

"Look to the stars!" He begins to chant.

Everyone raises their glasses. "Aim!" they cry.

I swallow, raising my glass. "Ignite!" I add, and we cheer to the twenty-three days of hell and then down our champagne.

Once Donna rubs the makeup off me for the last time, I head to wardrobe, where Nicky is busily hanging all the costumes, treating them as delicately as he did the first day on set.

"Darien! You were perfect." Nicky shuffles up to begin unbuttoning my jacket, but I hold up my hands.

"Actually . . ." I scratch the back of my neck. "I know this is weird, but I was wondering..."

"If you could have it," he fills in. He stops unbuttoning and folds his arms. "You know, just because you wear it, it's not *yours*."

"I know." My cheeks get hot. "I mean, I heard George Clooney got to keep his Batnipple suit, and Ryan Reynolds got to keep his *Deadpool* . . . look, there's just this event coming up tomorrow, and I don't have anything to wear. So I guess I was sort of hoping you could let me borrow it at least?"

"And never return it?" Nicky looks stricken. I half-shrug, half-nod, and Nicky rolls his eyes to the ceiling with a sigh.

"I'm not a part of this criminal act at all." He flaps his hands at me to go change. "I must've misplaced your costume. Oh woe is me!" And with a groan, he throws his arm over his eyes in a fake swoon.

I thank him—quietly—and promise to get it back to him in a week.

Gail and Lonny find me as I'm tugging on my shirt. I can't wait until my clothes start fitting normal again and aren't uncomfortably tight around the chest. I can't wait to go back to all the familiar comics T-shirts that don't fit me at this bulked-out size.

"Well?" Gail says. "How is it? How do you feel?"

"I can eat bacon again!" I yell, throwing up a fist. "All the bacon! Bacon or bust!"

"Yes!" Gail cheers. "After your promo shoots, you absolutely can!"

My cries of glee turn into an actual sob. I quickly shove my face into my arm. Thank god it's just Gail.

She pats me on the shoulder. "I know," she says. "But you'll get to have it soon, and then—"

"No." I swallow and shake my head, wiping my eyes with the back of my hand. "It's not the bacon." I mean, it *is* but it's also not. I'm overcome right now with everything. These last few months leading up to the shoot, the mounting pressure, the twenty-three days of high stress and rabbit food and Elle. All of it. "Why does it have to be so hard?"

"Getting a six pack?"

I give her a feeble smile. "I am more than my body, thank you."

Gail squeezes my shoulder and even though she's only a few years older than I am, I feel a burst of kidlike affection, like she's the cool babysitter who lets me stay up late when Mark's not around.

"No, I know what you mean," she says. "You've worked hard, Darien. You've worked *so* hard." She looks at Lonny as if she expects him to add something.

Weirdly, he does. "You have, boss," he says. "Now let's get moving."

Five minutes later I'm out the trailer, costume rolled up in my duffel and headed home. I follow Gail and Lonny out of the lot, where an SUV is parked. Jess rolls down the front passenger window.

"Dare, you coming?" she shouts. "We're partying!"

"We?" I ask.

The window behind her rolls down. It's Calvin, and for once he doesn't look angry at me. "Come on, Carmindor. Don't wuss out on us now."

Maybe it's just the exhaustion-induced adrenaline rush, or maybe it's the thrill of finally having *done* something, but whatever it is, it's making me want to celebrate. But I can't just *go* anywhere. I glance at Gail and Lonny, my de facto parents. Gail looks instantly worried, but Lonny grabs her shoulder and whispers in her ear.

"Okay," she says. "We'll cover for you. Just this once."

I pump my fist into the air. "Yes!" I kiss her on the cheek. "I love you, Gee."

"Mm-hm."

"Dare!" Jess shouts again. "We won't wait forever!"

"Seriously," Calvin says. "Put on your big boy pants and hurry up."

"But remember"—Gail digs into my duffel for a plain black hat and hands it to me—"if you show up on so much as a Snapchat tonight—"

"I know, I know. Mark will kill me." I pull my hat low over my brow.

"I'll be fine, Gee. You worry too m—"

A ringtone cuts between our conversation like a knife. Gail and I exchange a look, but when she shrugs, saying it isn't hers, I dig into my hoodie pocket. All of my phone numbers have assigned ringtones, but this one is generic. The only person whom I never assigned a tone to is—

Elle, the caller ID reads.

My heart jumps into my throat.

"C'mon, Your Highness!" Calvin shouts. "Celebration time!"

She's probably not actually calling me. It's probably a butt dial or something.

"You gonna answer that?" Gail asks.

"Should I?"

It rings for the third time. Fourth.

"*C'mooooon*," Jess echoes Calvin. "You're only young once, Carmindor!"

I hold up a finger and slide my phone unlocked.

"Hello?"

I wait one second. Two. Three. But there's no one there. And then the line goes dead.

"Huh." I pull the phone from my ear. CALL ENDING.

"Nothing?" Gail asks.

"I guess not." I hide my disappointment with a cough. "Well, I promise I won't get into much trouble."

"Like I haven't heard that before." Gail looks unconvinced, still staring at my phone. I tighten my grip on it and instantly feel stupid. Elle obviously doesn't want to talk right now. Besides, she'll be there tomorrow. And tonight's the only tonight I'm going to get.

"Here." I give the phone to Gail. "So I can't make any underage drunk dials. Or Snapchats. Just don't lose it. Or snoop through it," I add. "Can I go now?"

Gail nods, looking relieved as she pockets my phone. "All right."

I jog toward the SUV, the night air brisk and vibrant, leaving all the baggage of *Starfield* behind me, taking only the parts that I want to remember—the fit of a stargun in my grip, the power of standing at the helm of the *Prospero*, the nights talking with a girl who calls me *ah'blen*—and leaving the rest of it behind.

ELLE

SAGE DOESN'T TURN DOWN THE ROAD to my house—the truck's way too loud. She stops at the entrance to the neighborhood as I loop my duffel over my head. 9:31 p.m. This is going to be one hell of a sprint. "What's the plan for tomorrow?" she asks.

"Meet you at the bus station? Six a.m.?"

"Six it is!" She leans over and hugs me tightly. I return it.

"Wish me luck!" I cry as I roll onto the pavement.

All the houses are dark with sleep. I cut across lawns. The motion lights pop on as my feet thunder across dew-covered grass, my heart thrumming in my ears. I can't be late. I can't.

Turning into our driveway, I realize with a wash of relief that Catherine's Miata isn't there. No one is home yet. What's today? Friday?

Wait. Friday. Shopping day. Holy sweet merciful credit cards, Batman.

I slow down and creep around to the side, hoping I won't wake Giorgio as I climb up the creaky branches of the Bradford pear by my bedroom window. Halfway up, my foot slips. I curse, grappling onto another limb for support.

I pause, making sure no one heard me, before climbing up the rest of the way. When I slide through my window, my knees go to Jello and I sink to the ground, my heart still thundering in my ears.

I made it.

Relief wells up inside me. I curl my knees to my chest and press my forehead against them, trying to catch my breath. That was incredibly stupid—tonight of all nights. So stupid I'm shaking. Because I'm so close, so close to going to ExcelsiCon. So close to my father I can almost see him, like a figure in the distant dusk.

Just one more night, I tell myself. *Just a few more hours.*

Then the lamp in my room flicks on. Startled, I glance up. My heart stops.

Chloe is sitting in my computer chair, legs crossed, waiting patiently. Her gaze is so sharp it could cut glass. "Oh look," she says coolly. "You're home."

"What are you doing in my room?"

She cocks her head. "Why're you sneaking into the house? Could it *really* be this late?" She mocks a look at her fake watch and *tsk*s. "Oh my, it really *is* late."

Downstairs, the garage door opens and Catherine calls out that she's home.

"Mom was with a client," Chloe says simply. Which makes sense— the only explanation why Chloe would be home when Catherine isn't. "But it seems you made it just in time."

I don't understand. "In time for what?"

She leans forward. "I know what you're trying to do, *geek*," she snaps. "You think you were so smart, going behind my back. How do you think Mom'll react when she finds out you've been hanging out with that *freak* after work? You've been lying to her. After all she's done for you."

My mouth goes dry. "But you already knew that, and I said I wouldn't say anything if you didn't, and—"

"Stop screwing with me!" she cries, slamming her hands on the chair's armrests. "Where is it?"

I get to my feet, dumbfounded. "Where's what?"

"You know exactly what!" she snaps. "You took it. You know you did. So where is it?"

"Where's *what?*"

"Don't play stupid!" She leaps out of the chair.

"I don't know what you're talking about!"

"*The dress*," she hisses. I've never seen her so angry in my entire life. "Where did you put it? What, you think *you* can wear it? Don't make me laugh." Then her eyes settle on the duffel bag slung by the bed. She leaps for it, and I quickly grab for the strap, not wanting to let it go, but she's too fast.

"What's in here?" she cries triumphantly.

"Stop it! It's not in there!" I lunge for the bag but she jerks away, unzipping it. She grabs a fistful of cloth and yanks it out.

I stand, horrified. Oh, oh god. She knows. Now she knows.

Her surprise quickly morphs into some sort of anger as she turns the fabric over in her hands. "Oh my god." Her eyes cut back to me. "You were going to *enter?*"

"I—I don't—" My throat constricts.

"You were! You were going to enter! And you took the other dress so we wouldn't win! A loser like you. God, you really are pathetic."

Something in me snaps. Maybe it was her calling me pathetic for wanting to enter. Or that her claws clutch my father's jacket like it's a cheap Halloween costume. Or maybe it's her look of mockery, reminding me of that day last summer when I finally realized that people weren't nice. That no one was nice. That everyone lied, and that my heart was just a token, and this universe was the one in the Black Nebula. The hopeless, terrible universe. The one no one wants to be in.

I rush toward her, grabbing the collar of the jacket. "Give it back! It's not yours!"

"It's not *yours* either!" Chloe replies, darting away from me. The collar slips from my grasp. "This was in *our* house, so it's *ours!*"

"Yours?" I cry. "None of this was ever *yours!*"

I grab hold of a sleeve and tug on it. Chloe repels against me, trying to wrench away, but something tears and comes off in my grip. At the sound, I drop the sleeve as if burned and stare down at it.

No—no no no no no no—

"Ugh," Chloe mutters, dropping the jacket. "Cheap garbage."

I gather it up and press it against my chest. Willing it back together.

"Wait a second." She spins around. "If you were going to the contest, that means you have a pass, don't you?"

My blood goes cold. I'm shaking.

"Of course you do." She tears a poster off the wall and it comes down in scraps. "Oops, not there. Or there," she adds as she knocks a frame off the hook and opens my drawers, dumping clothes onto the floor. I watch her, still shaking, still with my arms around myself because I don't want to let go of the jacket. My dad's beautiful, ruined jacket.

"Hmm, now where would you put it?" Chloe turns full circle and then pauses on a poster. She glances at me as I pale, then back at the poster, and tears it off the wall. Behind it, tucked into the frame, are my con passes.

I jump to my feet. "Give those back!" I snap.

"Or you'll do what? Run and tell Mom?" she mocks. Just then she sees the worst of it: my savings, balled up in a rubber band, and the bus tickets to Atlanta.

"What's this?" Chloe sounds practically gleeful as she scoops up the tickets. "Greyhound tickets? Gross. Oh no—oops."

With one swift motion, she rips them in half. And then in half again, and again and again until the tickets—the nonrefundable cash-fare tickets that Sage and I were going to use tomorrow morning at 6:30 a.m.—are a pile of confetti.

"This should do nicely." She takes the roll of bills and pockets it. "We can just buy a better costume. Thanks."

"You *can't*." My voice cracks. "You can't or I'll—"

"Or you'll *what*?" Chloe sneers.

"Or—or I'll tell Catherine you're going to the con! She won't let you. I'll make sure she doesn't." I grip my dad's jacket tightly. "I'll—I'll—"

I've never stood up to Chloe. I've never threatened her. Never in my life. And for a moment she's shocked that I am, but then she blinks and her face falls into the dead-eyed look I know so well. How she looked last summer when she asked me why I thought James could ever like me. When she asked how I could have misinterpreted his kindness. When she made me out to be the freak, when the answers were always on the tip of my tongue.

But that's peanuts compared to this. That was the appetizer. Now she has my con passes, my savings, my mom's dress—she *has* to have mom's dress, who else would?—Chloe has everything. She has *everything* I ever wanted.

"You'll do what?" she says, stepping over the piles of clothes strewn across the floor. "If you tell Mom, then so will I. How do you think she'd like hearing that her stepdaughter is hanging out with a druggie?"

"Sage isn't—"

"Or that she's been skipping work?"

"I haven't!"

"And who would believe you? You're *nothing*, Danielle. You're nobody. You never will be. No stupid dress can change that. You'll always be the friendless weirdo whose daddy died."

She shoves her free hand into my shoulder. I stumble backward, unable to catch my balance, and tumble onto my duffel bag. My duffel bag, where nothing is left but the beautiful crown Sage made me.

There is a loud solid *crack*, and my heart stops.

"Chloe?" Catherine calls up from the front door. "Calliope? I'm home!"

Chloe smirks. "Coming!" she replies, flipping her hair behind her shoulder, and leaves my room.

Slowly, I pick myself up, but the damage is done. I don't need to open the bag to know what I'll find. I do anyway—the crown that Sage spent hours crafting lies in pieces at the bottom. I pick up a few and they crumble between my fingers.

Bile rises in my throat.

Outside my door, there's a padding sound of footsteps. I look up just as Cal peeks in.

"Elle?" she asks timidly—and then gasps. "Oh my god—what happened?"

I curl into myself. I wish the Black Nebula would eat me whole. I wish it would take me away. Hot tears burn as I squeeze my eyes closed and then they gush down my cheeks. I just want to go away. I don't want to exist anymore.

"Elle . . . ?"

"Get out," I tell her, my voice wavering. "Get out of my room, Cal."

For a moment she doesn't move, wanting to stay. To, what, watch as I break down? Does she get a kick out of it, like her sister? But then she sinks away.

It's all ruined. Everything is ruined. Just once I thought I could have something for me. Just once I thought . . .

But I guess this universe doesn't have happily ever afters. I was stupid to think it could.

I find myself reaching into my back pocket, taking out my phone. I close my eyes, holding it against my chest, afraid it'll be taken away too. Everything's taken away.

Everything always is.

Even Carmindor.

It's past midnight. He might be asleep. I remember the way his voice sounded. Deep but young. Weightless. Sweet. I wonder what it would sound like if he ever called me *ah'blena* aloud.

That thought is what makes me tap the phone icon beside his number, put it to my ear as my heart races faster and faster, as the signal pings off a satellite far into space and sends my call back down to earth to the exact spot I wish I could be.

His phone rings once, twice, a mayday out into this impossible universe. And then it goes to voicemail. A generic one without his voice, so it could be anyone's. He must be busy. Or asleep.

I hang up and press the back of my head against the door, blinking back the tears to try to stop crying.

We don't look up often, I remember texting. *Maybe we should start.*

Only glow-in-the-dark stars whisper down to me, an imaginary constellation. It took Dad and me an entire weekend to hang them. Afterward, we stretched out on the floor and stared up at the ceiling and he asked me, "Where do you want to go? Pick a star, any star. Then set your course. Aim." He pointed at a star, one eye closed, and pulled his thumb down as though he was firing a stargun.

I stretch my hand to my destination, aiming with one hand, and falter.

"*Ignite!*" I hear my father say, even though he's not here and never will be again. Because this is the impossible universe. And there is no Carmindor, there is no *Prospero*, or Euci, or the Federation, or observation decks. There's just me, stranded on the wrong side of everything that I love.

Like Princess Amara, lost in the Black Nebula.

PART THREE

IGNITE

———

"You are not alone, ah'blena,
and your stars will guide me home."

—Episode 33, "A Nox to Remember"

ELLE

"Now GIRLS, I WANT YOU TO text me the moment you get to your tennis tournament." Catherine smiles over the breakfast—eggs with spinach—that I made. I stand at the counter, sipping my coffee. I barely slept last night, and I'm not particularly hungry, either.

"Oh, of course," Chloe says pleasantly. She throws me a look, as if to warn me to stay quiet. But the truth is, I've never been quieter. What's the use of ratting her out, anyway? "And isn't Elle going to clean the carpets today?"

"Oh, that's right!" My stepmother claps and turns to me. "Now you know what to do, right? You won't leave the carpet sudsy like last time?"

"No," I reply, staring down into my cup.

Chloe checks her phone. "Cal, we'd better hurry or we'll miss our ride. James'll be here any minute."

Cal, who hasn't said a word all morning, hesitates. "I don't . . ."

Catherine's tweezed brows pucker. "Are you feeling well, darling? You look a little pale."

"She's fine," Chloe answers, and prods Cal up out of her seat. "She's just nervous is all. Aren't you, Cal?"

Cal steals a glance at me. Then back down at her untouched plate of spinach and eggs. "Yeah."

I can't stand it anymore. I excuse myself to my room. A few minutes later, I watch James's car pulls into the driveway and the twins hop in, taking my savings with them. My stepmother doesn't come to check on me; she just yells up to tell me the steam cleaner is in the garage and she'll see me tonight. Then the front door closes and the steady hum of the Miata turns out of the driveway and down the street.

After who knows how many minutes of lying on my bed, my phone buzzes in my pocket. I pull it out.

Sage 7:03 AM

—*Hey! Where are u?*

—*I've been calling ALL MORNING*

7:04 AM

—*I'm not going. I'm sorry.*

Sword points begin to sting in my eyes. I blink back hot tears.

The first ExcelsiCon I remember was the year I turned seven. Dad had been going crazy planning it for the last nine months of our lives. He spent so many sleepless nights arranging the panels, guest appearances, security detail, talking about the con in circles until I was so sick of hearing about ExcelsiCon that I didn't even want to go when it opened.

That morning, I woke up to the sound of Dad playing the *Starfield* theme at full speaker volume. So loud it rattled the stuffed animals off my shelves. He swooped into my room in his starched coat and his crown and took me up in his arms, singing with tone-deaf accuracy.

"*DUN DUN-DUN-DUN DUN-DUN-DUUUUUUN-DUN*," he howled, waltzing me around my room in my moon-and-stars pajamas, and it was the beginning of the best day of my life. When I got my star-gun signed by Mr. Singh. When I first thought I could be Carmindor. When Dad told me, "Starlight, star bright, you can be anyone you want to be tonight."

Tears flood down before I can stop them. I wipe them away as quickly as they come with the back of my hand, but there's more. They won't stop. I'm crying so hard I can barely suck in a lungful of breath.

Outside, something rumbles.

Wiping my eyes, I stumble to the window. Out on the street, a large orange truck takes the corner tighter than Spider-Man's leotard, barreling down the one-lane road, a green-haired maniac at the wheel.

Oh, *no*.

When Sage bangs open the front door and stomps up to my bedroom, she finds me kneeling on the ground, my face in the crook of my arm because I don't want her to see me crying. I don't like anyone to see me cry. Not since Dad's death.

Crying doesn't fix things. It doesn't bring anyone back.

"Elle—it's okay. It's all okay. This'll be okay—"

I shove away from her. "No it w-w-won't!" I take one look at the crumpled crown and the torn jacket and start crying harder. "They th-thought I stole the dress—my own *mother's* d-d-dress. So they t-took my money and r-ruined my . . . our . . ."

Sage falls to her knees and tries to hug me, but I push her away.

"Don't," I say. "Get away from m-me. I'm weird and h-h-horrible and—and—and I r-r-ruin e-e-everything. C-Catherine's life. The t-t-twins'. I'll ruin y-your life too. I haven't yet, but you j-j-just wait."

She scoffs. "Elle, you can't ruin someone else's life. Are you nuts? *They're* the ones who wrecked your stuff." Sage studies me for a long moment, rocking back on her heels. "Why would you ever think *you're* the one who ruins things?"

I laugh a small, thin laugh. "Because I'm just a b-burden. I don't want to be here. I don't want to be a part of this. I'm not Carmindor, Sage," I admit, hiccupping. "I c-c-couldn't be. I'm the Black Nebula, I'm Princess Amara—and I destroy ev-ev-everything I touch."

She sits back. "Okay, then."

"Okay *what*?" She sounds way too calm. "Don't you get it? This is it, Sage. This is the end of it. I don't get good things in this life. None of it."

"I don't believe that." Sage stands up and reaches out to help me up too. "C'mon."

Her hand hovers, outstretched, waiting for me to take it. I hesitate, looking up at it, wondering what she sees in me as a friend, why she doesn't get it. Can't she understand?

"Why?" I say at last.

"Because you're right; you aren't Carmindor. You're Amara. And you know why you are? Because you've taken a crappy subplot and managed to live through it, and you are selfless and you're brave." She squats and takes me by the shoulders. "Elle, when I watched the last episode I didn't think Amara destroyed anything. She saved the universe."

"Carmindor saved the universe! All *she* did was die!"

"I thought you said there was another universe on the other side?"

"Does it matter?" I snap back. "I couldn't be Amara if I wanted to. The twins lost Mom's dress and—and—" A lump forms in my throat.

Sage rubs the back of her neck. "Well, they didn't exactly lose it."

"What do you mean?"

"Elle, I . . . have a confession to make," Sage says slowly. "I took the dress."

"You?" The realization begins to dawn on me. "*You* took it?"

"Yeah. When I said I was taking Franco out to pee that day." She looks ashamed and proud at the same time. "I didn't think your stepsisters would wig out like that! I'm so sorry. I didn't . . . I just . . . I couldn't stand the thought of those snotty girls wearing your mother's things. I couldn't do it. And I'll understand if you hate me for life because of it and—"

I sling my arms around her and bury my face into her shoulder. "Thank you," I sob. "Thank you, *thank you.*"

"You aren't mad?"

"I wanted to steal it myself but I couldn't! I didn't know how. I—I was furious. But I couldn't do anything."

"But Chloe took your tickets. She took your savings because I took the dress."

I nod. "She would've taken those anyway. I know she would've."

"Okay." She laughs nervously and stands, outstretching her hand. I take it and she pulls me to my feet.

She squeezes my hand. "Now let's get to that con, yeah? We're burning daylight just standing around."

"But how are we getting there? The bus left and—"

"We'll take the Pumpkin."

I gape. "Are you serious? We can't take the Pumpkin. Your mom would *flip*. One more parking ticket and—"

"Desperate times, girlfriend. Desperate measures. I'll deal with her once I get home. Now get your things. We're going on a road trip."

"But we don't have money. Or passes."

"We'll figure it out as we go. C'mon Bilbo, where's your sense of adventure?"

"You're crazy."

She wiggles her eyebrows. "I know."

Drying my eyes, I gather my costume into my duffel bag, leaving the broken crown abandoned in the middle of my room, and hurry down the stairs. Sage throws open the back hatch of the truck and there, hanging from the roof, is Mom's dress. I stare with unabashed awe.

"Okay," she says. "If you want me to fix this up for you to wear it, you're gonna have to drive." She tosses me the keys and digs out a small sewing set from her satchel.

"Wait—what?" I catch the keys.

"You," she replies, closing the truck doors, and rounds to the passenger side. "Driving. You know how to get to Atlanta, right?"

"*Me?*" I sprint around to the other side and take a running leap into the truck, half-expecting Catherine's Miata to come rolling down the street. I buckle up, inserting the key into the ignition. The speedometer and all the little buttons and dials loom in front of me like a complicated control panel. "I barely know how to drive!"

"You said you had a license."

"That doesn't mean I practice!"

"Then you can learn," she replies, taking my bag. "We got four hours, half a tank of gas, and a contest to slay. So tell me: are you ready to hijack the Pumpkin, Princess?"

Sage grins her wild grin and there's no way I can say no. I just can't. "Aye, copilot."

She grins bigger and flips down her Ray-Bans. I follow suit, positioning my cheap aviator knock-offs to hide my red-rimmed eyes. I give the key a turn in the ignition. The engine rumbles to life like a beast waking from hibernation and the Pumpkin coasts out of the driveway and down the road, black smoke belching from the tailpipe.

DARIEN

"It'll never be the right blue," I mutter to myself, straightening the collar. The uniform is hanging on a peg in a closed-off room at the convention center. I thought that after twenty-three days of filming in it, I would be utterly sick of this costume, but it feels wrong not wearing it now. Like a second skin.

I run my fingers along the brass buttons and polished starwings. Gail had the tails starched this morning as I nursed a cup of coffee. I can't remember how late I stayed up, but it was well after I dragged my costars' drunk, happy asses back to the hotel.

"You're such a good catch," Jess had slurred in the back of Lonny's black car. As it turns out, having a bodyguard does come with perks, and those perks involve having on-call limo service all the time. Lonny was *not* happy. "That girl's crazy to not see it."

"What girl?" Calvin asked, lying facedown across the other seat.

"The one Darien's in love with."

"I'm not—" I argued, but Jess pressed a drunk finger against my lips.

"Shhhhhh," she commanded, and promptly puked on my shoes. I threw them away in the lobby, trying to avoid Lonny's death stare for the rest of the evening as we corralled costars back to their rooms.

There's a knock on the door a moment before Gail lets herself inside. "You ready, Dare?"

I run a hand nervously through my hair. "Sure thing. Any sign of my phone?"

She shakes her head. As soon as I got back to my room—well, as soon as I'd gotten back and wiped the remains of Jess's barf off me—Gail had broken the bad news: my phone was missing.

"I have no idea where I could've put it," she gushes for the millionth time. "I even tried calling the number, but it goes straight to voicemail. I'm sorry, I know you said—"

"We'll find it," I tell her with more certainty than I feel.

"Right, we will."

She takes me by the elbow, knowing I won't move until I'm prompted to, and leads me down the hallway and past the green room, the only place where the con's guests can sit around without being constantly asked for autographs or selfies. Even veterans sit in there more often than not. No one goes out onto the con floor. It's an aquarium full of piranhas. It's the epicenter of this universe's Black Nebula.

As the green room door disappears behind us, I give it one last forlorn glance when a guy with thick brown hair and an even browner coat catches my eye.

"Gail!" I skid to a stop. "I think I see Nathan F—"

Gail yanks me toward her like a yo-yo. "You can get him to sign your first-edition *Firefly* comic later. After your panel and your, ah, your signing."

I dig my heels into the carpet. "Signing?"

Gail cringes and tugs at her ponytail. "It was, um, it was Mark's orders."

"Mark's . . . ," I strangle his name out. "My dad said I had to?"

"He insists. He says it'll be good publicity. He says you need it. I tried to argue with him but—"

"What if that blogger's here? The one who left the messages?"

"We don't know if it's the same person," she points out.

"Oh, so what if they're *both* here? Either of them could have a ticket for my line!"

"I—I'm sorry," Gail repeats, and instantly my fear turns to regret and my shoulders slump. The brown coat in the green room is gone. Another missed opportunity.

I shake my head. "No, no, it's not your fault. You can't go against Mark. Maybe the con office can do something. I'll handle it."

"But Dare—"

"I'll *handle* it."

At the end of the hallway, I throw open the doors and make my way through the crowded con, Gail clawing through the sea of people behind me. I refuse to pause for selfies or autographs or anything because I'm on a mission.

First Mark makes me do the con. Then he blames me for all the weird leaks that have been happening. And now he won't let me cancel a signing? And no Orange Crush soda. I've had it up to my eyebrows with things out of my control.

Mark can kiss it.

I am *not* going to sign.

ELLE

THE ATLANTA CONVENTION CENTER IS *HUGE*.

Sage lets me off at the front to go find us badges while she finds out where to park the Pumpkin. It sputters away as I gape at all the people. There are *so many people*. Not just people but Vulcans and Nox and Turians and Sith Lords. Groots, X-Men, Jon Snows, Marty McFlys, Disney princesses. Nathaniel Drakes and Indiana Joneses, *DOTA 2* avatars beside *League of Legends* characters, Browncoats and hero capes and Hogwarts cloaks. Sailor Moons and sailors of stars and Trekkies and swarming among them all, in coats the perfect navy blue, the sign of the esteemed Federation, are the Stargunners.

The impossible world. And—even better—no sign of the twins.

12:22 PM

—*You would NOT guess where I am right now, ah'blen.*

—*[1 photo attachment]*

I wait for him to respond because I think he's here too—probably talking on one of the cosplay panels—but he doesn't respond. At least not at first. He will when he sees it. But will he want to meet up? Do I want to?

I . . . I think I do.

Determined, I hike my duffel bag higher onto my shoulder and embark on my quest to commandeer a ticket. A bored-looking guy is the only one left at the ticket table, a fat red sign reading SATURDAY PASSES SOLD OUT hanging overhead. I take a deep breath and march right up.

"Look, I'm not trying to get a *new* pass, it's just that my old ones were stolen," I explain to the ticket guy. "All I want is to enter into the cosplay competition. I *promise* I won't pass Go, collect two hundred, what-have-you—"

He points to the sign.

"No, I know what that says, I can *read*," I say. "I'm just asking if I can—"

"Get special treatment?" he says, finally looking up at me. He blinks behind thick black glasses. "Maybe get tickets a little earlier next time, sweetie."

"Don't call me sweetie," I snap.

"Who called you sweetie?"

Sage emerges through the crowd in the lobby, straightening her outfit, which, today, is a blue tutu dress. She looks like a deranged punk-rock fairy—not that that makes her out of place at a con.

"Okay, so I couldn't get a space in the garage because the Pumpkin wouldn't fit under the clearance, but I found this place with a meter around the corner and raided the register for quarters. Operation Avoid a Parking Ticket is under way."

"I think that's illegal," says the guy at the booth.

"So's sexual harassment." I try to give him a mind-melting glare, but nothing fazes this guy. Hell could be rising up around him and he'd probably just think it was *so* last-year's Syfy.

He sighs. "Look, if you want to see what you can do about your 'stolen' passes, go talk to the organizers. They're in the office over there." He gestures toward the corner of the lobby. "Go bother them."

With a scowl, I turn on my heels, making my way to the offices.

"I'll wait out here, I guess?" Sage calls behind me. "Have fun storming the castle!"

I wave a hand over my head to signal that I heard her.

This is ridiculous. Of all the years that my dad organized Excelsi-Con, he never would've hired a brat like *that* guy. At least there are other ways of getting into a con, and I know they aren't at capacity yet. They always leave a handful of badges unattended just in case someone important shows up. Like the president. Or Tom Hiddleston.

I reach the office door and peek inside the little window. A harried older woman is counting bills onto a desk. She looks familiar, but it takes a moment to remember.

"Miss May!" I knock and wave through the window. She jumps at hearing her own name, spinning around to me in her rolly chair. She's in the regulation purple ExcelsiCon T-shirt and blue jeans, and I swear she hasn't changed her Keds in the ten years I've been gone. Her gray eyebrows scrunch together as if trying to place where she's seen my face before.

I flash her the promise-sworn salute, and her eyebrows shoot up into her graying-brown hairline.

"Oh my word—*Danielle*!" she cries, jumping up from her chair. She rushes around the desk and throws her arms around me. "Danielle, you've grown so much! You look just like Robin. Just like him," she echoes, holding me at arm's length. "Goodness, it's been, what, six years?"

"A little over," I reply. Seven years. How has it been that long? I wonder if she blames me too. I pull a smile over my face. "And it's high time I came back, right?"

"Right as rain!" she replies. "Robin could never keep himself away. I knew you'd be around again."

"Actually, Miss May, that's what I need to talk to you about. I—we—"

Suddenly, the office door opens and slams against the knob with a bang. A tall, youngish guy—dark hair, swaggery walk—breezes past me.

"I need to speak with the manager," he says, his voice icy. "*Please*."

My mouth falls open. Because Holy Federation Prince, Batman. It's Darien *effing* Freeman.

Miss May looks surprised. "Well now, hold on a moment there . . ."

A flustered-looking woman—his handler, I'm guessing—trips into the office after him and closes the door quietly. "Darien, it's okay—"

"Gail, it's not okay." He turns back to Miss May. "I just need to talk to the director, *please*. That's all. I'm sure it's a big misunderstanding."

"The director's out on the floor," Miss May says.

"Excuse me," I interrupt him.

"One second, okay?" He barely glances over.

I feel like I've just gone invisible. It's one thing to feel invisible at home, but this—this is my dad's con. I shouldn't feel invisible here. I *won't* feel invisible here.

"Is there any way to get in touch with him?" he says. "Call him? Something?"

"Dare, you're running late to your panel," his handler pleads. "Maybe we can get this straightened out later . . ."

"But the signing's right after the panel," he says, trying to reason with her.

I set my jaw. First he gets cast to ruin Carmindor. Then he has the indecency to show his abs on national television to *sell* Carmindor. And now he's barging into the office interrupting *me* and pretending I'm invisible? This is why I blog. There are things in this life that I can overlook. Catherine, the twins, the crap at the country club. But you don't mess with my *Starfield*.

"Aren't you a little ungrateful?" I say.

He finally glances over as if seeing me for the first time. *Oh, hello there,* I think. *Nice of you to finally notice.*

"I'm sorry?" he says.

"Aren't you," I enunciate, "a little ungrateful?"

"I'm sorry, uh, miss, I'm in a bit of a hurry—"

"And I'm *not*?" I fold my arms over my chest. "I was here first and there's no reason for you to barge in here and throw a hissy fit because you can't sit your pretty butt down and sign for thirty minutes. That's *disgraceful*. In the grand scheme of life, what's thirty minutes to you?" I put my hands on my hips. "What's thirty minutes to make someone else's day pretty stellar?"

His shoulders stiffen. "You don't understand. You couldn't—"

"Couldn't I?" I laugh. "Give me your paycheck and *I'll* sign *for* you."

He opens his mouth to retort, but then closes it again and turns back to Miss May. "Please, is there any way you can talk to your manager? We can work out a deal. I just don't want to sign—"

"Well maybe you *should* sign," I reply for Miss May, who's growing paler by the moment. "Maybe that's *exactly* what you should do, Darien Freeman. Maybe you should've realized that being Carmindor is more than just putting on a pretty face."

It's a good line, because I happen to be quoting directly from my blog post. And when his gaze hardens into a glare, I realize he must recognize it. Well, good.

"You're just a spoiled star like all the rest of them," I add, waving my hand toward the door. "So why don't you *work* for once and go sign some autographs! It's the least you can do, if you call yourself Carmindor."

His handler—bless her, she looks overworked and underpaid in those terribly old sneakers—puts a hand to her mouth to stifle a gasp.

Darien Freeman faces me for the first time. I kind of see the allure— he's beautiful in person, especially with the scar, and those eyes—but his personality is the biggest turn-off I've ever had. He's definitely been working out for *Starfield*. I don't remember him looking so, um, imposing in *Seaside Cove*. He folds his arms over his chest, shoulders straining his T-shirt. "*You're* that blogger, aren't you. The one who hates me."

"I don't *hate* you."

"Then what's your beef?"

I stand taller—which, next to Darien, is not very tall. "What I *hate* is that you're being a bully!"

"I'm not being a *bully*."

"Oh, so going up and demanding things from nice people is what you consider normal, polite behavior?"

"I said 'please'! Didn't I say 'please'?" He asks in disbelief, looking back to his handler for confirmation. She purses her lips tightly, and something silent passes between them. When she doesn't come to his rescue, he throws up his hands. "Fine! Okay! Look Miss, uh—"

"Miss May," I interject. "Her name's Miss May."

"Miss May," he repeats. A muscle twitches in his jaw. "I'm sorry for being forceful. It's been a long day—"

"It's barely one o'clock," I mutter. Darien glares at me.

"—but I just want some free time at the con, you know? Just a few hours, and I won't have that with the signing. Could you *please* get your director on the walkie-talkie and tell him to find me? I'll be at the *Starfield* panel"—he looks back to me—"*working*."

Then he turns on his heels and leaves. A flood of fans has amassed outside and tries to overtake him as he exits the office, but a beefy guy—probably his bodyguard—shields him from the fans and guides him and his handler through the lobby. The door closes behind them, successfully shutting out all the people crying his name.

I roll my eyes and scowl. But Miss May is grinning at me.

"You really are your father's daughter."

"He acted like I was invisible," I say. "I just did what anyone would do."

"Nope, that was all Robin." She shakes her head. "I worked with him for so many years I can see when he comes out in you. You barely gave that boy a snowball's chance in hell."

"He was being *really* rude to you," I point out.

"Mm-hmm." Miss May nods and swivels back and forth in her chair, picking up a walkie-talkie. She radios the new director—Herman Mitchs, one of Dad's old buddies, balding, beer gut, loves to cosplay as Chewbacca—about Darien Freeman before turning her attention back to me. "So what can I do for you?"

"Well . . ." I wring my hands. "See, things happened and my passes were stolen—two of them, for me and a friend. I have the receipt here, but the guy at the ticket booth said—"

"*Receipt?*" Miss May laughs, leaning back in her chair. "Elle, the daughter of Robin Wittimer never needs to *buy* a pass! You're part of this con, honey. You're family."

From her desk, she draws out a badge. The top is marked yellow, the highest type of badge you can wear—the all-access kind that tells everyone else you're not just *somebody* but you're *somebody important.* This is the Stan Lee of badges.

She extends it to me and I take it, my fingers gliding over the black name printed at the bottom. *Robin Wittimer.* Tears sting my eyes.

"We've printed one for him every year," Miss May says. "Just in case you decided to come."

"Every year?" I ask, my voice distant. "But—"

"Didn't your stepmother tell you?" Miss May frowns. "For the first few years we sent them to your house, but when we kept getting them back we just decided to keep them here."

So Catherine knew I was welcome at ExcelsiCon all this time? She knew I had a badge just for me—from my dad—every year and *sent it back?* I chew on my bottom lip, trying not to cry.

"I had no idea," I whisper. "If I'd known . . ."

Miss May sees my face crumple and offers up a bowl full of butterscotch candies. "Well, you're here now. And your friend can wear this one," she adds, taking out one of those extra badges I knew they had lying around for special guests. "What's the occasion, anyway? Here to see the *Starfield* panel? Because I'm afraid you're missing it . . ."

"Actually, I'm here for the cosplay contest."

She smiles, unwraps a butterscotch, and pops it in her mouth.

"Your father's daughter, indeed."

DARIEN

"You need to calm down, Dare."

Thanks for that, Gail. Understatement of the century.

We're walking out of the giant auditorium, away from the panel that just let out. Spots blink across my vision from the flash of a zillion selfies that people who just *love* me in *Seaside* couldn't wait to take (even though, if they really loved me, they would've *not* had the flash on). All the audience questions from the panel are swimming in my head like the insides of the Blob.

How do you feel being the new Carmindor?

What do you bring to Carmindor that Mr. Singh didn't?

Since filming just wrapped, can you tell us a little about what to expect from your take on Carmindor?

Why did you think you could be the Federation Prince?

Jess didn't get those questions. Calvin didn't either. And every time Amon got asked why he cast *me* as the Federation Prince, he would simply say, "Did I cast the perfect person for the role? I think I did."

Which is, of course, media interviews 101. When you're asked a question you don't want to answer, you redirect it by asking your own question and answering that one instead.

So between that blogger in the convention office and the panel, I'm in a pretty terrible mood. I can't believe I ran into the *Rebelgunner* blogger. And it was a *girl*. Fate must be trolling me. Not even seeing Nathan Fillion will help this dark cloud over my head.

"That girl really got under your skin, didn't she," Gail says, shuffling behind me. Lonny follows behind us like a hulking shadow.

"She wasn't a girl so much as the spawn of Satan," I mutter, opening the GUESTS ONLY door to one of the private hallways.

"She had a point, you know," Lonny rumbles.

Gail nods. "Darien, you're usually so good with fans. *Darien*." When I don't stop, she grabs me by the arm to halt me in the middle of the hallway. The dude from that demon show passes, and I give him a bro nod. When he's out of earshot, she whispers, "What's *really* wrong?"

What's *really* wrong?

A muscle in my jaw feathers. "Gail, my phone is still missing and I haven't gone this long without talking to Elle since we disagreed about the solar flux capacitor, *Rebelgunner* is a girl, and I have a signing in less than"—I check my invisible watch— "*ten* minutes where a guy who's left threatening messages at my hotel might or might not show up."

Plus—and I know it's crazy—I can't shake the feeling that I'm being watched. I mean I know I'm being *watched* but . . . this feels different. The same way I felt all throughout filming. Like when the guy locked me up on the roof and then those clips and photos got leaked.

"But I'll be there," Lonny rumbles, cracking his knuckles. "I'll turn them into sailor knots."

"Thanks, bro." I exhale a long, stressful breath. "It'll be fine. Absolutely copacetic. As long as I don't sign anything that could be described as a *mound*."

ELLE

I MEET UP WITH SAGE IN the lobby and crown her with the extra-VIP badge—the same kind of badge I show to the ticket booth guy as we walk through the security line. His mouth falls open at the yellow band across the top of mine.

"Eat it," I mouth, and do the one-finger-at-a-time wave as the security guard checks my duffel—and the costume—and lets me inside.

"Okay, so we need to finish up your costume and get you ready for this contest," Sage says, patting the strap of the bag. "Still gotta make sure the stitching's right on your shoulder and glitter up your coat and—"

"Sage." I pull her to a stop.

She hasn't even looked up at it all. "Yeah? . . . Oh." She stares out at the expanse of showroom floor. Her mouth goes slack jawed. "*Ohhh.*"

Floor to ceiling, spanning the entire convention center. TV network and studio and game booths line the walls, lifesize replicas of *World of Warcraft* characters and Funko figures. People with pleasant smiles staff the tables that stretch from one side to the other, banners for *Star Trek* and *Star Wars* displayed overhead, waving gently in the air-conditioning. The crowd shuffles around photo ops mid-aisle, snapping selfies with cosplayers wielding cardboard swords and scythes, light sabers and phasers and starguns. A Deadpool bumps into me as he dodges out of the way of four Ewoks scuttling behind a mammoth Hulkbuster, their cellphones recording the event. And still no sign of the twins. Which is a good sign.

Sage and I slowly turn our eyes to each other. "Holy shit," she says. "I'm in nerd heaven."

"Oh, young Padawan," I tell her, waving my hand toward the room, "everything the light touches is our kingdom. Let's go explore it." I pull her into the din of fantasy and sci-fi denizens and we get lost in the shuffle.

"God, *look* at all these people—so many Carmindors! Do you think yours is here?"

"Maybe," I reply as we pass a booth selling *Assassin's Creed* robes.

"Seriously? Are you going to meet up?"

"I don't know. He hasn't answered."

"Mm." She nods toward a group of cosplayers gathered at the far corner of the showroom. One is holding a sign that reads TEAM FOUR STAR. "Do a lot of internet groups meet up at conventions?"

"Sure."

"How about your *Starfield* peeps? The online ones you talk to?"

"Oh—well, yeah. A few of them are here." We break apart for a moment as an elf with a scythe squeezes between us. "Anyway, we should get to the costume contest area and sign in, what do you say? And try not to run into the twins."

"If we do I'll shove them in a closet," Sage mutters.

I laugh. "Ready to kick some Nox butt?"

She scoffs. "Elle, I'm ready to tell them to get down on both knees and call you Queen."

"I thought you were going somewhere completely different with that."

"Eh, this is a PG sort of moment."

"Fair enough."

She consults a convention map that she found on the showroom floor, but I take it from her with a scoff. "Oh *please*, I know this place like the back of my hand."

"Yeah, how *do* you know this place so well?"

"Because my dad started this con," I reply, grab her hand again, and follow my feet into the crowd, the map of the convention floor burned into my memory like the glow-in-the-dark stars on my bedroom ceiling.

DARIEN

Scrawling my name over another headshot of my character on *Seaside Cove*, I thank the pretty brunette for standing in line and hand the photo back to her. She hugs it to her chest like it's made of gold, tells me she loves me in *Seaside*, and hurries off with her friends. It's pretty amazing. I thought I'd be tired of fans gushing up to me, but there's just something earnest in fandom that's never boring. Sure, having fans inflates my ego, but I like to think that I'm not *that* shallow. I appreciate this job because I'm making things that people—all kinds of people, from the looks of my line—enjoy.

"So the blogger was right," I mutter to myself, tapping the end of the permanent marker on the table. It's annoying just how right she was. My time is way less important than making these people happy.

Gail hovers just out of earshot, talking animatedly on the phone, setting up meetings and photo ops and all the things I'm too busy to handle. After all this, she deserves a break. Or a promotion.

At the front of the line is Lonny, looking as stoic and badass as ever—even in a Powerpuff Girls cap he swiped from a nearby booth to make him look less suspicious. He keeps getting strange looks.

A fan slides a book toward me and I begin to say that I don't sign other people's work when I recognize the graphic novel.

Batman: Year One.

I grip the marker, slowly turning up my eyes to a redhead in a Kilgrave T-shirt. He's taller than I remember—and older, obviously; his hair close-cropped, eyes dark.

My heart sinks. I sit back, capping the marker. "Brian?"

"Hey, Darien. Long time, yeah?"

I glance behind him. There are at least twenty people still waiting to get something signed. I can't just walk out now and Gail has her back turned, so she can't see the trouble even if I Hulked out and waved Brian over my head by his foot. I have to keep my cool. Which is hard, considering I want to punch him in the face.

Instead I nod and reply. "Long time. Do you have something for me to sign? You know I don't sign other peoples' work."

He licks his lips. The start of the Empire's insignia from *Star Wars* peeks up from the collar of his shirt. Of course he'd get the Empire's. He wasn't ever good enough for the Rebel Alliance. "I just want to talk to you—just for a minute. I've been trying to get in touch with you. I left voicemails at your hotel—"

"That was you? I thought—" I don't finish my sentence. Because what I thought was ridiculous. Of course it would have to be Brian.

He smiles. "Did you listen to them?"

"Can't say I had the time," I say, trying to keep my voice steady.

He makes an aggravated noise and squats so we're eye level. If that's not condescending, I don't know what is. "Look, I didn't know they'd try to take you down like that. I thought it'd just be a quick piece in some small tabloid. I didn't think, like, *People* magazine would get a hold of it. He said I'd get to keep the money, and . . . I don't know, dude, I thought you were in on it!"

"*In* on it?" I can't believe this. "In on what—you selling me out?"

"It was a lot of money. You understand, right? You have to understand."

I want to tell him off, but the frakking truth is that I *do* understand. I understand why he'd sell me out for paparazzi money. When someone gives you enough cash to cover a good chunk of your college tuition, you take it. And then there was me, the geeky son of self-crowned Hollywood royalty. We were outliers. So we became friends.

So yeah, of course I understand him. I understand him better than I understand myself. That's what pisses me off the most. That he couldn't understand me the same way. Wasn't that what best friends were? He was like my brother. Brothers don't rat each other out, and yet here we were.

I look down at my marker, twirling it in my fingers. "Yeah, Brian, I understand."

His face breaks open with relief. "Oh, good! So, listen, if we're cool and, like, friends again, I think—"

"No."

His eyebrows shoot up. "But you just said—"

"I'm not trying to be a dick. You *were* my best friend. I trusted you." The people behind him are getting restless. Gail is still yacking on the phone with whomever. It better be Mark or I'm throwing all of her underwear in my mini-freezer tonight when we get back to the hotel.

But Lonny—he's zeroed in on us, arms crossed over his chest, waiting for me to give him a signal. He arches a strong black eyebrow. Do I want him to show Brian the door? Yes, yes I do.

But that's not going to end things. I need to do that.

I push his copy of *Batman: Year One* back across the table. "I forgive you, Brian, but I don't think we can be friends again."

We both got our copies the first year we went to a con, before I ever became famous. We cosplayed as Carmindor and Euci and stood in line for two hours just to get David Singh's autograph on our old *Starfield* DVDs. It was the first time we really hung out outside of school, the weekend we became friends. The kind of friends that would become shoot-the-shit, drinking beer in the back of pickups on the beach friends. The kind of friend that recorded my first audition tape that Dad—Mark—used to get me the role of Sebastian on *Seaside Cove*. That first con was the start of it.

Then . . . then my life happened. *Seaside Cove*. Then *Starfield*. Then suddenly what I thought was true wasn't anymore, *who* I thought I was I wasn't anymore. And who I was to everyone else shifted. Changed.

"Enjoy the rest of the con," I tell Brian, motioning for the next person to step up in line.

"Are you kidding me?" Brian scoffs. "You're going to give me that *don't have time bullshit* when you've been texting some random girl for the last month?"

I look at him sharply, and his eyebrows jerk up. He's surprised, caught off guard, and suddenly it clicks—all those moments during filming, all my suspicions of being watched. I *wasn't* crazy.

"You," I say quietly. "*You* were there. You locked me on the rooftop. You leaked those shots." My head spins. "How did you even get on set?"

"You haven't figured it out?" His teeth gleam. "All I had to do was drop Mark's name and no one would mess with me. Your costume director seems terrified of him. Oh and by the way." He holds up something—my phone. "Your handler left this behind."

I lunge for it, but Brian yanks it away.

"Nah, not so fast. Because until like ten minutes ago, I was gonna bring it to you as a peace offering, even though you never answered my messages at the hotel."

"Look, I was busy shooting and—" I reach for it again. "Just give it back."

But he doesn't. He's looking at the screen. Reading.

"Elle's here, you know," he says.

My stomach plummets. It must show on my face because Brian grins.

"Don't worry. I'll let her know you're too busy to connect with friends." Before I can stop him, he types something out and drops my phone right into my lap. "You're welcome."

Then he raps his knuckles against the table and leaves, pushing his way through the crowd as a big guy squeezes in beside him and slides a *Starfield* poster onto the table for me to sign.

I look at the phone. It's open to a text message. One sent to Elle. But I didn't send it. I swallow the rock in my throat.

"Big fan, so excited for the movie!" gushes the guy.

I slide my phone to the side, trying to be nonchalant so Brian can't get the benefit of rattling me, and uncap my marker. "Yeah? What're you excited about the most?" I swoop my signature across the bottom of the poster.

"The observation deck," he says, grinning, "is nice this time of year."

"Only on the south side of Metron," I reply, sliding the poster back. "Thanks for coming," I tell him and look to the next fan. Keep looking ahead, keep looking ahead, I repeat the mantra to myself.

Don't ever look back.

Finally, Lonny lumbers over and hovers until Brian slinks away out of the line. He stays in my peripheral vision for a while until my body-guard cracks his knuckles. Finally Brian disappears. I hope for the last time.

Maybe that's what fame does. It corrupts everything around you until even your best friends see you more as a name than as a person, a commodity instead of an individual. Maybe that's just my life now.

But then what about Elle? Will the same thing happen when she finds out who I am? She already hates Darien Freeman—but will she hate me too? As I look up at the guy who used to trade Pokémon cards with me behind the cafeteria Dumpsters, I begin to wonder if I really want to take that chance again.

It'll only end up the same way. Maybe worse now. Maybe worse because I actually have feelings for Elle—deep feelings—and I realize that's what Gail was trying to warn me about. Not because Elle is a stranger, or because she might be a bad person, but because she's nor-mal. She's like everyone else.

And like everyone else, she couldn't possibly understand.

Gail finally gets off the phone and wanders back to me. "How're we doing?" she asks happily.

I strain a smile. "We're doing *great*." I show her my phone. "Found it."

The last message I sent—that Brian sent—is harsh, a hard farewell. But the thing is—and this is what kills me—it's right. I *can't* see her anymore. What did Elle say—that this was the impossible universe? I had scoffed at that, but now I'm not so sure it's silly. My life is impossible. My *luck* is impossible.

And me and Elle? Together? That's probably the most impossible thing of all.

Gail gasps. "No way! Where was it?"

"Pocket," I lie. Gail wilts with relief.

"Thank god." She straightens. "Well, you ready?"

"Ready for . . . ?" I try to keep my vision straight as I welcome another fan, toting what looks like an action figure of me. Good god, I'm an action figure now.

"The whole point of this con?" Gail shakes her head and takes me by the elbow. "Come on, Carmindor. You've got a contest to judge."

ELLE

I SMOOTH THE YARDS AND YARDS of night-sky fabric to disguise my trembling hands. Through the smudges in the mirror, Sage frets with my hair. It never does what anyone wants it to do, and today is no exception—it's not staying in its braid at all. When a lock falls out again, she throws up her hands.

"I'm sorry," I say. "I should've warned you my hair sucks." I try to thread my fingers through the strands to remove the rest of the braid, but they wrap around my fingers and the more I tug, the knottier the knots get.

"Ten minutes!" yells a stagehand. "All contestants to the wings—in order!"

Sage curses.

The other Amaras and Eucis and Carmindors—some genderbent, some AU, some strictly canon—shuffle around us and out of the bathroom until only one other Amara cosplay remains. I wonder if my Carmindor is in the lot. He has to be, right? He has to be in a contest or on a panel here or something. Otherwise he never would've texted me about the con in the first place.

The other Amara fixes her black lipstick in the mirror and pauses. She glances over. "Oh my gosh. I'm sorry, this is probably super creepy but . . . are you the girl who writes *Rebelgunner*?"

"I—um—yeah?" I'm too shocked to be embarrassed.

"Oh my god, I *love* your blog! I loved it before it got popular!" She envelops me in a hug, even though I don't know her at all. Is she a commenter? Or just a reader? Does it matter? It feels like a real hug. Friendly. I hug her back.

"I recognized you from your avatar—I hope that's not weird." She steps back and looks at my costume. Yards and yards of Amara's fabric, and the scraps of my father's jacket as the shoulder pads, golden tassels dangling. "Is this your costume? The one you were talking about in your post?"

I hesitate. "Sorta. My dad's, and my mom's. Kind of a mashup. It doesn't matter, though. This is all just so . . . so cool." I say, motioning out of the bathroom to the larger con. "It's everything Dad hoped it would be."

A thoughtful look crosses the girl's face. "Your dad?"

"He started ExcelsiCon," I reply. "Well, one of the people who did—"

"Wait. You're Robin Wittimer's daughter?"

"I—yeah." I nod. "He would've loved your outfit, by the way. I mean, it's amazing. You look like Amara."

"Thank you, but . . ." She flicks her eyes down the length of my costume, from the torn uniform to the broken starwing badge to the noticeable lack of a crown, and then, to my utter surprise, she plucks her own crown from her head.

"There." She rests it on my brow. "Better."

"What?" I touch it gingerly. "I can't take this—"

She holds up a hand. "Don't say no. I've been coming to this con for years. I love it. So consider it a thank-you."

In the mirror, behind my mess of hair, Sage's face flickers. I wait for her to complain about a new crown throwing off her whole look, but instead she snaps her fingers.

"That's it!" she cries.

"What's it?"

She digs a pack of makeup removal wipes out of her bag. "Wipe that makeup off. I've got a new idea."

"But—"

"Shush! We're against the clock. The contest starts in literally ten minutes." Then she turns to our new friend. "Do you think you can get us a—a starwing? Or maybe a gold rubber band?"

"I can get you more than that," she replies and hurries out of the bathroom.

I give Sage a strange look. "What are you doing?"

"Do you trust me?"

"Is that a trick question?"

"Do. You. Trust. Me?" She enunciates slowly.

What can I say? "Yes. Of course."

Behind her, the bathroom door bangs open, bringing in a flood of Carmindors and Amaras and Eucis and Nox Kings. So many Starfield characters, crowding around me, some I recognize from the message boards, new faces and old. They pick off pieces of themselves, handing them to Sage.

"If it wasn't for Mr. Wittimer . . ." I hear them say.

"This was the first con I ever went to . . ."

" . . . For the first time in my life . . ."

" . . . felt like I belonged . . ."

" . . . thanks to your dad."

My dad.

My dad.

I smile at all the cosplayers handing over bits and pieces of their costumes, because otherwise I might cry. They're just small things—Amara's gloves, licorice-colored earrings in my ears, even a sticky star under my left eye—"Because in the Black Nebula she's galactic," says a petite girl with a wink—and then, through the throng of people, an Amara with dark hair and purple glasses pushes through.

I do a double take. Oh—Holy Batnipples, no. It's Calliope.

We lock eyes. Cal stares at me, frozen as though she's just been ejected into space. She's wearing such an expensive cosplay gown. It's Princess Amara to the works—the best money could buy. It fits her beautifully, a deep blue with inlaid sequins and a draping neckline, silver-metal shoulder pads and clasped at her breast a brooch in the shape of starwings. I'm sure she doesn't understand what any of it means.

The chattering crowd goes quiet. Sage freezes mid-braid. Cal steps up and looks at my dress—the dress she was supposed to wear—and the jacket that Chloe tore apart, and her eyes water.

"It looks so much better on you," she whispers.

"Where's Chloe?" My voice warbles.

"Out in the audience. She wants to get the best view for when . . ." She hesitates. "I'm so sorry, Elle. I didn't think Chloe would go this far. She just . . . she really wants to be famous. She wants to be someone."

"She *is* someone," Sage snaps. "She's the queen of awful."

Cal looks at her helplessly. "She really isn't that bad."

"She is." Sage folds her arms. "And you just go along with it."

Cal blinks. And then, after a moment, she shakes her head. She takes a deep breath and says, "I'm so sorry, Elle. I think these are yours too. They're really tight on me and . . ." She lifts her dress and steps out of my mother's sparkling starlight shoes. "I think they'll fit you better."

Hesitantly, I slip out of the black flats Sage let me borrow and slide them on, one foot at a time. And for a moment I'm back in the living room, waltzing around on my dad's feet as he twirls me, around and around, in Mom's dress made of starlight and universes and love sewn into the seams.

The shoes fit perfectly.

"Contestant forty-two?" calls a stagehand, poking her head into the bathroom. "You're on next! Hurry up!"

Sage looks me square in the eye. "You ready, Princess?"

"I—I think so."

"Good." She finishes wrapping my hair into the crown and snaps back her hands. "Take her away!"

I glance over at Cal one last time, and she gives me a small wave before the stagehand spirits me out of the bathroom. I dodge a long-eared Nox. I don't even have time to look in the mirror, to look at what Sage and the other cosplayers did to me. I just know that she took the knots in my hair and folded them into the crown, and there are pieces of costumes on me that aren't mine and glitter on my starched tailcoat that sheds like stardust as I'm pulled down the hallway, the folds of the universe billowing around me. My face feels too light. Not enough makeup. There's too much me. I can't be Princess Amara.

We pass the contestants that just went on, and they turn to look at me with strange, thoughtful looks. I try to ask if there's something wrong, but the stagehand just keeps pulling me forward—and then we're at the mouth of the stage and the emcee shouts, "Contestant forty-two: the Black Nebula Federation Princess Amara!"

"Go," whispers the stagehand, and she nudges me gently.

My feet take the lead. One step. Then another.

My mother's starlight slippers echo across the stage like glass against the ground.

Chin up, Elle, I hear Dad's voice say in my ear. *Look to the stars. Aim . . .*

My hands fall out of their fists, my shoulders ease back, straight, relaxed. I'm half of my father. Half of my hero. And I am half of my mother. Half soft sighs and half sharp edges. And if they can be Carmindor and Amara—then somewhere in my blood and bones I can be too. I'm the lost princess. I'm the villain of my story, and the hero. Part of my mom and part of my dad. I am a fact of the universe. The Possible and the Impossible.

I am not no one.

I am my parents' daughter, and then I realize—I realize that in this universe they're alive too. They're alive through *me.*

Fashioning my hands into a pistol, I point it at the ceiling, lifting my chin, raising my eyes against the blinding stage lights, and I ignite the stars.

DARIEN

I'ᴛ's ʜᴇʀ ᴇʏᴇs. Tʜᴇ ᴡᴀʏ sʜᴇ looks at you like you've got all the time in the world and yet you're still running out. Her gaze is steady, her shoulders held high even though she's carrying the weight of the Federation on them. Her hair glows red, like the body of a dying sun, snarled and wild, around the golden crown.

As she walks, slow and steady, the clip of her sparkling heels on the stage, her dress swirls around her, fluttering, yards and yards of universe wrapped around her curves and edges. Her mouth, thin with determination, sits against her pale face like a rigid dark line. She comes to a stop in the center and raises her hand in the form of a phaser, aiming it to the sky, and then lifts her eyes to me.

Her gaze strikes a familiar chord, but I can't for the life of me think where I've seen it. I think it's from the show, from the princess herself, the way her shoulders ease back and her chin rises.

Defiant, like in the final episode.

She's wearing Princess Amara's ball gown, like the one Jess wore in that scene where we danced in the ashes for eight hours. But this Amara is a little different, a little changed, just a step to the side. What Amara would look like, perhaps, on the other side of that great Black Nebula. Not just a princess but the commander of the *Prospero*, the captain of her own life, with Carmindor's jacket draped over her shoulders, the collar crisp, the coattails starched and flaring behind her, the tips glimmering with a dusting of gold like a comet tail.

Her jacket—of a blue you see at dusk, a hue that makes you wish you could fly off into it—is the perfect shade. The right shade. The brass buttons along it are polished, gleaming, not because they're new but simply from being cared for. The starwings pinned on her lapel glimmer in the stage lights.

This is Amara. The true Amara. The one Carmindor fell in love with. The one he would have looked back at two seconds earlier. She makes me remember why I fell in love with *Starfield,* the hypothesis that in every universe, in every world, there is a Carmindor and an Amara.

In any universe, in any world, as anyone—we are them. They are us.

I glance over at the other two judges. They gape at her, enthralled. I begin to grin. *Right?* I want to tell them. My thoughts exactly.

ELLE

THE MOMENT I WALK OFFSTAGE I shake out all my limbs, trying to get
the nervous sizzle out of them. I feel like I just touched a live wire. But
I actually did it. I walked out there. I stared up at the judges, blind as
a freaking bat, and hoped like hell I made eye contact with at least one
of them.

And I sort of hope Darien Freeman didn't recognize me.

"Your Highness!" Sage whisper-yells, throwing herself at me. We
hug and she prances, throwing her arms in the air. "That was stellar!
You were stellar! Everything was stellar! There were some other good
ones, but oh god, I'm feeling good about this. Really good!"

"You are? Because I think I blacked out," I whisper back. "Do you
think Chloe recognized me?"

"She didn't," says Cal's voice. She's behind us, hovering. "I—I texted
her at the last minute about an emergency with my costume, so she had
to leave the theater. There's a good chance she won't be getting back in."

I look at Cal, full of surprise and gratitude. "Thank you."

"Don't." She shakes her head. "I really don't deserve it. It'll take a
long time before I do."

"Contestants?" The stagehand calls us all back toward the stage.

Sage hugs me one last time and whispers "Good luck!" before I'm
ushered back into the bright glaring lights. I glance at her in the wings,

unable to stop the grin spreading across my face, and in that moment I sort of realize it doesn't matter if I win. We made it this far, we competed, and nothing can take that away.

Third place goes to a Euci, who looks exactly like the movie promos. Not me. I knew it wouldn't be me, but still. I had a little hope. It was a good run. When I glance back at Sage, how come she's smiling? Does she know something I don't?

It's just the residual high of competing. There's forty-three of us and only three winners. Cal stands beside me, nervously twitching.

"I hate this," Cal whispers. "It reminds me of tennis tournaments."

"My dad used to say it was the best feeling in the world." I look out over the crowd, my heart thundering in my ears and lungs expanding in short, frantic puffs.

Cal looks at me strangely. "What, this?"

"Being your favorite character. I don't care if I win. I'm just glad I'm here," I whisper back.

"I wish I'd known him better," she says, picking at her nails. "I wish I knew *Starfield* better."

"I can teach you," I offer.

She looks over at me. "Yeah?"

"Yeah. Sage and I both can."

A blush tinges her cheeks. "I wouldn't mind that."

It must be a strange thing to say because she's just about to ask another question, her face twisted in concern, when the emcee cries, "Second place goes to . . . number forty-two, the Black Nebula Federation Princess Amara!"

The crowd cheers.

I don't hear him at first. Like, my ears didn't register those sounds in that order. But then Cal elbows me and jerks her head toward the front. Her lips move around the words "That's you."

That's *me*?

I look back toward the audience. The crowd. They're cheering so loudly it rattles in my ribcage. The emcee gives me a patient smile, nudging his head toward the front of the stage. I take one step. Every great journey always begins with one, doesn't it? All it takes is one. Then another. And another.

"Congratulations!" the emcee cries, handing me the prize. Two tickets to the Cosplay Ball. Second-place prize. Second place. I clutch the tickets tightly to my chest.

The emcee takes the last card from the envelope and looks down at it. His eyebrows jerk up into his hairline. "And first place, with a five-hundred-dollar prize and exclusive tickets to the premiere of *Starfield* is . . . number seventeen, Princess Carmindor!"

From the other side of the lineup, a cosplayer gathers up her tattered Federation uniform dress and sways up to retrieve her prize, waving to the audience. Even without her crown, she still nabbed first.

That's good cosplay. Fantastic cosplay. Gender-bending Carmindor? She was amazing. I clap with the rest of them, smiling.

The judges come out from the wings to congratulate us. I'm in a daze, trying to soak in everything but at the same time just trying to keep breathing. I didn't win. I don't have the cash prize. I'm not going to L.A.

But . . .

I look down at the golden tickets in my hand and my eyes begin to tear up. The Cosplay Ball.

"Good job," says a deep voice. It sounds familiar.

I glance over. *Darien Freeman.*

"You were amazing—I mean, that costume. You did a jood gob. I mean, a good job. Thank you—I mean—"

"Nox got your tongue?" I say before I can stop myself.

His eyes widen. His hands go slack. "You—you're the girl from the office. Rebelgunner."

There's a strange control to his voice that makes me want to both apologize for calling him spoiled and scold him for treating Miss May like an idiot.

Instead I just ease a smile onto my lips—he was one-third of my second-place vote, after all. "Glad you didn't try and chicken out of this too."

His eyes darken and his lips twist slightly downward, as if he's about to say something incredibly bratty, when Sage slings her arm across my shoulder and the other cosplayers—Nox knight and Steampunk Euci and Lord Dragnot (episode 3, minor character), along with a rainbow of others, flood around me with promise-sworn cries of joy.

How come I feel like I won even though I didn't?

Sage pulls me into a hug. "Second, yeah! I can take second."

"So who's your date?" Cal asks, nudging her chin toward the tickets. "For the ball."

"I don't know . . ." I chew the inside of my cheek. "I mean, I guess I figured Sage would—"

"Oh no," Sage interrupts. "You're *relishing* your winnings. Besides, I don't have a costume, duh."

"Sage'll be too busy hanging out with me," Cal blurts out. I barely understand what she says.

Sage's mouth drops open. "I . . . um . . . ," she stammers. And then she blushes beneath already-rouged cheeks.

My stepsister turns to her. "I mean, um, what do you say? Maybe we could grab a bite? If you want to." She stares at the ground. "With me, I mean."

Sage's mouth is moving but nothing's coming out. So I help her along and press the heel of my starlight slipper onto her toes. It must kick-start her brain because she yelps.

"Yes! I mean—like a date? I mean, um, yeah. Yeah, that'd be cool." And then she smiles, her eyes trained on Cal like she's the North Star.

Cal smiles. "Cool." Then, as if remembering her other half—or sensing evil, who knows—she glances into the crowd. "Elle, you might want to hurry off before Chloe comes up here. I know she's on her way."

"Let her come." Sage juts out her chin. "I'll punch her in the face."

"No, I think I should just go," I say. "Thank you again," I say to Cal, even though she'll just tell me that she doesn't deserve to be thanked.

Which might be true, but I'm half my mom, and my mom was always kind and always thankful. And my dad would want me to be like her.

Sage hands over my duffel bag and I pick up my dress, hurrying out of the throng of people. I know Carmindor hasn't responded since last night, but I've been busy too with the con. I can't imagine who else I'd bring to the ball.

In the bathroom, I drop my bag and splash water on my face. When I look up, a terrible thought strikes me.

What if he says no?

The girl in the mirror, with the crown of stars knotted in messy hair, with her mascara bleeding, in her hand-me-down cosplay jacket and her mother's dress, whom no one wanted, no one ever wanted, not since Dad died. But at this con, surrounded by the makings of my dad's dream . . .

Maybe he'll say yes. Maybe at this con the worlds are colliding, and nothing is impossible.

I reach into my duffel bag, building up the courage to ask him. Even if he says no, it'll be all right. Even if he doesn't want to meet me, I'll understand. But as I take out my phone, I see there's a message already waiting for me.

> *Carmindor 1:47 PM*
> —*I'm sorry, Elle.*
> —*I don't think we should talk anymore.*

My excitement, my anticipation, my hopefulness slowly slide down to rest like a lump of coal in my stomach.

DARIEN

I SLIP OUT OF THE CROWD onstage, toward the wings. *It's done*, I tell myself, looking back at all the fans, some with cameras, flashes on, others with GoPros and video recorders, their tiny black eyes aimed at me. *There's nothing you can do about it. It's sent.* I duck behind a stage curtain to get out of the line of sight.

"You okay?" Gail asks. She's the closest thing I have to a friend— and I have to pay her. "You're looking a little pale."

"I'm fine. Just . . . overwhelmed." I swallow and try to make a joke. "Some contest, huh? Pretty sure I showed my fans that I'm an excellent judge." When Gail doesn't laugh, I clear my throat. "Where's the bathrooms in this place?"

She nudges her head toward one of the stage exit doors. "I think through there. Do you want me to call Lonny over to go with—"

"*No*," I quickly interrupt. "I draw the line at bathroom escorts."

She shrugs. "All right. Just hurry back." Then she turns back to the crowd to deflect a group of girls storming me for a selfie.

I head toward the door, feeling queasier by the moment. This is the right thing to do. Just cold turkey. I could've ghosted her instead, let myself slowly fade from her life and that would've been truly harsh—

The stage door cracks me right in the face. I stumble back, clutching my nose as the person who opened the door curses.

"Ohmygod!" she cries, catching me by the shoulder. "I didn't see you—"

I curse, my hand coming away with blood.

"I am so sorry!" she goes on as I right myself again, pressing the backside of my hand gingerly against my nose. Sharp pain shoots up my face. "I was just coming from the bathroom and—oh . . . it's you."

I glance over. My stomach sinks to the bottom of the Black Nebula.

"Oh no," I groan.

Of all the people, the blogger. The second-place winner I embarrassed myself in front of once—well, twice—already. She quickly takes her hand off my shoulder. As if I burned her.

"I—I really didn't see you," she says.

"Obviously," I snap, and then instantly regret the sharpness.

"I'm sorry, okay?" She drags the heel of her hand over her eyes. They're puffy. From crying? Why is she crying?

"I—um—it just—are *you* okay?" I ask, and then she must realize it looks like she's crying, because she scrubs harder at her face.

"I'm fine!" She sniffs. "*You* should watch where you're going."

"Me?"

"I was opening the door!"

"So was I!" I argue. The blood leaks into my mouth and down my chin and onto my favorite T-shirt. Of course she has to ruin my favorite T-shirt. "Excuse me," I grind out, pushing past her into the hallway.

"I said I was sorry!" she shouts, her voice following me down the hallway. I shove my way into the bathroom and try to wipe up the blood with a few dozen paper towels.

"Crap," I mutter, twisting a piece of toilet paper and shoving it up my nose. I go to sit on a toilet so I can lean my head back. "Nothing like a good nosebleed to remind you you're an idiot, Darien."

I'm talking to myself in a bathroom stall. That is how far I've fallen into Tom-Cruise-Jumping-on-Oprah's-Couch territory. And that is pretty far in the span of a few weeks. Compared to the beat-up guy now sitting in a john at ExcelsiCon, the guy stuck in that New York hotel room seems saner than ever. Hiding out in the stairwell and everything. Talking with a girl I barely knew. Thinking I could—what?—*be normal* with her?

I was fooling myself. I began to believe my own lie. And now I have a broken nose to explain to Mark.

I take out my phone and pull up the message Brian sent her.

I'm sorry, Elle.

I don't think we should talk anymore.

I could reply again. Tell her it was a mistake, a joke, something. Maybe she'd understand—this girl who's normal and nice and funny. Who always finds a way to make me laugh. Who knows what to say and exactly when to say it, sending up words like constellations to guide me through deep space.

"I'm sorry," I mutter, trying to compose some semblance of an apology, thinking of something, anything, that doesn't sound douchey. "I wasn't thinking. I was stupid. But if you knew who I was, would you still talked to me? You hate Darien Freeman."

I sigh, massaging my temples.

"*I* hate Darien Freeman," I add, my thumbs bouncing along the touch-screen keyboard. The cursor blinks back at me. "And I *am* Darien Free—"

The door swings open right onto my kneecap. I clutch my leg with a yelp as Lonny glares down at me, his shoulders taking up the entire stall—wall to freaking wall. I sink down on the toilet, puddling into his shadow.

"Oh." I sound just like him—emotionless. "Hi there, big guy."

"Gail told me you came in here." He narrows his eyes. "Get into a fight?"

"With a door."

"I didn't think I needed to protect you from doors too."

"No, it wasn't *this* door," I say. "I was walking here and some girl shoved past me and . . ." But looking up at my bodyguard, I realize that even explaining won't help my case. I sigh and pull myself up on the seat. "Just forget it."

"Don't tilt your head back," he says as I do exactly that. "It won't help. Pinch your nose at the bridge. I'll tell Gail you need some ice. And painkillers. Do you want me to tell her you won't make it to the masquerade thing tonight?"

"It's not just a masquerade, it's a cos—" I let my shoulders sag. "Never mind. I . . . guess I have to go."

"The threat has been neutralized," Lonny agrees. "You ought to be safe."

"Yeah. And I'll be wearing a mask anyway, right? How much worse could today get?"

He shakes his head. "You know every time you say that, it just gets worse, right?" he replies, and leaves the bathroom.

I take out my phone and read my unsent text.

I am Darien Freeman.

I think of all the things she could do with the texts we have. All the places she could sell them. All the news stories she could cover. All the secrets I've told her. All the half-lies. All the times I called her *ah'blena*.

But I *am* Darien Freeman. And I lied to her. Maybe I didn't write that text, but Brian was right—I was going to have to write it one day anyway. It had to be done. For Elle's sake and mine.

I tap my thumb against the backspace a hundred and three times, erasing every space, every letter of my unsent apology. And then, with shaking fingers, I delete her number.

In an instant, the history of Elle and me is gone.

ELLE

I DON'T THINK WE SHOULD TALK ANYMORE.

There really isn't any other way to interpret that.

I see myself into the lobby outside the Cosplay Ball, shifting on my glass slippers. It's inside a huge hotel in the center of Atlanta. I stare up and up and up at the skyline, clutching the tickets close.

It's funny, but now that I've realized Carmindor doesn't want me, my heart isn't rattling around in my chest. I feel weirdly calm. I guess it's because I knew—like with James—that I'm not good enough.

Every person who walks in through the revolving doors could be Carmindor. They all look familiar yet still strange, like funhouse-mirror versions of the characters you know. A Klingon comes escorting a Vulcan, Dean Winchester with the angel Castiel, two *World of Warcraft* Orcs, Harry and Hermione—so many pairs of people so that when someone enters alone, I stand a little straighter, squint a little harder, wondering if maybe this one is him. . . .

I readjust my mask. It's Cal's, because in all my planning and plotting and saving, I forgot about that one small detail. Or maybe, deep down, I didn't really think I'd win.

Cal's mask is heavier than I thought, and smooth to the touch. When she gave it to me glitter came off on my fingers. I blinked, my eyes burning.

"I . . . don't know where Chloe is," Cal told me hesitantly. "I didn't see her after the, um, the contest."

"You didn't?"

She shook her head. "While you were in the bathroom she kind of came up and, um, lost her cool. A little."

I paled. "Do you think she's going to tell Catherine?"

Cal shook her head. "If she does, she'll get in trouble too. So I don't think she would, but just—Elle—watch out. Chloe doesn't take losing lightly."

"What could she do at a dance party?" I scoffed.

Sage shrugged. "It'll keep you on your toes. And when you meet Darien, please don't do anything rash."

I gasped. "You wound me! I'd never!"

She gave me a level look.

"I'll be nice," I mumbled.

"Mm-hmm. We'll pick you up at eight? It'll be cutting it close to get you both home by midnight but . . ."

"Eight is great," I assured her with a smile. I still wished they would come to the ball, but if my best friend and my apparently not-psycho stepsister want some alone time, who am I to stand in the way? "You two have fun."

And then they had left me in the gold-plated lobby, absolutely alone. Dressed up as Black Nebula Federation Princess Amara, shedding glitter from her starched coat like stars.

After one more person, I'll go in, I tell myself, nodding to another couple emerging through the revolving door. *Or maybe one more.*

But the minutes tick by, and after a while the music from the ballroom grows loud enough to echo inside the lobby, and I'm still standing here.

Deep breath in, deep breath out, I think. *I can do this.*

I don't know what'll happen once I go inside. I don't know if the ball will live up to all the ideas in my head, to all the memories of my parents waltzing around the living room, to what Dad always wanted it to be.

But if I never go in, I'll never find out. And I'm tired of being afraid of things I can't control.

I turn toward the music at the end of the hallway and show my ticket to the volunteer at the gilded doors. She tears it in half and hands it back.

"So do a lot of people go stag?" I ask, trying to sound chill. My voice comes out in a squeak.

"I mean, it all depends." She pauses. "But I don't think you're alone at all."

She gives me a promise-sworn salute and the nervousness building in my chest slowly ebbs. I return the salute, curl my fingers around the doorknob, and push.

The ballroom is dark, decorated in shades of purple and blue. Pinions of light spiral around like shooting stars. And it's full, so full of people. I stare at them in unabashed wonderment. Dad told me about this ball. How he pictured it. He used to sit on the foot of my bed and paint a picture in the air with his hands.

"It'll be huge—grand! Dark, like space, but not dark enough that you can't see. And everyone dressed up. Look, there's a Spock over there! Is he dancing with Chewbacca? A Turian with a Nox! Can you believe that, Elle? The things you never thought you'd see right there. It'll be a universe inside our universe that exists for only a few hours. Only," he added, "until the stroke of midnight."

I slowly wander to the steps leading into the saturated ballroom, staring down at the people with glowing drinks and pointed ears, the dark lights that make purple armor and blue sneakers and white teeth glow. A heavy fog hangs over the dance floor, swirling around dancers, wrapping around legs.

A smile slowly spreads across my face. "You made it, Dad," I whisper, and then follow the steps down into the ball.

DARIEN

LIKE FEDERATION PRINCE CARMINDOR DURING THE Brinx Devastation, I just gotta live through this.

Ten more minutes, I think, standing in the middle of a throng of fans. I'll give the *Rebelgunner* girl ten more minutes to get here. The meet-and-greet with the first-place winner went fine: she was polite, totally nervous, here with her girlfriend dressed as CLE-o. Third place was very . . . bro-ish. We bumped fists. It was cool.

Now Gail is perched beside me, the glow of her phone illuminating her face as she texts mercilessly. She can't still be going through emails or contacting Mark. It must be something else.

"Darien, can I get a picture?" asks a girl I can barely see. She pulls me into a selfie before I have a chance to say no. I smile and the camera blinds me.

"Thank you!" she squeals as the next girl pushes her way to the front and we repeat the process all over again.

I lean back toward Gail. "Can I go yet?"

"You said you wanted to judge the contest, right?" She doesn't even glance up. "Well, half of that job is being here. The other two judges aren't leaving anytime soon."

"Yeah, but they aren't getting nearly as much attention," I point out.

"Darien?" says the next girl, dressed as Princess Amara. Her dark hair is pulled up into a braid and her makeup is incredibly spot-on, but she just makes me think of the Black Nebula Amara from the contest, and running into the blogger, and then rereading the text to Elle, and I start to feel sick again.

I was never that guy to just drop someone. I didn't think I could be. Not until I was.

"Darien, I'm a *huge* fan and I run a beauty vlog. I would really love it if—"

That's when I see her out of the corner of my eye—the girl from the contest, the one from the office, gorgeous eyes and a sharp tongue—and once I turn to look, I can't look away.

At the top of the stairs, the girl with glowing red hair stares down at the rest of us from behind a sparkling golden mask. Her bowlike lips are painted the flaming color of a red giant. She's beautiful.

"Excuse me," I tell the vlogger and move closer through the throng of people.

As the girl descends, the crowd begins to turn and look. It must be the glint of her crown, the way her coat glitters. They bend to each other to wonder if she came alone.

"Who *wouldn't* want to go with her?" a Nox near me whispers to his date.

She takes each step gracefully, even under the weight of every eye on her—even alone. This is where, in all the movies, the guy sees what he's been waiting for the entire plot. This is where his life clicks into place. The meet-cute where he falls in love. This sequence.

But this isn't a movie, and I've already missed my meet-cute. The sky doesn't suddenly crash in around us. The world doesn't lose sound.

Because this isn't where I fall in love. I fell in love across the cell signals and late-night texts with a girl I barely knew.

ELLE

WHEN I REACH THE BOTTOM OF THE STAIRS, a tall boy in red offers his hand. "May I?" he asks. His uniform is neatly pressed, a Starfleet insignia pinned to his chest and a mask tied behind his Vulcan ears. Not a Stargunner, but close enough. Beggars can't be choosers.

"Sure," I reply, and take his hand. He whirls me into the fray as the DJ starts another 8-bit anthem. We dance for two songs, but it's not the dancing I thought it'd be. It's not like Dad waltzing Mom around the living room. He's a pretty awkward dancer, and I'm not much better. Besides, there's some kind of cyborg next to use trying to grope his way to home base with a Night elf, and I'm not sure how I feel about that sort of union.

"So what's your name?" redshirt shouts.

"Amara," I reply.

Redshirt does not look amused. "No, I mean your real name."

"Oh—well, what's yours?"

He's doing the redshirt equivalent of the white-man's shuffle. Head bobbing, elbows in toward the chest, moving like a T-rex on drugs. I can't take him seriously.

"Dave," he replies. "Saw your costume at the contest today. You were . . . really something."

"Thanks. It was my dad's—"

Someone taps me on the shoulder and I spin around. A guy dressed as a young, soon-to-be-married Han Solo offers his hand. "Can I have the next dance?"

Then a girl in *Final Fantasy* garb asks after him, and then a humanized Pikachu after her, and then—there are just too many. Too many songs, too many dances, too many faces. I have never been popular before. I'm a nobody, just an extra in someone else's movie. But no one here seems to have gotten the memo. It's overwhelming and it's sort of uncomfortable. If this is the kind of attention Chloe was after, well, she can have it. Give me my blog. Give me a dark theater. Give me *Starfield*.

Halfway through a pop-infused "I Will Always Love You," I excuse myself from the din of the dance floor and make my way to the concessions. Most everything is picked over, but I grab a cracker with cheese and a small glass of punch.

I find a corner of the ballroom that's dark and less populated and sit down against huge bay windows. My cheeks are hot from dancing, and I've been sweating in this jacket for three songs now. I tug at the collar and press the cool side of the glass against my neck, closing my eyes for one sweet second.

But then I hear footsteps. Walking toward me. I peek open an eye. Shiny black boots, embroidered at the calves with the Federation symbol. My heart's already beginning to sink as I slowly look up. Black pants and a coat that buttons on the left side, golden knobs and shiny golden lining. Three chains draw out from one of the pockets, looping around under the left arm to the back of the shoulder, hiding under the golden epaulette.

Even in the dim lighting I can tell the coat is the wrong shade of blue, but what it lacks in color it succeeds in measurements. It hugs his slim waist and broad chest, tight across his shoulders—and he does have commanding shoulders. I'm sure even the collar would fit perfect around his neck if it wasn't unbuttoned (which is actually a good idea; it's way too hot for a wool jacket). The starwings clasped to the lapel glint in the city lights shining in through the window. It's like the coat was made for him. And given that this is a cosplay ball, it probably was.

My eyes trail all the way up to his face, his brown skin and strong jawline, his piercing dark eyes beneath the black eyelet mask, and my heart sinks into my gut like a stone.

"Cheese and crackers," I mutter. "*You* again."

Darien Freeman puts his hands on his hips, cocking his head. It's not adorable. It's really not. "I came to ask the second-place winner for a dance, but I think I'm a little late, Princess."

"It's Princess Amara to you," I snap back. "And yes, but I'm taking a moment. Alone."

He puts up his hands. "All right." And, miraculously, he turns to leave.

I close my eyes again, thankful for the moment of silence. Dad would love this ball. He'd love everything about it, even the crappy pop music. He would love the costumes, the intermingling of species, the heart and soul of people being something else for a little while. But I don't feel like Amara right now. I feel exhaustedly like myself.

"Hey, that costume's pretty amazing," someone says.

Two minutes of peace—all I ask for is *two*.

"The details are so sweet. Was it expensive? Who did it?"

My eyes snap open. I glance up at whoever's asking. He's my age, dressed in one of the most ostentatious cosplays you could choose. Black robes, large shoulder pads, makeup that looks like scales. The ends of his adhesive ears blink purple and blue almost in time with the music. The Nox King.

"What do you mean?" I ask.

"I mean, what's the name of the guy who made it?"

"It couldn't have been a girl?" I ask.

"You know, I didn't think I'd seen you around a con before," he replies, as if that's some sort of explanation. "Darien Freeman fangirl, right?"

"What?"

He scoffs. "Come on. You're too cute to play dumb."

I stare at him, suddenly very aware that Darien Freeman isn't as far away from this conversation as I'd like him to be. I set down my punch, trying to work out the right words to say.

"For your information, the costume was my dad's before he died, and my friend and I did a few alterations to it." I don't include the part where it almost got destroyed. "Actually, a few other cosplayers helped too, so you could say it was a cosmic effort."

"Knew it." The Nox King looks way too happy. "There's no way you could've made that."

"Oh?" I cock my head. "And why's that?"

"Chill out, I'm not trying to be offensive." He laughs. There's a spot of black lipstick on his teeth, but I'm not about to tell him. "You just dressed up to get some attention and hey, it worked—"

"Excuse *you*." I jump to my feet. "*Starfield* is one of my favorite shows of all time and—"

"You don't have to try and explain yourself to me, okay? Fake geek girls like you always win."

He turns away but in I grab him by that stupid tattered cape—why does the Nox King have a cape, anyway? I never understood that in the show—and jerk him around. He's surprised for a moment but quickly turns angry. I guess no one touches his costume without permission. Well no one calls me a fake, either.

"You're right, I don't have to explain myself anyone, but especially not to some left-testicled Nox like you. Do you think you're funny? You couldn't even cosplay as Euci! You'd bring shame to every slapstick secondary character in the omniverse!"

"Yeah, coming from someone who's just here to play princess, that's a little rich, isn't it? What's wrong—couldn't think up anything more original?" He shakes his head. "Poor little fake cosplayer—"

"Excuse me." It's Carmindor—*Darien*—back in his wrong-blue uniform.

"Stay out of it," I snap.

Darien arches an eyebrow. "Easy, Princess." I make a *hmph* sound, but he keeps talking. "I was just going to ask what episode you're from, sir?"

The Nox King scowls, lipstick smearing over his teeth even more. "Episode sixteen."

"Huh," says Darien.

"What's it to you?" The cosplayer crosses his arms.

"Nothing." Darien shrugs. "Just that the Nox King doesn't wear a cape in episode sixteen."

"Yeah, so?" Nox King says. "I improvised."

"Cool, cool." Darien frowns, then taps his own shoulder, then gestures to the shoulder guard on the cosplayer. Now that he points to it, I realize what's wrong.

"But what about the insignia?" Darien says. "Because I seem to remember it on the other side. In every episode. And it's not a small detail. It's pretty big, actually. How can your followers kiss the symbol of their religion if it's on the wrong shoulder?"

The cosplayer opens his mouth, then closes it again.

"That is why you didn't win," Darien Freeman goes on, "because you were careless. Not because you're a 'real fan.' We're all real fans. This girl most of all."

The cosplayer advances on Darien. "Yeah? Then who the hell are you? Her *boyfriend*?"

Carmindor Darien simply smiles in the face of the Nox King—how I wish that the movie revolved around *that* plot arc instead—and stands his ground. Shoulders straight but easy, his chin slightly inclined, a smirk tucked into the side of his lips.

I don't mean to stare—and I'm not staring, I'm merely looking—but for a moment, in the dim light of the disco ball and the fog machines and the glow from the sconces on the walls, he actually looks the part.

Like . . .

"I'm Federation Prince Carmindor to you," Darien Freeman replies, and the irony isn't lost on me, "but also just a fan. Like you. And no, she isn't my date, but now that you mention it"—he extends a hand to me—"I wouldn't mind some fresh air, would you?"

I freeze, until I remember I'm part of this whole thing and not just watching from the wings.

Darien's eyebrow arches higher over his eyelet mask. "Well, Princess?"

My gaze raises from his outstretched hand to the coy look glimmering in his eyes, asking me to play along. Okay, I'll play along. I take his hand. "Only if I don't have to walk through a Black Nebula."

"Once is enough," he jokes, and leads me out onto the balcony. "Let's get on with our meet-and-greet, shall we?"

DARIEN

I DON'T STOP UNTIL WE'RE OUTSIDE on the small veranda connected to the ballroom. Two Vulcans are making out by the peach tree (everything in Atlanta is peach themed, apparently), so I lead her to the other side. Beyond the balcony, the city stretches out like a map of lights.

Princess Amara unravels herself from my arm, leaving a strange sort of hollowness. I brush it away.

"You didn't have to step in and save me, you know," she begins, retreating to the bench. "I can save myself."

"Self-rescuing, are you?"

"Sorry to disappoint."

"I'm not disappointed at all." I sit down beside her. "It's just one of my pet peeves is all—someone accusing a fan of being a fake. I know about that way too well."

She chews on the inside of her mouth. "Look, about that blog post . . . I didn't—I didn't think . . ."

"Please, you know you thought I was only in it for the money," I tease, and her cheeks redden even more.

"I didn't know you," she replies. "I mean, I *don't* know you, but—"

And there's the problem. That's always the problem, isn't it? Nobody knows me. I should go back inside. I should tell Gail that we need to go. The meet-and-greet is over. I've done my part. I shouldn't linger here long enough for people to snap photos and begin making assumptions, selling the gossip. Maybe she'll get some TV host or DJ to pay for an interview. Cash in and get her five seconds of fame, like Brian.

But this girl seems nothing like him. And neither did Elle.

I clear my throat. "You probably know enough about me. I'm sure you've read a few interviews, watched a few talk shows."

"The dunk tank one was really good."

I grimace. "Yeah, that was a good one."

"But . . ." She hesitates. "That's not really *you*, is it? I don't mean to be blunt. I just—I just don't believe that the guy who stuck up for me back there is Darien Freeman."

"I assure you I am, Princess."

"But that's not Darien Freeman. That's not—"

"The guy you wrote your blog posts about?" I finish. "Great pieces of journalism, by the way. All incredibly searing. Each one hurt worse than the last."

She winces. "Okay, I deserve that. I feel like a complete jerk for it, and I'm sorry. But if you're not that guy . . ." She starts to braid a piece of hair behind her ear, like she's nervous, which is kind of adorable. " . . . then who *are* you?"

"Who am I?" I echo, surprised.

She nods. "We could, um, call it an exclusive? I'll even redact the other posts."

I shift uncomfortably, thinking of Elle and of what Brian said. In all our texting, I hadn't been truthful to her—not once—because I was lying by omission. If I really valued her, cared about her, would I have at least told her the truth?

Maybe I can get a second chance.

"I don't think you got me wrong at all," I tell the princess.

"Try me."

"Honestly? I'm . . ." I take a deep breath, looking down at my feet. "I'm no one."

She tilts her head toward me as the eyebrows behind her golden mask scrunch together.

"I always thought I was no one too," she replies. "But we're wrong. We're anyone we want to be. Anyone we can be."

"Yeah? Do you think I could be a good Carmindor?"

The couple snogging in the other corner giggle, pulling each other to their feet. They stumble inside to dance out Michael Jackson's "Thriller," and silence settles between the princess and me. We're the only two people on the balcony. It's so quiet we could be the only two people left in the world.

"My dad said that anyone could be Carmindor," she says. "That anyone can be Amara. That we have bits and pieces of them inside us. We just have to shine them off and let them glow."

"He sounds like a great guy."

"The best. He . . . he died when I was little."

"I'm sorry, I didn't . . ."

She ignores my apology. "This was his cosplay, you know." She fondly touches the starwings on her lapel. "And my mom's. They used to come to ExcelsiCon dressed as Carmindor and Princess Amara every year. ExcelsiCon was Dad's brainchild. He had all these big dreams for it, you know? He would've loved to have seen this ball. He used to talk about it after Mom died. I miss that the most, I think, how much he talked about this con and this ball—a masquerade of stars, he'd say. I didn't think he meant literally." She elbows me in the side.

A ghost of a smile begins to tug at the edge of my lips—the first real one I can remember in a long time—and she begins to mirror it, but then it falters.

She looks away. "I know I wasn't the best cosplayer at that contest. Did I get second place because I'm the old con-director's daughter?"

I chuckle to myself, shaking my head. She can't even begin to understand the irony in all this.

She frowns. "What's so funny?"

"Princess, I voted for you because when you walked out on that stage you made me believe it."

"Believe what?"

"What your father said—that anyone can be Carmindor and Amara. You just gotta find that piece of them inside you and let it glow."

A flush rises in her cheeks. She looks down into her lap, where her fingers are weaving the ends of her hair into a million braids. Why does she seem so familiar? Not from the blog. Not from the office. From somewhere else. I've heard these stories before, played out at a slower pace, like a waltz unwinding.

I begin to open my mouth to say something when she jumps up from the bench and spins around to me, hand outstretched. "Do you want to dance? With me, I mean. Would you want to dance with me?"

Do I?

"Only if you lead, Princess," I reply. I take her hand and she pulls me to my feet.

Her smile broadens. "I was hoping you'd say that."

ELLE

I lead him—Carmindor, Darien Freeman, *whoever*—into the ballroom, into the crowd, straight to the epicenter. The DJ spins a new tune and the crowd disperses until only couples remain.

His fingers curl tighter around mine. The song is soft and slow, and with a shiver I realize it's the *Starfield* theme song. Darien seems to notice at the same time, and he grins. "What good timing."

"Sometimes the universe delivers," I say, and then realize it's true, though only in other universes.

"Maybe we're secretly in a movie," he mock-whispers.

"Maybe the universe just likes playing tricks."

People around us turn to watch. Their eyes fall on us like laser pointers, as hot and focused as the moment I stepped onto that contest stage. My skin tingles, as though every move I make is the wrong one.

He lowers a hand to my hip and we begin to sway slowly. My cheeks get hot as the music soars. It's full strings, the woodwinds, and the swell of an orchestra rising, rising, whisking you across the galaxy. It's the sound of Dad dancing Mom through the living room, around and around, as she laughed and stumbled along. It's the sound of Dad waltzing me through the living room after Mom's turn is over, telling me about a grand ball, this dream of his, where for a moment—a breath of time—you're the person you always dreamed you could be.

Like the Federation Prince, unafraid of anything. Like a daughter, living up to her father's memory. Like a self-rescuing princess, dancing with . . .

My eyes flicker back up to his, and I swallow hard. "Do you even know how to dance?"

"Do *I* know?" He laces his fingers through mine, pulling me closer. He smells like cinnamon rolls and coat starch. "I am Carmindor."

As the orchestra crescendos into the second verse we step out in unison, catching the note in one fluid movement; the ballroom becomes a whirl. We spin across the dance floor, around swaying couples, our feet in sync in this strange sort of cadence, as if I know every step he's about to take—or he knows mine. Flickers of light twinkle around us, cutting through the fog that swirls in our wake. It feels like the entire universe orbits us in an impossible moment.

An impossible moment in an impossible universe.

What would it be like to dance with my Carmindor? The one I've bared my soul to? Would it be anything like this?

"Thank you," I whisper, looking into Darien's masked face.

"For what?" He leans closer.

"For tonight. For—for everything."

"I thought you said you were self-rescuing," he jokes, grinning.

"Even self-rescuing princesses sometimes feel like no one."

We're so close I can feel his breath on my lips, and my heart is tugging, telling me to kiss him even though I don't know him. Even though my heart, battered and bandaged and taped together, is still rattling from the text a few hours before. But there's something familiar in the cadence of his words, the way he phrases sentences, the way he articulates thoughts, like a voice I've heard before.

Closer, closer—

Then, as always happens in the impossible universe, the moment disappears. Someone grabs me from behind and spins me around. Suddenly I'm face-to-face with Chloe.

And she is *not* happy.

DARIEN

IT'S THE BEAUTY VLOGGER FROM BEFORE. She grabs the arm of Princess Amara—jeez, what's up with me not knowing anyone's name? Ever—and jerks her away.

"You!" the vlogger girl sneers.

"Chloe," Princess Amara whispers.

The vlogger girl—Chloe—looks her up and down with disgust. "You *did* steal it," she hisses. "I knew it. I *knew* you took my dress!"

A wave of murmurs ripples across the crowd. The music carries on but this Chloe is impressively loud, and the hairs on the back of my neck start to rise.

Princess Amara wrenches her arm away. "I didn't steal anything, Chloe."

"Of course you did! And now you're dancing with *him*!" She jabs a finger at me.

I hold up my hands. "Whoa, now—"

"Stay out of this!" Chloe snaps at me. I step back. Okay. She glares at Princess Amara, her pretty made-up face warping with fury. "You got everything, you know that? You had *everything*. And just for once—for once!—I wanted something too."

"Chloe, I don't know what you're talking about—"

"Don't you?" she advances toward Amara, who steps back defensively.

I look around for a security guard—where's Lonny when you need him? "Can we get some security over here?" I say behind me, but that only serves to enrage the girl even more.

She glares at me. "Don't bother. Once you find out who she *really* is, you'll run for the hills."

"Stop it, Chloe," Amara replies. "I'll leave."

"Oh no! Stay all you want! I just think you need to tell him the truth, yeah? How you're an orphaned, friendless little worm whose father was a loser geek who liked weird space crap more than his family!"

Amara's eyes widen and she freezes. Her mouth falls open. "Wha— what?"

The crowd begins to thicken, murmur.

"Oh come *on,*" the girl says with a laugh. "Your dad was weird and you know it. He was the cream of the crop in weird! He treated you like you were *so* special, just because you were bizarre like him. Like you were his *only* daughter. But did we hold that against you? No. And what do you do? You steal *my* dress. I worked hard for that!"

Amara snaps. "Liar!"

"You stole it! I'm sorry if you messed up your life, but don't mess up everyone else's. And now you think you can get with *Darien Freeman?*" She snorts. "Dream on, Elle. You're no one."

Elle?

I stand in the crowd, growing cold.

Her name is *Elle?*

The text message, Amara's puffy eyes, the costume—oh man. She can't be my Elle. She can't.

"And," Chloe adds, advancing on Elle, who, like a flower in winter, curls up, shrinking, "you never will be anyone—"

"Stop it."

Chloe turns a wide-eyed gaze to me, not believing I'd take her side. Elle's side. A part of me can't believe it either, but not for the same reasons.

I remember the nights talking with Elle—my Elle, the Elle in my head, the one who apparently doesn't exist. Wanting to text her. Waiting

for her to text me. The first time she called me *ah'blen*. The nights we
stayed up late, and how little we really knew about each other, and how
much I wanted to know about her.

Me and her—that girl. That Elle.

Us.

How could I ever mistake Elle for someone like Brian? Think they
were the same person? I was blind and stupid and she had been here all
along.

"Don't you want to know who she *really* is?" Chloe asks. She's horrible, just like I imagined Elle's stepsisters. She described them perfectly.
"She's just some weird little *geek.*"

"I know who she is," I reply. Elle glances over to me. I can see her
tears. I can't take back that text message, but I can give her what she
gave me over these last few weeks. I was such a doofus. "She's kind, and
she's smart, and she's stubborn and very, very passionate. But not in a
bad way. In a good way. In a way I aspire to be. She grew up in a universe without anyone to appreciate her—and what gives *you* that right?
What gives you the right to treat her like she's no one?"

"I—I—" Chloe looks from me to Elle and then back to me, as if
trying to puzzle out why I'm standing up for her stepsister. Do people
really think I'm that selfish?

I grab Elle's hand and squeeze it tight. It's assurance that I'm not
just saying that. I mean it. Because if she's the girl I think she is, she'll
understand. She deserves to know who I really am.

"Oh, and her father?" I say. "He started this convention. This cosplay ball. So if you think *he's* a weirdo, then I think you're in the wrong
crowd."

And with that I give her the promise-sworn salute.

A Torturian beside me mimics my salute. And a Nox. A Jedi. A
Vulcan. A Dark Elf. The entire Fellowship of the Ring. Everyone, in
their different-colored hair and costumes and masks, lifts their hands in
promise-swears to show that underneath the robes and breastplates and
Spandex are people whose hearts beat together. We might all be differ-

ent—we may ship different things or be in different fandoms—but if I learned anything from twenty-three days in a too-blue uniform playing a character I thought I could never be, it's that when we become those characters, pieces of ourselves light up like glow sticks in the night. They shine. *We* shine. Together.

And even when some of us fall to different universes, those lights never go out.

Finally, Elle gives her salute. And I squeeze her hand even tighter.

"We're all geeks here," I say.

ELLE

CHLOE WHIRLS AROUND. NO ONE IS dancing, even though the music keeps spinning. Everyone has a promise-sworn outstretched, even cosplayers who aren't dressed in *Starfield* regalia. Chloe chews her bottom lip to keep it from wobbling, her nails digging into her starchy dress. I don't know how she got it, or how she got in here, and my heart twists because I know this isn't how she wanted things to go.

"I hate you!" she cries. Then she pushes her way out of the room. The crowd begins to applaud as she stumbles up the stairs and disappears, chased out by a roar of hoots and hollers.

I think to go after her but then stop myself. Chloe wouldn't go after me. She wouldn't even try.

Beside me, Darien sighs. "Man, that was a pain."

"You humiliated her," I say.

He squints at me. "She humiliated you too."

"I know but . . ." I glance back to the ballroom door. "I'm used to it."

"And that makes it okay?"

"No . . ."

He sighs, and slowly the crowd begins to go back to whatever they were doing before. Dancing, mingling, eating those delicious finger foods I have yet to try. Maybe I should at least eat a puff pastry before they're all gone. He rubs the back of his neck. "Listen, I—I think I need to tell you something."

"That you're a *serious* fanboy?" I try to joke, but my heart is still racing from the argument. I can't get the watery look in Chloe's eyes out of my head. We really destroyed her. Maybe she's like that, but I'm not.

"Well, that too," he says, laughing, and then turns my hand over in his. "But really it's about—"

The ballroom doors swing open with a deafening groan. A blue-green haired girl sprints inside, followed by a pair of door attendants, shouting about how she needs a ticket.

"Sage?" I let go of Darien's hand as she reaches me. "What are you doing here?"

She bends over, hands on knees and trying to catch her breath. "*Jesus*! Haven't you been checking your phone? I've been looking every-where for you! We need to go!"

"What? Why—oh god, the time!"

"Yeah, Cinderella, the *time*!" Sage grabs my wrist and yanks me toward the exit.

"Wait," Darien says, attempting to come after me. "Elle—"

"I'm sorry," I say, but I let Sage pull me away. A hundred thousand possibilities of what Catherine will do to me are running through my head. And all of them give me a vomitus feeling.

Please let me get home in time, I think as we thread our way through the ballroom. I don't look back at Darien. I can't. I push his look of hurt—actual, gut-wrenching hurt—out of my head.

Because I'm as good as dead.

"What time is it?" I yell to Sage. She cuts through the crowd like a knife, her grip so tight I know it'll leave a mark.

"Nine o'clock!" she calls back.

"Nine?" Panic grips my chest. Even if we gun the Pumpkin to 80 M.P.H., it's at least a four-hour drive. "We'll never make it!"

She shoves open the ballroom door and we flee into the golden-hued lobby, across the plush carpet and toward the revolving door. The Mag-ic Pumpkin is idling outside. In a no-parking zone. And there's a cop heading toward it from across the street. Cal leans out the passenger window, motioning us to hurry. Footsteps follow behind us, and just as I career out of the revolving doors, I spin back to see who—

Darien.

"Wait, please!" he cries, slamming his way to the revolving doors. His mask has fallen off and I can see the shiner on his nose, dark as a rainstorm, and the alarm in his eyes. The kind where you're afraid you'll never see someone again.

"Wait—*ah'blena!*"

Ah'blena?

I stumble, and one of Mom's shoes slips off.

"What are you doing?" Sage grabs my hand when I bend for the shoe. "Come on! We have to go!"

She's right. We have to go. *I* have to go. Pull myself out of this—this—whatever this is. This dream. This moment. A shoe is a shoe—it's not worth the wrath of Catherine.

I take off at a run just as Darien rounds out of the revolving doors. Jumping into the driver's seat, Sage slams the truck into gear and I grab ahold of the handle bar for the passenger foothold. The truck heaves forward as I swing open the door and climb inside, next to Cal.

In the rearview mirror, he's still running after us. But as we pick up speed his feet slow to a stop and he doubles over, resting his hands on his knees, my name on his lips a moment before he disappears behind a building. I turn to face the road, chest tight and head pounding.

He'll get over me. All we had was a moment. Just a moment in an impossible universe waltzing that beautiful, impossible waltz.

DARIEN

I'M ABOUT TO VOMIT.

My lungs burn with every breath, but I right myself, looking down at the glittery slipper. I swipe it off the ground. I'll drop it off at the hotel desk. Maybe they can hold on to it until Elle can pick it up. Or I can tell her.

A knot forms in my throat.

I almost did—I almost told her who I was. I was so close. Tapping the bottom of the shoe against my palm, I turn back toward the hotel.

And freeze.

The Nox King is standing in the way, phone out and recording the entire thing under the harsh light of a streetlamp. He smirks, and that's when I recognize him. I curse as he grins wider.

"Nice cosplay, Brian," I spit out at him.

"Had you fooled at least."

"Can you stop recording?"

"Why don't you ask your dad?"

I sigh. Yeah, Mark is going to kill me. But I'll deal with that later. "You can just not sell it, you know. Pretend to be a decent person."

"Still so blind, man?" Brian shakes his head. "I kinda feel sorry for you."

I'm too angry to play games. Elle was right here—right beside me— but then suddenly she wasn't, and when she left it felt like she took the air from around me until I could barely breathe.

Brian's still talking. "I'm sure we'll get a lot for this footage, too. What should the headline be, you think? Darien Favors Contestant? Geek Girl Will Do Anything to Win? Renowned Cosplay Competition Upended by Star Darien Freeman's D—"

That's it. If one good thing has happened over the last several months of preproduction and soulless salads and protein shakes and four a.m. workouts with Arnold Schwarzenegger's cousin, it's that I learned to throw a punch. Thumb out, clench fist—

Swing.

Brian stumbles from the force of it. Clutching his jaw, he waves his phone at me. "It's still recording, stupid! You want assault and battery on the headlines too?"

"ASSAULT *THIS*." And with a wild yell, I charge at him.

Brian spins around and dashes toward the revolving doors. I slam into the same wedge with him, like two sardines in a tin can, pulling at his obnoxious Nox ears.

"Ow, ow, ow! Hands off!" he cries. "Those were expensive!"

"We were friends!" I manage to rip off one ear before he pushes the revolving door far enough to escape into the lobby. "You just said you wanted to be friends!"

"Yeah, until you turned out to be a better-than-everyone-else ass-hole!" he shouts over his shoulder, circling an expensive-looking couch. The upholstery is really nice, but screw it. I climb over the cushions—he thought I'd go around—and grab him by that *stupid* nonsensical cape. I always said the Nox King didn't need a cape.

"And *you* sold me out! You were jealous!"

"*Seriously*, man?" He whirls behind another chair and shoves it at me. "Your head's so far up your dad's ass it's unbelievable."

I catch the chair before it slams into my crotch. "Take that back."

"You're daddy's little boy. Doing everything he wants. He *manu-factured* you, you know that?" He grabs a handful of magazines and throws them at me.

I duck as a *Teen Vogue* with me on the cover sails over my head. "I said *take it back*."

"What, not proud of being his little b—"

I charge at him again. He cuts through a family of four and shoves their luggage cart between us. I grab the other side. "So you took a picture of me face-planting into a dock and sold it? That really made everything better!" I try to jerk the cart away, but he holds fast. "Why'd you do it?"

His dark purple makeup begins to flake off as his face scrunches in anger. "Why don't you ask your father?"

"Mark's got nothing to do with it—"

"*He* planted the pictures!" Brian roars.

I gape.

"Never thought of that, huh?" He sneers. "Don't you think the timing was a little *too* good? Just wrapped up the second season of *Seaside*. You'd auditioned for Carmindor and people kinda knew who you were—"

"Frak you."

"—but they didn't *really* know you. No one cared outside of your SeaCos or whatever the hell they're called."

He's lying. I know he is. But his words begin to constrict my throat, making it harder to breathe.

"I took them as a joke—something to give you shit about later. But then Mark confiscated them, told me they could get me paid," Brian says. "And he was right. One big story and you were on the map. You were everywhere."

"It was hell!"

"It was *business*, man," Brian says. "I thought you'd get over it eventually."

"And I thought I could trust my best friend."

The dad of the family whose cart we've commandeered tentatively reaches for their luggage, glancing between us as if we're crazy monsters. At the check-in desk, the clerk is already on the phone, probably with security. I can see the headline now—*DARIEN FIGHTS WITH SLEAZY PAPARAZZO AND MURDERS HIS ASS.*

"Sure," Brian says, "blame *me* for all this. Can't stomach to blame yourself, can you?"

I spin the cart away from Tourist Dad and attack with a Conan the Barbarian cry of rage. Brian retreats through the ballroom doors, disappearing into the dark mist of the dance party. He skids to a stop at the balustrade leading down to the dance floor and glances back.

"Oh sh—"

But I've already taken a flying leap. My shoulder slams into his chest and we tumble over the railing like King Kong off the Empire State Building. The ten-foot drop takes a lot longer than I expect. Long enough for me to regret this entire decision.

Well, at least I'm insured.

We crash onto the floor with enough force to knock the breath out of me. The DJ scratches a Pokérap remix to a halt. Avengers and Night elves and Jedi circle us. I roll onto my back, groaning. I don't think I've broken any bones, but I can't tell. It feels like I've cracked absolutely everything. Beside me, Brian rolls over too, and we stare up at the ceiling. It's actually a pretty nice ceiling. Golden chromed like the rest of the hotel, fancy . . .

I must've hit my head harder than I thought.

"You know what?" I sit up unsteadily. I've been bruised and beat up today more times than I ever was on set. I knew I wanted to stay away from this con for a reason. "We could've been friends. But it never would've worked, and not because I'm famous. Because you're a dick, Brian. You stalked me, you yelled at me in front of my fans, you stole my freaking phone . . ."

Somewhere in the back of the ballroom I hear Gail yelling at people to get out of her way; she's already calling our insurer to make sure my abs are covered for battle wounds.

Brian inhales a long, shuddery breath. "Maybe." He glances over. "But I'm telling—*ow*—the truth." He slowly gets to his feet. His lip is bloody from where I nailed him. He stretches out a hand and I take it, painfully standing up (okay, so I might've sprained something, or bruised something very, very bad). "He controls you, man. And you were gonna let him take that girl away too."

Gail finally finds her way to us and takes me by the face. "*Dare*! Are you okay? Are you hurt? How many fingers am I holding up?"

"Three," I reply, realizing that Brian is no longer there. I whirl around, looking for him, but all I see is a black cape as he slips between two Orcs and disappears.

Gail yanks my face toward her again, inspecting my nose, then my lips, and muttering to herself in her mother-hen way about how much Mark is going to chew us out this time. "I always get into the worst trouble with you, Dare. We're heading back to L.A. and I'm locking you in your apartment until the premiere. That's a *promise*."

"Actually . . ." I remember the words on the side of the food truck that Elle left in. The Magic Pumpkin, "Charleston's Best Vegan Food Truck!" It's all beginning to make sense now. The chimichangas. The jokes. She was already so close. Brian's words echo like warning bells in my head.

You were gonna let him take that girl away too.

I should've told her the truth in the beginning. I shouldn't have been so scared of the consequences because I'll live through them, whatever they are. I just want to be real. For once. Without a mask, unscripted, unknown. I would rather live my life knowing that Elle hates me than live as fake Carmindor in her head.

"We're going to take a nice long vacation. It's going to be perfect—"

"No." I hold my ribs, trying not to grimace. I think I definitely bruised them. "I need to talk to my dad first."

THE PHONE RINGS ONCE, TWICE, BEFORE Mark picks up. I check my watch. 12:31 a.m. Way early out on the West Coast. He should still be up partying. Or going to some event sponsored by this film studio or that production company. Networking, he says. I remember the years he did nothing but network, night after night. My entire childhood was filled with it. I had more babysitters than I could name. And then one weekend, long after the divorce, he got me that toothpaste commercial gig, and three months later an audition for this OC-esque TV series called *Seaside Cove*. Then the headlines happened.

I rub the scar on my chin absently. I don't know how much I believe Brian, but I don't know whether I want to believe Mark either. I can't remember much from those weeks in the tabloids. It was a whirlwind of paparazzi and press and headlines, and it never really died down afterward. There was my life before the headlines, and after.

I wonder, in Elle's possible universe, who I would've become without them. Maybe in that universe I'd still have a father, and maybe I wouldn't have blamed Brian.

Maybe I'd be no one at all.

"Hello?" Mark grumbles.

"Hey, old man," I say brightly.

"Darien? What are you—what time is it?" I hear him shuffle around, and then he groans. "Darien, it's late over there. Aren't you supposed to be catching a flight?"

"Supposed to," I say. "It's probably taking off. I don't know."

There's an edge to his voice. "You don't know?"

I swallow the knot in my throat and concentrate on my polished leather boots. They're Carmindor's boots, actually. I haven't changed out of them yet. I'm fooling myself into thinking that maybe if I'm dressed like a hero, I can still act like one, holding on to the last ragged shred of courage left in me.

Lonny, sitting in a cushy hotel-room armchair, quietly sips a glass of sparkling water. Gail, in the chair beside him, scrolls through her phone. They're both listening, and I don't care. When I asked if they could stay in the room when I called Mark, they agreed without hesitation. It's a comfort. I guess because they're the closest thing I have to friends. Or parents.

"How do you *not* know? You are getting on that plane. You are coming home. Do you realize how much money those tickets are—"

"Did you leak those photos?" I blurt out. "The ones Brian took? From the yacht?" Gail looks up from her phone, her face pale with surprise. Mark stays quiet for a long moment.

"I realized that you needed to pick your friends carefully," he replies slowly, choosing his words carefully, just like he wants to pick my friends. My career. My girlfriends. And everything else. My entire life. "When I saw he had those photos, I had to do something. So I did. That way we stayed ahead of the news."

I sink onto the edge of the bed and stare at the beige carpet. "So you sacrificed my pride and privacy for a little fame."

"Those headlines got you Carmindor, Darien."

They got me Carmindor.

The words feel like a knife twisting in my gut; I remember the weeks after the headlines broke. Staying in my apartment, locking the doors, feeling the walls closing in around me. Then outside, wearing sunglasses and a hat everywhere, trying not to scroll through the headlines but reading them anyway. Feeling the shame solidify inside me, becoming hard, forming a wall.

"Were you ever going to tell me?"

"Darien, it's compli—"

"*Were you?*"

"Darien, I wanted what was in your best interest."

"And the pictures from the shoot? Was that you too? Or did Brian leak those on his own?"

"Don't be naive. All leaks are fake," Mark scoffs. I can practically see him drawing the air quotes as he says the word *leaks*. "Brian was hard up for cash, so I found him a PA gig on set. Told him to keep his head down and maybe snap a few things. Spy on your phone, if he could get it."

"You lied to me. You let me get slandered. Again. For what? A few minutes of fame?"

"To keep you relevant," my father says.

"Congrats," I reply bitterly, "it worked."

There's a long pause. "I know you probably hate me," Mark says. "You have every right to. But I'm not the bad guy here, I swear. I never wanted to be. The leaks, the attention, you and Jess—we're better because of it, yeah? It worked out perfectly. We survived."

"I guess," I say. He's right: I did survive. The film's in the can. I'm going to be a star. But Elle, losing Elle. That's the aftermath.

"Now," Mark continues, "I'm going to book you another flight. You've got a photo shoot in the morning, then a sit-down with a few press junkets and—"

"No."

"No?"

I take a deep breath, screwing my courage to the sticking place. "Rebook the shoot. Tell them something came up."

"Don't be ridiculous. You've got contracts to uphold for this movie. There's money on the line—"

"Dad, I don't want to be Carmindor for the money."

"Darien, this is a *job*."

I clench my jaw. "It's not about the money. Or the contracts. Or the photo shoots. Or the headlines. Or the notoriety. Or my insured abs— why the hell insure my abs, anyway? It's like Taylor Swift insuring her legs. It's *ridiculous*."

"Every precaution," he says. "It's just—"

But I cut him off. "Headlines or no headlines, I took the gig because of Carmindor. Because of *Starfield*. Because we used to sit down and watch the reruns together. Remember?"

"That was a long time ago, Darien."

Maybe. But sometimes it still feels like yesterday, when he was still my dad. "To me it's about the characters. It's about the story. The fans. It's about—" The words catch in my throat as I remember the conversations Elle and I had, about the Black Nebula, about the world, about the what-ifs.

"—it's about the impossible universe," I finish.

"What are you talking about?"

For once I manage to swallow my anger. "I want to be part of my own story again, and I—"

I realize that I can't stay in this limbo anymore. Between not having a father and having one. Unlike Elle, who would do anything to get her father back, I still have one.

"I want a new manager," I say at last. "I want my dad back."

"Are you . . . firing me?"

"Yeah. I am. I love you, Dad, but I am."

His voice turns hard. "Darien, listen to yourself. Your career. You can't just—"

"I am," I reply, and then I hang up.

Gail begins to collect her things from around the room. From the look on her face, she thinks she's fired too. "I'll be out of here soon. Mark said I'm supposed to—"

"Forget Mark," I tell her. "You are officially promoted, effective immediately." Her eyebrows shoot up. I toss her my phone, and she fumbles to catch it.

Gail's jaw goes slack. "You mean . . ."

"I mean I'm probably going to need you to go to L.A. and make some apologies at that photo shoot tomorrow," I say. "You can still catch a flight if you—"

"But I'm horrible at apologies!" She could not turn any paler. In fact, I think she's actually turning green. "What happened to Mark? Why can't—"

I grab her by the shoulders and turn her to face me. We lock eyes. "Gee, you're my number one. Always have been. You're the only person I trust. Now, if you don't want to, I understand, but I want to ask you anyway. We're a team, and always will be. Will you be my manager?"

"I . . ." Her mouth works silently, and then she closes her eyes and breathes deep. Some of the color returns to her cheeks. Finally, she opens her eyes and nods curtly. "You bet, Dare."

I grin, squeezing her shoulders. "You're the best."

"*Miss* the Best to you," she replies, returning my grin—but just as suddenly she drops it. "Oh, the flight—I have to catch that flight!" Spinning out of my grip, she grabs her purse from the floor and darts for the door. She pauses and turns back to me. "I promise I won't let you down."

And then she's gone, the door slamming behind her.

Lonny finishes his drink and stands. "So what's our plan?"

"You don't have to go," I tell him, shrugging out of Carmindor's jacket. "I'm sort of going AWOL, so it's not in your contract."

"Then as far as I'm concerned, I'm off the clock," he says, straightening his suit. "I can do whatever I want with my time, and I want to help you out. So what's the plan?"

"First," I say, "to the vending machines. With all this good luck, they gotta have an Orange Crush."

And holy gods of soda, Batman, by the glowing light of the great vending machines on the third floor, I spot a beautiful Orange Crush button, and when I push it an orange bottle rolls out. I crack the seal and drink to the sweet, sweet taste of victory.

"That's your plan?" Lonny says. "To drink a soda?"

I cap the bottle and shake my head, a half-crazy idea now fully formed in my head.

"I'm going to do what Carmindor should've done in the last episode of *Starfield*," I tell him. "I'm going after the girl."

ELLE

THERE HAVE BEEN ONLY THREE INSTANCES in my life that I thought I'd never get through. The first was when Mom died. I was too young to remember much, except the memory of Dad hugging me on a cold September morning and the smell of sterilized hospital rooms.

The second was that moment before Catherine came outside, while I sat on the porch waiting for Dad to come home. The air was humid and sticky, and I couldn't wait to show him the story I'd written about Carmindor and the Nox King. It was the best one yet. I was so happy.

And then my stepmother came outside, with the phone pressed to her shoulder, and said, "Come inside, Danielle. Robin isn't coming home."

I can't remember where I put that story. I stopped writing after that. I guess the blog came out of that hole—a little good in the impossible. And those two moments, I made it past eventually. But the third . . .

I'm not sure I'm going to make it through this one.

Because I lost my mother's shoe, I'm late for curfew, and as Sage turns onto my street I see my house, my parents' house, with the ugly FOR SALE BY OWNER sign that Catherine put up. All the lights are on and Catherine's Miata is in the driveway. On the porch, my stepmother stands with her arms crossed, hands cupping elbows, her face a stony unreadable expression. And on the Pumpkin's dashboard, the clock reads 2:05 a.m.

I am Princess Amara, and this is my Black Nebula.

Cal leans forward. She's pale and clearly nervous, wringing her hands. I don't want her to get in trouble at my expense—but I don't know what else to do. She seems adamant about going in with me, even though I told her she can sneak in through my window. There's no reason for both of us to get punished.

"You don't have to go." Sage slows down but doesn't stop entirely. She's being a good friend. She's the best friend. I'm glad I got to know her. "Or I can go with you."

But she can't go with us. I thought I'd be panicking more; that it would be clawing up my throat, stinging my insides like jellyfish kisses. But I'm surprisingly . . . calm. A few moments stranded in the eye of the hurricane.

Cal squeezes my shoulder. "I'll be right here too."

"Cal, you don't have to—"

"Stop trying to take all the blame," she interrupts. "I'm not my sister, and I'm not my mom. I'm sick of being put in this box. I'm not a box person. It's time Chloe and Mom learned that."

The Pumpkin comes to a full stop.

"God, she looks like a wet cat," Sage mutters.

"That's her normal look," I tell her.

Sage leans over and hugs me hard. "I'll see you tomorrow at work?"

"Yeah," I croak. "I mean, maybe." I hug her back and open the truck door, but Cal lingers for a moment, unsure how to say goodbye to Sage. I quickly avert my eyes. It's not my business, and it feels private.

As I step out onto the lawn, Catherine narrows her eyes at me. But then Cal follows me out of the truck, and Catherine's face morphs into anger—like a firework exploding. Just me is one thing, but me and Cal? Dread curls in my stomach like snakes. *She can't do anything*, I tell myself. *Don't be scared of her.*

But I am. I'm scared of her like Carmindor is scared of the Nox King, like Amara is scared of the Black Nebula. Before I found my parents' costumes and met Sage and found some kind of happiness, I didn't think Catherine could possibly take anything away that hasn't already been taken. But standing here, wearing my parents' things, the taste of watermelon punch on my tongue and David Bowie crooning "Ziggy Stardust" through the Pumpkin's speakers . . . I realize she can take away a whole lot more than I realized. I have a *life* now. I have things that matter.

I pull my dad's jacket over my shoulder. It smells more like Darien than me, like cinnamon and starch and sweat and a night I won't ever forget. Behind us, Sage forces the Pumpkin's into gear and, with a loud belch of black smoke, coasts down the road.

"Calliope . . ." Catherine looks down at her daughter from underneath her lashes. "I believe we need to talk. Chloe told me everything. I am very, *very* disappointed."

"Mom, I can explain," she says, but her mother cuts her off.

"Inside, please, before we make more of a scene."

Cal ducks her head and hurries into the house. Catherine's lips curl in disgust as I quietly follow. She slams the door shut, and Cal whirls around.

"Mom, I can explain. It's not what it looks like—"

"Oh I know what it looks like. I just didn't think you would lie to me so *blatantly*, darling," Catherine replies, her voice eerily cool. "Sneaking out of your tennis tournament? To go hang around with some druggie and your stepsister? Don't you want this varsity position? A future? Chloe seems to be the only one who does."

It clicks then, in an instant. Chloe arrived home before us and told Catherine the exact lie that would throw Calliope under the bus with me. I can't believe it for a second, because why would Chloe do that? They've been inseparable ever since I can remember.

Cal seems just as shocked. "But—that's not—Chloe—"

"Told me everything," Catherine finishes. "Upstairs. Now."

"But Mom—"

"Now!" Catherine snaps.

For a moment, I don't think Cal's going to go, but then she disappears, hurrying up the stairs. When the door to the twins' room slams, Catherine turns her gaze on me, sharp and hard.

"Where did you get those clothes?" Her voice is like knives. I stop in the foyer to wipe my bare feet, Mom's shoe—the one shoe I have left—is in my hand, and Catherine looks at me with disgust. Glitter is falling off around me, stuck in the folds of my dress, pasted to my skin as though I am part stardust too.

"They're mine," I say. "My parents'."

"And you had the audacity to drag Calliope into your nonsense?"

"It wasn't *nonsense*, it was a convention. We entered a contest."

"A *contest*?"

"A cosplay contest. Remember ExcelsiCon? Dad's dream? I wanted to be a part of—"

"I don't care what *you* want, you little brat!" Catherine exhales so hard it sounds like a hiss. "You *knew* Calliope was impressionable. You knew you could get her to go along with your schemes. This all started when you started working at that filthy food truck."

"It's not filthy!"

"The girls at the country club told me I had you on too loose a leash to let you work there, but I trusted you." She draws herself up full height, her silk robe gleaming. "You will never see that girl again, Danielle."

"Sage?" My heart plummets. "But it's not Sage's fault!"

"I will nip this in the bud before you disgrace all of us," she continues, raising her voice to drown mine out. "You will never, ever see her again. Do you hear me?"

The word hits me like a punch to the stomach. Never see Sage again? Ever?

"And you will quit that job," she adds, "effective immediately. You'll work somewhere *respectable*, where I can keep an eye on you."

"But—but it's my job!" I try to argue, my voice cracking. Quit the Magic Pumpkin? It's one of the only things I ever fought to have. One of the only things I got by myself—one of the only things I could get by myself. "I earned it! I like that job!"

"I can't trust you, Danielle," my stepmother says, "and if I can't trust you, you don't deserve what I give you."

"All I did was go to the convention my dad built!" I blink back the tears burning at the edge of my eyes. "And it's *my* con too! I went because he's my father! He's mine! I finally I felt like he'd be proud of me—why can't you?"

Catherine crosses her arms. "I can't be proud of a daughter who lies to me."

"*Daughter?* You never let me do anything! You've punished me for—for I don't know what! For *years!*" Tears burn my cheeks. "Why do you hate me?"

"Hate you?" She blinks slowly, as if it's the most absurd thing she's ever heard. "Danielle, I don't hate you."

I clench my jaw. "You sure haven't acted like it. All I ever wanted from you was one thing—just one. I wanted you to be proud of me. Like you're proud of Cal and Chloe. I just . . ." I squeeze my eyes closed, trying to stop the tears. I hate crying, but I can't stop. "I just wanted—wanted you to love *me*, too."

I put my face into the crook of my elbow, stifling my sobs. The mascara and glitter and all the good things from the con rub off onto my skin, leaving wet streaks.

When I finally manage to look up, Catherine's blue eyes are glittering in the foyer light. She doesn't respond for a long moment.

Finally, she tilts her head, smiling like she's trying to be gentle. "I've tried to love you, sweetie, but you make it so hard."

My sobs catch in my throat.

"Your obsession isn't healthy," she says briskly. "It wasn't healthy for your father either, living in a world of make-believe. That's all he ever did. That's all he ever was. It was only ever you, and him, and *Starfield*. And I hate how much you are like him."

My arm drops away and I stare at her, trying to see the lie behind the cream makeup and dark mascara, but her lips are set in a thin line and her eyes are dark, and I don't think she's lying.

"There were just so many things I wanted to change about him," she says. "And you."

"Change? To what?" I ask, my mouth running before I can stop it. "To the perfect daughter? To some cookie-cutter version of you? To someone you think is acceptable and worthy of your love? Why do I have to prove to you that I'm worthy?"

"Danielle, I only want what's best for you—"

"No, you want what's best for *you*!" I snap, my voice rising. "You never wanted me, admit it! I'm a *burden*. After Dad died, that's all I was. And if you hate me for being like him, *fine*, but I'm the best parts of my father. He raised me to fight for what I believe in and to be a good person—and he raised me to see the best in other people!" My voice is so loud, it's cracking. "But I let you trample over all the good things he gave me. But not today—today at the con, for the first time I felt like I belonged somewhere. And that's more than I've ever felt here! In my own parents' house! The one you're *selling*!"

Her eyes narrow. "*Starfield* isn't real, Danielle. The sooner you learn that, the better off you'll be."

Of course it's not real. I know it's not real. It's just as fake as the Styrofoam props they use and the cardboard sets and the tinny laser sounds and the ice cream machines they try to disguise as "data cores"—I know it's all fake. But those characters—Carmindor, Princess Amara, Euci, and even the Nox King—they were my friends when everyone in the real world passed around rumors behind my back, called me weird, shoved me into lockers, and baited me into thinking I was beautiful only to push me away just before we kissed. They never abandoned me. They were loyal, honorable, caring, and smart.

But I realize that trying to explain *Starfield* to Catherine is like trying to explain the sky to an anglerfish. Because she's none of those things, and never will be.

"Now you will go upstairs and take off that *ridiculous* outfit," she commands. I turn to leave, defeated, but Catherine isn't finished.

"And," she says, "you will give me your phone."

I freeze.

"Danielle!"

I reach for the phone in my jacket pocket. For a brief, crazy moment, I imagine that dream I had of me and Franco. Setting off west, never looking back. I knew it was just a dream, because this house can't move and without it I'm not sure who I would be. This was the last place I belonged, and I don't even belong here anymore, and soon it won't even be my home. I won't belong anywhere.

But if I have nowhere to go, what's the use in fighting?

Like ripping off a Band-Aid, I hand her my phone. Her manicured fingers curl around it. "Good. Now go to your room."

Tears come back before I can stop them and I take the stairs two at a time. Catherine doesn't come after me. I'm not worth the energy, and there's really nothing left for her to take. In my room, I press my forehead against the door and squeeze my eyes tight.

I can't take this anymore. I have to leave—now. But I don't have my phone. I can't call Sage and tell her what happened.

And Carmindor . . . In the end even *he* knew I was no one worth talking to.

When Darien called me *ah'blena* I almost thought it was him. That Darien Freeman was my Carmindor. But it couldn't be. The universe can't be that cruel. And Darien, like Carmindor, wouldn't talk to a nobody.

I clutch my dad's jacket and sink to the carpet, crying into the costume harder than ever. Because now the glowing constellations above me just look like fake glow-in-the-dark stars. And the coat just smells like sweat. And the house, old and creaky, is just cold. And the living room will never be waltzed in again.

That is why this universe is impossible: because all the good things are impossible to keep. The universe always takes them away.

DARIEN

Turns out, Charleston isn't the easiest place to go hunting for a food truck.

"I think this's it," I say, and tap the back of Lonny's seat. He pulls onto the side of the road. I think he's relieved. We've already been to three other food trucks before someone—at a shrimp and grits truck—had an inkling about where we might find one that's orange and yellow.

"Oh, you're lookin' for the Pumpkin," the older woman had said, rubbing her greasy hands on an apron that read G.R.I.T.S.: GIRLS RAISED IN THE SOUTH. "I think that old girl's somewhere over by the market today. That way," she pointed in the opposite direction—Kings Street, apparently—and gave us directions.

Travel tip: if you're visiting Charleston, know where you're going ahead of time. There are so many one-way streets, once you go down the wrong way you'll never want to drive in this town again. After nearly grilling a baby stroller and double tapping a marathon runner, we finally found an orange and yellow truck parked at the far side of the market toward one of the touristy piers.

Lonny flicks on the hazard lights. "I can wait," he says. "Or come with."

"I think I got this."

"You sure?" he rumbles, looking at me through the rearview mirror.

"Unless you *want* to come," I say. "For moral support?"

"I'm good, boss."

"Real pal you are. I'll call you when I need you." I get out of the car and watch Lonny pull away before I make my way over to the Magic Pumpkin. It's horrendously orange. You can see it a mile away, which is probably the point. Its entire body is painted to look like a pumpkin, with yellows and reds and blacks highlighting the drawn-on curves and ridges. A girl with bright teal hair leans against the counter, and my heart leaps when I recognize her—the same girl Elle drove away with.

"We're all out of fritters today," she says as I get close, without looking up from her magazine.

"I wasn't coming for the fritters."

"Well, I hope you aren't coming for the sweet potato fries either. Because we're out of those too."

"I'm not coming for food at all," I say. This girl kind of scares me.

"Huh." She still hasn't looked up. "So what do you want? I'm understaffed and irritated."

"I, um." I try to catch a peek into the back of the truck. Where's Elle? She has to be in there somewhere, doesn't she? I don't remember her ever talking about a day off. "Actually, I . . ." I swallow hard. "I thought I could find Elle here."

That piques her interest. She finally looks up at me. "Huh."

I shift. "Huh what?"

She shows me her magazine. My promo shoots from after *Hello, America*. I wince. "You look way better Photoshopped."

"That's a first," I say. "Hearing it out loud, I mean."

"Everyone probably thinks it." She puts down the magazine and cocks her head. "What're you doing here?"

"You wouldn't believe me even if I told you."

She lifts an eyebrow. "You're right."

I take a deep breath and pull out Elle's lost shoe. Her eyes widen. "Okay. I'm interested."

I explain everything—from the first text to someone I hoped was Robin Wittimer to the weeks talking with Elle to ExcelsiCon to the ball to the moment the truck pulled away. "I want to find her and tell her the truth. I want to apologize."

She leans farther over the counter, debating. "Why? So you can clear your conscience? You just gonna run away again, *Carmindor*?"

It's irony, we both know. Carmindor never runs away from anything. He stays and he fights and he deals with the consequences. And I think we all have the chance to be him.

I think this is my chance, now.

"No," I reply. "I won't run away from her again. Unless she's chasing me with something and then I'll probably run—but never from *her*."

Teal-hair girl debates for a second, chewing on a chunk of bright pink bubblegum. "Well, Elle quit. Or her stepmother quit for her. And she's not answering her phone and she isn't at home. I have no way of contacting her."

My heart begins to sink.

"But," she holds up a finger, "I thiiiink know where she might be. If you're interested. I can take you there."

I hesitate. "Now? But aren't you—"

"It's a restaurant on wheels, Carmindor. It's *supposed* to move." She closes the serving window, climbs through the middle to the cab, and pushes open the passenger door with her foot. I climb into the seat. The entire vehicle smells like pumpkin fritters and oil and twenty-year-old leather seats.

"I'm Sage, by the way," she says, as she cranks up the monster of a truck, "and I suggest you buckle up."

The Magic Pumpkin roars to life with a belch and begins to rattle like it'll come apart at the seams. I quickly heed her warning and wrap the seatbelt around me. She forces the truck into gear and slams on the gas, swirling onto a one-way street with the speed of a NASCAR driver. My eyes dart to the rearview mirror—I see Lonny has fired up the rental car and is hot on our tail. Sage tears through historic Charleston, the crowds simply peeling out of the way, and points us out of the city.

"So . . . where are we going?" I ask, once I'm sure I'm not going to die.

"This country club over in Isle of Palms. It's horrible."

"Then why is she working there?"

"Because she wasn't supposed to go to the convention," Sage says. The truck jostles across one of the many bridges in and out of town, their white suspension cords intertwined overhead. "Her stepmother didn't want her to, but we took the truck—I got in major trouble for that by the way, grounded until the sun rises in the west. Like hell I am," she adds under her breath, before going on. "But we went anyway and entered that contest. We thought we could make it home but—"

It begins to make sense now. "That's why you left in such a hurry."

"Bingo." Sage grins. "And now I'd bet the Pumpkin that her step-mom's got her chained up at the club."

Sage turns off the bridge, following the signs to Pointe Greene Country Club. Everything suddenly grows greener, with lush grass and dense foliage. The roads improve, too. She follows the winding route up to a checkpoint and eases the truck to a stop in front of a yellow barrier arm. She leans out as the guard on duty opens his window.

"Business?" the guard asks.

"Just here to look around," she replies. "I think I might want to become a member."

He twitches his mustache. "I'm sorry, I can't let you in without permission."

"From who?"

"People who belong to the country club," he says slowly, as though Sage is stupid or something, and gives her a lookdown, from her teal hair to her piercings to her *Killer Queen* halter top. "And I don't think you're a member."

Her hands tighten around the steering wheel. She scowls. "I'll show you what I'll do to your *member* if you—"

"Excuse me," I interrupt, leaning forward in my seat. I flick up my Aviators and put on my best smile. Slipping into Darien Freeman in the blink of an eye. I never thought I'd actually be happy for the mask.

The security guard narrows his eyes. "What?"

"Hi. Darien. You might know me. *Starfield?*"

His eyebrows dart up. Ah, *bingo*.

"I've got a friend who works here, and I'm in town for just a little while. Do you think you could, you know, let us in to see her? Please?"

He begins to nod—*thank you* Starfield, *thank you*—but then his eyebrows collapse down again. "I don't care if you're the prince of England," he says. "You can tell your friend to back her pretty truck up. You ain't getting in."

"Well that's rude," I mumble.

Sage mutters something under her breath and slams the truck into reverse. The security guard sits back triumphantly and begins to close the window.

My shoulders slump. "I guess I'll wait until she gets off work."

"No."

"Why not? It's only a few hours, right?"

"Because the only way Elle can get home is with her stepmom. And if the security guard won't let us in, what do you think Catherine'll do?" She eases the truck to a stop and slowly slides it into gear. The engine belches black smoke.

"What else can we do?"

Sage narrows her eyes. "This day, we fight."

She slams her foot on the gas pedal. The truck's tires squeal, burning rubber, before they catch traction with a jerk. I grapple with my seatbelt. You'd think by now I'd be good with stunts. You think I wouldn't want to kiss my butt goodbye.

You'd be wrong.

Sage pulls the truck to the side and we curve around the barrier, barely squeezing through. The security guard throws open the window, his face beet red, and shouts after us, but Sage just slams the PLAY button on the stereo and cranks the music as loud as it'll go.

The *Starfield* theme roars from the speakers like the trumpets of war.

ELLE

THE COUNTRY CLUB IS ALREADY STIFLING. This morning, Catherine
yanked me out of bed at six and made me clean out the attic for good:
all of my *Starfield* DVDs, the statue of Carmindor, the replica communi-
cator toy that Dad got me as a kid, and a few posters and postcards and
collectibles (including one hella rare Pez dispenser). Then she drove me
over here, chatted up the manager, and five hours later I'm stuck at the
café on the veranda in a sweat-stained green shirt and khakis, bored out
of my mind. I hated this job when I had it before, and I hate it now. But
I've given up trying to fight.

The café overlooks most of the greens at the country club. To the left
is the pool, to the right is about a mile of shorn golfing hills. Most of the
morning I've been serving middle-aged golfers with too much time and
money on their hands, but they're not the only ones here today. Chloe
and her friends are sitting at a corner table, gossiping so loudly I know
it's on purpose. James sits right beside her, but unlike last year when it
seemed she couldn't be close enough (while he was pretending to fall in
love with me), today she couldn't be less aware of him. She's too good
for him now. Or something. Cal's there too, in her usual chair, but she's
completely silent.

She had come up to me when I was cleaning this morning, when
Catherine wasn't looking, and held something out.

"Chloe and I found this with the dress in the trunk upstairs. Did . . . did you write this?"

The paper was yellowed with age, but I would remember it even if a hundred years had passed. Tears welled up in my eyes, even though I didn't think I could cry anymore, and I took it, nodding.

"It's—it's a story. Fanfiction. I used to write them for Dad all the time." I blink back the tears and sniff. "Where did you find this again?"

"In the trunk. There are a billion of them. He must've saved them all."

"All of them?" I look down again at the piece of paper. "Thank you, Cal."

She smiled, shyly, as if she shouldn't. "It's the least I can do."

But now Cal is silent. And the sound of Chloe's voice is blasting across the veranda like a foghorn.

"He was *such* a dream," she gushes. "And *so* nice. And *way* sexier in person. Gives you a run for your money, James," she adds, playfully patting his knee. "I wish y'all could've been there. Like, it was a *blast*."

"How did you get tickets?" James asks.

"I bought them."

"I didn't know you liked that kind of stuff," says Erin, the twins' second-in-command. "You're always picking on your sister about it."

The pictures went viral overnight: two dancers at a cosplay ball, a movie star and a regular girl in a dress made from the night sky. "Darien Freeman, Prince Charming?" the headlines read. And the girl they're calling Geekerella. I can't say it isn't catchy. You'd think everyone would be freaking out, seeing me with Darien Freeman, but the girl in those pictures? She's wearing a mask. And Chloe, surprise, came down this morning with dyed-red hair—just like mine.

Her YouTube channel gained ten thousand followers literally overnight. Her views have skyrocketed. She's gone from internet nothing to internet celebrity at warp speed. There's even an online petition to get Darien to come meet Chloe again so they can have their "happily ever after," which I wouldn't be surprised if Chloe started herself. Honestly, I don't know what's funnier: Chloe pretending to be me, or that Excelsi-

Con me is famous. Or as famous as internet celebrities go. *The girl who danced with Darien Freeman.*

Chloe waves her hand. "*Step*sister. And it's not my fault she's weird. Speaking of my which—Elle!" She calls out, glancing over her shoulder at me. "Elle! Another latte!"

With a sigh, I dog-ear the page in my book. "Whip or no?" I ask, taking the milk out of the fridge under the counter.

"What do you *think*? And it better be soy."

I fix up her drink and walk it over to her. She can't be bothered to come get it herself.

"I had to escape out of there so fast, though." Chloe takes the cup without even thanking me. "I didn't even have time to give him my name! And now all these other girls are pretending they're me. Look." She holds out her phone, flicking through a bunch of hashtagged photos. "Posers."

"I hear she lost a slipper," I say. Chloe's eyes narrow to slits but I shrug it off because what have I got to lose now? I've totally given up. "Maybe the real girl has the slipper?"

"You didn't say she lost a slipper," another friend, blond hair with purple tips, says. "Chloe, that's it! You should totally—"

"I lost the other slipper," Chloe grinds out. She sips her coffee, gags, and spits it out. "Ugh, I said nonfat, not soy!"

She shoves the mug back at me. Liquid sloshes over the rim, all over my apron and green polo shirt. Hot—scalding hot. I yelp, jumping backward. The latte splatters across the floor.

"*Oops,*" she sneers, whipping her head around to ignore me. "As I said, I lost the slipper, so the point's moot."

I grab a handful of napkins from a dispenser on another table and begin mopping up the coffee. James takes a few napkins too, gets out of his chair, and helps me. Chloe glances over. "James, you don't have to do that. That's why she's *working.*"

"I know but—" James cocks his head. "Is that . . . *thunder?*"

"Of course it's not thunder. It's gorgeous outside." Chloe rolls her eyes as I finish cleaning up the spill. "Honestly. Let's just get going."

She takes a club from her golf bag and twirls it in her hands as she heads onto the green. Then she snaps her manicured fingers for us to follow, and we do. With a sigh, I hike her golf bag onto my shoulder and set off down the grassy slope. Of all the days for Phil the Caddy to be sick, it had to be today. Or any day. And of course my boss doesn't care if I leave my post at the café—not if Catherine's daughter needs a caddy.

Once we're out in the sunlight, Chloe drops the ball on the grass and squints into the distance. Then she pulls back and swings. The balls arcs high into the air and plops down five hundred feet away, in a sand trap.

"Oops," she drones. "Elle, fetch that for me, would you?"

The thunder is getting louder, even though the sky is crystal clear. I wonder if Carmindor is looking at the same sky. And then, with a pang, I wonder why I care.

"Elle!" Chloe screeches. I start after her but the noise is so loud now, and I swear I've heard it before. A deep rumbling, like a dragon. Or . . . *no.*

No way.

Suddenly, one of the gardeners setting out the sprinklers for the evening yelps and throws himself to the side. Over the bushes to the parking lot, emerging like the great pumpkin in flight, flies an orange and yellow truck. It hits the ground with enough force to carve a dent in the immaculate grass and tears across the greens toward us, the bright-green fender smiling with a mouthful of leaves and twigs. And with the truck, blaring from the open windows so loud I can hear the speakers pop, is the *Starfield* theme.

"Ohmygod, what is *that*?" Chloe gasps.

James blinks. "A food truck?"

Cal beams. "I think it's called the Magic Pumpkin."

The truck skids to a stop in front of us. The windshield wipers flick on against the leaves, and Sage gives a whoop from the driver's seat. "That was SO AWESOME!"

I drop the golf bag and run up to Sage and throw my arms around her. "I'm so sorry!" I croak, hugging her tight. "Catherine took my phone and I couldn't explain and—I'm sorry. I'm sorry, I'm sorry . . ."

She returns the hug, smelling like the place where I belong—pumpkin fritters and day-old coconut oil. "I missed you too! You wouldn't *believe* who I picked up today."

"I told you not to pick up hitchhikers," I say.

She shrugs. "I'm trying to turn over a new leaf—"

Just then a black-haired young man falls out of the passenger door and all but kisses the ground. He rights himself quickly, leaning against the truck. Even though he's a little green, everyone immediately recognizes him.

Chloe's blond friend gasps. "Ohmygod . . ."

"Is that . . ." James says.

Chloe stands a little straighter, her eyes wide as saucers. "*Darien!*"

At the sound of his name, Darien Freeman quickly pulls back his shoulders and jerks his head toward her. There's a subtle shift in his face—a rehearsed set to his lips, a levelness of his eyebrows—that makes me think of the masquerade. A mask.

He turns to me. "Elle—"

"Darien!" Chloe cries again, as she drops her club and hurries over to him. "Ohmygod it *is* you!" She looks around at her friends, her smile broadening in an *I Told You So* sort of way. "James—James, get this on video!" She slaps him on the arm to get him moving, and he pulls out his phone. She flips her hair back and rushes up to Darien. "Darien! I didn't know how you would find me—was it the petition? You know I started that petition . . ."

"I can't believe she was telling the truth," Erin whispers to James, who nods, shocked. They're literally speechless. I never thought I'd see the day.

My heart is in my throat when I tell it not to be, it's speeding up when I tell it not to expect much. I don't know why he's here—he knows Chloe isn't the girl he danced with—but of course he's succumbing to her charms. Who wouldn't?

"It took a while. I—I just wanted to formally apologize," he says.

Chloe feigns shock. "Apologize? For what? And how did you find me?" she asks, touching his biceps, leaning toward him. To her, flirting comes as natural as breathing.

Right. Because she's the one who wanted him anyway. Not me. Maybe in some other universe. But here—not me.

But then he tilts his head and glances over. At me. And the mask begins to slip away, little by little, until I can see something familiar underneath. He smiles at me. "I just came to return something to Elle."

"*Elle?*" Chloe echoes.

He holds up a slipper made of starlight.

"Well, *ah'blena?*" he asks, offering it to me.

Ah'blena. There's only one person who's ever called me that, who's ever wanted to.

My heart rises into my throat like a balloon.

Carmindor.

In front of Chloe and her friends, in front of James who pretended to love me and Cal who learned to love herself, and Sage who taught me that being who you are is okay, I slip a foot out of my boat shoe (ugh, country club rules) and set it before me.

He kneels and gently takes my heel, and then slips my mother's starlight slipper right onto my waiting foot.

DARIEN

SHE STARES DOWN AT ME, HER messy braid of dyed-red hair spilling over her shoulder. She pushes up her boxy black glasses and steps forward, hesitant, like I'm playing a trick on her. A light brushing of freckles dot her cheeks. I noticed them before, but now I want to connect them like constellations, a starry sky on skin that is slowly but surely turning red. Glowing.

Elle.

Not Princess Amara, not the girl from the convention who broke my nose (still blaming her, don't argue), not a stranger I can't trust. I don't know how I imagined meeting her—really meeting her, without a mask or a costume or a facade—I don't even remember what I thought she might look like. How I imagined her. How I thought she'd be.

Because this is the only Elle I could ever imagine. She's the only possibility that could have ever existed. I won't say that she is perfect, or that she is the most beautiful girl I have ever seen, but the moment her gaze finds mine, she's the best parts of the universe. She's a person I would love to spend a lifetime with on the observation deck of the *Prospero*.

She swallows hard, her lips tightly together. The damp grass begins to seep into my jeans and I hear Lonny's distinctive "keep back, please," behind me, but I don't want to get up. I want to stay locked here in this moment. I wait, wondering if she could—ever—forgive me. The Carmindor me, the actor me, the human me—Darien Freeman and Carmindor combined.

Finally, so quietly I almost can't catch it—although I don't need to, I'm watching her lips and read the words in the air—she speaks. Says what I never thought I'd hear from her.

"I hear the observation deck is nice this time of year, Carmindor."

ELLE

HE DOESN'T ANSWER FOR A MOMENT, but then he laughs. It's soft and deep, like a velvet cake wrapped in creamy mousse. Eventually he replies—like I hoped he would, like I wished he would, my heart soaring up and up and up into space, "Only on the south side of Metron."

He doesn't look like Darien Freeman. He looks like any guy with dark curly hair, wearing a *Starfield* shirt that's a little too small, faded jeans, and old Vans. He looks like someone who could play Carmindor if given the right color uniform, or someone you could meet at the mall.

There's a scar on his chin that Carmindor doesn't have, and a purpling bruise spreading around his cheeks, which—oh right. I guess that was my fault. He's rubbing the back of his hand against one of his eyes like he has something in it. Like tears, maybe. Oh, Nox's ass, is he crying?

"I thought you'd hate me," he says, standing up. "I didn't write that last text message—it's a long story but I didn't write it. But I didn't own up to it either. I was scared. I thought if I told you who I was you'd hate me."

"Oh you big dork!" I wrap my arms around him in a hug. He puts his arms around me too, and buries his face in my hair. "Stop crying, you're gonna make me cry."

"I'm not crying," he strangles out, clearly crying. "Just to clear the air, I won't always look this good. So if you're just charmed by my killer abs . . ."

I press my hand against his stomach. "We both know they're air-brushed."

"How dare you. I won't look as good is what I'm saying."

"Well, it's a good thing I didn't fall for your charming looks."

He hesitates. "So you can forgive me? For lying to you? For—"

I press a finger to his lips. It's a good question. One I don't know the answer to, but I remember our waltz, and his coming to my defense, and I think . . . "I think I *could* forgive you if . . ."

"If?"

"If you call me *ah'blena* again."

He takes my hand and steps closer, so close my bones are jittery. He smells like the Magic Pumpkin and fresh deodorant and cinnamon, and it's a scent I want burned into my memory. I want it on my clothes. I want his gaze, the way he looks at me—like I'm the last star in the night sky and the first one at dusk—branded on my heart. He's tall, but not so tall that I'm looking up his nose into his cerebral cortex. And he's unsure and he's courageous and conflicted and so very . . . Darien.

The real one.

"*Ah*' . . . ," he begins, enunciating every syllable, raising his hand to my chin, "*blen* . . . ," tilts my face up, slowly drawing toward me, like two supernovas about to collide, " . . . *a*."

And somehow, in this impossible universe, his lips find mine.

"Got it," James says somewhere behind me. "And . . . uploaded!"

"Uploaded?" Chloe echoes, her voice bordering on a shriek. "No—no take it down! Take it down right now!"

"Excuse me, miss?" A huge burly guy in a suit—Darien's bodyguard, I guess—claps a giant hand on her shoulder. "I'm going to need you to calm down." When he sees me looking, he shoots me a subtle thumbs-up.

Darien slowly pulls away from me, smiling. We can't stop smiling, can't look away enough to care. The entire world could be falling to the invasion of the Nox and we wouldn't be the wiser. "I've wanted to do that ever since you called me *ah'blen*."

"I'm glad you know what it means," I reply, tongue-in-cheek, remembering *Hello, America*. "But what if I was bald? You didn't even know what I looked like."

"Shared it," Cal confirms, looking at her own phone.

Sage peers over her shoulder and nods. "Nice. Twitter, Tumblr—want to hashtag it?"

"Done."

"Stop it! This isn't funny!" Chloe cries. "You are the worst! I can't believe you're *ruining* this for me! You all are!"

Darien chuckles. "You're behind *Rebelgunner*. That's worse."

I scrunch my nose. "Is it, really?"

"Oh yeah. You're the enemy."

"I'll just keep you on your toes."

He mock-gasps. "I wouldn't want to jeopardize the integrity of a critic!"

I grin against his mouth. "Then you better kiss me again. I want to make sure I get that part right for my next post."

"Now *that* I can do, Princess." And he kisses me again. It isn't the kind of kiss to end a universe of possibilities. It's the exact opposite.

It's the kind of kiss that creates them.

ELLE

EIGHT MONTHS LATER

I STARE OUT THE TOWN CAR window in amazement.

"They're monsters," I mutter to myself, looking at all the fans. I imagined myself getting out onto the red carpet with the greatest of ease, but there's no way that's happening with this crowd—let alone in this dress. I couldn't even wiggle out of the Magic Pumpkin at prom, and now I'm supposed to just casually slip myself out of the back of a black SUV? *Ha*.

Sage and Cal gaze out their windows too, their hands laced together. I don't think they've stopped holding hands since that day at the country club. And I don't think they're going to stop anytime soon. They're even going to the same city for college. I mean, New York is a huge place and there are tons of colleges there, but they'll still be in the same city. Sage even designed their wardrobe for the premiere tonight: a sleek pantsuit—with a subtle print in the shape of starwings—for herself, and a slinky dark-purple dress that swirls in and out of itself like the Black Nebula for Cal.

"I've never seen so many people—uh, *dog*!" Sage scowls, shoving the brown Dachshund off her pantsuit. "This is premium quality! Next time you jump on me I'll skin you and wear you as a hat!"

Frank the Tank swishes his tail and gives a yip. I pick him up and stroke him under the chin. "Shhhh, Auntie Sage didn't mean that."

"Oh like hell I didn't!"

"You'd clash with her wardrobe," I whisper into the Frankenator's ear. "You'll never be a hat."

He barks again, tongue lolling happily out of the side of his mouth, and Sage scowl-smiles. Under her thorny exterior, she's actually grown attached to the Frank.

After the con, Catherine was still . . . well, she was still Catherine. She never apologized for her words, but I never expected her to. I just began treating her with the exact courtesy she showed me. Which was none.

So on the night of my eighteenth birthday last September, I packed my bags, got into the Magic Pumpkin idling in the driveway (surely drawing the ire of all the neighbors), and left. I didn't even write a note. For the rest of my senior year I lived with Sage and her mom. At night, I missed my house. I missed the way it creaked and groaned. I missed the leaks. But I learned that when I closed my eyes, I was still home. I still saw my parents waltzing in the living room. I still smelled Dad's burnt roast in the oven. I could still remember following him around as I read my fanfics. It was all still there, tucked tightly away inside me. The house might have belonged to my parents, but Mom and Dad weren't the house. They were in me, and wherever I went I carried them along.

The car slowly moves up in the cue line. There are so many people out there, waving signs and shouting Darien's name. Some say I HEART DARIEN, others I WANT TO WABBA-WABBA WITH YOU. It reminds me of the crowd I first saw on *Hello, America*.

I lift Franco so he can see all the crazy people too.

"So is your lover boy gonna meet you on the carpet?" Sage asks.

I shrug. "I think so."

"You *think* so?"

"Uh, I've been a little preoccupied, remember?" I put Franco back down and scrub him behind the ears. "That whole cross-country move?

Not to mention orientation at school. And Darien's been insanely busy with promo. So I've mostly just been talking with his manager, Gail."

Long-distance relationships are hard. I found that out right away. The video got an enormous number of views, but reality soon settled in and Darien went back to postproduction, promo, and the next season of *Seaside Cove*. Sometimes I would see him with other girls in magazines—just friends, I knew—and I pushed down the jealous part of me. I tried not to think too much about it. Senior year was busy anyway, between SATs and college prep and applications and scholarships. Plus, I had Sage and Cal to hang out with, and I even went to a party or two. No country club people there, of course.

So it was okay that Darien went along with his life, and I mine. We never missed saying goodnight to each other, though. Not once.

But now that we'll be on the same side of the country, in the same city, it makes me nervous. Nervous because of his larger-than-life persona. Nervous because I don't know if I want to be part of that circus. Nervous because I have my whole life ahead of me, and this is just one small part of it. An important part, but a small one.

I don't know if I can keep balancing on the tightrope. I'm starting at UCLA in the fall, film studies, because apparently my blog garnered the attention of some film professor and he liked my *Starfield* critiques enough to vouch for me despite my grades. My entire world is about to open up and bloom. Do I really want a famous boyfriend on top of all that?

I bounce my knees nervously as our car reaches our destination. Cameras flash like strobe lights in a haunted house. I stare down the red carpet like a too-long hallway. I gulp.

Finally, the car stops. "Okay, misses," the driver says, "here we are."

Sage and Cal look at me expectantly. "So: question," Sage says. "Does this mean we can't gripe about his bad acting anymore?"

"Since when did I say his acting was bad?"

Sage raises an eyebrow, and my smile fades.

"Not a word, you hear me?" I poke a finger in her face.

"My lips are sealed." She grins. "After you, Geekerella."

I sigh—one BuzzFeed article and you've got a nickname for life, apparently—and wrap my free hand around the door handle. Breathe in, breathe out. The world is watching. Even Catherine and Chloe, somewhere, on that giant TV of theirs. Or maybe they're sitting in their new condo in Mount Pleasant, in an immaculate living room, looking for someone else to make miserable.

You can do this, Elle, I tell myself. *You went to a cosplay ball alone. A red carpet's* nothing.

Channeling my inner Princess Amara, I open the door to a raging flash of cameras. I slide out, only slightly stumbling on the curb, and clutch Franco tightly to like he's a football and the theater door is the goalpost. I just have to get there.

I strain my lips over my teeth in something that I hope is a smile, and move down the red carpet. Thank god I decided to wear my Doc Martens instead of those three-inch heels Sage suggested. I'd have done fallen flat on my face.

"What's your name, gorgeous?" asks a paparazzo.

"Here with someone?" another asks.

"Oh look, over there! I think that's the contest winner!" someone else adds, pointing to a tall dark-skinned woman making her way down the red carpet—the girl who won, way back at ExcelsiCon—and they flutter off to her like moths to a flame.

I close my eyes and take a deep breath. Holy overload, Batman, how can Darien do this twenty-four-seven?

I hold Franco a little tighter to my side. "Talk about star-crazy, huh, buddy?" I whisper to him. "C'mon, maybe I can get you a hotdog at the concessions stand—if there *is* one."

Behind me Cal gasps, grabbing Sage by the arm. "Oh my god, that's Jessica Stone!" She points down the red carpet to a beautiful dark-haired girl signing a fan's *Starfield* poster. "God I love her—not as much as you, though."

"Oh no, I'd be okay if you loved her more," Sage replies. "Maybe we can share her. Hey, Elle, is that Darien with her?"

A knot forms in my throat. It *is* Darien. He came to my high school graduation a few weeks ago—briefly, in sunglasses—but seeing him across the red carpet feels like I haven't seen him in years. He looks so different in his natural habitat, relaxed and magnetic, an arm around Jessica as he talks warmly to a news camera. Everyone around drinks him in, wanting more. And for a moment, I feel so, so small.

"We should go over," Sage says, but I catch her before she can. She shoots me a strange look. "Why not?"

"I just—he's busy. It's fine. I'll find him later."

"But he's right there now," she insists, furrowing her eyebrows.

"If she doesn't want to go, she doesn't have to," Cal says. "I mean, he does look busy."

"Too busy for his own—"

I cut her off. "Ssh. We're not, like, official. To the press."

Sage glowers but quickly gets distracted. "Ooh is that Calvin What's-His-Face?" She loops her arm through Cal's and pulls her down the red carpet.

I swallow the knot in my throat and look down at Franco. "Well, at the very least, you'll be my date tonight, right, Frankie?"

"Replacing me already, are you?" asks a velvety voice above the din of the crowd.

I glance up.

Darien, standing a few feet away, puts his hands in his pockets. His suit cuts him at all the right angles, sharp and acute. He's not quite as bulky as last summer, his hair is a little longer for the new season of *Seaside*. He raises a single dark eyebrow. It's infuriating how well he does that.

A blush burns the tips of my ears. "I mean, he is a better actor than some people."

"Ouch."

"And he matches me perfectly," I add, fanning out my dress with my free hand. I told Sage to sew me a dress the exact color of Darien's Carmindor jacket. Brass buttons line my corset, glitter sweeping up the bottom hem as though I ran through a puddle of gold. Franco has a matching blue vest that almost doesn't fit around his belly.

The edges of Darien's lips quirk up. "It's the wrong color blue, you know."

I glance up into his eyes. "I dunno, I hear the Carmindor in this new film wears it right enough."

He smiles. It's wide, unabashed, no secrets tucked into the edges. "You look beautiful."

I return his smile. Why am I so nervous talking to him here? Like I'm balancing on a tightrope, afraid I'll fall. "You look—you know how you look. I don't have to inflate your bratty ego. You look terrible. That's how you look. Like you didn't go to sleep until 2 a.m."

"Actually four-thirty, and you know your nose twitches when you lie, right?" He touches his own nose, approaching me slowly.

I scrunch my nose and look away. "It was around four-thirty for me too."

His shoulders sag a little. "I'm sorry I texted so late last night."

"It's fine! Seriously. I know you were off saving the galaxy—" I wave my hand toward Jessica. Getting my drift, he gives me a level look. "I know things are going to get crazy for you for a while—"

"Exactly," he interrupts, "which is why I wanted to ask you . . ."

A reporter calls his name. "Who's that girl?" the reporter asks.

"Are you two a couple?"

"Where's she from, Darien?"

"Is she the girl from last summer?"

Another chimes in, then another—or maybe it's a paparazzo, they all look alike now. Even blogs are considered newspapers here. Everything is. Tweets and instas and tumbls and snapchats being fired off faster than warp speed. The sooner we axe whatever rumor is brewing, the better.

"We're just fr—" I say when Darien steps closer, taking his hands out of his pockets. He reaches for my free hand and laces his fingers through mine. My words catch in my throat.

He turns his face down toward mine, pressing his lips against my ear. "Quick, when the Nox invaded District Eleven in episode thirty-four, what did Carmindor and Princess Amara do?"

My eyebrows furrow. "They . . . joined forces?"

He nods gravely. "Elle, would you join forces with me? Together we can defeat the Nox."

I stare at him wordlessly. Cameras continue to flash. Franco woofs, his tail spinning like a windmill.

"Elle?"

Do I want to? Do I really want to? I try to imagine the opposite—a universe without Darien. A universe without his goodnight texts, and teasing words, and those secret smiles he reserves only for me—the ones that are crooked and caring—and suddenly I realize that I don't like that universe at all. It wouldn't be nearly as impossible.

And what good is this universe if it isn't impossible?

"But what about—what about your promo stuff?" I grapple for words. "And marketing? And making alliances and playing the field and—"

He brings my hand up to his lips and kisses it. "I want you, *ah'blena*. I want to try this thing with you, whatever this is. I want you to be my co-pilot. And I want to ask you before the movie, in case you really hate it."

Of course he would be afraid of that. Of course he'd be that big of a doofus. I press my forehead to his, the paparazzi snapping so many photos they blind me like stars. "If you screw up Carmindor," I say between my smile, so it looks like we're whispering sweet nothings instead of throwing shade, "then I will personally make your life a living hell on my blog."

Beneath us, Franco sticks out his tongue, looking from me to Darien expectantly.

"Do you really mean that, *ah'blena*?"

"I promise-swear, *ah'blen*."

He bends close, despite the crowds, despite the cameras, despite

Franco's nose-diving into his suit pocket where he's probably keeping a snack, and kisses me. Around us, the flashes flare like the thrusters of the good ship *Prospero*, sending my heart rocketing into the farthest reaches of this impossible universe.

STARFIELD IGNITES THE STARS

By Danielle Wittimer

PREVIOUSLY PUBLISHED ON
REBELGUNNER.COM

WITH A LEGACY A BRIGHT AS *Starfield*'s, expectations are high. Decades have passed since the series first aired, but *Starfield* still stands on its own beside such behemoths as *Star Trek* and *Star Wars*, and fist-bumps with *Firefly* and *Battlestar Galactica*. Though the fandom was small, it was passionate. We Stargunners believed that we would follow Carmindor anywhere—even into the Black Nebula.

And going into this film, I thought that was where it was leading us—into the unknown. Nostalgia can't compete with newfangled lens flares and artistically shaky camera angles. I hardened my heart for disappointment, I lowered my expectations, I gave in to the knowledge that my Carmindor would never be on the screen. And although I was not wrong, I was surprised.

The film opens with an attack on the Federation ship *Prospero* by unknown enemy forces. And anyone who has seen the TV series will know what happens next. You will gird your loins and you will cross your heart—and the Black Nebula will open, and you will be sucked in with it.

For viewers, and especially for fans, it's a moment of considerable trepidation; the fate of the universe literally hangs in the balance. And then he steps onto the bridge: Federation Prince Carmindor, black boots shined and polished, the insignia of the Federation impressed into the leather, clad in a blue a little *bluer* than his original uniform. But beyond outward appearances, Darien Freeman plays Carmindor a little differently. A little more unsure, a little more self-doubting when it comes to his own judgment. It's the one thing I miss from his character in the original, that utter confidence in everything he was.

But Darien Freeman brings a depth to our Federation Prince that David Singh left untapped: a flawed and deeply human side of a character we all know and love. Freeman's Carmindor is younger, brasher, and less heroically self-assured, but he's still Carmindor, always thinking, always striving to be better than the person he was moments before. Maybe there's room to grow, but that's how I fell in love with this character in the original, because of his idealism, his belief that you could be bigger than your bones. And with Jessica Stone's self-possessed, sharp-tongued Princess Amara and Calvin Rolfe's wisecracking Eucinedes beside him at the helm, this captain is driving a considerably entertaining ship.

Not everything in the movie is perfect. The catch-up expository dialogue can get wooden (especially for already-informed Stargunners), and the cliffhanger ending may leave some viewers unsatisfied. But even with its shortcomings, the reboot manages to capture the heart of the TV series everyone fell in love with: that if you believe in yourself and have a few good friends, then you can do anything. You can *be* anything. So, as the saying goes:

Look to the stars. Aim. Ignite.

Starfield opens nationwide this weekend. The sequel is slated for next summer.

ACKNOWLEDGMENTS

THIS BOOK WAS A STRANGE GIFT to me, and this fangirl has a bajillion people to thank—especially my agent, who brought this gift to my in-box, and my editor, who told me to run wild.

But most of all?

This story would never be possible without fandom. And I would never have picked up a pen if not for fanfics. That was my community, where I grew up—in the midst of flaming reviews and shipping wars and OTPs and AU!fics and headcanons and songfics and half-baked homages to *My Immortal*. In high school, when I was sad or felt helpless, the comments and reviewers and friends I met in fandom helped me realize that I wasn't ever as alone as I thought.

And yeah, there might not be real magic in this world, but there is the power of fandom—the power of passionate people who, when working together, can birth movies out of canceled one-season sci-fi shows, resurrect fictional towns like Stars Hollow, and create endearing fan-musicals that will last far longer than its Muggle counterpart—and that kind of magic will never disappear.

So I want to thank you. You, the reader. You, who cosplays and writes fanfiction and draws fanart and runs a forum and collects Funko-Pops and must have hardcovers for all of your favorite book series and frames for your autographed posters. You, who boldly goes.

Never give up on your dreams, and never let anyone tell you that what you love is inconsequential or useless or a waste of time. Because if you love it? If that OTP or children's card game or abridged series or YA book or animated series makes you happy?

That is never a waste of time. Because in the end we're all just a bunch of weirdos standing in front of other weirdos, asking for their username.

So, as Carmindor always says: Look to the stars. Aim. Ignite.